Dear Reader,

It's hard to believe that the Signature Select program is one year old—with seventy-two books already published by top Harlequin and Silhouette authors.

What an exciting and varied lineup we have in the year ahead! In the first quarter of the year, the Signature Spotlight program offers three very different reading experiences. Popular author Marie Ferrarella, well-known for her warm family-centered romances, has gone in quite a different direction to write a story that has been "haunting her" for years. Please check out *Sundays Are for Murder* in January. Hop aboard a Caribbean cruise with Joanne Rock in *The Pleasure Trip* for February, and don't miss a trademark romantic suspense from Debra Webb, *Vows of Silence* in March.

Our collections in the first quarter of the year explore a variety of contemporary themes. Our Valentine's collection—*Write It Up!*—homes in on the trend to online dating in three stories by Elizabeth Bevarly, Tracy Kelleher and Mary Leo. February is awards season, and Barbara Bretton, Isabel Sharpe and Emilie Rose join the fun and glamour in *And the Envelope, Please....* And in March, Leslie Kelly, Heather MacAllister and Cindi Myers have penned novellas about women desperate enough to go to *Bootcamp* to learn how not to scare men away!

Three original sagas also come your way in the first quarter of this year. Silhouette author Gina Wilkins spins off her popular FAMILY FOUND miniseries in *Wealth Beyond Riches*. Janice Kay Johnson has written a powerful story of a tortured shared past in *Dead Wrong*, which is connected to her PATTON'S DAUGHTERS Superromance miniseries, and Kathleen O'Brien gives a haunting story of mysterious murder in *Quiet as the Grave*.

And don't miss reissues of some of your favorite authors, including Georgette Heyer, Joan Hohl, Jayne Ann Krentz and Fayrene Preston. We are also featuring a number of two-in-one connected stories in volumes by Janice Kay Johnson and Kathleen O'Brien, as well as Roz Denny Fox and Janelle Denison. And don't forget there is original bonus material in every single Signature Select book to give you the inside scoop on the creative process of your favorite authors!

Enjoy!

Marsha Zinberg

Marsha Zinberg
Executive Editor
The Signature Select Program

MINISERIES

KATHLEEN
O'BRIEN

FIREFLY
GLEN

HARLEQUIN®

TORONTO • NEW YORK • LONDON
AMSTERDAM • PARIS • SYDNEY • HAMBURG
STOCKHOLM • ATHENS • TOKYO • MILAN • MADRID
PRAGUE • WARSAW • BUDAPEST • AUCKLAND

ISBN 0-373-83691-0

FIREFLY GLEN

Copyright © 2006 by Harlequin Books S.A.

The publisher acknowledges the copyright holder of the individual works as follows:

WINTER BABY
Copyright © 2001 by Kathleen O'Brien

BABES IN ARMS
Copyright © 2002 by Kathleen O'Brien

This edition published by arrangement with Harlequin Books S.A.

® and TM are trademarks of the publisher. Trademarks indicated with ® are registered in the United States Patent and Trademark Office, the Canadian Trade Marks Office and in other countries.

www.eHarlequin.com

Printed in U.S.A.

CONTENTS

Dear Reader,

Home. It's a small word to mean so much. And yet that one syllable holds the power to inspire writers and poets, philosophers and painters.

But what is it, really? A hundred people will give you a hundred different answers. It's a house, a city, a parent, a husband, a friend. It's where you retreat, sick and frightened, and come out brave and well. It's where you can finally take off your armor, lay down your sword and rest.

Sometimes the treasure of home is handed to you at birth, gift wrapped with love and laid at the foot of your cradle. Sometimes, though, you have to search for it on your own.

Sarah Lennox, the heroine of *Winter Baby*, has almost given up searching. The child of a home that was broken and broken again, she has decided that for her, *home* is a dream that will never come true. The closet she ever came to knowing that security was one magical summer in Firefly Glen, a tiny town in the Adirondacks.

So when she finds herself pregnant and alone, that's where she turns. She needs a peaceful place to hide while she sorts things out.

But instead of being swaddled in solitude and silence, Sarah finds herself instantly caught up in the madness and mayhem and pure sparkling magic that make up Firefly Glen. And somewhere between building ice castles and visiting puppies in the local jail, she finds herself doing the one thing a confused, abandoned, pregnant woman should never do. She falls in love.

And, most surprisingly of all, she finds a home.

Because when you peel away all the poetry and the philosophy, that's what home really means—love.

Warmly,

Kathleen O'Brien

WINTER BABY

To Renie, with a kiss to put in your hand.

CHAPTER ONE

SARAH LENNOX WASN'T SURPRISED the soufflé fell. It was difficult to focus on creating frothy dinner concoctions when you'd just discovered you were pregnant.

Minutes later, the soufflé began to burn, but she didn't get up to rescue it. Instead, she sat on the edge of the tub, letting the acrid odor of scorching eggs fill her nose while she stared stupidly at the little pink *x* on the test strip.

It must be a mistake. It *had* to be a mistake.

She wasn't going to have a baby. Not right now. She wasn't even getting married for another fifty-nine days. And she wouldn't begin having children until two years after that. That was the plan. The master plan. Ask anyone who knew her. Check any of her diaries since she'd been twelve years old. College. Career. Marriage. Wait two years just to be sure. *Then* children.

That was the plan. So this…this *nonsense* had to be a mistake.

But the counter was lined with these little strips, and they all had pink *x*'s on them. This was the fourth home pregnancy test she'd used tonight.

It was a mistake, all right. But it was *her* mistake, not the test's.

The master plan was toast, just like her soufflé. She was definitely, disastrously, terrifyingly pregnant.

In the living room, the stack of Christmas CDs she'd put on an hour ago clicked and shifted and began playing "What Child Is This?" *Cute. Very cute.* She felt a faint urge to get up and break the CD in two, but she didn't have the energy to follow through. Apparently shock and horror worked like a tranquilizer dart. She couldn't move a muscle.

When the doorbell rang, she was confused, momentarily unable to remember whom she'd been expecting. It rang again, then again, short and hard, as if whoever it was didn't much like waiting.

Her subconscious recognized that irritable ring. Of course. *Ed.* Her fiancé was coming for dinner. They'd had an 8:00 p.m. date. It was now 8:01, and he didn't like tardiness. He had a master plan, too—and, if anything, it was even more rigidly scheduled than Sarah's own. It had been one of the reasons she chose him in the first place. It was definitely one of the reasons she stuck with him, even though lately their relationship had been…a little rocky. Just a tiny bit unsatisfying.

Still, all relationships had their rocky moments. And Ed would make a good husband. She wasn't the type to run around breaking off engagements. She wasn't like her mother. When she gave her word, she meant it.

And now she had no choice. She was pregnant with Ed's child. *Pregnant.* She made a small gasping sound, as if she couldn't breathe around the fact.

She stood numbly, instinctively sweeping all the tiny test strips and empty pink boxes into the wastebasket. For a long moment she stared down at the debris, which seemed to represent the bits and pieces of her shattered master plan. How solid could the plan actually have been, she asked herself numbly, if it had been so easily destroyed?

Ed had given up ringing and was knocking now. Sarah actually half smiled at the frustrated annoyance in the sound. Poor Ed. If he didn't like her being slow to answer the door, he was going to really *hate* the rest of his evening.

"Good God, what is that *smell?*" As Sarah opened the door, Ed started to signal his annoyance by one disapproving glance at his watch, but almost immediately his horror at the odor in the apartment superseded everything else. He wrinkled his aristocratic nose into a disgusted twist. "Sarah, for God's sake. Have you burned dinner?"

"I think so," she said. And then, because he was looking at her with an expression of complete incredulity, she realized that something else probably needed to be said. She wondered what it was. She felt as if she were speaking a foreign language. "I'm sorry?"

"Me, too," he agreed curtly. "I haven't eaten since breakfast." He sniffed the air again. "Have you turned off the oven?"

"I don't think so," she said, trying to remember. "No. I don't think so."

He narrowed his eyes. "Are you all right?" He didn't wait for her answer. He moved into the kitchen with the assured purpose of a man in charge in his own home. But it wasn't his home, Sarah thought suddenly. It was her home. Why did he feel that he was in charge?

Because somebody had to be. She obviously would burn the whole apartment complex down if somebody didn't take over. Already the kitchen was filling with smoke.

After he flicked the thermostat off and determined that dinner was completely ruined, Ed let the oven door slam impatiently. He punched the exhaust fan to High, then returned to the living room, closing the kitchen door tightly behind him. The Christmas CDs were still playing, and the gentle pine scent of her tree fought with the nasty burned smell of dinner.

"I'm sorry," Sarah said again, although she no longer felt very sorry. It was just a soufflé, after all. Why was Ed making such a big deal out of it? His handsome face couldn't have looked sterner if she had just charbroiled the original copy of the Magna Carta. "Maybe we could order pizza."

He looked at her silently, as if he didn't trust himself to speak. Sarah felt the beginnings of rebellion stir. Was burning dinner really such a sin? In the early days she had thought Ed's perfectionism was admirable, a sign that he possessed high standards. He expected a lot from others, but he required a lot of himself, too. For instance, Sarah knew that he would require himself to be a faithful, reliable husband, which was exactly what she wanted. What she needed. She had no intention of repeating her mother's mistakes.

After Sarah's father had been caught cheating, when Sarah was only eight, her mother had promptly divorced him. She'd spent the next several decades trying to find a replacement. But she was a rotten judge of men.

Sarah couldn't remember a time when she hadn't been determined to choose more wisely. She wanted someone sensible. Strong. Faithful. Someone with a plan.

Several times during the past few weeks, however, traitorous thoughts had crept in. He had sometimes seemed not admirable, but…pompous. Petty. Dictatorial.

Out of nowhere came a chilling thought. Someday he would turn that expression, that cold, unforgiving blue gaze, upon their child. Over a broken toy, a soiled diaper, a C in math. She felt a quick, primitive burning in her legs, as if they were straining to run somewhere far, far away—somewhere he couldn't find her. Or the baby.

But this was crazy. It must mean that her hormones were already acting up. She'd better pull herself together, or she'd never find the courage to tell him.

"Chinese. How about Chinese?" Ed liked Chinese food. Maybe he was just hungry. Maybe he'd be less tense after he ate something. She smiled as pleasantly as she could. "My treat."

"No." He sighed from the depths of his diaphragm. "Oh, maybe it's just as well. I really shouldn't stay very long anyhow. I've got a lot to do tonight."

He gestured toward the sofa, which was decorated with small needlepoint pillows that read "Peace on Earth" and "Joy to the World."

"Sit down, Sarah," he said somberly. "I have news."

"Oh," she said. She moved the pillows out of the way and sat. She looked up at him, trying to find the man she had fallen in love with, that handsome, twenty-eight-year-old former math teacher whose extraordinary maturity had made him the youngest high school principal in the state of Florida. That worthy man couldn't have disappeared overnight.

She smiled the best she could. "I have news, too, Ed."

He sat on the chair opposite her. "Let me go first," he said. "Mine is very important." He winced. "Oh, hell. I didn't mean it like that."

Somehow, still smiling, she waved away the insult.

He'd know soon enough that her news was important, too. Life shattering, in fact. She tried to compose her face to look interested, but her mind couldn't quite focus on anything except the new truth inside her.

What would he say? How would he feel? How, for that matter, did *she* feel?

After a moment she realized he wasn't speaking. She glanced over at him, surprised to see him looking hesitant. Ed was rarely at a loss for words. At Groveland High School, where they both worked—Ed as principal, Sarah as Home Economics teacher—Ed was legendary for his ability to subdue hostile parents. He smothered every complaint under a soothing blanket of verbiage.

He cleared his throat, but still he didn't begin. He looked around her tiny living room, then stood abruptly. "I can't breathe in here, with all this smoke. Let's go outside."

Sarah felt a new unease trickle through her veins. What was this news that he found so difficult to share? But she followed him out onto the small balcony that overlooked the complex swimming pool. The air was balmy, typical December weather in south Florida. The colored holiday lights looped along nearby balconies blinked rather desperately, as if reassuring themselves that it really was Christmas, in spite of the heat.

Ed went straight to the railing and leaned against it, looking down at the turquoise pool, where several of Sarah's neighbors were having a keg party. They were all dressed in Santa hats and bathing suits.

Sarah was suddenly eager to postpone whatever Ed had to say. Eager, too, to postpone her own devastating news. "Uncle Ward had hoped we could come spend

Christmas with him in Firefly Glen," she said. "Wouldn't that have been lovely? White mountains and sleigh rides, and marshmallow roasts, and—"

"And four days snowed in with a bad-tempered, senile old man?" Ed shook his head. "No thanks."

Sarah stared flatly at the stranger in front of her. "I never said he was senile."

"Well, he's almost eighty, isn't he? Besides, I didn't have the time, you know that." Ed turned around, squaring his shoulders as if he had finally come to a decision. "Sarah. Listen."

She stood very still and waited. A drunken chorus of "Grandma Got Run Over by a Reindeer" wafted up from the party below, but she could still hear Ed's fingers drumming against the railing.

"All right," she said. "I'm listening."

"They offered me the job, Sarah. The superintendent's position. I'm going to California."

She didn't take her eyes from him. But she had heard the telling pronoun. *"I'm" going to California. Not we. "I."*

"Congratulations." She'd known he was applying for the job, a plum assignment as superintendent of schools in a small, affluent Southern California county. But she hadn't really believed he'd get it. He was so young. He'd been a principal only a couple of years. But apparently he had wowed them in California, just as he wowed people everywhere, with his good looks, his sharp mind, his glib conversation.

"Sarah, do you understand? I'm going to California. Next month. Maybe sooner."

"Yes, I understand." But she didn't, not really. "Are you saying you think we should postpone the wedding?"

He set his jaw—his square, well-tanned jaw...he really was so incredibly handsome—and licked his lips. "No. I'm saying I think we should call off the wedding."

"What?" She couldn't have heard him correctly.

He shook his head. "It's not working, Sarah. I know you've sensed that, too. You must have. It's just not the same between us. I know we haven't wanted to admit it, but I don't see how we can deny it any longer. And now, with me leaving..."

She waited. Her whole body seemed suspended in a weightless, airless space.

He looked annoyed, as if he had expected her to finish the sentence for him. "Well, now, with me leaving, it's the right time to just admit it isn't working, don't you think?"

"What's not working? What exactly isn't working?"

He made an impatient noise, as if he felt she were being deliberately dense. "*We're* not working. You've changed lately, you know that. You've been—well, to put it bluntly, Sarah, you've been bitchy for months. You criticize everything I do, for God's sake, at school and at home. And it's been weeks since you've wanted to make love, really *wanted* to. I know some of it is my fault. I've been busy. Preoccupied. Maybe I haven't been as thoughtful as I should. I know I forgot your birthday."

She closed her eyes on a small swell of nausea. *He* hadn't forgotten her birthday. His florist had. For every major holiday, anniversary or birthday, his florist had a standing order to send her white roses. Ed had never even asked her whether she *liked* white roses. Which she didn't.

She hated white roses, especially hothouse ones,

which never quite opened and had no real scent. Why hadn't that told her something, right from the start?

"Anyhow, it's obviously not going to work. I'm sorry, Sarah. But this seems like the perfect time to make a clean break. Don't you think so? With me leaving. Next month. Maybe sooner."

She felt herself trembling with shock. And beneath the shock, but rising…something that felt like anger.

"No, actually, I *don't* think so. Remember I said I had news, too? Well, here it is. I'm pregnant, Ed. I'm going to have a baby. Next July." She smiled tightly. "Maybe sooner."

For a moment, he reacted as if she had produced a gun and aimed it at his heart. He blinked. His mouth dropped open. He felt blindly with both hands for the metal railing behind him.

But he recovered quickly. He straightened to his manly six-four, a full foot taller than her own height, as if he could intimidate her into withdrawing her accusation by sheer size. He narrowed his eyes, closed his jaw and squeezed the railing so tightly his knuckles grew white.

"That's ridiculous," he said through clenched teeth. "It's simply not possible. I have never had unprotected sex with anyone in my entire life. Never."

She lifted her chin. "And I have never had sex with anyone but you," she said. "So obviously we're part of that small but unlucky percentage for whom the *protection* wasn't quite infallible."

He was shaking his head. "Impossible," he said firmly. "Simply impossible." After a moment, his face changed, and he moved toward her, his eyes liquid with a false pity. "Sarah. If this is some pitiful attempt to hold on, to try to keep me from going to California—"

When he got close enough, she slapped him. The sound rang out in a momentary lull in the partying below. Several Santa hats looked up toward her balcony curiously.

Ed rubbed his cheek, which was probably stinging. It was definitely red. "Good God, it's true." He looked bewildered. "It's really true?"

"Yes, you bastard," she whispered furiously. "Of course it's true."

He worried his lower lip, his unfocused gaze darting back and forth unseeingly, as if he were scanning his mind for options. "Well, no need to panic," he said softly. She knew he was talking more to himself than to her. "It will be all right. There are lots of ways to fix this. It's not even very expensive anymore."

For a moment she thought she was going to be sick. Morning sickness already? At night? But then she realized it was pure, unadulterated disgust. *Fix this?* As if she were a bad bit of plumbing.

"Get out." She pulled the sliding glass door open behind her with a savage rumble. "Get out of my house, and don't ever come back."

"Sarah, calm down." He reached out to touch her shoulder, but she jerked away. "This isn't the end of the world. Let me help you. At least let me write you a check—"

"Get out."

He moved through the door, but at the threshold he paused again. He was trying to look concerned, but under that fake expression she glimpsed the truth. He was relieved that she was throwing him out. Relieved that he could scuttle away from the problem and still blame her for being unreasonable.

"I want to help you deal with this," he said. "I'll pay

for whatever it costs. But remember, I won't be here for long. I'm heading out to California next month, maybe—"

"I know," she said. "Maybe sooner. As far as I'm concerned, it's not soon enough. Or far enough. *Now get out.*"

A WEEK LATER, the gynecologist confirmed what the little pink x's had told her so clearly that night. Sarah was going to have a baby next summer. Probably late June or early July. *Congratulations.*

But it still seemed unreal. Like a very, very long bad dream. As she entered her apartment, Sarah dropped her purse, her mail and her *So You're Having a Baby* brochure on the coffee table. Then she dropped herself onto the sofa, like a puppet with cut strings.

Her answering machine was blinking. One call. It was probably Ed, who had left one message every day this week. Each time he said the same thing. "I've looked into it, and your insurance will cover the procedure. I'll write you a check for any out-of-pocket expenses. But you need to hurry, Sarah. The sooner the better, as I'm sure you know."

She pulled her feet up underneath her and rested her head on the softly upholstered arm, hugging her "Peace on Earth" pillow to her chest. Maybe she ought to call him back. Surely two people who were close enough to create a baby ought to be able to discuss what to do about having done so.

And perhaps Ed didn't really mean what he was suggesting. He was shocked, just as she was. Maybe even a little frightened, though he'd never admit it. Neither of them was acting quite rationally.

Maybe she should call him. It was only six. He

would be at home. His schedule was as familiar to her as her own. She could pick up the telephone right now. Yes, she should probably call, try to talk calmly.

But she didn't move. She felt suddenly exhausted, as if she hadn't slept in weeks. She didn't want to talk to Ed. She didn't want to talk to anyone. He had already planned to leave her, she reminded herself. He had already decided he didn't want her. She felt her mind recoiling, rejecting the overload of emotion.

Her half-focused gaze fell on the coffee table, where the week's mail still lay where she'd dropped it as she came in every day, unable to work up the energy to open it.

A few bills, a dozen Christmas cards.

But now she saw that one of the cards was from Uncle Ward. His brief return address was written in his familiar arrogant black scrawl: Ward Winters, Winter House, Firefly Glen, NY.

The sight was strangely comforting. She reached for the card, wondering if Uncle Ward had included one of his long, witty letters chronicling—and sometimes sharply satirizing—the goings-on in his little mountain town. How lovely it would be to escape, even for a few minutes, into Uncle Ward's world.

The envelope was bulky. There *was* a letter. She settled back to read it, smiling her first real smile all week, suddenly hungry for the sound of her uncle's voice.

The letter was filled with rich, amusing stories and with vivid, tempting descriptions of the beautiful snowy winter they were having. She came to the end reluctantly.

...And I can't seem to make anyone see reason about the damned ice festival. Greedy politicians, all puffed up and self-important. I guess I'll have to take matters into my own hands. But what about you, Sarah? Aren't you ready for a real winter? Florida! Bah! What do palm trees and cockroaches have to do with Christmas? If your stick-in-the-mud fiancé won't come, come without him. I'd like that even better, actually. This Ed guy sounds as if his life view is a little constipated.

Sarah caught herself chuckling. Ward was actually her great-uncle, and, while Ed had been wrong to call him senile, he'd been right to call him bad tempered. Ward was crusty and sardonic and demanding, but he was also tough and practical and wise. And entirely right about Ed.

She sat up, wondering how much a flight to Upstate New York cost these days. She didn't feel quite as exhausted anymore. Maybe a dose of Uncle Ward was just exactly the bracing tonic she needed.

And maybe his quaint and quirky Firefly Glen, with its white mountains, its colorful architecture and its silly, small-town squabbles, was just the sanctuary she needed, too.

Firefly Glen. She had spent one summer there, back when she was thirteen. Her mother and her husband had been fighting through a nasty divorce, and she had been packed off to Uncle Ward while the grown-ups settled important matters, like who would get possession of the Cadillac and the mutual funds.

Her memories of that summer were emotional and confused, but they were surprisingly happy. Long, green afternoons walking with Uncle Ward in the town square, hearing rather scandalous stories of Firefly Glen's

history. Talking with him late at night in the library of
his fantastic Gothic mansion, huddled over lemonade
and popcorn and chess, and feeling understood for the
first time in her life.

He was acerbic and affectionate, hot tempered and
honest, and she had adored him. In August, her mother
had collected her—in the Cadillac, of course. Her
mother was very good at divorce, and would only get
better with each failed marriage. Sarah's life hadn't
allowed another long visit, but to this day, when she
wanted to speak the truth—or hear it—she had called
her Uncle Ward.

He and Firefly Glen had restored her then. Perhaps
they could do the same now. She picked up the telephone. Surely somewhere in that gentle valley town,
amid all that snowy silence, she could figure out what
to do with her life.

CHAPTER TWO

AT EIGHT-THIRTY on Christmas Eve, both downtown streets of Firefly Glen were wet with an icy sleet, the shining asphalt crisscrossing at the intersection like two ribbons of black glass.

The temperature on the bank clock said twenty-nine degrees, but the garlands strung between the streetlights had begun to swing and twinkle, which meant the mountain winds had found their way through Vanity Gap and into the Glen. Sheriff Parker Tremaine, who was headed toward the large red-brick City Hall at the end of Main, huddled deeper into his fleece-lined jacket and decided that the real temperature was probably more like two below.

Still he took the street slowly. Every couple of minutes a car would crawl by, and the driver would wave or honk or even pull over to offer Parker a ride. But Parker would shake his head and wave them on. Call him crazy, but he wanted to walk.

He liked the cold, liked the swollen bellies of the clouds overhead—they'd probably deliver snow by morning. He liked the pinpricks of sleet against his cheeks and the tickle of wool against his ears.

He liked the peace of the hushed streets. He liked the way the stained-glass windows of the Congregational Church beamed rich reds and blues into the darkness.

Most of all, he liked knowing that most of the 2,937 "Glenners," whom he'd been hired to protect, were safely tucked in for the night. The rest, the Fussy Four Hundred, as they were known in the Sheriff's Department, were gathered in the assembly room of City Hall for an ice festival planning session.

Parker, who had just responded to a prowler call at the park—a false alarm, of course—was a little late to the meeting, which had begun at eight. By now the planning session had probably escalated from civilized discussion to hotheaded shouting, and Bourke Waitely was undoubtedly brandishing his cane like a weapon.

But the image didn't make Parker hurry. As long as he got there before nine, he'd arrive in time to forestall any actual violence.

And when it was all over, he'd be off duty, and Theodosia Graham, who owned the Candlelight Café, had a hot, thick slice of pumpkin pie waiting for him.

"You're one damned lucky man, Tremaine."

Realizing he'd spoken out loud, Parker had to laugh. The chuckle formed a small white puff in the icy air, like a visible echo.

Lucky? Him? That was pretty damn funny, actually.

He was the thirty-four-year-old divorced sheriff of a tiny Adirondack town that gave bad winters a new meaning, and he was looking forward to spending Christmas Eve alone with a seventy-five-year-old spinster and a piece of pie.

Plus, apparently he'd begun talking to himself on the sidewalk, which back in Washington, D.C. would have scared all the other pedestrians into crossing the street.

Who in his right mind would call this lucky? He looked at himself in the window of Griswold's Five and Dime. The only guy out here, shuffling along in a freezing rain, no wife waiting at home, no kids dreaming of sugarplums, not even a girlfriend dreaming of a diamond. The textbook illustration of a loser.

So what the hell did he have to be so smug about?

Nothing. He grinned at the guy in the window. Nothing except for the fact that, after twelve years of exile, he was home again. He had ditched a career he hated, even though everyone told him he was crazy to give it up. And the beautiful, bitchy wife he couldn't please had finally ditched him, though everyone had told him he was nuts to let her go.

But he didn't care. He liked being alone, and he liked being the sheriff of Firefly Glen. In fact, he was so damn pleased with his life that he decided he'd give Theo Graham a great big sloppy Christmas kiss.

"Sheriff! Sheriff, come quick! It's an emergency!"

Parker looked over toward the emphatic voice. It was Theo. She had climbed down onto the front steps of City Hall, and she was leaning forward into the wind, her sweater wrapped tightly but inadequately around her bony shoulders.

He loped up the icy steps carefully, wondering what the problem was. Could he have misjudged the timing? Could Bourke Waitely actually have thumped someone with his cane? God, he hoped it hadn't been Mayor Millner. Alton Millner would slap Waitely in jail just for the fun of it.

"What's happened, Theo?"

"It's Granville Frome," Theo said as they hurried through the doors. "He was boring everybody to tears

with tourism figures, you know how he is. So Ward
Winters called him a greedy little pea-brain, and before
you could say 'stupid old coot' Granville came around
the table and knocked Ward to the floor. They were still
down there, wrestling like a couple of crazed teenagers, when I came out to look for you."

Parker shook his head. Ward Winters was usually
smarter than that. Everybody in Firefly Glen knew that
Granville Frome, who owned half the downtown
property, wasn't a greedy little pea-brain. Frome's brain
was much bigger than a pea, and his ego was considerably larger. And his temper was bigger still.

The scene inside was pure melee. So many people
were standing around, waving their arms and shouting,
that Parker had a hard time finding Ward and Granville.
Finally he pushed his way through to the center of the
room, where he saw the tangle of flannel and denim,
long, bony limbs and mussed silver hair that constituted
the two elderly combatants.

Granville's grandson, Mike Frome, was leaning over
the two old men, begging his grandfather to stop and
plucking at any arm or leg that stood still long enough.
Mike looked up as he saw the sheriff enter the room, and
Parker could tell that the teenager had received a shiner
for his efforts. Poor kid. He'd look like hell by morning.

"Sheriff! I've been trying—"

"Greedy son of a bitch!"

"Cave-dwelling Neanderthal!"

"Oh, God, Granddad, stop. Please, just stop!" Mike
looked harried and embarrassed. "He won't listen to me,
Sheriff."

"He probably can't hear you." Parker pointed to a
couple of other men. "Sam. Griffin. Give us a hand here."

It was a struggle, but the combined efforts of the four relatively young males finally pulled the two old scrappers apart. And then it took all four of them to keep them separated—two on Ward, two on Granville. The old men glared at each other, their chests heaving and their arms still straining to land one more punch, until gradually their breathing slowed.

Parker, who was in charge of Ward's right arm, felt the slow return of common sense. The shoulder relaxed slightly, and the fist dropped to the old man's side.

"Oh, all right, damn it," Ward Winters said gruffly. "You can let go now. I won't kill the stupid son of a—"

"You couldn't kill me if you tried, you pathetic old bastard!"

The four guards tightened their grips as Granville Frome tried to lunge forward once again. Parker glanced over at Mike, who held his grandfather's left shoulder in a determined clutch. "Mike, can you get him home?"

Mike nodded. He turned to Granville. "Grandmother is going to be really mad," he said. "You promised her you'd behave if she let you come tonight."

Ward Winters made a scoffing noise. "I should have known you'd let your wife tell you what to do, Granville, you pitiful little—"

Parker let his hold on Ward's elbow tighten painfully. "Enough," he said firmly, and Ward subsided with a low, unintelligible muttering.

Parker turned to the crowd. "This meeting is over, folks," he said, raising his voice to be heard over the din. "The weathermen are calling for six inches by sunup. Might be a good idea for everyone to head on home now."

No one resisted, but still it took a while. Goodbyes between friends were slow, with warm Christmas messages sent home to loved ones. Between enemies, parting was even slower, with all parties vying to have the last word. And then it took forever for coats, scarves, hats and mittens to be divvied up and donned.

While Ward and Parker stood there, about ten women—all between the ages of sixty and eighty—stopped to be sure Ward was all right. Parker had to smile as he watched the ladies fuss over the old guy, smoothing his thick shock of wavy white hair, tenderly brushing dust from the sleeve of his blue flannel shirt and offering to deliver everything from aspirin to chicken soup in the morning.

Ward, whose lanky good looks had attracted women like this for most of his seventy-seven years, brushed them all off brusquely, but Parker noticed that a subtly flirtatious charm lay beneath the gruff exterior.

Add that to his mansion and his millions, and it was no wonder the ladies were enchanted. Roberta Winters, Ward's wife, had died last year, and the women of Firefly Glen were lined up at the gate, hoping for a chance to be the next Mrs. Winters.

Parker wished them luck. But he had a feeling that Ward would be single for a long time. There weren't many women in Firefly Glen—or in the entire world, for that matter—who could compete with Roberta Winters.

"So tell me the truth," Parker said as he and Ward ambled out of the nearly empty meeting room. "Why are you so hell-bent on stopping the ice festival?"

Ward winced as he shoved his hand into his glove. "That blasted fool damn near broke my wrist."

Parker let the silence stretch, waiting for his answer. Finally Ward turned to him with a scowl. "Why do I want to cancel the festival?" He growled under his breath. "Because I don't want a bunch of morons crawling all over my town, clogging my streets and my air with their dirty cars. I don't want the café crammed with their slobbery children. I don't want to have to fight through a noisy horde of them to buy a stamp at Griswold's. I don't want to find them tramping across my lawn taking pictures of my house—*my private house!*"

He pulled his muffler tight around his neck, achieving an amazingly rakish look for a man his age. "And I damn sure don't want them to move here. I don't want them thinking that pretty patch of woodland over by Llewellyn's Lake would be the perfect spot for their tacky new mansion."

Parker chuckled. "You know, Ward, two hundred years ago the land where Winter House stands was probably forest, too."

"I don't care." Ward waved his hand, then winced. His wrist must really be hurting him. "I don't want them mucking up my town." They were passing the one bar approved by the cautious city council, and Ward jabbed his forefinger toward its sign irritably. "Look at that! *Cricket's Hum Tavern?* What the hell kind of name is that? Ever since we've started bringing in the tourists, we've become so damn cheesy I could just throw up."

He started reading the signs as they walked. "Frog's Folly Children's Fashions. Candlelight Café. Black Bear Books. Duckpuddle Diner." He made a face. *"Duckpuddle Diner?"*

"Yeah, I thought that one was a little much myself."

"Well, if we've already sunk to Duckpuddle Diner,

can Sweet Sally's Smut Shoppe and the Lorelei Landfill be far behind?"

Ward wasn't really expecting an answer, and Parker didn't give him one. He knew it was a legitimate debate, whether the town leaders should go looking for growth and prosperity or whether they should concentrate on keeping Firefly Glen safe and clean—and *small*.

The argument had been going on for two hundred years, and it wasn't going to be solved tonight.

Besides, it was cold, it was late, and the two of them were basically on the same side of the debate anyhow. The Tremaine clan had been living in Firefly Glen just as long as the Winters family, and Parker's love for this town was every bit as possessive and protective as the old man's could ever be. Maybe more—because Parker had tasted life away from Firefly Glen, and he had found it bitter.

They reached Ward's car just as the church bells rang out ten o'clock. Both men stood quietly, listening to the clear tones echo in the crisp silence of the Christmas air. The first few drifting flakes of snow fell slowly around them.

"You're a good man, Parker," Ward said suddenly. "I'm glad you decided to come home. And you've been a good sheriff, even if you were one of those damn political appointees, which are usually just about worthless."

"Thanks." Parker smiled, surprised. Even that backhanded compliment was uncharacteristically effusive for his crotchety friend. Had the sweetness of Christmas bells softened the old man up, or had Granville Frome landed a big one to Ward's head?

Anyhow, it was ironic that Ward should say such a thing, on this same night when Parker had already been feeling so lucky. "Me, too. I like it here. I wasn't sure, when I first came back. You know, after being in Washington. And I knew how Glenners felt about political appointments. But I like being the sheriff."

"Yep. I thought you did." Ward sighed. "That's why I think it's a damn shame your own brother-in-law would be such a son of a bitch as to run against you."

Parker frowned, completely confused. His own brother-in-law…run against him…for what? He squinted. "What are you talking about?"

"About that snake Harry Dunbar." Ward pointed toward the front window of the stationery store, which was run by Parker's younger sister, Emma Tremaine Dunbar. "Sorry, son."

And right there in the window, next to the display of Christmas cards and smiling Santas, was a sign. A campaign poster, to be precise.

Vote Dunbar For Sheriff, it said in red, white and blue letters. Because It's Time For A Change.

SARAH GUIDED HER RENTAL CAR slowly, making her way through the sharply twisting curves of Vanity Gap without a lot of confidence. This wasn't at all like driving in Florida. The narrow path was closely bordered by rugged, ice-capped granite walls, and though the road had obviously been cleared lately, new snow was already falling, obscuring the tarmac.

Now and then the granite walls would part, giving her a dizzying view of the steep mountainside that brought on a fierce wave of morning sickness. She tried to keep her eyes on the road, her breakfast down and her courage up. But what, oh, what had made her think she could handle this?

She had hoped to get here in time to spend Christmas with her uncle, but the details had swamped her. Arranging for a six-week leave of absence from her teaching position hadn't been easy, and then the minutiae of closing down her apartment—stopping mail and electricity, farming out plants, throwing out food and saying goodbye to friends—had seemed to take forever.

Still, she had managed to free herself by New Year's Day, which had felt like a good omen. The perfect time to be making a new start.

She had landed at the Albany airport this morning with fairly high hopes, but now, after two hours of mountain driving, she was beginning to wonder whether she should have stayed in Florida. What exactly had she accomplished by running away? And why here, so far from home and everything she understood? What if her memories of Firefly Glen were romanticized by time and youth? What if it was just a grim, bleak, cold little hole in the mountains?

All of a sudden, like a spectacular surprise designed by a movie director, her car finally broke through the gap, revealing the valley below.

Sarah pulled onto the overlook, letting the car idle as she stared, utterly enchanted. Firefly Glen lay before her like a toy village arranged on a coffee table, too perfect to be true.

It was a clear, crisp morning, the sun round and winter-white. The snow glistened like crushed diamonds on the branches of trees, the rooftops of houses and the steeples of the churches. That tall one, on the eastern edge of town—that was the Congregational Church, Sarah remembered suddenly. The golden bells in that steeple had rung out the hours here for more than two hundred years.

The whole village was heavily wooded, as if it had nestled itself into these mountains back in the 1700s without disturbing a single leaf. On the western border of town, the Tallulah River winked in and out of white-frosted elms and hickory pines like a ribbon of silver sequins.

The entire scene exuded beauty, permanence and peace. Sarah leaned her head against the car window, overcome by a strange sense of longing. It would be good to belong to a place like this.

But she didn't. She wasn't sure she belonged anywhere anymore. Suddenly she felt intensely isolated here on this mountain, removed from the simple charm of Firefly Glen, exiled from those solid, cozy homes with soft gray plumes of smoke rising from their red-brick chimneys.

Alone. She fought back stupid tears and uncomfortable nausea with equal determination.

It's hormones. Just hormones, she reminded herself bracingly. Everyone knew that pregnant women were irrationally emotional. She had to stop giving in to it, stop this maudlin self-pity. She was alone on the mountaintop only because she had stopped to appreciate the view.

But the nausea…

That was very real.

She stumbled out of the car and lurched over toward the trees, her boots crunching on snow. In spite of the freezing air, sweat beaded on her forehead and upper lip. She leaned against the smooth white bark of a birch, closed her eyes and concentrated on taking deep breaths.

To her dismay, she heard another car approaching. She held her breath, hoping it would go on by, but it didn't. It paused, slowed, and then, tires rolling over the snow, eased onto the overlook.

It was a rather large black SUV that dwarfed her small rental car. Firefly Glen Sheriff's Department, the gold lettering across the side panel announced. Two people were in it, a male driver, and a female passenger next to him.

The driver had rolled down his window and leaned his head out.

"Everything okay here?"

"Yes, I'm fine," Sarah called, glad to discover that it was almost true. The wave of nausea was passing. It would return, she knew, but for now the relief was blissful. She smiled at the man, noticing the gleaming gold star on his black leather jacket.

The sheriff himself. She tried to remember any stories her uncle might have told about this man, but came up blank. She moved closer to the Jeep, to demonstrate that she was safe and unharmed…and harmless. "I'm really fine. I was just enjoying the view."

He smiled back. Even from this distance, she could tell it was a dynamite smile, white and wide and charmingly cocked toward one side. For just a flash of an instant, she forgot she was a recently ditched, slightly desperate, pregnant schoolteacher. For one lovely second her stomach did a very different, very pleasant little flip, the kind it used to do when she was a teenager.

"It's nice, isn't it?" He glanced toward the Glen below them, then returned his smile to her. "We look even better up close," he said, apparently completely unaware of any double entendre. "So. Are you headed our way?"

She nodded, knowing that underneath the friendliness he was appraising her, as any good sheriff would, deciding whether she was a problem that needed controlling. "In a few minutes."

"If you'd like, we can follow you." He waved a hand toward the winding mountain road. "Make sure you're okay."

But she didn't want to do that. Her stomach was settled for now, but what if it started acting up again once she was back in motion? She couldn't imagine herself screeching to a halt, tumbling out of her car and getting sick on the snowbanked side of the road—all right in front of the horrified eyes of this man.

It had nothing to do with how good-looking he was, she assured herself. In her condition, she was hardly in the market for any man. It was just—well, it just wasn't the first impression she wanted to make on the residents of this town.

"I'll be fine," she assured him. "Really. I don't want to hold you up."

"I'd hate for you to get lost," he began, but suddenly the woman next to him broke in.

"For heaven's sake, Parker, maybe she doesn't want a sheriff's escort. It's one road, less than a mile. A straight shot. No forks, no detours, no nothing. Even a woman can handle that."

Sarah looked curiously toward the female who was speaking, but the shadows in the SUV were too dark to make out much. One of his deputies? She wasn't taking a very subservient tone for a subordinate.

The sheriff shook his head and tugged at his ear in

frustration. He looked a little embarrassed. But he was still smiling. "It has nothing to do with whether she's a man or a woman, Emma."

"Oh, really?" The female voice was equal parts amusement and sarcasm. "Is that so?"

With a sigh, the sheriff turned back to Sarah. "I'm sorry. I certainly didn't mean to…to be patronizing…I mean, to imply…" He gave up, chuckling helplessly. "Well, anyway, welcome to Firefly Glen."

Then, with a smile, he shifted his Jeep into reverse and prepared to exit the overlook.

He paused in a shaft of sunlight that spotlighted the most amazingly gorgeous man Sarah had ever seen. Black hair, blue eyes…and that smile so sexy it had the power to transform a beleaguered woman into a giddy teenager. But, she saw now, it also had warmth. Warmth enough to make a total stranger feel suddenly befriended.

"I'm Sheriff Parker Tremaine," he said. "And if you need anything at all while you're visiting our town—"

The woman, a pretty twenty-something with hair as dark as the sheriff's, leaned back, letting out a laughing groan. "Oh, brother. Dudley Do-Right."

The sheriff shook his head. "Sorry. This is my sister. She's a little crazy. Recently escaped. I'm taking her in." He lifted his right elbow to fend off a friendly blow from the woman. "But don't let her scare you away. Most of us down there in the Glen are perfectly sane."

EMMA HAD ATTRACTED quite a crowd with her story, and Parker thought if she didn't shut up pretty soon he really was going to toss her in jail.

Not that they had any room in the jail. Suzie, his part-time clerk, had turned the one holding cell into a replica of the Bethlehem manger, complete with papier-mâché cows and a baby-doll Jesus that, if anyone touched him the wrong way, said in a rather disturbing, machinelike voice, "Betsy needs a new diaper."

He had hoped that Suzie would take it down now that the new year was here, but she had bristled at the suggestion. Suzie, a seventeen-year-old high school junior, was gunning for an interior design scholarship to NYU, and she expected her manger to clinch the deal. She wasn't letting anyone dismantle a single straw of hay until she had good pictures for her résumé.

So Parker really had no choice but to let Emma keep regaling the customers of the Candlelight Café with her reenactment of Parker's rescue on the mountaintop.

"But won't you let me escort you down the mountain, miss?" Emma's voice was a syrupy, annoying imitation of Parker's own. "I am the valiant Sheriff of Firefly Glen. I can protect you."

Parker growled. Even though Emma was now twenty-six and about to celebrate her first wedding anniversary, she would always be his annoying little sister. They had lost their parents in a car accident three years ago, and the tragedy had been one of the reasons he'd decided to come back to Firefly Glen. He hadn't liked the idea of Emma here without any family at all. But the move had certainly left him at the mercy of her irrepressible teasing and, even worse, her incessant matchmaking.

"Damn it, Emma, give it up. I just asked the woman if she needed help. It's my job, remember?"

Emma grinned and tucked into the pumpkin pie Theo Burke had just placed in front of her. "Yeah, but if she'd been a three-hundred-pound logger with a face like a gargoyle, I'll bet you wouldn't have stopped." She turned to her audience. "This lady was gorgeous. Petite, honey-blond hair, great body. Dudley Do-Right here was practically drooling on his boots."

Parker held out a napkin. "Shut up, Emma. Don't talk with your mouth full."

While she chewed, somehow he diverted the conversation, subtly leading Theo and the other customers in a debate about the ice festival, a subject that was always good for a distraction. Eventually the others wandered off, and he breathed a sigh of relief.

Emma could be a royal pain. But he had to admit—at least to himself—that she had been right about one thing. The woman on the overlook had been a knockout. He found his thoughts circling back to their encounter, over and over. She'd been underdressed for the weather, with only a green turtleneck sweater, jeans and a pair of boots. But the sweater had outlined a body that was darned near perfect. And her face had been more than pretty. He remembered the vulnerable curve of her cheek, almost as soft as a child's. It made an interesting contrast with the strength he had glimpsed in her hazel eyes, the hint of determination in her chin.

Fascinating. He wondered who she was visiting. But that was the advantage of living in such a tiny town. Sooner or later, he'd run into her.

"What's the matter with you, Emma Tremaine?" Theo Burke had appeared at their side, holding a second piece of pie for Parker. He grimaced. After a sugar rush like this, he'd have trouble staying awake all afternoon. But Theo would be hurt if he didn't eat it. And besides, it was the food of the gods.

Emma looked up questioningly, her mouth still full of pie.

"Trying to get Parker interested in this woman on the mountain." Theo scowled. "You don't want to hook him up with another out-of-towner, do you?"

Emma shrugged, tossing her dark brown bob, the same haircut she'd had since high school. "Well, we've got to get him hooked up with someone, don't we?" Her blue eyes, so like Parker's own that it was like looking into a mirror, began to dance. "I'm not getting any younger, Theo," she said plaintively. "I want to be an aunt."

Theo narrowed her eyes, considering. Though she herself was a spinster, she had appointed herself the official town matchmaker, and she took her job seriously. "Still, there must be a suitable woman here in the Glen—"

Down the next row of tables, someone dropped a plate with a splintering crash. Theo didn't bother to finish her sentence. She rushed over, ready to comfort her inconvenienced customer and to chasten her clumsy employee with one quick, deadly look.

Parker and Emma shared an amused glance. Theo Burke was famous for treating her customers like royalty. The Candlelight Café lived up to its name. Every table really did have an ivory taper set in a silver candlestick. And real linen, too. Theo trained her teenage waiters to what she called "French standards." It amused the customers, but it kept them coming back. Where else could you get five-star service with your French fries?

"Seriously, though, Parker—" Emma toyed with the last bit of piecrust on her plate "—aren't you interested in ever getting married?"

"I've been married," he said calmly, drinking his coffee. "It wasn't that much fun."

"Yeah, but you married a bitch." Parker gave his sister a quizzical look, and she bristled defensively. "Well, I'm sorry. But you did. The way she acted when you decided to come back to the Glen! Man, was she ever a witch."

Parker put his coffee cup down. "Well, you can't really blame her. Tina liked being married to a member of the Secret Service. It impressed her friends. And she thoroughly enjoyed having affairs with all the cutest politicians in Washington." He grinned at his sister. "Apparently she couldn't work up much enthusiasm for cheating on the sheriff of Firefly Glen."

Emma eyes were as dark as mud. "I'd like to find that woman and—"

"Let it go, Emma," Parker said lightly. "A lot of it was my fault, too. She didn't start out being a bitch."

That was true. He remembered how hypnotized he had been by Tina's exciting body, her cover-girl face— the sophisticated pampering she'd showered on him, purring and seducing and flattering.

And he'd never forget how hot they had been for each other. Or how alarmingly fast that heat had burned itself out.

"That's partly why I'm not eager to try it again." He heard the sober note in his voice, and he was sure Emma recognized it, too. "Not unless I'm sure. I would have to be one hundred percent positive it's the perfect woman."

Emma's expression was suddenly wistful, her earlier effervescence dissipated. "I don't think that's possible, Parker," she said softly. "Nothing's ever really perfect."

He could have kicked himself. Though Emma never

outright acknowledged it, he knew something was wrong in her marriage. She'd married Harry Dunbar, Parker's deputy sheriff, just last year, and for a few months, things had seemed fine. But lately Emma's natural buoyancy had flattened out. Something was definitely wrong.

Harry had been out of town since before Christmas, visiting his family in New York City. Emma hadn't gone with him, something Parker couldn't understand. Their first Christmas, and they spent it apart?

And there was the problem of the upcoming election. Apparently Harry had decided to run against Parker, which made for a damn sticky family situation. Harry had been pretty ticked off last year when, after the old sheriff's death, the governor had appointed Parker to take over. Harry had fully expected to get the nod. After all, he'd been the deputy sheriff here for years.

So it was not really a shock to discover that Harry planned to oppose him in the election. He might win, too. Harry had lived in Firefly Glen all his life—a real plus with the voters. Some people around here considered Parker a traitor. It was okay to go off to college—everyone did that—but you were supposed to come right back. Parker hadn't. He'd stayed away for eight extra years, getting his law degree, being a "big shot" in Washington. A member of the Secret Service. "Putting on airs," Mayor Millner had called it once when he thought Parker wasn't listening. Glenners didn't care for "airs."

Obviously Harry hadn't consulted Emma about his decision. Rumor had it that Emma had ripped down Harry's campaign poster the minute she saw it. She had apologized to Parker, and her repressed anger was obvious. He wondered what she had said to Harry.

But she wouldn't talk about it. In fact, she still insisted everything was fine. And when Harry wasn't around, like today, she was so much her normal playful self that Parker could forget.

"I know nothing's perfect," he said, reaching across the table to lay his hand over Emma's. He was horrified to discover that it was trembling. "But we don't have to settle for anything really *bad,* either, Emmy."

She looked up and tried to grin. It was such a failure that Parker suddenly wanted to find Harry Dunbar and beat him senseless. "I mean it. We have a right to be happy," he said tightly.

"Then get married and make me an aunt," she said, banishing her gloom with an obvious effort. "That's what would make me happy."

CHAPTER THREE

AFTER HER ODD but appealing encounter with the sheriff, Sarah's mood changed completely, and she entered the township of Firefly Glen with a light heart and a happy sense of New Year optimism.

She hardly recognized the place. Winter had completely transformed the summer playground of that visit so long ago. Carrot-nosed snowmen stood sentry at each corner of the town square where she and Uncle Ward had once played Frisbee and licked their melting ice cream from sticky fingers. And the leafy green maples where the Frisbee had finally gotten stuck were now just delicate brown skeletons against the dove-gray sky.

For a lifelong Southerner like Sarah, the sight was pure magic. She drove slowly, drinking in every detail. The shopkeepers here obviously didn't feel that the arrival of January meant that Christmas decorations must come down. Windows, doorways, streetlights and storefronts were looped with deep green pine garlands threaded with velvety red ribbons. The large tree in the center of the square shone with huge red balls and small twinkling white lights.

And to Sarah's surprise, the placid serenity she had imagined as she stood on the mountain looking down had been merely an illusion. What a world of teeming life these few blocks held, in spite of the freezing cold and the snow that still fell lightly.

The sign she'd passed on the way in had proclaimed that Firefly Glen had 2,937 residents. Surely every one of them was out here today, bundled up in puffy blue coats, cherry-red knitted hats, green-and-navy-checkered mittens and bright yellow mufflers.

As she watched one little toddler struggle to walk, as stiff-legged as the Michelin Man in his padded snowsuit, she cast a doubtful look at her own light gray wool-blend coat, which lay across the back seat of the rental car. It had been the best she could find at the department stores in Tampa, but she suddenly realized that it wasn't going to be nearly warm enough for the rigors of a New York winter.

She thought of the long, twisting walk up the path to the front door of Uncle Ward's medieval mansion. In that flimsy coat, she'd be frozen solid before she had a chance to rap the massive brass knocker. They might not find her until spring.

She began searching the names of the stores she passed, looking for something that might save her.

Adirondack Outerwear. Yes, that sounded perfect. Gratefully she slipped the car into one of the designated parking spaces. Clenching her teeth against the sharp bite of wind, she darted into the store, hoping her charge card could handle the extra expense.

A sweet-toned little bell announced her arrival, but no one came to greet her. In fact, at first sight, the store seemed deserted, the coats hanging abandoned on circular racks, the multicolored mittens lying in neat, forgotten rows under empty glass countertops.

But as Sarah made her way toward the back, she realized that she was not alone. Something was going on at the back of the shop, near the cash register. All the salesclerks—and several people who looked like customers, as well—were clustered around the counter.

A sales meeting? It didn't sound like it. In fact, as she stood, wondering, the voices grew louder. It quickly became clear that she had stumbled into some sort of fracas. One person was waving a newspaper, and about four other people began talking at once.

Feeling like something of an intruder, Sarah considered trying to sneak out again. But her curiosity got the better of her. What, in an idyllic hamlet like this, could be making everyone so hot tempered?

She fingered a few coats not far from the action, shamelessly eavesdropping. She couldn't help being curious about the people here. The anecdotes in Uncle Ward's vivid letters had made her feel as if she knew them.

"It's libel, I tell you. It's actionable. I can prove damages—"

"He can't do this! I won't make it through the winter without the profits from the festival!"

"Damn it, Tremaine, if you can't do something about that bad-tempered old hermit—"

Tremaine? Sarah looked up, wondering if it could be the sheriff she'd met on the mountain. It was hard to see through the crowd, but finally the agitated people shifted, clearing the way. And there he was.

Sheriff Parker Tremaine, his gold star still resting on the soft black leather of his jacket, was the man at the core of the debate, the authority to whom they all appealed. No question it was the same man. Same wavy, dark hair, same startlingly blue eyes. Same tip-tilted smile on the same generously chiseled lips she had admired once before. Apparently he wasn't exactly terrified of the annoyed crowd around him.

Sarah caught her breath. She had found him fairly eye-catching before, but obviously seeing Parker Tremaine from the neck up didn't tell the whole story. As she watched him leaning back against the cashier's counter, listening to the escalating complaints, Sarah finally got the full effect of his long, lazy limbs and tight, narrow hips.

He was even better looking than Ed, she realized. And yet, he had a kindness in his expression that Ed hadn't ever exhibited. Even more appealing, he seemed comfortably indifferent to his looks. His jacket was well-worn, fitting his broad shoulders with a fluid familiarity. His hair was just wavy enough to be unruly, but she saw no sign that Parker cared. Where Ed had always been obsessively gelling or spraying, Parker's hair was merely cut and combed and then ignored. But the result was an unintentional sexiness, as if that slight disarray invited someone to smooth it into place.

Her hands unconsciously stroked the silky fabric of the coat she held. Yes, she concluded, Parker Tremaine wore his sex appeal the same way he wore that shiny badge on the breast of his black leather jacket—lightly. As though both of them were fun but ultimately unnecessary.

She hadn't realized she was staring until she saw that Parker was looking right at her. Even from this distance, she could tell that there was a pleased recognition in his gaze.

Maybe she could help. In a way, she owed him. He had offered to rescue her on the mountain, and he had, without realizing it, actually done so. She hadn't needed a jump start or a can of gas or a new tire. But she had needed that smile, that simple gesture of welcome. He had rescued her confidence, her optimism. He had given her the courage to make it that last mile down the mountain.

She spoke up quickly, just loud enough to be heard over the clamor of voices. "Excuse me? I'm sorry to interrupt, but is there anyone who might be able to tell me about this coat?"

Everyone turned toward her, apparently shocked to discover that there was a witness. Sarah felt herself flushing, slightly uncomfortable at being the center of attention, but then she caught Parker Tremaine's eye one more time, and he was giving her that special smile. She smiled back, but she felt the flush deepen.

"I'm sorry. May I help you?" Two salesclerks came over instantly, chagrined. The rest of the people dispersed edgily, talking to one another in lowered tones, as if wondering what imprudent comments this stranger had overheard.

Sarah pretended to listen to the saleswoman extolling the virtues of Polarweave technology—something about storm cuffs and synthetic insulation and temperature ratings—but she was really watching as Parker Tremaine made his escape through the confused crowd.

As he passed her, he winked conspiratorially in her direction. "Thanks," he mouthed, and she found herself grinning stupidly back, as if she really had done something heroic.

"Damn it, Tremaine, you can't get out of here without promising you're going to do something about that selfish old bastard."

One of the men from the crowd, a seventy-ish, self-important type with a red face and a snub nose, had followed the sheriff to the door and was obviously not going to give up easily.

Parker sighed, pulling on black leather gloves as he shouldered open the shop's front door. A blast of freezing air hit the front of the store, driving the older man back, as the sheriff had no doubt expected it to do.

"I'll take care of it," Parker said firmly as he zipped up his jacket and prepared to exit. "This festival is going to take place even if I have to lock Ward Winters in the county jail until spring."

Ward Winters?

But Sarah was too shocked to say a word. And with a melodic ringing of door bells, Parker Tremaine departed, leaving her standing there, with an expensive black Polarweave coat in her arms and a stupid, disbelieving smile fading from her lips.

FOR THE THIRD TIME, Emma Tremaine Dunbar sat down in the back office of her stationery store, The Paper House, to proof the copy for the Kemble baby announcement.

She prayed that the front door chimes didn't sound. It seemed ridiculous to hope for bad business, but she couldn't afford to get called away again. She had promised Harry that she'd close early. He wanted to have lunch at home together. He wanted to have a "serious talk."

But this announcement had to get to the printer today, or the Kemble family would be justifiably furious. If only she thought Harry would understand. He liked the money her store brought in, but he seemed to think it took care of itself. He didn't accept that Emma should ever be busy when *he* needed her.

Darn. There were three typos. She swiveled to the computer, punching in the keys as fast as she could, trying to call up the Kemble file. She glanced nervously at the clock overhead. It was one. She was already late.

The door chimes rang out. Emma stifled a groan, mentally begged the file to open more quickly, then stood up to return to the sales floor.

But this time it wasn't a customer. It was Harry.

He wasn't in uniform. Harry didn't work on Monday. His days off were Monday and Tuesday, about which he complained bitterly, blaming Parker for designing an unfair schedule. Emma had pointed out once that Parker's own schedule was even worse—he didn't even get two days off in a row—but Harry didn't care. Whenever anything displeased him these days, it was always Parker's fault.

Or Emma's. She looked at Harry's tight face and wondered why he was still so unhappy. Last year had been so different. Back before Parker had moved home and snagged the job Harry had wanted. Before the other bad news, before they had discovered that they…

Well, just *before*. They had been happy then. They had laughed—a lot. Now she couldn't remember the last time Harry had even smiled.

And yet, in spite of his frown, he looked so darling today, in that brown suede jacket she'd given him for his birthday, which matched his brown hair perfectly. Her heart did a couple of hot little thumps, thinking how much she loved her husband—and yet how little she seemed to be able to comfort him.

"I knew I'd find you here," he said stiffly. "I knew you'd forget I had asked you to come home for lunch."

"I didn't forget," she said, vowing not to take offense. "I had customers."

He looked around the empty store, commenting silently on its emptiness.

"And then I had an order to proof." She felt her patience giving out on her. "Come on, Harry. You aren't always able to get home on time, either. Do I give you this kind of grief about it?"

He tightened his lips. "I don't think you can really equate the two, do you? I think enforcing the law might be just a little more significant than sending out invitations to Birthday With Bozo."

Emma stared at him helplessly. She wanted to go up to this sour, embittered man and grab him by his suede collar and shake him until he told her what he had done with her real husband. Or else she wanted to go up and kiss him until he thawed, until he remembered that he was special, no matter what had happened to make him feel so insecure. Until he remembered that she loved him, and she always would.

But she'd already tried those things, more or less. And they hadn't worked. They'd only driven him deeper into his emotional hole. Apparently he didn't want to get better. And he didn't like it that she seemed to be able to move on, to put together a happy life in spite of the grim disappointments they had endured this past year.

Her strength didn't sustain him. It only made him feel even more inferior.

But she wouldn't be weak just to please him. She wouldn't drown with him, no matter how much she loved him.

"Well, we're together now. How about if I lock the

door, and we can have our conversation here? What did you want to talk about?"

He raked his hand through his hair. "You know what. The poster. I want you to explain to me why you took it down. I want to know why you aren't willing to campaign for your own husband. I want to know why, when the income from my career supports you, too, you can't do even that one little thing to help me win."

Emma's heart was beating rapidly. Stalling, she arranged herself on the edge of the nearest table, careful not to dislodge the large sample books of cards and invitations. She took a deep breath and gave Harry a steady look.

"That's not a conversation," she said. "That's an interrogation."

"I don't care what you call it. I want some answers."

"So do I." She folded her hands in her lap, to help her resist the temptation to choke him. "I want to know why you'd put me in the embarrassing, distressing position of having to choose between my brother and my husband."

Harry narrowed his eyes. "And I want to know," he said, his voice acid, "why that choice should be even the slightest bit difficult."

The urge to shake him grew stronger. Was it possible he really didn't understand this? That his self-absorption had become so complete that he couldn't imagine what she was feeling?

"Because I love you both, you idiot. Because you and Parker are the two most important people in the world to me. I can live with the fact that you are competing for the same job. But I will not be forced to take sides."

"You're already taking sides. If you don't publicly

support me, it makes me look bad. Everyone will know what that means."

"I disagree," she said, still striving to be rational. "I think it makes you look good. It shows that you're not eager to make this campaign any more uncomfortable for your family than it has to be. It makes you look as if you're sensitive to your wife's dilemma. *Even if you're not.*"

He made an angry gesture. "Oh, so now I'm not sensitive, either?"

"Harry, for heaven's sake—"

To her dismay, the front door chimed, and a customer walked in. Oh, God, she had forgotten to lock the door. The tension of living with this new Harry was making her absolutely crazy.

It was a middle-aged woman. A tourist. You could tell by her deep copper suntan, something you never saw on the faces of locals. She was dusting snow from her shoulders, oblivious to the fact that she was shaking it onto the Valentine's display Emma had just begun to assemble, where it would melt and ruin everything it touched.

The woman patted her big, teased helmet of preposterous yellow hair, transferred her huge designer purse from one hand to another and scanned the store avidly. "Have you marked down your Christmas cards yet?"

Emma stood politely. "Yes," she said. "I'll show you where they are. Just give me a minute to—"

But Harry was already gone.

THE COAT HAD COST her three times what she could afford, but as Sarah trudged up the winding path toward Winter House, which sat at the top of a small, snow-covered hill, she decided it was worth every penny.

Though it was only about two in the afternoon, the temperature had begun to drop, and the light had taken on a bluish cast, as if twilight were impatiently pressing against the sun. The falling snow was thicker now, and with every step Sarah's feet sank into several inches of fresh white powder.

Looking up toward the mansion, Sarah saw that it, too, had been transformed by winter. In that long-ago summer, to the thirteen-year-old Sarah who had harbored here, Winter House had seemed like a happy, honey-colored, sun-kissed castle. The hill it stood on had been kelly-green, and the surrounding lush parkland of oaks had softened the mansion's asymmetrical lines.

It was different now, in this stark setting. It was more like some mysterious, silent abbey—dark and complicated and vaguely forbidding. For the first time, she could see that the mansion had been aptly titled. Even if its owners had been named Smith, this would have been Firefly Glen's Winter House.

It was a typical nineteenth-century Gothic mansion of fawn-colored stone. Its eccentric, disorderly silhouette of crenellated towers, steeply pointed arches crested with fleur-de-lis, wide oriel windows, turrets, spires and gables stood out boldly against the low, oppressive pewter sky.

Rising from its bare and snow-covered hill, it looked like the ultimate temple of winter: cold and hauntingly beautiful.

When Sarah finally reached the huge oak doors, which were decorated with bold iron strap hinges and a brass lion's mouth knocker, she almost expected it to swing open with a creak, revealing a shuffling, half-mad hunchback.

Instead, the door was answered by a charming woman of about sixty-five, with silver hair impeccably groomed, pink lips, sparkling brown eyes, and a trim figure displayed to advantage in a shirtwaist dress patterned in giant yellow tulips, as if in defiance of the weather.

At the sight of Sarah, the woman smiled sweetly and swept the door wide.

"Oh, how wonderful, you must be Sarah. Ward has told me so much about you. It's just marvelous to meet you. Just an absolute delight. Come in, come in. You must be freezing. Give me your coat—what a lovely coat. Your uncle will be so happy. I'm Madeline Alexander, dear, a great friend of your uncle's."

Apparently without drawing a breath, she whisked Sarah's coat away, hung it on a large oak hall stand and kept talking.

"Yes, a very great friend. In fact, dear, I'll tell you a secret," she said as she led Sarah by the arm through the enormous, wood-paneled front hall, moving so briskly that Sarah barely had time to register the ribbed, vaulted ceiling and thick tapestries draped along the walls. "I'm probably going to marry your uncle Ward someday."

Sarah hesitated without thinking, pulling the older woman to an abrupt stop. "What?" Her uncle's letters had never even mentioned anyone named Madeline.

Madeline smiled peacefully. "Well, he doesn't know it yet, of course. And you don't need to mention it to him—it would only upset him." She patted Sarah's shoulder with a beautifully manicured hand. "It'll just be our little secret, all right?"

Sarah began walking again, unsure what else to do. Madeline seemed quite in control of the situation, and completely at home in the mansion. "Your uncle is in the library. He does love the library, doesn't he? Although I think it's rather gloomy. Those stained-glass windows may be quite valuable, but they do strange things to the light, don't they? Right here, dear. I keep forgetting it's been so long since you've visited. You probably don't remember where the library is."

But Sarah did remember. The library had been her favorite room, too. She and her uncle had spent many a happy hour here, lost in deep, philosophical conversations over a game of chess. Uncle Ward had been the world's best listener, and his young, unhappy great-niece had had much she wanted to say.

Suddenly she was so eager to see her uncle that she wanted to burst through those doors and wrap her arms around him. She felt a burning behind her eyes, thinking of him living in this huge, strange mansion, all alone now that Aunt Roberta was gone. She wanted to hold him close, to apologize for letting Ed stop her from coming to Aunt Roberta's funeral. And she wanted to thank him for extending his friendship, opening his haven—on that long-ago summer, and again today, when she was almost as vulnerable as she had been at thirteen.

But that was probably just the hormones acting up again. With effort she restrained herself. Effusive boiling over of affection wasn't Uncle Ward's style. If such feelings were ever to be shared between them, it would be more subtle. Indirectly, through a seemingly impersonal discussion of art or literature or theater, they would make their emotions understood.

So Sarah hung back, letting Madeline, who obviously relished acting as mistress of the mansion, throw open the ornate doors and announce her formally.

It took a moment for Sarah's eyes to adjust to the

light, what little there was. Red and yellow stained-glass windows made up one whole wall of the library, and the winter sun was just barely strong enough to penetrate. The result was that everything—leather-bound books, mahogany tables, Oriental carpets and people alike—seemed washed in a watery golden glow.

Sarah had been expecting to see her uncle enthroned here in lonely splendor. But as her vision cleared she saw that at least four other people were in the room.

Two women of approximately Madeline's age perched in the window seat, pouring tea from a tea set that probably was silver but glowed an eerie bronze in the strange light. Her uncle sat in his usual chair—his throne, Aunt Roberta had always teasingly called it. It was a heavy, carved monstrosity with serpent arms and lion's claw feet.

And in the chair beside him sat another man. This had been Sarah's chair, that summer. The chair of honor. The chair of the chosen chess partner, the lucky confidant, the favored friend.

She squinted, unable to believe her eyes. But it was true. The man who sat in that chair today was the sheriff of Firefly Glen. The man who, just half an hour ago, had threatened to put her uncle in jail.

CHAPTER FOUR

SARAH WENT FIRST to her uncle, surrendering in spite of herself to the overwhelming impulse to envelop him in a tight hug. For a long moment, she remained there, silently drinking in the comfort of his wiry strength, his familiar scent of soap and leather and pipe tobacco. Oh, she was so glad she had come. She hadn't felt this safe in a long, long time.

He accepted her embrace with uncharacteristic patience and warmth, as if perhaps he, too, had found the years apart too long and lonely. But just when she began to fear she might dissolve into overemotional tears, he patted her back briskly and chuckled in her ear.

"If you don't let go soon, Sarah, my love, you'll ruin my reputation as a prickly old bastard. And then I'll have to beat the Alexander sisters off with a stick."

Sarah grinned and pulled away, finally remembering her manners. Turning, she faced the others. "I'm sorry," she said, smiling. "Hello."

Madeline took over. "Oh, my dear, you mustn't apologize. Of course you want to say hello to your uncle, after all these years. It's just the sweetest thing. Well, now, I'd like you to meet my sisters. Flora and Arlene, Flora's the eldest. I'm the youngest, of course—" this with a flirtatious double blink in Ward's direction. "I know they'll be happy to pour a cup of tea for you. You do like tea, don't you? It's just the thing on such a nasty day."

The two women over by the stained-glass window immediately began clinking cups and saucers and pouring steaming, aromatic liquid. The sisters were every bit as lovely as Madeline, though they couldn't match her rippling stream of charming chatter. They didn't, in fact, seem to try. They merely beamed at Sarah and nodded their heads in agreement that, yes, it was delightful finally to meet her.

"And the guy with the badge over there," Sarah's uncle said from behind her, "is Sheriff Parker Tremaine. Tremaine, this is my niece. Keep away from her. I haven't had a long visit with her in fifteen years, and I don't plan to share her visit with anybody."

"Hello, Sarah." Parker, who had stood at Sarah's arrival, smiled that cockeyed smile she remembered all too well. "I was hoping I'd get a chance to say thank you in person. Your niece and I have already met, Ward," he added blandly. "She saved my life about an hour ago."

"She did what? How?" Ward looked irritated. "No, don't even tell me. Sarah, I'm going to have to ask you not to fall in love with Tremaine here. It would be just too boring. Every other female in the Glen already has beaten you to it. Hypnotized by the badge, I guess. You know women. Anything that sparkles."

Madeline made a small, offended noise. "Not *every* woman, Ward," she sniffed, but the old man just rolled his eyes and ignored her.

"Besides," Ward went on, obviously enjoying himself, "he's kind of a half-ass sheriff, and lately he's been annoying the hell out of me. But he's a passable chess player, so I haven't thrown him out. Yet."

"Actually, I think you should hear this story." Parker Tremaine was clearly undaunted, as amused by the bickering as her uncle was. He tossed a wink at Sarah. "It's a good story, Ward. You'll love it—it's all about you. See, your niece rescued me from a lynch mob. That's right, a lynch mob, ready to string me up in the town square. And you know why? Because I haven't slapped you in jail yet."

"Ha! Put *me* in jail?" Ward raised his shaggy black eyebrows. "You and whose army?"

"The Chamber of Commerce army, Ward. Every one of the Firefly Glen innkeepers, shop owners, ski renters and hot chocolate vendors who had planned to get rich from the ice festival. They think you're trying to destroy them financially, and they don't plan to lie down and let you do it. I'm pretty sure the words 'libel' and 'punitive damages' were mentioned."

So that was what it had all been about, all those tense faces and strained voices at the clothing store. Sarah looked over at her uncle, perplexed. She wondered what he'd done.

"Oh, what a bunch of babies," Ward said, waving his hand in a symbolic dismissal of the entire argument. "It was just a couple of little letters to the editor. Just one man's opinion. This is America, isn't it—even this far north? Since when did it become libel to express your opinion?"

"I'm pretty sure it's *always* been libelous to imply that there's something dangerously wrong with the Glen's tap water."

To Sarah's surprise, her uncle looked sheepish, an expression she didn't remember ever seeing on his rugged face before. "Well, mine tastes funny, Tremaine, and that's a fact. Try it. Tastes like hell."

"It's always tasted like hell. It's the minerals. You know that. And honestly, Ward. Ten newspapers? Including the *New York Times?*"

"Well, I didn't think they'd *run* it," Sarah's uncle said, his voice a low grumble.

"Tea, Ward?" Madeline chirped merrily. Ward glared at her, but she kept bustling around, gathering up his cup and saucer, tsking and fluffing his napkin. Sarah couldn't tell what had set the older woman into such a dither. Was it because the topic of the ice festival upset her, or was she just tired of being left out of the conversation?

"Flora, do pour Ward a fresh cup. His is cold. Do you think it might be a little chilly in here? I do." She shivered prettily. "I think we might have let the fire burn down too far. I'll fix it. I just love a good strong fire, don't you?"

Brass poker in one hand, Madeline opened the heavy metal screen that covered the flaming logs and began stirring carelessly. The fire surged in a whoosh of sound, one of the bottom logs collapsed, and embers flew out like red and orange fireworks.

Just as Madeline turned away, one of the embers settled on the bright yellow tulips of her flowing skirt. Sarah noticed it and felt a faint stirring of alarm, but before she could say a word, the frothy fabric began to blacken and curl. A lick of flame started traveling with hideous speed up the back of Madeline's dress.

"Oh!" Madeline was turning around, trying to see what was happening. She was clearly too rattled to do anything sensible. With a whimper of fear, one of her sisters tossed a cup of tea over the flame, but it was half empty, and managed to extinguish only one sizzling inch of fabric. The rest still burned.

Sarah began to run. Ward began to run. But miraculously Parker was already there, gathering up the skirt in his hands and smothering the flames.

It was out in an instant. Just as quickly as it had begun, the crisis was over. Half-crying with nervous relief, Madeline collapsed helplessly into Ward's waiting arms. She murmured weak thanks to Parker, but she didn't lift her face from Ward's shoulder and so the words were muffled and, it seemed to Sarah, just slightly grudging.

It was as if Madeline resented the fact that Parker, not Ward Winters, had stepped forward to be her hero.

But Parker didn't seem to care. He accepted Madeline's thanks, and that of her sisters, with a comfortable lack of fuss, as if he did such things every day. Marveling at his indifference to his own courage, Sarah stared at the sheriff. He was still down on one knee, his hand resting on a lean, muscular length of thigh, graceful even at such a moment. His careless waves of black hair fell over his broad forehead as he checked the carpet for any live embers.

Sarah swallowed against a dry throat. Madeline might prefer her heroes to be silver haired, craggy faced and over seventy. But if Sarah had been in the market for a hero, *which she wasn't,* Parker Tremaine would have been just what the fairy tale ordered.

A minute ago, he had joked about how she had saved his life. But he had *really* saved Madeline just now. With his hands. His bare hands— She looked at those hands. Blisters had begun to form on the palms. Everyone was clustered around Madeline, oohhing and aahing over her near escape. Why wasn't anyone worrying about Parker?

She touched his shoulder softly.

"Sheriff," she said, trying to force out of her stupid mind any thoughts of fairy tales, to think only of ointment and bandages, aspirin and common sense. "Come with me, and I'll find something to put on your hands."

LUCKILY, PARKER KNEW where the first-aid supplies were kept at Winter House. Madeline, who was glued to Ward's shoulder, was making a hell of a racket. Sarah Lennox, inquiring politely where the bandages were stored, was no match for her.

Parker knew he didn't really need a bandage. The damage to his hands was minimal—just one small blister on each palm. He got more torn up chopping wood every week or two. But Sarah looked so sweetly concerned he just couldn't resist. And besides, it would give him a couple of minutes alone with her, something he'd been hoping for ever since he first glimpsed her on the mountain this morning.

He had fully expected to meet her again sooner or later. Firefly Glen was too small for any two people to avoid each other for long, even if they were trying. But what a piece of luck that she should be related to his good friend Ward.

"The supplies are upstairs," he said, cocking his head toward the doorway, inviting her to follow him. "I'll show you."

Back before indoor plumbing, the bathroom had been a small bay-windowed bedroom adjacent to Ward's own suite. When the mansion had been updated to include all the modern amenities, this room and several others had morphed into bathrooms and walk-in closets.

As a result, it looked like the bath in some fantastic monastery. It was painted Madonna blue, with a ribbed, domed ceiling forming a Gothic arch over the claw-footed bathtub. The bay windows were blue and gold stained glass.

Sarah smiled as Parker opened the door. "I'd forgotten how amazing this house is," she said. "When I was here as a kid, I was a little afraid of it. I was always getting lost."

"I'll bet. I still do. I'm convinced the place was designed by a lunatic." Parker unlatched the medicine chest with the tips of his fingers, revealing a well-stocked supply of ointments and bandages. He held out his hands and smiled. "Okay, then. Be gentle."

Sarah smiled back and, as she leaned forward to assess the damage, he could just barely smell her perfume. Nice stuff. Sweet and modest, but with a hidden kick to it. A lot like the impression he got of Sarah herself.

Not that he'd know anything about that. Not really. Not yet.

"Oh, dear," she said, running the tips of her fingers across the pads of his palm, tracing the outline of the biggest blister. "Does it hurt a lot?"

He couldn't decide whether she'd be more impressed if he suffered agonizing pain stoically, or if he professed himself too tough to feel pain at all. So he settled for the truth. "It's pretty minor. Stings a little. I used her skirt to do most of the work. The worst of the fire never got to my hands."

Guiding his hand toward the basin, Sarah turned on the water and let its soft, cool trickle run over his palm. The pain stopped immediately, and he had to admit it was something of a relief. She kept his hand there, cupped within hers almost absently, while she scanned the labels of the available ointments.

"She was lucky you were nearby." Sarah frowned at the cabinet, as if she didn't see what she wanted. "At least you knew what to do and weren't afraid to do it. I think the rest of us were paralyzed with shock."

"Oh, I don't know," he said. "Ward was only a step or two behind. And I'm not at all sure Madeline wouldn't rather have waited for him."

She glanced up, and their eyes met in the mirror. She had great eyes—hazel, with deep flecks of green. And they seemed to have so many moods. On the mountain, he would have called them sad. Vulnerable. But then, in the shop, he'd been struck with how perceptive they looked. Now they were uptilted, dancing with amusement in a way he found absolutely adorable.

"I noticed that, too," she said with a small laugh. "Incredible. Madeline's clothes are on fire, and she's thinking about romance?"

"She's in love." Parker allowed Sarah to place his other hand under the spigot. "You know how that is, I'm sure."

Until he saw the guarded expression fall over Sarah's face, he hadn't even realized what he was asking. But she knew. She had instinctively sensed the question behind the question.

Are you already spoken for? Should I back off—or is it okay to take another step forward?

Well, heck, of course she knew. She was beautiful, smart, sexy, interesting. She probably saw that question in men's eyes every day. And, judging from the way the amusement had flicked off behind her eyes, she didn't much like it.

But because he was a fool, and because he suddenly itched to know, he pressed. "Come on. Admit it. Hasn't love ever made you do anything really, really stupid?"

"Of course," she said tightly, turning off the water and reaching for the nearest hand towel. She took a deep breath, and finally she smiled again. "But I think I can safely say, Sheriff, that if there's a man in this world worth setting myself on fire for, I haven't met him yet."

Parker laughed. "Good," he said. He was absurdly satisfied by her answer. What was going on here? Was he flirting with Ward's niece? That would be dumb.

But he hadn't been this fascinated by a woman since the day he met Tina.

Well, everyone knew where *that* had landed him. In six years of hell, and then in one ugly, pocket-draining day of divorce court. You'd think he would have learned his lesson.

Still…Sarah Lennox was inexplicably intriguing. Maybe it was that hint of her uncle's determination in her jaw, so at odds with her fragile femininity.

Or more likely it was just his own hormones growing restless. He had actually enjoyed his year of celibacy. It had been a relief after Tina, a time of emotional and physical R and R.

But maybe, just maybe, a year was long enough.

Wow. He pulled himself up with an embarrassed yank. That was damn cocky. And way off base. Sarah Lennox didn't look at all like the kind of woman who would find it fun to share the sheets with some relative stranger during her winter vacation. Even more to the point, while she was friendly and polite, she hadn't shown signs of being one bit overwhelmed by his manly dimples.

Not to mention how Ward would react if Parker started exercising his hormones again with the old man's favorite great-niece. Ward might be in his late seventies, but he was still plenty tough enough to scatter pieces of Parker's body all over a tri-county area.

Parker returned reluctantly to reality. While he and his ego had been taking that stupid mental flight, Sarah had already smoothed on the ointment. Now she was ready for the bandage. She gingerly placed a snow-white square of sterile gauze against the first blister, then started winding a strip of bandage around his hand to keep it in place. She seemed completely focused on her task, eyes down, lower lip clasped between her teeth intently.

Parker felt a little silly. It was just a blister, for Pete's sake. And he was damned glad that Emma couldn't see him. He probably looked like an overeager lapdog, holding out his blistered paws so Sarah could make them better.

But he had to admit it was kind of sweet.

"Tell me," she said as she tied off the bandage. "What's really going on with my uncle and the ice festival?"

She let go of his hand and began on the other one. Parker flexed his fingers for a moment, testing the bandage, before he answered. He didn't want to upset her. But maybe she could help him make Ward see reason.

"He's putting up some serious opposition this year. Some of the merchants in town think he's damaging them financially. They're pretty steamed up over it."

Sarah looked thoughtful. "But I thought Firefly Glen has always had an ice festival. I remember my uncle telling me about it when I was just a little girl. He made it sound charming."

"Yeah, he and Roberta used to love it. They were even king and queen one year, back when they were first married. But the festival keeps getting bigger. New events are added, bringing in more and more tourists. Ward's been grumbling for years now, saying it's going to ruin the Glen."

"Is it?" Sarah looked up from her work, her eyebrows arched in a serious query. "That would be tragic."

She sounded sincere. Maybe she understood, Parker thought. Maybe she already felt a little of the magic of this peaceful valley. After all, she lived in Florida, a tropical paradise that wobbled on the same environmental tightrope.

"I don't know," he said honestly. "It could. All you have to do is look at some of the big tourist spots around here to see how tacky and congested things could get. But I guess it's human nature. If you're a businessman, you always want more business."

He sighed, feeling as conflicted as he did whenever he tackled this conundrum. "Anyhow, this year the city council voted to open some of the events to outsiders, and to advertise big time. I think, for Ward, that was just the last straw. He's making it his mission to ensure that the festival fails."

Sarah was finished with his hands. He held them up, eyeing the white gauze skeptically. He looked like a prizefighter, taped and ready to don his gloves. His deputies would get a good laugh out of this. They already liked to tease him about being a "city kid," even though he was born and raised right here in the Glen. Those years in Washington had really cost him.

Sarah put her supplies carefully back in the cabinet. She lowered herself to the edge of the large white tub and looked up at him, her expression more somber than ever.

"He actually wants it to fail? That must make a lot of people very angry," she said.

He nodded. "It does."

"How angry?" Her voice was quiet. "Do you think my uncle is in any danger?"

What should he say? He didn't think so. He knew these people, had known many of them all his life, and they weren't wicked. They weren't violent. They were, for the most part, people who valued solitude, people who revered nature, people who believed in individualism. That was why they had chosen to live in such a place, where nature was raw and beautiful, so dangerous it taught you courage, so powerful it taught you humility.

But he couldn't be sure. He had experienced enough to have learned that you never *really* knew how far a person would go if you pushed him. And Ward was definitely pushing.

"I can't be sure," he said carefully. "I don't think so, but I'd be a whole lot happier if Ward would back off a little. It's true that love makes people do some pretty weird things. Well, so does money."

Sarah studied his face for a long moment, as if she were trying to read between his lines. Finally she took a deep breath and stood, smoothing her honey-colored hair back with one steady hand. She was only about five-four, and she probably didn't weigh a hundred and ten pounds dripping wet, but she looked like a force to be reckoned with. She also looked sexy enough to make Parker's palms tingle where she had dressed them.

"I see," she said. "Then maybe it's a good thing I came when I did."

Parker couldn't have agreed more.

IT WAS NINE O'CLOCK. Snow had been floating outside the library windows for hours. Sarah and Ward had long ago fallen quiet, in that lovely way good friends do, when comfortable intimacy has no need of words.

Plus, the chess game had reached its climax. Sarah had just realized that her uncle's king was only two pawns away from her undefended queen.

But then the telephone rang.

Its metallic trill was jarring, an ugly crack running through the glassy silence. Though the phone actually had been sitting on the table beside Ward's chair all along, Sarah stared at it as if it had landed there from outer space.

Ward didn't seem to share her confusion. He answered it without skipping a beat, taking her pawn with an evil grin even as he said, "Hello?"

Then, to her surprise, he held the phone across the chessboard. "It's for you."

Sarah's heart thumped uncomfortably in her throat. For her? Who could it be? She mentally scanned the few possibilities. She had told the school, of course, in case her replacement teacher had questions. And her mother, on the off chance that she and Husband Number Four would worry.

And Ed.

But Ed wouldn't call. Would he? She had left a curt sentence on his answering machine. *I'm going to stay with my uncle for a while.* And then, almost an after-thought. *I know you'll be gone by the time I get back. Have a nice life.*

So it couldn't be Ed. He was officially off the hook, and he'd probably take the fastest jet he could find to California, thanking his lucky stars she hadn't made a scene. Of course, someday they would have to talk. She didn't want any money from him, but still…someday there would be issues of what to tell the baby. And would Ed want to know when the baby was born? Would he want information, pictures, visits…*rights?*

She knew she had taken the coward's way out, leaving that message. Perhaps in their future lay unpleasant negotiations with lawyers, difficult conversations with their families, wrenching decisions about a thousand little things. But not yet. Please. She wasn't ready yet.

She must have looked frozen, because Ward frowned, tilted his head and gave her a quick, assessing glance. Then, before she could will her hand to reach out, he brought the telephone back to his own ear.

"Sarah's not available," he said in a voice of gruff authority. "I said she's not available. If you'd like, I'll take a message."

He listened a minute, muttered another syllable or two, then pressed the disconnect button and lay the phone facedown on the end table.

"That was Ed," he said casually, his gaze on the chessboard. "He still sounds constipated. Your move."

Obediently Sarah studied the pieces, but she couldn't help smiling. Oh, how she loved this tough and wonderful old man! She could just picture Ed right now, staring in outraged disbelief at the dead receiver. He wasn't accustomed to being thwarted. He liked being the boss—at work, and, she realized now, even at home with her.

In a twisted way, he probably would actually have

enjoyed fatherhood. All that power, all that sheer physical superiority.

She shuddered slightly, thinking of it. She stared down at her doomed queen and came to a decision.

"You know, it may be inevitable, but I don't feel like surrendering tonight." She looked up and gave her uncle a crooked smile. "Let's finish this tomorrow."

He leaned back in his chair, stretching so broadly it made the old wood and leather creak. "Good idea. I think we both could use some fresh air," he said. "Feel like taking a walk around the lake?"

She darted a glance at the windows. "It's still snowing, isn't it? Won't it be awfully cold?"

Ward laughed as he headed across the room, making for the hallway, where the coats and hats were kept. "Of course it's cold, Short Stuff. That's the point, isn't it? Otherwise you'd be back in Florida, working on your suntan and bickering with your boyfriend."

He was right, of course. The minute they stepped outside, she knew it. Here was a new world, a world of such mysterious beauty that Ed and his temper immediately faded to total insignificance. Even her pregnancy seemed merely a simple, uncomplicated truth, one small detail in the huge, unstoppable rhythms of nature. She couldn't worry. She couldn't plan. She could suddenly do nothing but admire this amazing, magnificent landscape.

With a strange sense of excitement, she curled her fingers inside the cashmere-lined gloves her uncle had loaned her. "I love it," she said, tucking her arm through his. "And I love *you*."

He made a low growl in his throat. She had violated one of his basic rules—No Mushy Stuff. But then he chuckled, forgiving her. "Come on. You ain't seen nothing yet."

They walked slowly, their feet sinking into the brand-new snow with soft crunches. Though slow, fat flakes fell all around them, it was easy to find their way. The moon was huge and blue, so close it seemed to be pressing its face against the treetops, peering in at them, trying to make contact.

"There's the swinging tree," Ward said, pointing to a gigantic cottonwood, its gray, ridged bark bright in the moonlight. No rope-and-plank swing hung there tonight. "Remember? That means the lake's not far now."

During Sarah's summer here, they had walked around Llewellyn's Lake almost every day. Afterward, she'd seen it in her dreams a hundred times, reliving the green-and-gold hours of laughter, the kites, the picnics, the scarlet cardinals blinking between the trees, the clumsy ducks clamoring for crusts of bread.

But when they finally reached the lake, she could hardly believe her eyes. It was frozen solid, a hard, vast expanse of blue and white and gray, as if a chunk of moon had fallen to the earth. They stopped at the edge, between two snow-heavy pines, and stared over its eerie contours.

"See that little white light over there?" Ward pointed toward the north. "Brighter than the others—straight across the lake from us? That's the light at the end of Parker Tremaine's dock. Just in case you were curious."

Sarah could barely make it out. It winked in and out of snowflakes. She turned to her uncle with a quizzical smile. "Curious about what?"

"About where the sheriff lived." His voice was bland, but Sarah noticed he didn't meet her gaze. "It's not one of the Season houses. But it's a respectable spread anyhow. The Tremaines have been around the Glen forever. They're good people." He paused. "He's a good man."

Sarah took a deep breath—then wished she hadn't, as the freezing air burned into her lungs. She coughed slightly, hugging her uncle's arm a little tighter. "You wouldn't be thinking about matchmaking, would you, Uncle Ward?"

"Matchmaking?" He sounded indignant. "Hell, no. Why would I do that? You're getting married on Valentine's Day, right? Nope, I just thought you might like to know where the sheriff lived. You know, in case there's ever any trouble."

She pressed a little closer, using his strong body to block the wind. "What kind of trouble? You mean about the ice festival? Surely it won't come to that."

"Well, now, you can't tell. One of those greedy apes in town might decide I'm too much of a nuisance. Take Bourke Waitely. He owns the hotel, and he's got a temper like a wet weasel. Smells like one, too. He might get some dumb idea that he could stop me."

She stared out at the lake. The snow was letting up, and moonlight flashed off its icy surface.

"I don't really know many of the details," she ventured carefully, "but would it be so terrible if you let the festival proceed? I mean, rather than risk getting anyone so angry that…" She sighed. "I just want you to be careful."

When he didn't answer, she looked up at him, her concern deepening. Snow dusted his broad shoulders and sparkled against his navy blue ski cap. He looked as if he belonged in this harsh landscape. Tough and rugged and alone.

And yet, though he looked almost the same as he had fifteen years ago, the truth was that he was getting older. He wasn't as invincible as he once had been. She found that she couldn't bear the thought of any harm coming to him.

"The year Firefly Glen was incorporated," he said suddenly, his voice edgy and bitter, "there were only fifty residents, all loggers and trappers. Simple people. And there was one tiny path scratched through the mountains, just wide enough for a wagon. But then a bunch of New York millionaires decided the Glen was the perfect place to escape from the crowds and the dirty air. And before you could say *hell no,* they were everywhere, building mansions just like the ones they were so eager to get away from."

He clicked his teeth irritably. "They even had to cut a new road through the pass just so they could fit all their fancy furniture and gew-gaws. That's why the loggers named it Vanity Gap, because it was the hole those rich fools squeezed their egos through."

Sarah chuckled. She'd heard the story before, but she never tired of it. It always amused her to hear her uncle's indignation, as intense and righteous as if he'd been one of the original loggers himself—when, in fact, he was a direct descendent of one of those pesky millionaires.

"And what exactly does this have to do," she said, nudging him gently, "with the ice festival?"

"Oh, I don't know. I guess it's just more of the same. More change." He sighed heavily. "Too much change. You know, your aunt hasn't been gone a full year, but I wonder whether she'd even recognize some things around here today. They're building a new subdivision in the woods where I asked her to marry me."

He squared his jaw hard. "I look around, Short Stuff, and I wonder how long it will be before there's nothing left. Nothing left from before."

"I know how much you must miss her," Sarah said quietly, beginning to understand her uncle's fierce opposition to change. "I miss her, too. She was always so happy. She made everyone around her happy, too. You two had the most beautiful marriage I've ever seen."

"She was too damn good for me, and that's the truth." Ward finally turned to Sarah. "Listen. It's none of my business, but I've just got to say something. Just this one thing, and then I'll shut up, I promise."

"You don't have to," Sarah broke in, anticipating where he was heading. "I already know what you're going to say."

Ward looked grim. "I doubt it. You don't use words like this."

She chuckled. "Really, I *do* know. And it's okay. I'm not going to."

He tilted his head. "Not going to what?"

She smiled. "I'm not going to marry a constipated son of a bitch who doesn't give a flying flip about anything except himself."

Ward whooped with laughter. He gathered her up into his arms and swung her around until she felt lightheaded, just as he had done when she was only thirteen. "Well, darn it, Short Stuff. Why the hell didn't you say so?"

CHAPTER FIVE

"YOU TELL YOUR UNCLE I want to know how he likes that book," the tall, slim, silver-haired owner of Black Bear Books said as she handed Sarah her change. "Tell him he's overdue for a visit. I've been keeping hot chocolate ready for him ever since Christmas."

Sarah smiled. She'd been in Firefly Glen only three days and she was already getting used to this. Every spinster and widow in town seemed to have a line out, hoping to catch her rich, rugged Uncle Ward. As soon as they realized Sarah was Ward's great-niece, these women turned relentlessly chummy. They tucked little treats under her arm and whispered little messages into her ear, all sent with love to the owner of Winter House.

Somehow Sarah managed to get out of the shop without committing her uncle to anything. She'd learned that, too—the women might be angling for him, but Ward had no intention of getting snagged on any of those sugary hooks.

Sarah wasn't due back at Winter House until lunchtime, so she walked slowly, browsing the shop windows. It was cold, but the air was crisp and clean, and the sunlight was neon-white. She'd had to buy a pair of sunglasses. Naively, she had never guessed that a cold

New York sun shining on snow was every bit as blinding as a hot Florida sun reflecting off the water.

Shifting the load of Ward's novels to her other arm, she paused at the entrance to *Bewitching Stitchery*. A nursery display had been set up in the window, with a beautiful rainbow of yarns cascading over the lacy canopy of a gleaming white cradle.

The colors were enticing, and Sarah was tempted to go in. She hadn't ever knitted much—there was little need for sweaters and mittens in Florida. But suddenly she could imagine what fun it would be to create pale pink booties, or baby-blue blankets, or soft, doll-sized caps with fuzzy pompoms on top.

She had her hand on the doorknob before her better judgment pulled her back. That idyllic nursery in the window was just fantasy. And Sarah didn't have time for fantasy. This vacation was supposed to be an opportunity to face reality calmly. A chance to sort things out and make some tough decisions.

Like…what on earth did she think she was doing? Was she strong enough to meet the challenge of single parenthood? She didn't feel strong. She felt downright cowardly. She couldn't even bring herself to tell Ward. How was she going to tell her co-workers, her friends? *Her mother?*

And, when the truth was admitted, then what? She had arranged a six-week leave from Groveland High but was she really going back? What was the point in that? As soon as her contours began to change she would undoubtedly be fired.

And yet, if she didn't go back to Florida, didn't go back to teaching—what *would* she do? How would she support herself and this new life, too?

She felt a tightening of anxiety in the pit of her stomach, a sensation that was becoming all too familiar. She hadn't realized she was still holding on to the knob until the door lurched under her hand and another customer rushed out of the store, clutching bulky shopping bags stuffed with packets of blue and green yarn.

Surprised, Sarah backed up, but her feet slipped on a patch of ice that coated the sidewalk. She had no experience with ice. As if in slow motion, she sought her footing, but she had on the wrong shoes, and there wasn't enough tread to help. The armload of Ward's books unexpectedly tilted her center of gravity. Her arm grabbed for the rapidly closing door—and missed.

She fell helplessly into an undignified heap on the icy sidewalk.

The exiting customer was horrified.

"Oh, I'm so sorry. I didn't see you there! Oh, dear. Let me help you up."

Sarah tried to smile, though her elbow was already aching and she knew she looked ridiculous. "It's nothing. My own stupidity. Don't worry, really. It's nothing."

But as she tried to pull herself to her knees, something in her stomach protested. A white knife of pain shot from her ribs to her hips. Startled by the intensity of the pain, she froze.

"Are you all right?" The woman looked worried. She dropped her bags. "Have you broken something?"

Stay calm, Sarah told herself. She had probably just strained a muscle. She tested her legs and found that she could, indeed, find her way to her feet. But the pain was still there, intensifying as she straightened up completely.

Her mind throbbed, too, registering a formless, wordless fear. She put her gloved hands across her stomach numbly, not even thinking to help as the other woman picked up the scattered books and handed them to her.

She took the books. Her fingers were trembling.

The woman clearly wanted to go, but apparently something in Sarah's face stopped her. "Gosh. I just—are you sure you're okay?"

Sarah nodded numbly. "I'm fine. But could you tell me—" She paused. "Is there a doctor nearby?"

AN HOUR LATER, as she redressed behind the cheerful, soft blue paisley drapes at the ob-gyn's office, Sarah had begun to feel silly.

Not that the obstetrician, a surprisingly young, auburn-haired beauty named Heather Delaney, had said anything to embarrass her. Dr. Delaney had been nothing but soothing and supportive. The office staff had worked her in immediately, and the doctor had checked her out thoroughly, finally pronouncing that the baby was just fine. It was merely a strained muscle. It probably would be better in a couple of days.

But Sarah felt stupid anyhow. She knew that she had foolishly overreacted. She'd panicked at the first small mishap. She'd let the first twinge of pain send her rushing to the doctor, who, in spite of her warm, professional bedside manner, probably thought Sarah was a hypochondriac.

She was buttoning up her green corduroy jumper, arranging the ivory turtleneck sweater beneath, when Dr. Delaney came back into the room, holding a small piece of white paper.

"If you need something for pain," the doctor said, "this should help." She smiled. "Though of course you probably already know that the less medication you take, the better. The baby gets a dose of whatever you swallow, whether it's alcohol or aspirin."

Sarah smiled back. "I don't need anything," she said. "It doesn't really hurt all that much. I was just—" She tugged on the sleeves of her sweater self-consciously. "I guess I'm just so new at this. Everything about it scares me."

Dr. Delaney leaned against the edge of the counter, which was filled with parenting magazines, tissues and silver jars of mysterious instruments. Though Sarah knew the doctor had a waiting room full of patients, she acted as if she had all day to address Sarah's concerns.

"It's pretty overwhelming, isn't it? The idea that you're responsible for creating anything as complex as a human being, somehow insuring that it comes out perfect." She chuckled. "But you know what, Sarah? The baby is definitely in the driver's seat on this one. And believe me, he knows what he's doing. All you have to do is make sure you don't interfere."

Sarah laughed, imagining this determined little being, intently steering his way into existence. Into her life. What a delightfully fantastic image! It made her feel strangely lighthearted about the whole thing for the first time since she had glimpsed that terrifying little pink x on the test strip.

"Wow." She raised her eyebrows. "You mean I'm not the boss here, Dr. Delaney? In a way, that's kind of scary, too, isn't it?"

"You bet!" The doctor grinned. "Because from what I hear, the little darlings are pretty much in control for the next twenty years or so." She wadded up the pain-killer prescription and lobbed it into the gleaming silver trash can in the corner. "But you really have to call me Heather. Everyone does. And I'm a good friend of your uncle's, so—"

"You are?" Why on earth hadn't Sarah thought of this possibility? She obviously hadn't fully absorbed just how *small* a small town really could be. "Oh, I see. I hope you'll—" She wasn't sure how to put this. "Dr. De—I mean, Heather. I—I hope you won't mention that I've been here. You see, I haven't told my uncle about the baby yet."

Heather's green eyes widened, and she looked younger than ever. Her skin was as pale and flawless as if it had been made of ivory satin. But her gaze was intelligent and probing. "I'm a doctor, Sarah, not the town gossip. But do you mind telling me why you haven't said anything to Ward? I've known him all my life, and I'd be willing to bet he'll be absolutely thrilled."

Sarah threaded the straps of her purse around her fingers. This was the difficult part. It was going to be the difficult part for rest of her life, admitting that she had made a terrible mistake, a mistake she and her child were going to have to pay for forever. How could she explain it to others when she hardly understood it herself?

And how could a woman like Heather Delaney understand what a muck-up Sarah had made of her life? After watching her for a mere twenty minutes, Sarah already knew that Dr. Delaney didn't make mistakes. She was serene and beautiful, focused and professional, educated and successful. She wouldn't in a million years have allowed a faulty condom to derail her life plans.

But, as the sages always said, it wasn't the falling

down that was the problem. It was the *staying* down. The mistake was made. Sarah's job now was to face the consequences. And to do it with at least some semblance of grace.

She straightened her shoulders and met the doctor's serious gaze steadily.

"I am going to tell him. Soon. But it's complicated. As you may have guessed, this pregnancy was unplanned. My fiancé and I just broke off our relationship. He's very angry that I intend to keep the baby."

Heather frowned gently. "I'm sorry," she said simply. "That must be difficult."

"Yes. It is." Sarah cleared her throat. "I need a little time to get used to it privately before I share the news with other people. Having a baby alone is a huge responsibility. I honestly don't even know how *I* feel about it yet."

The doctor's frown smoothed out, transforming slowly into a wide, engaging smile. "Oh, I think you know, Sarah." She laughed softly. "I think you know exactly how you feel about it."

For a second, Sarah didn't answer, surprised by the absolute confidence of the other woman's voice. Then she tilted her head. "Really? What makes you think so?"

"The fact that you're here." Heather shrugged, undaunted by the chill in Sarah's tone. "Tell me. What went through your mind when you fell? How did you feel when you thought you might have harmed the baby?"

Sarah swallowed, remembering. "Terrified," she said. "Panicked."

"And why were you so frightened?"

Sarah put her left hand over her stomach. She stared

down at the bare hand, with its naked line of untanned skin where Ed's ring used to be.

"Because I thought I might lose the baby. Because I thought this—this miracle—might be taken away from me."

She shook her head, almost unable to believe the words she was saying, or the sudden clarity that was sweeping through her like rain, cleaning out the fog and the fear.

Sarah looked up, and she knew her surprise was registered on every feature. She could hardly see around the sudden rush of warmth behind her eyes. "Because I can't imagine the rest of my life without this baby."

When her gaze cleared, she saw that Heather Delaney was grinning, and that her lovely green eyes held a hint of moisture, too.

The doctor held out her hand. Still feeling slightly weak with the unexpected emotion, Sarah did the same.

"Congratulations, Ms. Lennox," Heather said, shaking Sarah's hand with a firm, bracing warmth. "You're going to be a mother."

THE FIREFLY GLEN Sheriff's Department was a fairly modern red-brick annex attached to the east side of City Hall. It looked kind of silly, actually. The architect had decided to get creative with the roofline, which tilted up against the bigger building like a tired youngster leaning against its mother.

But Parker wasn't complaining. About a hundred and fifty years newer than City Hall, the department was comfortable and up-to-date. And it was generously proportioned, especially considering the fact that Firefly Glen had almost no crime.

Four deputies, one secretary and a part-time file clerk shared the large main area, which was flanked by Parker's office on one side, and the holding cell on the other. More than fifteen hundred square feet total. There should have been plenty of room for everyone.

But the way Harry Dunbar and Parker were getting along these days, Yankee Stadium itself probably wouldn't have been big enough for both of them.

Parker had taken to scheduling the two of them in different places, on different days, as often as possible. He didn't want to hear Harry talk to Emma on the phone anymore. He didn't think he could stand listening to Harry's cold, distant tone without wanting to plug the son of a bitch. Who the devil did he think he was, treating Emma like that?

Unfortunately, creating distance hadn't been possible today. Their new budget was due at City Hall tomorrow, and it would take both of them to prepare it. Consequently, by four-thirty in the afternoon, the air in the Sheriff's Department stank of tension.

Suzie, who had come in after school to dismantle her manger, sized the situation up the minute she opened the door.

"Oh, great," she said, dropping her electric-purple backpack on her desk in disgust. "Both tigers in the same cage. I guess it'll be a laugh a minute around here." She adjusted her eyebrow ring. "You know, I could have had a job at the Sweet Shoppe," she reminded them.

Harry ignored her, but Parker looked up from his paperwork with his best attempt at a smile. "I'll be glad to write you a reference," he offered.

Her only answer was the trademark Suzie Strickland

withering glare. She stalked into the holding cell and began her work. For the next hour or so, they heard only an occasional muffled curse and the now-familiar electronic lament, "Betsy needs a new diaper."

Parker and Harry continued to work side by side, crunching department budget numbers, without saying a word. When a call came in from Theo Burke, it was almost a relief.

Parker asked a few questions, then hung up and turned to Harry. "That was Theo. She says she's got burglars in her basement."

"No kidding." Suzie stuck her head out of the cell and laughed sarcastically. "I knew she had bats in her belfry, but—"

Parker waved her back into the cell. Suzie's first job had been at the Candlelight Café, but her sarcastic tone had never quite met Theo's exacting standards, so she'd been fired. Apparently the rejection still rankled.

He turned to Harry. "Can you check it out?"

Harry closed the file he'd been working on and stood. "Sure. Fine." He grabbed his jacket and headed for the door.

"Good riddance," Suzie muttered as the door swung shut behind him. She peered around the barred cell door. "That man has some serious attitude going. What is *with* him, anyhow?"

Parker didn't look up. He wasn't going to discuss this with Suzie. There was a slim chance he might not have to discuss it with anyone. After the one aborted attempt to put a campaign poster in Emma's shop window, Harry's campaign had seemed to stall. Almost three weeks had gone by, and he hadn't announced anything officially yet. Maybe he had changed his mind.

"Well, okay, fine." Suzie's voice was huffy. "*Don't* answer me."

"Don't worry. I won't."

The peace didn't last long. Within twenty minutes, Harry was back. And he had Mike Frome and Justine Millner, the mayor's gorgeous eighteen-year-old daughter, with him.

Parker raised his eyebrows toward his deputy.

"The burglars," Harry said succinctly. "I caught them wedged between rows of canned tomatoes. They apparently weren't expecting company. They weren't dressed for entertaining, if you know what I mean."

Oh, good grief. Parker transferred his gaze to the teenagers. Mike met it bravely, but he was struggling, redfaced and miserable. Justine looked down at her hands, modestly weepy and winsome.

At that moment, Suzie rounded the cell corner again, awkwardly dragging two large mannequins behind her. "Could somebody please take Mary and Joseph back to Dickerson's for me? I promised I'd return them today, but I can't do the whole thing alone."

She broke off, finally noticing the other kids. Parker could see that she read the nuances accurately. Suzie, for all her posturing, was actually smart as hell.

"Oh, brother," she said, scanning Justine Millner's graceful slump and disheveled hair. She snorted rudely. "I *swear,* Mike Frome. You are so *lame.*"

"Suzie, back to work." Parker intervened quickly, taking pity on Mike, whose flush had deepened to a deep maroon. "Haul those mannequins over to Dickerson's for her, will you, Harry? I'll take care of our burglars."

Harry agreed readily. Harry wasn't a fool, either. He

knew that busting the mayor's daughter was not the kind of job that won you any medals. He was obviously happy to let Parker do the dirty work.

Finally Parker was alone with the terrified teens. He let them stew a minute, shuffling papers around on his desk and making notes on his calendar. Finally, as Justine began to fidget, he swiveled his chair and faced the guilty pair.

"So, you and Justine were down in Theo Burke's storeroom after hours." He gave Mike a hard look. The kid worked for Theo, for God's sake. He knew that the old woman owned a dainty but perfectly lethal handgun. And she knew how to use it. "What kind of dumb pills have you been taking, Frome?"

"I know, sir," Mike said, hanging his head. "I know. But I was just—I mean we were just—"

"I know what you were just," Parker said. "You were just hunting for your retainer."

Mike looked bewildered. He glanced over at Justine, but that was no help. She had decided to cry. Probably dissolving into charming weeping had been her strategy for every tough situation she'd ever encountered. Mike looked back at Parker. "My retainer?"

Parker shook his head. Had he been this dense when he was eighteen? Would he ever have chosen a spot like Theo Burke's storeroom to romance his girlfriend? Had he ever been horny enough to find industrial-sized cans of stewed tomatoes an aphrodisiac?

Oh, well, hell yes, he had. All teenage boys were exactly that horny.

But this one was about to be in big trouble, unless he started thinking a little faster. Justine had begun to cry noisily, which, if she didn't muffle it quick, was going to annoy Parker so much he'd change his mind about saving her spoiled and, to his mind, somewhat overrated ass.

"That's right. Your retainer." Parker stood, walked over to the sink along the far wall and plucked a paper towel from the dispenser. He held it out toward Mike. "Sadly, you left your retainer in a paper towel in the café's break room. You were almost home before you realized you'd accidentally thrown it away with the night's trash. Right? You didn't want to bother Miss Burke, so you came back to look for it. I can call and explain that to her right now."

Mike was finally catching on. He took the paper towel, retrieved his retainer from his pocket, and folded it up carefully. "But…" He put his arm manfully around Justine's shoulders, though he cast Parker a rather endearing, imploring look. "What about Justine?"

"Justine wasn't there. I think Justine was home doing her schoolwork, don't you?"

Justine, who apparently had been listening intently even through her tears, beamed a beauty queen smile Parker's way, the tears miraculously drying. "Oh, thank you, Sheriff! Thank you so much! I'm going to tell my dad he shouldn't vote for Deputy Dunbar! I don't know why anyone would vote for him anyhow. He's so strict about stuff. He was downright mean tonight."

"Right. Okay, then, we've got that settled." Parker had to work at staying professional. "I'll call Theo. Mike, you stay here in case she wants to talk to you. Justine, you have a car, right?"

"Yes, sir, I do. My dad's BMW is outside." Justine was dabbing at her eyelashes, making sure the tears hadn't caused any makeup damage. "You're so sweet, Sheriff. I know my dad donated money to Deputy

Dunbar's campaign, but I'm going to tell him he should vote for you instead." Justine smiled radiantly toward Parker once more. "You *aren't* a lousy sheriff."

Mike groaned under his breath. "Justine," he begged.

"Well, he's not," she insisted. She leaned over and kissed Mike, then checked her lipstick with her forefinger. "Bye-bye. See you tomorrow."

Parker and Mike watched her go in silence, locked in their own thoughts. Mike, with the single-mindedness of a teenage boy, was undoubtedly lamenting his aborted seduction and wondering when he'd get his next chance.

Parker's thoughts were a little murkier. The mayor was aligned with Harry against him? Well, how about that.

This was what he got for being so moronically self-satisfied with his life recently, he thought. He'd been imagining himself the heroic town lawman, beloved by all, opposed by none—presiding over his idyllic little hamlet with even-handed justice.

Then, on Christmas Eve, the truth had hit him like a shovel. His own brother-in-law was running against him. And now the mayor—and God knows who else—was contributing to Harry's campaign.

Heck, with a war chest like that, Harry might even win.

"I'm really sorry about what Justine said, Sheriff," Mike put in tentatively. "She doesn't think sometimes." He breathed a lovelorn sigh. "But she sure is pretty, isn't she?"

Parker started to make a caustic comment, but who was he to criticize? He'd actually been fool enough to *marry* his mistake.

"Yes," he agreed. "Very pretty. But maybe you two

ought to slow down a little, huh? You wouldn't want to find yourself standing in front of a preacher with Mayor Millner's shotgun in your back."

Mike frowned. "No," he said slowly, as if he found it hard to process the mixed signals his hormones and his common sense were sending him at the same time. He looked at Parker sadly. "But she's gorgeous, you know?"

Suzie made a rude sound from the cell. Both males looked over, surprised. Parker had forgotten she was still here. Clearly Mike had, too.

"Hey, Mike," she called out. "Do you know what Vanity Gap is?"

Mike threw the cell a dirty look. "Yes, weirdo. I know what Vanity Gap is. It's just outside town. It's that road between the mountains."

"Nope." She poked her head out. Her glasses were crooked, and her dark, lanky hair was covered in straw. "It's that space between Justine Millner's ears."

Mike growled and made a pretend lunge, but Suzie darted back into the cell, chuckling evilly.

Parker almost laughed himself, but he managed to turn it into a severe throat-clearing. "Well, maybe we'd better call Theo now."

But Mike hadn't stopped feeling bad about the election. "You know, it's just a rumor," he said. "About Deputy Dunbar running against you. Maybe it isn't even true. You know how rumors are."

Though he knew Harry's campaign was far more than rumor—he'd seen the poster with his own eyes—Parker grinned. "Around here they're as reliable as sunrise. I don't think they've been wrong in two hundred years."

"They're definitely not wrong about Justine," Suzie's disembodied voice rang out.

Mike squinted, then set his jaw, determined to ignore her. "It's mostly about the ice festival, I think. You know, the way old man Winters is trying to get it canceled? Justine said her dad is really mad. He says the festival is super important to people around here. He says you should find a way to make Mr. Winters stop making trouble, like lock him up or something."

Parker chuckled. "Mayor Millner always was a little fuzzy about how the Constitution works."

Mike looked confused, which didn't surprise Parker. The day the teacher covered the Bill of Rights, Mike had probably been obsessing about Justine's tight red sweater.

But he also looked worried. Touched by the boy's sincere concern, Parker patted his shoulder reassuringly. "Hey, don't worry about it. Deputy Dunbar can run if he wants to. It's called democracy. Now come on, let's explain things to Theo before she comes down here and shoots us both."

"AND TEN. And hold it. Excellent, ladies. Excellent. *Hold it!* You can do it!"

Could she? Sarah realized her leg was shaking as she tried to keep it elevated in a donkey kick, the same donkey kick the aerobics instructor was somehow holding so effortlessly.

Amazing how out of shape you could get in just a month.

"And relax! Okay, ladies, very good. Let's take five."

Sarah collapsed in a damp heap on the floor of the gym. She had to be kidding. It was going to take a lot more than five minutes to get her jellied muscles under control again.

"She's tough, isn't she?" Heather Delaney, who had

been right next to Sarah for the past half an hour, smiled sympathetically. It was some consolation to Sarah that the exquisitely toned Dr. Delaney was breathing rather fast herself.

Sarah closed her eyes and groaned. "If this is 'low impact' aerobics, I'd hate to see the hard stuff."

Heather shook her head. "As your doctor, I'd have to forbid it. Her advanced class is only for Amazons and eighteen-year-olds."

The two of them wandered out into the anteroom, where chilled juices and warmed towels were available. For a community center exercise class, the setup was fairly ritzy—and these little niceties reminded Sarah that this definitely wasn't your average community.

As her uncle was always pointing out, though it had started out as a community of loggers and trappers, for more than a hundred years now Firefly Glen had been a favorite hideaway for millionaires. Apparently millionaires even *sweated* in splendor.

"*There* she is!" Heather pointed toward the door, which was just shutting behind two new arrivals. "Well, it's about time. Come with me, Sarah. I want to introduce you to Emma Tremaine. She's supposed to be my best friend, but somehow she always manages to leave me to face the donkey kicks alone."

Sarah smiled and started to follow, but within a fraction of a second the name finally registered.

Tremaine. And not one Tremaine, but two. The sheriff and his sister.

CHAPTER SIX

EMMA LOOKED SO MUCH like Parker it was startling. Where he was tall and uncompromisingly masculine, she was petite and feminine. But otherwise, they could have been twins. Same dark hair, same blue eyes, same charismatic vitality that could reach across the room, or across a snowy mountain, and *make* you notice them.

Good genes. But dangerous. You had to handle that much sex appeal carefully. You couldn't just let it loose in a crowded room.

Like this one. Sarah noticed that several of the women milling around stopped talking and stared at Parker, who wore a marvelous blue muffler that was probably the exact color of his eyes and a black leather jacket, which fit like a supple second skin.

Sarah swallowed raggedly, suddenly miserably aware of her sweaty, tousled hair and her total absence of makeup. And her brand-new exercise clothes, which she'd let the salesclerk talk her into, and which she be-latedly realized were *much* too green and *much* too tight.

But it was too late now. Heather was striding toward the Tremaines, and Sarah could only follow, praying that the warm towel she draped over her shoulders covered the deep, ridiculous vee of her neckline. What had she been thinking? This shade of green looked positively radioactive. She looked like that shiny, feathery green thing her uncle attached to his fishing hook. What had he called it? *A lure.* Good God, she looked like a lure.

As they drew closer she could hear Emma talking. Or not *talking,* exactly. More like yelling very quietly.

"Damn it, Parker, I've told you a hundred times to stay out of this!"

Parker jammed his hands into his pockets. "Make sense, Em. What am I supposed to do? Just sit back and let him talk to you like that?"

"That's right." Emma was scowling fiercely. "I told you—this is between Harry and me."

"Em—"

But finally the Tremaines noticed they had company. Emma looked over sheepishly. "Heather." She made a visible effort to compose herself, finally removing her heavy silver-wool coat and hanging it up. "Hi. Sorry I'm late. I had to stop by the department and see Harry for a minute."

"No problem." Heather smiled smugly. "I told Svetlana the Sadist that you'd be glad to do an extra fifty donkey kicks after class as makeup." She ignored Emma's groan. "Meanwhile, I'd like you to meet Sarah Lennox. She's Ward's great-niece. Remember he told us she'd be visiting for a few weeks?"

Sarah sent the other woman a mental thank-you. She appreciated the smooth implication that they had met through a common connection to Ward rather than across the obstetrician's examination table.

Emma seemed to have sloughed off her temper. She

grinned broadly. "Of course! The damsel in distress!" She put out her hand enthusiastically. "I see you made it down the mountain."

Sarah laughed. "And I see you escaped from the mental hospital."

"What? Oh, that's right. He told you I was a nutcase that day, didn't he? Well, Parker's all talk," she said, tossing her brother a narrowed glance. "He doesn't really want to lock me away behind bars. He'd rather bundle me up in bubble wrap, so I never get bumped or bruised. Isn't that right, Parker?"

"That's right, Em." Parker seemed to be recovering from their tiff more slowly. His handsome face still looked tight and worried. But he gave Sarah a fairly dazzling smile anyhow. "Hi," he said. "I've been meaning to call you, to thank you for the first-aid."

"Oh, no. It was nothing," Sarah said stiltedly, tugging on her towel. "I was glad to help."

"Are you the one who taped up his hands?" Emma looked delighted. "I was *wondering* who did that. Usually Parker is way too macho for a bandage. He'd rather just bleed all over the furniture like a *real* man."

"Emma." Parker's voice was quiet iron. "Don't you need to go in there and get some ass-kicking?"

Emma scowled at him. "Donkey-kicking," she corrected icily. "I need to go *do* some *donkey*-kicking."

"Well, don't let me stop you," he said politely. He turned back to Sarah. "Actually, I really was hoping you'd be here."

Out of the corner of her eye, Sarah saw Emma elbow Heather. "Told you," Emma whispered loudly to her friend.

Sarah felt herself flushing, but she refused to speculate on what Emma might have meant. She dabbed at her face with the towel calmly. "Really? Did you need to talk to me?"

"Yeah." He looked around, noticing as if for the first time the room full of damp, spandex-wrapped women, many of whom were watching him from behind their sparkling water bottles. "But not here. What about tomorrow? Maybe we could have lunch?"

"That would be fine," she said, thinking it through hurriedly. "I could make sandwiches. Uncle Ward is having lunch with Madeline tomorrow, so we could have the house to ourselves."

Emma choked, and Sarah sensed that even Heather was smiling curiously.

Damn. She felt ridiculous. This was like junior high school, when a cute boy stopped by your locker, and every word became a double entendre, and your friends giggled mercilessly, till you wanted to crawl right into that narrow metal compartment with your books and slam the door behind you.

But she wasn't in junior high school. She was a grown woman. A very grown-up, very *pregnant* woman. However much Emma or Ward or *anyone* would enjoy playing matchmaker here, she was not looking for a boyfriend. As the little pink *x* proved, she had already had one boyfriend too many.

"I meant, I thought perhaps you'd rather he weren't around. I'm sure you want to talk to me about him." She hoped she didn't sound too defensive. "About the problems with the ice festival?"

"Sure," Parker said easily. "Among other things. See you around noon, then."

As the three women walked slowly back toward Madame Svetlana's torture chamber, Emma was practically humming with excitement. "Did you see his face, Heather? Absolutely amazing. I haven't seen Parker this revved up about anyone since the divorce, have you?"

Heather shrugged. "I haven't been monitoring his heart rate, Em," she said. "And neither should you. Stop meddling."

"I'm not meddling." She turned toward Sarah earnestly. "I'm really not. I'm just thrilled that he's finally interested in somebody."

Sarah couldn't help smiling at the openhearted eagerness she saw in the other woman's face. Obviously there was a lot of love running deeply between brother and sister.

"I'm afraid you're misreading Parker's interest, Emma. He's only interested in finding an ally to help rein in my uncle. That's it. Honestly, it's nothing personal."

Emma shook her head. "I *never* misread Parker. I know him too well. It's personal, all right. And I'm delighted. He's been alone too long. A whole year. But his divorce was tough on him. She was such a—"

Emma caught Heather's eye and swallowed the word she'd been going to say. "Anyhow, ever since Tina, Parker's decided he's got to have the perfect woman, the perfect marriage, the perfect life. I keep telling him, there's no such thing. But he won't gamble. He says it's the perfect woman or nothing."

She dropped her towel on the floor, turned and eyed Sarah with a friendly speculation. "And apparently, Miss Sarah Lennox, *you're it.*"

IT WAS EASY, when living at Winter House, to settle into a lazy, luxurious rhythm, to pretend you were one of those earliest millionaires to settle in Firefly Glen.

No problems your money couldn't solve. No worries, no responsibilities, no tomorrow. Just the sweet smell of wood smoke in the fireplace, the warm cinnamon taste of morning tea in a Sevres cup, the smooth spill of your satin robe against your arms. And, in a couple of hours, lunch with a handsome man whose sister thought he liked you.

Sarah leaned back against the headrest of the silk chaise and stared at the ceiling. It was her favorite feature, out of the hundreds of interesting quirks in Winter House's eccentric design. The beautiful ceiling was only half painted. The left half was crowded with floating cherubs and simpering angels. The other half was as blankly white as new snow.

During her first visit, Sarah had asked her uncle about the ceiling, and he had said it was a grown-up story. He had promised he'd tell her when she was older.

Well, she was older now. She'd have to remember to ask him this time.

Sarah's lunch with Parker was set for noon, so when someone rang the doorbell at ten o'clock, she assumed it must be for her uncle. She stayed where she was, sipping tea and watching the snowflakes, until the rapping became a pounding, and she realized her uncle wasn't going to answer it.

Tightening the sash of her long robe, she hurried to the door, a little embarrassed to be caught lounging this late in the morning. But this deep, silent snow was like a blanket wrapped around the house, lulling her into a slower pace, the same way it urged the wild animals into hibernation.

It was Parker. And he didn't look lulled by the snow, or anything else. He looked crisp and official. And out of sorts. He was in full uniform, his badge gleaming in the sunlight. And why was he so stilted? Gone was the languid ease of the friendly small-town sheriff. Instead his lanky body was ramrod alert, the official posture of any ticked-off big-city cop.

Something was wrong. She checked the grandfather clock in the foyer, wondering if she'd mistaken the time. But the clock was ticking steadily, and it really was only ten in the morning.

"Parker," she said, confused. "I wasn't expecting you—"

"I'm not here for lunch," he said tersely, glancing past her into the hall. "In fact, thanks to your Uncle Ward, I probably won't be having lunch at all today. Where is the bullheaded son of a—"

"I don't know," she said quickly. "Maybe getting ready for his date. I haven't seen him—"

"I'm right here, Tremaine." Her uncle's voice thundered out from the staircase behind her. Sarah swiveled, her hand still on the doorknob. Ward was coming down the stairs, fully dressed in a thick black fisherman's sweater and gray corduroy slacks.

He was smiling. The expression had a disturbingly smug quality, Sarah thought, watching him uneasily.

"Well, let the man in, Sarah, and for God's sake shut the door. The sheriff has something to say, and I'm not going to let it snow all over my hallway while he says it." Ward moved toward the gold parlor. "Want a cup of tea, Sheriff? We've got some herbal nonsense that is supposed to calm your nerves. Looks like you could use it."

"What do you think you're doing, Winters?" Parker had come in, but he wasn't moving toward the parlor. He was standing in the hall, just over the threshold, his feet planted squarely on the checkered marble tiles as if he were a piece in a chess game. His shoulders were stiff, snow dusting them like epaulets. "What are you trying to accomplish by this foolishness?"

Ward stopped and gave Parker a sly grin. "What foolishness? Oh. Could you possibly be referring to the small issue of the sleighs?"

"The sleighs?" Parker looked surprised, and not pleasantly so. "Damn it, Winters. Have you done something to the sleighs, too?"

"Not really. I rented them, that's all." Ward sauntered into the gold parlor, apparently confident that Parker would follow.

Which the sheriff did, his eyes narrowed and his jaw set into hard right angles. "You *rented* them? What do you mean? *All* of them?"

"Every last one." The older man grinned. "It took a while, but I tracked down every sleigh in a hundred-mile radius, and I rented the darn things. Just for one week in February, of course."

"The week of the ice festival."

"The man's quick." Ward turned to Sarah with a rakish tilt of one eyebrow. "He may look like the half-wit sheriff of a pokey little town, but he's always thinking. *Of course* the week of the festival, Tremaine. It's the only week that matters."

Parker ran his hand through his dark hair and let out a deep, exasperated exhale. "It won't stop anything, you know," he said in a tired voice. "They'll bring some in from *two* hundred miles away, if necessary. Or they'll dig them out of people's barns. They'll build new ones. Believe me, they'll manage."

"Maybe."

"And even if you stopped the sleigh rides completely, so what? It's stupid, Ward. The rides are just icing. The festival can go on fine without them."

Ward shrugged. "Maybe," he repeated. "But it'll annoy the hell out of Bourke Waitely, which is reason enough for me."

Parker cursed under his breath, and Sarah felt compelled to intervene. "Wait," she said, moving into the room to stand between the two men. "I don't really understand. You seemed upset from the moment you arrived, Parker. If you didn't know my uncle had rented all the sleighs, why are you here?"

Ward was busily pouring himself a cup of tea. With his back to the others, he said, "Probably because of the billboard. Right, Tremaine?"

Parker just nodded, pinching the bridge of his nose with his thumb and forefinger.

Ward chuckled. "Tell her, Tremaine. Tell her about the billboard."

Parker looked up, his blue eyes weary. "Why don't you tell her yourself?"

"Well, modesty wouldn't allow me to do it justice." Ward arranged himself comfortably in one of the biggest satin armchairs and smiled up at Sarah. "It was quite an inspiration, if I do say so myself."

Parker growled under his breath. "Your uncle, who may just be the biggest fool in the Western Hemisphere, has put up a billboard at the edge of town, on an empty but rather conspicuous lot."

"That's *my* lot, by the way," Ward interjected, his forefinger raised warningly. "A man can do what he wants with his own property, can't he?"

"I know," Parker said. "We already checked that out. Anyhow, your uncle has put a ten-foot picture of himself across that billboard. Must be the worst picture ever taken of him. He looks like the ugliest, meanest old coot you'll ever see. And above it, he's printed, Last Seen In Firefly Glen. Do Not Attempt To Apprehend."

"Damn, I'm good!" Ward laughed. "It's a thing of beauty, don't you agree, Sarah? Simple. Effective. Ten little words, and every one of them true. Best of all, there's not a thing Bourke Waitely or any of those money-grubbing sellouts in this town can do about it."

"Don't be too sure about that," Parker put in grimly. "Mayor Millner's looking into it even as we speak. There are ordinances. Zoning. Height restrictions—"

"I comply with every one of them," Ward said, waving his hand dismissively. "Damn, man, don't you think I looked into all that? I'm not stupid."

"Well, you're sure *acting* stupid." A slow, heavy vein was throbbing in Parker's jaw. "For God's sake, Ward, use your head. I don't know whether you're just trying to piss off Bourke Waitely, or whether you've just plain lost your marbles, but a lot of people down in that town are boiling mad. And I'm not going to be responsible if a mob of them decides to march up this hill some night and stuff one of those sleighs right down your throat."

"Okay." Ward looked bored. "You're not responsible. Now was there anything else you wanted?"

Parker stared at the older man for a long moment, apparently caught in a strangely inarticulate impotence. Then he slapped his hat against his thigh, muttered something short and furious under his breath and wheeled around to head for the door.

Sarah cast one pleading look at her uncle. She met nothing but his bland, poker-faced answering stare. With a sigh, she, too, gave up and rushed out of the room.

Her robe was whirling around her legs, and her bare feet made small slapping sounds as she ran lightly across the hallway. She caught Parker just as he was opening the door.

"Wait," she said, grabbing his arm. "Please. Tell me. You mentioned a mob. It hasn't come to that, surely. Has it?"

He shook his head, more in frustration than in denial. Anxiety squeezed at Sarah's throat. She wished she could follow Parker outside, so that they could talk in true privacy. Standing here at the door was no good. Snow was already falling on his shoulders, and cold air rushed in through her inadequate satin nightclothes, making her shiver uncomfortably.

Her sloth this morning had been a mistake. She should have dressed early. She should have been prepared for anything, the way she always had been back in Florida.

"I don't know." Parker sighed. "They're mad, Sarah. And they have reason. He's way out of line here."

"Can't you control them? I mean, you *are* the sheriff."

He tossed her an irritable glance as he efficiently turned his collar up against the cold. "Sorry. My uniform didn't come with a magic wand to wave over angry mobs and turn them into flocks of geese."

"I didn't mean that. I just meant, surely they'll listen to you. Surely they'll back off if you tell them they should. His behavior may be childish, but he hasn't done anything illegal, has he?"

Parker slid first one hand and then the other into soft, black leather gloves. "Well, you can bet that Bourke Waitely and all the other lawyers in town are finecombing the city code book right now, trying to prove that he has. They want him neutralized. And that's Bourke's own word."

"Neutralized?" Sarah frowned. "That sounds a little threatening."

Parker zipped up his jacket with a frustrated metallic growl.

"Right," he said tightly. "*Now* you're catching on."

EMMA LIT A PATCHOULI CANDLE, put Dean Martin on the CD player and dimmed the lights. Yes. That was perfect. *Yes.*

Then, five minutes later, *no.*

She blew the candle out and raised the lights. It was too much pressure—it would just make things worse. But she left the music. Corny old Italian music was Macho Harry's embarrassing little sentimental secret. For the first six months of their marriage, he had warbled "That's Amore" in the shower every morning.

But not lately. Emma touched Dean Martin's smiling face on the CD case. "Come on, Dino," she whispered. "I could really use some help here tonight."

Tonight was the night. Tonight, come hell or high water,

she was going to make her husband notice her. Make her husband *want* her. Make her husband be a husband.

But how?

She'd thought about buying one of those black leather teddies Ginger sold down at Sweet Dreams, the lingerie shop that was directly across the square from Emma's paper store. But she had decided against it. She didn't mind a little playful costuming now and then. In fact, the night they'd gone to a Halloween party dressed as Mulder and Scully from *The X-Files,* the sexual tension had been terrific. Harry had kept her awake all night, protecting her from aliens.

But that was *before.* This was *after.* And, given the current state of their love life, the teddy was risky. What if it didn't work? What if Harry still walked away and flicked on the television? How demeaning would that be? She could just picture herself standing there, tricked out like a two-bit dominatrix. She'd probably feel like killing him.

So she'd settled for her prettiest pink underclothes and Harry's favorite dress. When she heard Harry's car come up the driveway, she knocked back the rest of her wine for luck, and poured herself a second glass. She added another ice cube to his Scotch and water, and arranged herself with what she hoped was casual sensuality on the sofa.

"Hi." She looked up from the magazine she'd brought over as a prop. She pretended to glance at her watch in surprise. "Gosh, it's late, isn't it? You must be starving. I've kept a plate of roast beef warm in the oven. Do you want it now, or after you change?"

Harry tossed his coat over the arms of the hall tree. "Neither," he said, dusting the snow from his hair. "I knew the city council meeting would go on forever, so I grabbed a sandwich at the café."

Emma counted to ten silently, hoping she would keep her big mouth shut. He could have called. He could have spared her the effort of fixing a meal no one would eat. Not to mention he could have invited her to join him at the café. Just a few months ago, he would have.

But she mustn't say any of that. Nagging wasn't exactly an essential ingredient of any love potion she'd ever heard of.

Harry took his wet boots off and propped them in the corner next to the coats. Their house was too small to have a mudroom, so they had created a mud corner. He straightened wearily, twisted his back until his spine released a cascade of small cracking sounds, and sighed.

"Is your back bothering you?" Emma folded her magazine. "Come sit over here. I'll massage it."

Harry shook his head. "No, thanks. I'm fine. It's just those god-awful metal chairs at City Hall." He moved over to the CD player and punched the power button. "Do you mind if I turn this off? I've got a headache."

Okay, that was enough. Emma stood, forcing herself to stay relaxed. She went to Harry and put her arms around him, ignoring his subtle stiffening.

"Poor guy," she said, resting her cheek against his chest. Though he didn't return the embrace, it still felt so right. If only he knew how much she loved him, loved the familiar contours of his body, the jut of his collarbone against her temple, the thump of his heart under her hand. "It must have been a tough day."

"Not really. Just long."

She tried not to be discouraged, but she knew this mood. Passive, unreachable, yet steadfastly contrary. He would disagree, politely but firmly, with whatever she said. If she mentioned that it was Thursday, he'd say, no, it's just the day after Wednesday.

Even worse, though she had begun to softly knead the tense muscles along his spine, he remained completely wooden. She might as well have been hugging a life-size doll.

But she refused to take offense. She refused to give up. It had been three months now since they had made love. If he defeated her tonight, those months could stretch into four, then a year—and then what? He'd be like a boat whose tethers had been sliced, drifting further and further away from her on a tide that would never turn.

She kept rubbing softly. Her hands knew him so well. She knew what he liked. She knew where the little kinks of tension were hiding.

"Emma, stop it." Harry put his hands on her shoulders. "I know what you're trying to do here."

"Good," she murmured, her face half-turned into his chest. She let her hands drift toward the small of his back, then down, over his belt, grazing the tight curve of his very sexy rear. She nuzzled him, encouraged by the skitter of his heartbeat. "Then help me do it. This kind of thing is usually a duet, you know."

"Stop it." He pushed a little with the heels of his hands, forcing her away from him. She lifted her head and looked at him. His face was so tense the muscles practically screamed. "Damn it, Emma, stop it. You know this is pointless."

She took a deep breath, but she was at her limit. *"Pointless?"*

"That's right. You know what the doctor said. It's never going to happen, Emma. We can't have a baby." He tightened his mouth. "No, correct that. *I* can't. I can't give you a baby, no matter how hard I try. You heard what he said."

"Yes, I heard him say that we probably can't have children." *Oh, Harry.* How could she want to strangle him and make love to him all at the same time? "But I *didn't* hear him say that we can't have sex."

For a minute she thought he might give in. He looked at her with such longing in his gaze that she was sure he couldn't resist. But, after only a few seconds, he muttered an oath under his breath and pulled away.

"What?" All the frustration she'd been smothering came roiling to the fore. This was so wrong. It was one thing if he had lost interest in her. That would be terrible, even heartbreaking. But she was strong, and she would survive it if she had to.

But when he so clearly still wanted her, how could he let this business about his sperm count come between them? As if she gave a *damn* about his sperm count!

"Harry, for heaven's sake. Stop making this so complicated. You are my husband. Not my baby-making machine."

He was facing the fireplace. "I know that you don't understand why it's complicated, Emma. Maybe that's because you're not the problem. I am."

"You certainly are." He was so unbelievably blind. And she was so damn mad. "I'm going nuts, Harry. I love you. I want to have wild and crazy sex with you. I'm talking about panting, sweating, up-till-dawn sex. Remember that? Believe me, babies have absolutely no place in this picture."

He shook his head. "I'm sorry. It's just not that simple for me."

"Well, it is for me. I'm only twenty-six years old, you know. I'm not quite ready to become a nun."

He didn't answer her. She clenched her fists, so frustrated that she was starting to feel slightly light-headed. Wasn't there anything she could say that could break through his shield of self-pity?

"I'm warning you, Harry. Maybe you should see someone. Talk to someone. Because if you don't work through this—if you don't stop pushing me away, then—"

He gave her a tired glance. "Then what?"

She set her shoulders. "You know what. If you won't make love to me, sooner or later I'll go looking for someone who will."

It was, of course, a lie—a deliberate jolt of electricity designed as a crude kind of shock therapy. She wanted to scare the apathy right out of him. She wanted to shock him straight into her bed.

Instead, he shocked her.

"Maybe," he said slowly, "that isn't such a bad idea."

CHAPTER SEVEN

PARKER LIKED WORKING AT NIGHT. He liked working alone. He could get about ten times as much done when he wasn't distracted by Harry's sullen tension, Suzie's sarcasm, or the endless phone calls from the Fussy Four Hundred.

Not that he was exactly *alone* tonight. He actually had six companions, though they were all asleep. Suzie had turned the holding cell into a temporary pet store.

Yep, he thought, smiling to himself. He now worked in a zoo literally as well as figuratively. And he had no one but himself to blame.

Suzie had come in one day last week, practically in tears, her arms full of puppies. Apparently she had decided to raise a little "easy" money for her college fund by breeding her female golden retriever. The results had been five adorable, but not quite pure-blood, puppies. After several weeks of trying to be patient, Suzie's mother had finally thrown a fit and threatened to send the animals to the shelter.

Parker had been fool enough to feel sorry for the girl. Consequently, all five puppies, and the mother dog, now called the holding cell home. Suzie planned to trot potential customers in and out of here every day next week.

First the nativity, now this. He clearly wasn't ever going to get his cell back. Good thing there was no crime in the Glen. Unless, of course, Parker's own criminal stupidity counted.

When he heard the light knock on the front door, which he kept locked at night, he assumed it was the dispatcher, coming in to take over the graveyard shift. But, to his amazement, when he opened the door he saw that it was Sarah Lennox.

She was so thoroughly bundled up against the fifteen-degree freeze he almost didn't recognize her. The pale oval of her face peeked out from a dark green hood, and her honey-colored hair was escaping in wisps that looked even softer than the hood's golden cashmere lining.

What was she doing, coming down to the Sheriff's Department after dark? It was supposed to snow soon. Almost everyone was at home by a roaring fire.

"Hi," he said, too surprised to be very suave. Then he had a sudden troubling thought. "Is anything wrong? Is it Ward?"

She smiled. "No. Nothing's wrong." She shivered a little and bit her lower lip. "May I come in?"

Apologizing, he stood back and let her enter. She brought cold air with her, and something else, too. He sniffed the tantalizing aroma, trying to identify it. Perfume? No. *Food.*

Chinese food.

As she paused, scanning the office, apparently looking for a spare surface, he finally noticed that she was carrying a large brown bag with the logo of the local Chinese restaurant stamped on it—*The Firefly and the Dragon.*

His favorite.

It was too good to be true.

"I guess I've been working too long," he said, awe-struck. "I'm hallucinating. I actually think I saw an angel walk in here holding my favorite takeout."

She laughed. What a pretty laugh she had! It had a cool sparkle, like a clear, sun-shot creek. It was a laugh you could wash yourself in and clean away the grime of the day.

"No hallucination," she said. "It's real food. I asked around. Apparently in a small town everybody knows everyone else's habits." She dug in the bag and pulled out a small container. "There's even a piece of pumpkin pie for dessert."

"Wow." He closed his eyes for a moment, imagining how good it would taste. Then he opened them, met hers and smiled. "But why?"

It was a simple question, but a fair one. They hadn't exactly parted this morning on the friendliest of terms.

Her answering smile was a little sheepish.

"It's an apology. For this morning. I should never have said that about how you should control the people around here. It was rude, and it was ungrateful. I do understand that you are trying to protect my uncle, and I wanted you to know that I appreciate it, even if he doesn't."

Parker didn't respond for a moment, marveling that anyone could be so humble and generous. He tried to imagine his ex-wife apologizing with such simple dignity about anything. But why would Tina ever say she was sorry? She wasn't. Tina didn't waste time re-gretting any of her sins. She was too busy committing new ones.

"That's okay. Just please warn your uncle that he'd

better not get caught so much as jaywalking around here for a while. Or he and I will end up playing chess through the bars of a holding cell."

"I know," she said. "I have told him. It doesn't seem to sink in. Frankly, I'm stumped. I just don't know what to do."

"Do *anything*. Get him therapy. Drug his tea. Tie him up."

She smiled ruefully. "Put him in jail?"

"It's crossed my mind."

"I thought it might have. So I brought you a book, too." Sarah looked just slightly mischievous now. "I got copies for both of us." She held out a small paperback, a current self-help bestseller. *Make Anyone Do Anything—A Primer of Persuasion.*

He had to laugh, but he took it. "Thanks," he said, riffling the pages, catching the occasional psychobabble buzz-phrase. "I'm not sure the book's been written yet that can outsmart Ward Winters, but I'll give it a try."

"Me, too. We can compare notes later." She gave the bag of Chinese food one last nudge to make sure it was secure on the table. "Well, enjoy. I guess I'd better get back before it starts snowing."

"What?" He frowned. "You aren't going to stay and eat?"

"Oh, no." She looked uncomfortable. "You obviously have a lot of work to do. I'd just be a distraction."

A distraction. Well, she had that right.

It was ridiculous how often in the past couple of weeks he'd found himself thinking about her. Dumb stuff, like whether her hair was as soft as it looked. Whether that determined chin of hers meant she had her uncle's stubborn streak. Why she had looked so fragile, so sad, up there on the mountain that day. Whether she was always kind to strangers, the way she'd been when she tended to his blisters, or whether she had singled him out for special treatment.

And then of course there were the X-rated thoughts, the kind he hadn't had about anybody in a long, long time.

Yeah, she was a distraction, all right. If she only knew.

"I was almost finished with work anyhow." But he wasn't convincing enough. That two-foot stack of files on his desk probably didn't help. She was already putting her gloves back on. "Really, Sarah. You'd be doing me a favor. It's not much fun eating alone."

She was shaking her head, smiling politely, but, as if it had been a choreographed ballet of persuasion, at that very moment the dogs decided to wake up.

The soft, scuffling sound of clumsy puppy feet on shredded newspaper came first. Sarah looked toward the sound curiously. And then the master stroke—a series of the cutest little baby yelps imaginable.

Parker smiled. Hadn't he been clever to say yes when Suzie brought the puppies in? He might just have to buy one himself out of sheer gratitude.

"I'll show you," he said, answering her unspoken question, "if you'll stay."

She hesitated, but the puppies were clamoring now. They probably smelled the Chinese food, the little beggars. They were getting big enough to want more than mama dog had to offer.

"I didn't really buy enough food for two," she said doubtfully, but he could tell she was hooked.

"That's okay. I've got some leftover pizza in the refrigerator. You like green peppers? At least I think it's green peppers." He grinned at her. "It's green something."

She screwed up her nose. "Yum," she said. "Parker, I really should—"

"Please." He took her right hand and, holding her gaze with his, began easing off her glove. *Go slow, go slow,* he reminded himself. But it was hard. Something about her made him want to go fast. "Please stay."

She didn't stop him. He got both gloves off and dropped them onto the closest desk. Then he reached up and slipped his hands inside her hood. Slowly he eased it away from her head. Without it, she looked suddenly naked. Vulnerable.

He smiled reassuringly as he touched the top button of her coat. "Why don't you take that off?" The puppies were going crazy now, slipping and jumping and yipping for attention. "There are some guys over there who seem pretty eager to meet you."

She tilted her head. "Are you sure you haven't already read that book I brought you? You seem pretty good at getting your own way."

But she wasn't really annoyed. He could tell. She took off her coat, draped it over Harry's desk, then turned to him, her hands on her hips and a small smile on her lips. "Okay. Show me. And they'd better be every bit as cute as they sound."

He took her hand. "They are."

He felt pretty safe making that promise. And she clearly wasn't disappointed. When he unlatched the door and brought her around the corner, she let out a short gasp of delight.

"Oh, Parker," she breathed. "Oh, how darling."

Then she went down on her knees and was immediately swarmed by five pale blond fur-balls, all huge tongues, oversize paws and yelping excitement.

She didn't seem to mind the muss and the slobber, their paws clawing at her soft green sweater or their little teeth tugging at her shoelaces. She laughed and cooed and cuddled each one of them in turn. And from the quiet corner of the cell, mama dog looked on without the slightest bit of anxiety.

Parker watched, too, and as he did a liquid warmth seeped into his veins, a sensation he only dimly recognized as desire, because it came so gently, so comfortably, as if it was a perfect match for his own blood, as if it belonged there.

But once inside him, the feeling grew, flooding him with its light. He couldn't take his gaze away. He couldn't move at all. He could barely breathe.

When one of the puppies tried to climb up the front of her sweater, licking her throat as if she were made of sweet cream, Sarah flung back her head, eyes shut, lips curved in an innocent pleasure.

He couldn't stop himself. He bent over that blind, smiling, beautiful face. "Sarah," he said softly.

She opened her eyes, and they were full of laughter. "What?"

He didn't answer. He touched her chin. And then, before either of them could think better of it, he kissed her.

It wasn't a long kiss. It wasn't pushy or intrusive or threatening. And yet he felt the delighted smile fade from her lips as if his kiss had been a frost, forcing the petals from the rose.

He pulled away, of course. It would have been impossible to persist in the face of such a reaction. It was a bit of a shock, actually. Ordinarily his kisses weren't greeted as if his lips had been dipped in poison.

She lowered her head and stared down at the puppies. Her whole body had gone strangely still.

"I'm sorry," he said. "You just looked—cute. I didn't mean to make you uncomfortable."

"You didn't. Really." She set the puppies back down carefully. She managed to extricate herself, and she got to her feet. "But I was thinking—I just remembered that my uncle will be waiting up for me. I really should get going."

He didn't move as she slid past him, exiting the cell as if she feared he might try to lock her in. He still didn't move as she hurried to Harry's desk and scooped up her coat and gloves.

Slowly he pulled the cell door shut to keep the puppies in. He leaned against it, deliberately passive, watching her from a safe distance without making any sudden movements. He couldn't figure out exactly why she was so skittish, but he knew he had been clumsy, like a poacher crashing and stomping through a silent, untouched wood.

He kept his voice light. "Too bad. No Chinese, then?"

"I'd better not," she said, fumbling with her gloves in an awkward haste. "I'm sorry. It's just that I had completely forgotten about Ward."

She couldn't quite get the gloves on.

"Sarah," he said gently, as she threaded her fingers incorrectly for the second time. "Sarah, it was just a kiss."

"I know," she said, smiling at him with an intensity that was obviously manufactured. "It isn't that, really. I just don't think I should leave my uncle alone too long."

The buttons closed. The deep green hood swallowed

her up once more. And then, with a polite exchange of goodbyes and small, firm click of the door, she was gone.

A puppy snuffled, scratching at the cell door.

"It's okay, buddy," Parker said softly. "We goofed, that's all. We'll get another chance." The puppy whimpered, as if he didn't have much hope that Parker would do any better the next time.

Parker glanced over at the paperback Sarah had left. *Make Anyone Do Anything.*

He chuckled under his breath. "I think you're right, little fellow. I think we'd better read this book after all."

ON SUNDAY AFTERNOON the temperature rose to fifty degrees, and the whole town of Firefly Glen came out to celebrate.

The square was a bustle of color—teens playing, mothers swinging babies, people walking dogs. The thermometer might drop to zero again by morning— weather up here was apparently famously unpredictable—so everyone wanted to make the most of this gift, this smiling hour of stolen spring.

In the Candlelight Café, Theo was serving Heat Wave Sundaes for fifty cents. Half the town was here. Sarah and Ward waited twenty minutes for a booth, and when they were finally seated, Sarah was dismayed to discover that she had an uninterrupted view of Sheriff Tremaine and his gorgeous brunette date, who sat at an adjoining table.

Of course he looked wonderful, in a casual blue cotton shirt with the sleeves rolled up to the elbow. Must be his day off. And he was smiling *that smile* at his date, who obviously was eating it up with one of Theo's silver dessert spoons.

Sarah studied her sundae, cutting into it with slow, surgical precision so that she didn't have to watch.

Just her luck. She had spent the past two days trying not to think about him. Trying to forget the flare of heat she'd felt when he kissed her. She had snuffed it instantly, of course, but for a split second there in the jail cell his sex appeal had sliced into her like a warm, sharp knife sinking into soft butter.

She might as well quit kidding herself that, as a pregnant woman facing major life decisions, she was beyond the tawdry urgings of mere physical desire. Apparently some deeply female part of her didn't realize that she was pregnant. Or didn't care.

So all right, denial was no longer an option. But self-control was.

And she'd start by refusing to look at him. She filled her mouth with sweet, oozing whipped cream and focused on her uncle, willing herself not to possess any peripheral vision.

"That's all right, Theo." A woman's voice broke into their conversation. "We can sit here, with Ward and Sarah. There's plenty of room."

Sarah turned at the sound. Madeline Alexander stood at the edge of their booth, wearing a shirtwaist dress covered in huge red roses and red earrings the size of Easter eggs.

But that was just typical Madeline. The real surprise was that she had three little girls in tow, lined up behind her like ducklings. The girls looked to be about eight years old, and they wore bright blue uniforms and beanies that read, Firefly Girls: Troop 637.

"They didn't have a table big enough for all of us," Madeline explained while she moved things around to accommodate the new situation. Sarah slid over, as it became clear that Madeline intended to sit with Ward, leaving the Firefly Girls to share Sarah's side of the booth. The girls looked embarrassed but obedient as they piled in, elbow to elbow, the last one half-hanging off the edge of the seat.

"Sarah, I'd like you to meet my girls. Well, not *my* girls really, but I'm their troop leader. This is half of our troop. The other girls are over there, see them? Hi, girls!" She raised her voice. "Girls! Girls, over here! Say hello to Sarah!"

If Sarah had hoped that Parker might depart without noticing her, those hopes were dead now. Half the customers in the café turned at Madeline's sunny outburst and the answering clamor of responses from the girls, who sat at a table nearby.

"Hi, Sarah!"

"Hello, Sarah!"

Amid the hullabaloo, Parker caught her eye. "Hello, Sarah," he mouthed silently, adding a wink for good measure.

Darned if she didn't blush. *Good grief.*

"Sarah, you're the very person I need," Madeline gushed as soon as the girls subsided, as if she couldn't bear a silence. "I need your help desperately. Tell her she simply must agree to help us, Ward. I know you don't approve of the festival, but you must tell her how important the costumes are to the girls."

Ward shrugged. "I haven't got any idea what you're talking about."

"Well, you know one of our assistant troop leaders has gone out of town. Her parents are sick or something. So now we don't have enough help. And with the festival coming up—and the costumes…oh, it's such a disaster!" She sighed, waving her hands in the air to illustrate the chaos she faced. "And I know you are a good seamstress—after all, you do teach Home Ec, don't you? Oh, please. Do help us, Sarah!"

Amazed that Madeline was discussing the festival so openly in front of Ward, Sarah looked at her uncle. He didn't look angry. He looked bored. And he refused to meet her eyes, the coward. But everyone else at the table was staring expectantly at her—Madeline with damp, desperate melodrama, and the three little girls with owlish curiosity.

"All right," Sarah said weakly. "I'll be glad to do what I can."

"Oh, thank you, Sarah." Madeline, the social maestro, called out merrily to the rest of the troop. "Girls! Girls! Sarah is going to be our new troop leader! Say 'thank you, Sarah!'"

A new chorus went through the café. By now the adult customers were grinning and joining in. A couple of people were clapping. Parker was openly laughing, though his date seemed less amused.

Sarah put her face in her hands helplessly. Why had she thought this was a sleepy little snow-shrouded town where she could hibernate until she decided how to handle her dilemma? She hadn't had a minute's real solitude since her plane touched down in Albany.

The little girl who had scooted into the booth right next to Sarah suddenly poked Sarah's arm rather insistently.

Sarah looked over with a smile. The girl was a pudgy, freckled redhead whose beanie was perched so high on her springy curls that it looked as if it might tumble at any moment. Sarah had noticed—as teachers always do—that she didn't seem to be very chummy with the other girls.

"Thanks, Sarah," the little girl said, as if by rote. Then she got down to business. "Are you going to eat that cherry?"

Sarah plucked the cherry out of her sundae and handed it over.

Madeline tsked and frowned in their direction. "Eileen O'Malley, if you keep eating everything in sight, you're never going to fit into your snowflake costume for the festival."

A couple of the other girls tittered, and Sarah felt her hackles rising on Eileen's behalf. But the spunky little girl seemed unfazed. She simply returned Madeline's glare and popped the cherry into her mouth defiantly. Madeline sighed and turned back to Ward.

The little girl munched quietly for a few seconds, then looked up at Sarah.

"Don't you think it's totally dumb," Eileen said, "for the *Firefly* Girls to dress up as *snowflakes?* It doesn't make one bit of sense, does it?"

"I don't know." Sarah made a show of considering it. Eileen looked deadly serious, as if this issue was her litmus test, and Sarah realized that she wanted to pass, if only to offset Madeline's cruel remark about the little girl's weight. "Snowflakes and fireflies. It does seem odd. But maybe firefly costumes were just too hard to make."

"Or maybe Mrs. Alexander is just a mean old poop." Eileen had spoken under her breath so that she couldn't be heard across the table. When Sarah didn't chastise her, she grinned suddenly, abandoning her grievance. "But that's okay. Are you going to lick that spoon?"

As Sarah handed her spoon over, she had a funny thought.

Her baby was going to be a girl. She knew it—somehow she just knew it. A little girl, maybe a lot like this one, full of spunk and laughter and loads of common sense.

And with that thought came a revelation. The baby wasn't an abstraction, a predicament. She wasn't a dilemma waiting to be solved. She was a person waiting to enter the world, where she would live and love and eat ice cream, laugh and cry and probably fail geometry.

And Sarah could hardly wait to meet her.

"IT'S LIKE RIDING A BICYCLE, damn it." Ward glared at Sarah, who was wobbling toward him on the ice. "You don't ever forget."

"Yeah? Well, tell that to my ankles," Sarah responded shortly, struggling as hard as she could to stay erect.

Why had she let her uncle talk her into this? She couldn't ice-skate. She was a Floridian, for heaven's sake. Maybe her brain dimly remembered using the indoor skating rink during her summer vacation here fifteen years ago, but her body had total amnesia on the subject.

Too bad Heather had assured her that a few spills wouldn't hurt the baby. Exercise is good, the doctor had said. The spills are worth it, as long as they're not from a ten-story building.

"Come on, come on. You can do it."

Ward was skating backward, holding both her hands, urging her on. The show-off. He looked so annoyingly dapper and fit in his parka and muffler and ski cap. Whereas she looked like an idiot. Her rear end was white with ice shavings, from all the times she'd landed on it, and her nose had started to run from the cold.

"No—I—can't." She tried to free her hands, but that was a mistake. The movement upset her precarious balance, and she began to weave and sway. She felt like a cartoon character with rubber legs that kept stretching in different directions.

And then, of course, she went down.

Ward laughed and skated a fancy figure eight around her. When she tossed a handful of snow at him he sped off, one hand tucked behind his back like a racer. He looked like a man half his age.

She, on the other hand, didn't dare try to rise to her feet. She was only a couple of feet from the bank, so she crawled on all fours toward safety.

Suddenly, there was a face just inches from hers. A golden, furry face with a huge tongue hanging out.

"What—?" The tongue darted out to touch her nose, and then she knew. It was one of the puppies she'd seen in the jail cell last week. He started dancing around her, grinning with pleasure. Apparently he thought she was a kindred spirit, down on all fours like an animal herself.

She couldn't help grinning back. He was almost unbelievably cute. But he was so little he must be freezing. She picked him up and scanned the perimeter of the lake, knowing that Parker had to be nearby.

He was. He was sitting on the bench just a few yards to her left, watching the pair of them. His dark blue jacket and black corduroy pants blended into the bench so well she hadn't noticed him.

She cuddled the puppy close to keep him warm. He accepted her embrace without resistance, nibbling happily at the string of her mitten. Then she climbed awkwardly to her feet and walked stilt-legged through the snow.

She plopped down next to Parker with absolutely no

grace. But she was too relieved to be on solid ground to care. "I'm trying to decide how embarrassed to be. How long have you been here?"

He grinned. "Long enough to know you won't be taking home the gold next year."

She had to laugh. She nodded toward her uncle, who was waving at them from the far side of the lake. "Hans Brinker out there is pretty disappointed in me."

Parker tilted his head. "Somehow I doubt that," he said. He tugged at one of the puppy's ears playfully. "So. What are you going to name him?"

"Me?" She looked down at the puppy, who had lost interest in her mittens and had started chewing on his own paw, as if he'd never seen it before. "You want *me* to name him?"

"I think you should," Parker said. "He's yours."

"Mine?" Sarah looked down at the puppy in horrified amazement. "He can't be *mine!* I can't own a dog. I don't even live here. I mean, I will be going back to Florida in a few weeks."

"Oh?" Parker looked politely curious. "I've never been to Florida. They don't have dogs there?"

"You know what I mean. I live in an apartment. I'm never there. I can't have a dog." She looked down at the puppy, who had decided to gaze up at her adoringly. "Why don't you keep him?"

"Can't," Parker said apologetically. "I already bought one of his brothers." He watched as the puppy began licking Sarah's neck. "Besides, anyone can see that puppy belongs to you."

"Hey, Sheriff!" Ward had skated closer now, and he came to a sharp stop right in front of them. He was grinning wickedly. "I thought of a new slogan for my billboard! Right under that great picture of me, it'll say, Hide Out In Firefly Glen." He chuckled. "Get it? Hide out? Like a criminal." When Parker didn't smile, Ward scowled and tilted his head back arrogantly. "It's sub-liminal. I guess you have to be subtle to get it."

And then, with a cackle and a flourish, he skated nimbly away, his silver blades flashing in the sun.

Parker shook his head. "I guess the how-to book isn't working." He raised one eyebrow. "Or haven't you reached the chapter on incorrigible, stubborn old geezers yet?"

Worried, Sarah gazed after her uncle, stroking the puppy's soft fur for comfort. "He listens to me, but then he just goes ahead and does whatever he wants. He really seems to hate this Bourke Waitely fellow. Who is he?"

"Bourke owns the only hotel in town. He probably stands to make more money from the festival than anyone. He and Ward are enemies from way back. I've heard rumors, but that's all. Best I can piece together, Bourke used to be in love with Roberta, and, even though Bourke eventually married, he never quite gave up thinking he could steal her from Ward."

"Fat chance of that," Sarah said. "I never saw two people more in love than Ward and Roberta were."

"I know." Parker reached out and touched the puppy's nose softly. The little guy had fallen asleep under Sarah's rhythmic stroking. "They probably had the only truly happy marriage I ever heard of. They always gave me hope for the human race."

They didn't say anything further for several long minutes. Instead, they shared the simple pleasure of watching Ward's elegant skating, the way tiny, sudden rainbows would flash from the snow, the way his skates kicked out pinwheels of spun glass. And in the silence, they could clearly hear the tiny tinkling melodies made by the wind as it blew icy pine needles against each other.

Though she was so cold her nose was numb, and she ached all over from her many tumbles, Sarah found herself strangely contented. She liked the warm comfort of the puppy's weight against her chest and the easy companionship of the man next to her. In her experience, very few men were as good at silences as Parker Tremaine.

But she couldn't let this one stretch too long. She couldn't let herself grow accustomed to it.

"I really can't keep him, you know." She shifted the warm bundle without waking him. "I appreciate the thought, but—"

"How about Frosty?" Parker eyed the puppy appraisingly. He gave no indication that he had even heard her. "That's what we always call the king of the ice festival. And Frosty here seems to love the snow."

"Parker, I—"

"Look at him, Sarah. He's already adopted you." Parker touched the limp, sleepy paws with his knuckle gently. "Tell you what. Why don't you just hang on to him for a little while, just as long you're here? Then, if you really don't want to keep him, I'll take over."

Sarah looked down at the sweet, rounded head of the sleeping puppy. Wouldn't it be terribly difficult to have him for a little while, then have to give him up? And what exactly was this all about, anyhow? Could something else be going on here? Were strings attached to this gift? Why would Parker Tremaine buy Sarah a dog, unless he hoped that she...that they...

Perhaps it was time to get it all out in the open.

"Parker," she began uncertainly. "I feel as if there's something we need to get straight. I don't know if you're hoping—if you are thinking that maybe you and I…"

He looked politely curious, maybe a little amused, but nothing more. God, this was awkward. He hadn't ever even asked her out on a date, not really. There was just that one impulsive kiss in the jail cell. It might have meant nothing. She might be making a fool of herself.

"I mean. It's just that I don't want you to get the wrong idea. I don't think it's a good idea for us to…to see each other. Except as friends, of course."

"You don't? Why?" Parker cast a smiling glance toward the lake, where Ward was still grandstanding. "Because of the insanity in your family? I'm prepared to overlook that."

"I'm serious," she said earnestly. "It wouldn't work, really it wouldn't. I'm here for such a short time. A month at the most. And I need, well, I need to keep my life as uncomplicated as possible right now. I have a lot of things I need to sort out."

Slowly, as he watched her face, Parker's expression sobered. "Ward told me there used to be a guy back in Florida. Something that wasn't good for you, something that wasn't working. He mentioned a broken engagement." He watched her carefully. "Is that it? Is that what you have to sort out?"

"Kind of." She looked away. "Among other things. I just really don't need any emotional complications right now."

"Okay." Parker smiled. "No emotional complications. Not from me, anyhow." He glanced at the puppy, who was waking up, wriggling like a baby in her arms. "But I can't speak for Frosty here. I have an idea this little fellow is a real heartbreaker."

CHAPTER EIGHT

AFTER DINNER, when the cook had gone home for the night and Frosty had finally tuckered himself out and fallen asleep in his crate, Sarah sat with Ward in his workroom while he put a new finish on an old English carved chair.

He had offered to play chess with her instead, or even watch TV. But she had been happy to forgo those pleasures. Newly sensitized to the dangers paint fumes might present to an unborn baby, she made sure the exhaust fan was on, and she sat a little distant from the action. She loved to watch him work.

The chair itself was exquisite—part of Winter House's original furnishings. But it was Ward himself she enjoyed watching most. His gnarled hands were still so deft, and the way he swirled the brush was so graceful, sliding slow across the broad planks, following the curve of a scroll, then dipping delicately into the ridges of a fleur-de-lis.

"It's beautiful." She picked up an unused brush and feathered its bristles against the palm of her hand. "It's like being an artist, isn't it?"

Her uncle snorted. "*Hell,* no. I'm no artist. I'm just a drudge. Your aunt…" His hand paused. "Now *she* was an artist. She always knew what colors to pick, what pieces to put where. I was just the hack who carried out her orders. And considered it a privilege, too."

Sarah smiled. She remembered that. Roberta could fuss over the placement of one picture, making Ward hold it first here, then there, then another inch to the left. Sarah had thought it silly back then. What was one picture in a house that possessed hundreds? But now she understood what a work of art Winter House was, and she realized that Roberta's careful attention had kept it that way.

Ward chuckled as he resumed his work. "Me an *artist!* Your aunt would get a good laugh out of that one. She always said I had the decorating eye of a circus clown."

"Aww." Sarah tapped her brush against his forearm sympathetically. "Don't feel bad. You can always make a living as an ice-skating instructor."

He glared at her. "You scoff, madam, but sometimes the problem isn't the teacher. It's the student."

"I know. I'm sorry. I'm hopeless." Her tailbone still ached from all those falls. "Did you know Parker Tremaine was there the whole time? It was pretty embarrassing to discover I had an audience."

"Oh, come off it. You know perfectly well that Parker Tremaine thinks anything you do is adorable. Although I bet he's never seen that face you make when you eat asparagus."

Sarah looked over at her uncle quickly. "Don't be silly," she began. He was still working, his gaze concentrated on the intricate carving on the arms of the chair, so she couldn't read his face.

"It's not silly. It's true. He's smitten." Ward glanced up suddenly, his brush poised in the air. "But I take it the feeling isn't mutual."

"Of course not." She beat the paintbrush nervously against her palm. "No, that didn't sound right. Parker is a very nice man. And I like him a lot. But he's just a friend. I don't think of him like *that*."

"Oh, yeah? Well, you'd be the first woman in Firefly Glen history who didn't." He went back to work. "That's how you'll go down in the record books, then. They'll say *She couldn't skate worth a damn, and apparently she was blind as a bat, too.*"

"Not blind," Sarah complained, half-laughing even though the subject made her a little uncomfortable. "I'm well aware he's handsome."

"Crazy, then? He's a fine man, Short Stuff. You could do worse." He grinned. "In fact, you *have* done worse. Don't forget the erstwhile Ed."

"I haven't forgotten him. In fact, that's why I'm not interested in Parker Tremaine, or anyone, right now."

"Nonsense. You fell off the horse, you get back on." He pointed the paintbrush at her, and a couple of dots of mahogany finish fell on her forearm for emphasis.

"Life's short," he said. He tilted his hand to look at his wedding ring, a simple, time-scratched gold band that she'd never seen him take off. "There are few enough years as it is. Ed's had three of yours already. How many are you going to let him steal?"

She squeezed the paintbrush in both hands, struggling with the decision about what to tell him. It didn't seem right to hide the truth any longer, not when he was obviously hoping that she might develop a romantic interest in his good friend Parker.

Besides, she would have to tell him about the baby sooner or later. Wouldn't it be more honest to do it sooner?

But she was a coward. She had never looked into her

uncle's eyes and seen disappointment. She dreaded the day when she would. She hated the thought of losing his respect.

On the other hand, if she didn't speak up now, she was going to lose respect for *herself.*

"It's not just Ed," she said, drawing a deep breath. She sat straighter, taking her courage by the reins. "There's something else, something important I've been wanting to tell you."

He obviously heard the serious note in her voice. He put his paintbrush down slowly, resting it across the lid of the finish can. "Okay," he said, giving her his full attention. "Let's hear it, then."

She didn't sugarcoat it, or lead into it with a meandering preamble. Ward was a blunt man who believed in meeting trouble head-on. And this was trouble with a capital *T.* He wouldn't admire her for trying to dress it up in a fancy hat and pass it off as anything else.

"I'm pregnant," she said simply. "I'm going to have Ed's baby later this year. He knows. He knew before we broke up. He would prefer that I get rid of it. He doesn't want me, and he doesn't want the baby."

Ward looked grim. "Man, this Ed guy just gets better and better."

She lifted her chin. "Well, that's the whole sad story, really. I'm pregnant, and I'm not going to be getting married. I'm going to have this baby, and I'm going to do it alone."

Her uncle narrowed his eyes. "That's it?"

She nodded. "I'm sorry. I know what you must think." She swallowed. "I know you're disappointed in me. But at least now you can see why I'm not in a position to date the sheriff or anyone else at the moment."

"I can?"

She looked at him, confused. "Well, of course. I'm pregnant—"

"I got that." To her surprise, her uncle was smiling. "You're pregnant, and you're not going to marry the jerk. I think that's wonderful. Absolutely *terrific!* Now if you'd told me you were pregnant and you *were* going to marry the jerk, well, that would be bad news."

"But I certainly can't be out dating—"

He shook his head woefully. "God, child, you're about as Victorian as this chair. This is the twenty-first century, isn't it? What, you think you're damaged goods? Not fit company for any decent man? I think I read a line like that in *Jane Eyre,* or some equally hysterical piece of antediluvian blather. But I've never heard a real human being say anything that ridiculous."

She could hardly believe his attitude. Where were the questions, the recriminations, the lectures? Where was the dreaded disappointment?

"But what about Parker? Surely if he knew about the baby, he—"

"I just said he had a crush on you, Short Stuff. I didn't say he wanted to marry you."

She couldn't speak. She had imagined a thousand reactions to her news. But never this...this uncomplicated pleasure. It still hadn't fully penetrated her anxiety. But there, on the edges of the guilt that had been smothering her, she glimpsed a thin border of sunshine.

Ward was already back at work on the chair, smiling down at the scrolled arms and dabbing his brush with new enthusiasm.

"Poor Parker," he said, chuckling. "Oh, give the guy

a break, why don't you? He thinks you're cute. He wants to take you to dinner." Ward tossed her a grin. "And I hate to rain on your hair-shirt parade, Short Stuff. But even fallen women have to eat."

HARRY HAD BEEN STOMPING around the department like a snake-bit elephant all day, and Parker had just about had enough of it. He didn't care if Harry was Emma's husband. If the damn fool didn't start acting civilized, Parker was going to take him out back and introduce him to Miss Manners the hard way.

The telephone rang. Suzie was working this afternoon, and she answered it with her usual singsongy, fake upper-crust accent. "Good Ahfahnoooon. Fiahhfly Glen Sheriff's Depahhhtment." Parker tried not to cringe. She'd been doing this schtick ever since he had dared to tell her that "Hey, this is the cop shop" wouldn't quite cut it as a greeting.

She listened a moment, then she punched the hold button. "Harry," she said, pushing her glasses up on her nose wearily. "It's for you. Again. It's Emma. Again."

Harry shook his head without looking up from his paperwork. "I'm not here."

Parker felt his fingers making a fist without even consulting his brain. "That's odd, Harry. Because I could swear I'm looking right at your ugly mug right now." When Harry didn't respond, Parker jammed the button for the incoming line and picked up the telephone himself. "Hey, Em. I'm sorry. Harry's here, but he's sucking a lemon right now. Maybe you'd better call back later."

She didn't like that, but, as he had known she would, she accepted it rather than give Parker a chance to say anything further about Harry.

Parker put the telephone down and looked across the room, where his brother-in-law was glowering at him.

"Why don't you just stay the hell out of this, Tremaine?" The deputy's voice was crisp with bitterness. "This is not your problem."

Parker didn't blink. "I think it is," he said levelly.

"Yeah, well it's *not*." Harry was getting red. "And if you'd like me to prove it, I can—"

Suzie stepped between them, holding her hands out dramatically, like the referee in a prizefight.

"Gentlemen." She rolled her eyes. "And I'm using that term loosely. Gentlemen, in exactly thirty seconds, Troop 637 of the Firefly Girls is going to walk through that door. They are on a field trip. They're working on a law enforcement badge. So unless you think they'd enjoy watching two grown men brawl on the floor like hoodlums, maybe you'd better chill out."

"Hell, Suzie." Parker took a deep breath. "Why didn't you tell me they were coming?"

"I told you last Tuesday, last Thursday, yesterday, and again two hours ago." She tossed her dark hair in wounded hauteur. "But no one listens to me. I'm just the clerk, what do I know?"

Oh, great. Parker could hear Harry taking the same deep breath he had needed himself. The two men carefully avoided making eye contact as the front door opened and a blue stream of beanie-topped little girls poured in.

Parker summoned a smile. He had better overcome his frustration quick, or else when they went to bed tonight these kids would be having nightmares about the mean policemen.

He was steeling himself to handle Madeline Alexander's compulsive cheeriness, but to his surprise the last person through the door was Sarah Lennox. And then he remembered. Madeline had recruited Sarah as a backup troop leader.

Sarah hadn't noticed him. She was talking to Eileen O'Malley, tilting slightly toward the little girl, listening to her conversation as earnestly as if they were discussing quantum physics.

And Eileen was glowing under the attention. Parker could picture Sarah in her classroom, offering that same easy affirmation to any child who needed it. What lucky kids her students were though they probably didn't know it. They were too young to recognize how rare true emotional generosity was. When they got a little older and had been knocked around by fair-weather friends, selfish lovers, vain bosses and narrow-minded neighbors, then they'd appreciate Ms. Lennox, who had always made them feel good about themselves.

Parker felt his sour mood lifting. He turned to the children and said, "Okay. Who wants to see where we put the criminals?"

A dozen hands waved in front of his face like little pink flags.

"Well, let's see. Who can I trust with the keys?" He scratched his chin, surveying the eager faces, looking for the one who needed it most. If Sarah could do this, so could he.

He saw C.J. Porterfield standing toward the back. She had her hand up, but halfheartedly, as if she already knew she wouldn't be chosen. C.J. was the daughter of an Internet millionaire, and she was just as brilliant and hopelessly geeky as her old man.

Parker crooked his finger at her. "C.J., you look

reliable. You come be the keeper of the keys. Deputy Dunbar is going to take you on a tour of the department, and when you get to the holding cell, you can unlock it for him."

C.J. took the keys solemnly, as if she had been handed a stick of dynamite. One of the keys was an antique, a big brass monstrosity that was more or less just for show. It had unlocked the jail cell Firefly Glen had used a hundred years ago, a cell long since torn down. Today, in this updated facility, the real cell key was small and silver and looked as if it might operate your mother's Honda.

You'd think a beady-eyed killer lurked in that cell right now, the way the other girls gathered around, eager for a chance to touch the brass key. And if Harry did his spiel correctly, they would get plenty of hair-raising stories about former inmates. Parker remembered from his own youth that field trips were considered a pathetic bust if they didn't include some blood and gore.

Luckily Harry had managed to rise above his mood, too. He took the kids away to show them the emergency radio. Parker had to smile, listening to him talk about mountain rescues at midnight, brushfires at dawn, coyotes caught snarling in the kitchen and fugitives caught streaking for the Canadian border.

Harry was good at this—he loved kids. He'd have them squealing and shuddering in happy horror before the hour was up.

It was a shame, really. Once, Parker had believed that Harry would make a great father to Emma's children. But now he wasn't even sure Harry made a very good husband. Damn the man. What was *wrong* with him?

"So have you ever really had any criminals in your

jail cell?" Sarah had wandered over to his side, and she was smiling. "Last time I was here, it looked more like a petting zoo."

"Of course we've had criminals," Parker said in mock indignation. "Once we held an escapee from the Albany prison for forty-eight whole hours. An *ax* murderer, no less."

She raised her eyebrows. "And that was—"

He chuckled. "Seventy-three years ago. But I haven't had a good night's sleep since."

"No sleep? Why, that must be just like when you have a new puppy," she observed, widening her eyes innocently.

He grimaced. "Uh-oh. You, too? God, I'm sorry. But I'm in the same boat. I took Frosty's brother, you know—he was the only one who hadn't been adopted. I swear that dog whines nonstop from dusk until dawn. Then, of course, he sleeps all day." He gave her a placating smile. "Good thing they're so darn cute, isn't it? Otherwise you might want to strangle the puppy and the guy who gave him to you, too."

"I'll try to control myself," she said. "Actually, I've found the answer. Frosty cries when he's in his crate, but if I let him sleep up on the bed with me, he's fine."

Parker held his face under control with a noble effort. "Really," he said politely, aware of all the little ears around them. "How about that?"

Sarah shot him a suspicious look, but she didn't comment. They watched Harry handling the kids for a few minutes in silence. C.J. had just locked Eileen O'Malley in the jail cell, and the other girls were snickering.

"Well, you totally won't be able to escape," Daisy

Kinsale, a pretty blonde, was saying. "Not by squeezing through the bars, anyhow!"

"But don't worry," Daisy's smug-looking buddy Harriet piped in. "The bread-and-water diet will be good for you!"

Parker felt Sarah's tension building. "Kids can be such monsters," she muttered under her breath. "That blond girl is Eileen's own stepsister, did you know that?"

"Yeah, I did." Parker eyed Daisy Kinsale with annoyance. Brad Kinsale was a friend of his, and he was a damn nice guy. Why didn't he teach his kid better manners? "These mix-and-match families can be pretty rough sometimes, can't they?"

She nodded. "Brutal. I have six stepsiblings, from three different stepfathers. Believe me, I know all about it."

He hadn't realized that Sarah's growing up had been so turbulent. Though Ward had talked about Sarah often, he had never mentioned this. Parker wondered if that might be what had made Sarah so aware of other people's needs. Being forced to get along with so many intimate strangers—it could either make you bitter as hell or intensely sensitive.

But what a rotten life for a kid. He wondered what on earth her mother had been thinking.

He sighed. "That's just one of the reasons I'm glad my ex-wife and I never had children. Divorce is always the hardest on them, isn't it? And it makes starting over so much trickier."

She didn't answer. She was staring at Eileen, apparently lost in thought. She looked so sad, as if she found Eileen's plight unbearable.

He suddenly wanted more than anything to make

her smile. "I wouldn't worry too much about Eileen, though, if I were you," he said.

Sarah turned. "Why not?"

"Well, she doesn't know it yet, but she's undoubtedly going to turn into a wild Irish beauty, like every O'Malley woman for ten generations behind her."

He chuckled, remembering that Eileen's aunt, Deirdre O'Malley, had broken his own heart a couple of times during high school. "In a few years, every boy in town will be trotting around after her with their tongues hanging out. Including the boyfriends of every girl in this room."

"Good," Sarah said fiercely. Her chin was set in that special tight square she reserved for her most intense emotions. Watching her now, Parker realized that, for all her air of gentle fragility and her occasional mournful moments, Sarah Lennox was at heart a very strong woman.

Her appearance was deceiving. She wasn't as dramatic as the O'Malley women—those tall, athletic women with their fiery hair and their flashing eyes. Sarah was petite and slim. Her honey-blond hair was pale and translucent, like a halo around the narrow oval of her face. Her eyes were round, wide-set and kind, with none of the flashing arrogance that made the O'Malleys look like Celtic warrior queens.

Those eyes said Sarah could be easily hurt.

But that chin said she could take it.

Yes, he thought. He would take sweet, stubborn Sarah over the O'Malley firebrands any day.

If only she'd let him.

BY NINE O'CLOCK THAT NIGHT, when Parker was getting ready to go home, he was so tired he could hardly button his jacket properly. It had been a long day, but he had managed not to kill Harry, so in his book that meant it was a good day.

Harry had left first, five full minutes ago. Parker had stayed behind, leaving some final instructions with the graveyard deputy. He had thought it was smart to keep at least five minutes between him and Harry at all times.

But when he finally closed the department door and stepped out into the crisp, starry night, eager to get home to his quiet house, his warm fire and his annoying but adorable new puppy, he saw that Harry hadn't gone anywhere.

Instead, Harry and Emma were standing beside Emma's car. Their postures were so rigid they screamed hostility. Parker would have known he had stumbled into a domestic disturbance even if he hadn't been able to hear their arguments clearly.

Which, unfortunately, he could.

"You're a coward, Harry Dunbar. That's why you've left. Because you don't have the courage to stay and work things out."

"Think whatever you want, Emma." Harry's voice was as jagged as broken eggshells. Parker stopped in his tracks. He'd never heard Harry sound like that before. "Say whatever you want. I don't give a damn anymore."

"You never did." Emma was trying to yell, but it came out hoarsely, as if her throat were raw from hours of crying. "If you had *ever* loved me, you couldn't give up on our marriage."

"That's right, Emma." Harry was trying to pull away, but Emma was holding fast to his arm. "You guessed it. I never cared."

"Hey." Parker moved into the circle of illumination cast from the streetlight. He went to his sister. "What's going on here?"

"Goddamn it, Parker, this is none of your—"

"He's moved out," Emma broke in, turning to Parker. Her voice was hard and furious, but her swollen eyes, streaming with tears, spoke of a dreadful anguish. "He hasn't got the guts to stay and work out our problems, so he packed his suitcase and left me."

"Our problems can't *be* worked out." Harry had finally extricated himself from Emma's clutch. "But maybe you should remember that they are *our* problems. Not Parker's. Leave him out of this."

"Listen, Harry—"

"Shut up, Parker." Harry sounded like a total stranger. "Just shut up. Emma, go home. I'm not going to have this fight in the middle of the street, in front of everyone. It's *our* problem. Our private problem."

Emma drew herself up with an attempt at dignity, but she was shivering. She hugged her coat around herself like a little girl. Watching her, Parker felt his blood pounding in his temples. No one was allowed to treat Emma like this. *No one.*

"They stopped being *our* problems the minute you walked out the door, Harry," she said thickly. "They are *my* problems now. And I can handle them any way I see fit."

Harry stared at her, his mouth slightly open, as if he couldn't believe what she had said. "You'd tell him, wouldn't you?"

"You're darn right I would, if I thought it would help. At least he wouldn't just run away from the problem, like you did. At least he's not *weak.*"

Harry's head snapped back, as if from a blow. "You *bitch*."

That was the last thing Parker clearly remembered. His vision blurred with something bright and red. He felt his arm go back, and then he felt the bones of his fist connect with the bones in Harry's jaw.

Harry must have been seeing red swirls, too, because he swung back like a madman, and before Parker could make sense of anything, he had slammed Harry's body against the wall. He had one forearm across Harry's throat, and his jacket bunched in the other hand. He swallowed, and he tasted his own half-frozen blood.

"Stop it, you crazy lunatics!" Emma was beside him now, tugging on his arm wildly. "For God's sake, stop it, Parker. Do you think it will help me if you kill him? *I love him,* you idiot. *I love him!*"

HALF AN HOUR LATER, Parker finally got home, but he didn't feel much like starting a fire or petting the puppy, which Emma had named Snowball. He was staring at the bunged-up thug in his bathroom mirror, wondering when he had become such a damn fool, when the telephone rang.

He started to curse, but the movement hurt his busted lip. It was probably just the new guy at the department, wondering how to handle some trivial little detail. But he couldn't risk not answering it, in case it was Emma. So he threaded his way around the scampering puppy and grabbed the bedroom phone on the fifth ring.

"Parker? It's Sarah. I'm sorry to call so late."

He plopped down on the edge of the bed, almost too tired to register his full surprise. Snowball began whining and trying unsuccessfully to leap up with him, but it was an old tester bed, and much too high.

"That's okay," Parker said, careful of his lip. "What's up?"

"I just wanted to say thanks for being so nice to the girls this afternoon. They had a wonderful time."

"Good. Me, too," he said politely. He waited, feeling sure she had something else to say. She hadn't called him at ten o'clock at night just to tell him that.

The hesitation on Sarah's side of the line was tense and expectant. He wondered if she was waiting for him to create an opening. But an opening for what?

"Anyhow," she went on finally. "I have also been thinking about what we said the other day."

Snowball began making a melodramatic racket, scrabbling at the bedclothes and whining, desperate to join him. Parker could hardly hear. So he reached over and scooped him up, one hand beneath his belly, and deposited him on the comforter. The puppy settled down instantly. He curled up against Parker's hip and rested his chin on his thigh, sighing blissfully.

"Don't get used to this," he whispered, his hand over the mouthpiece. Then he spoke into the phone. "And? What were you thinking?"

"That maybe I was being silly. You know, overreacting to the whole thing—the kiss, the puppy, the whole idea of dating. I meant to tell you this today, but the girls were always around and—"

"And?"

"And anyhow, I think maybe it would be okay. I'm not ready for anything serious, of course—and of course you aren't, either. But there's really no reason why we shouldn't have lunch, or see each other every now and then, if you want to."

She paused. "I mean, assuming you want to."

"Yeah," he said, softly stroking the puppy, who seemed to be asleep already. "I want to. How about dinner tomorrow night?"

She seemed taken aback. "Tomorrow?"

"Well, I'd say tonight, but it's a little late. You've probably already had dinner." He smiled. That hurt his lip, too, but he didn't care. "I'm calling your bluff here, Sarah."

"I wasn't bluffing," she protested.

"Okay, then. Dinner. Tomorrow night. Seven o'clock. Dress warm and come hungry."

CHAPTER NINE

JUST ONE DATE. Just for fun. Just as friends.

What harm could it do?

Reciting those simple phrases over and over, Sarah stood at the window of her bedroom in Winter House, waiting for Parker to arrive. She wished she could get rid of this edginess. It was a tight-chested, pins-and-needles anxiety, the kind you might feel right before a rough exam for which you hadn't studied nearly enough.

Maybe it was just the weather. All day long the sky had been heavy, riding low in the heavens like a boat with too much cargo. The cook had left early, complaining that her arthritis was acting up, as it always did before a snowstorm. Ward was eating out with Madeline, and Sarah would be with Parker, so the woman had nothing to keep her at Winter House.

Sarah's ears were tuned for the engine rumble of Parker's Jeep, so she almost missed the slight, silvery tinkling of sleigh bells. Even when the lovely sound pierced her consciousness, she didn't connect it with Parker. She thought at first, illogically, of wind chimes, like the ones on the balcony of her Florida apartment.

It wasn't until she saw the sleigh itself that she understood. Drawn by an elegant gray horse, it glided across the snow like something from another century. The curving metal runners were elaborately filigreed, like fine calligraphy, and the graceful, roomy body of the sleigh was painted a festive green, with sparkling silver trim.

Parker brought the sleigh to a stop in front of the house as easily as if he drove one every day. The horse tossed his head and pawed the snow, setting the bells along his harness jingling merrily.

For a moment, Sarah didn't move. This was another world, a world she'd never seen before. And she was enchanted. Then, remembering that this magic carriage had come for her, she let the curtain fall shut, grabbed her coat, hat, muffler and gloves and lightly flew down the staircase.

She made it to the front door just as Parker was lifting the brass knocker. "Hi," she said, feeling a little giddy from hurrying. She glanced at the sleigh. "Nice car."

"Like it?" He grinned. "It's a 1920 model S. One horsepower."

When he smiled, she noticed a dark bruise that ran along the lower edge of his lip. She looked more closely. His lip was slightly swollen, too.

"Oh dear," she said softly. "That looks painful."

He worked the lip carefully, as if testing it. Then he smiled again. "Nope. Apparently it's not serious. Just showy."

"What on earth happened?"

He shrugged. "Nothing, really. Occupational hazard. Much too dull to bore you with."

She could tell he wasn't going to elaborate. And she didn't want to pry. So, giving up, she wrapped her muffler around her throat and walked down the steps. Up close, the sleigh was even more charming, the wood weathered with age but freshly painted and gleaming. The interior was piled high with rugs and pillows.

"Is it yours?"

He shook his head. "The horse and the sleigh belong to the town vet—he's a friend of mine. I told him I was going to try to impress Ward Winters's niece so that she'd help us persuade him to release all the sleighs for the festival."

She looked over at him, smiling. "So, is that what this date is all about? Trying to enlist my support against my uncle?"

"Oh, absolutely," he agreed, his face poker straight. "For myself, I have no interest in moonlit sleigh rides with beautiful women. None whatsoever."

She laughed at that and tried not to let the compliment warm her too much. She wasn't beautiful, and she knew it. She was cute—occasionally, when she was at her best, even pretty in a tepid, monochromatic way.

But maybe on a cold winter night, with sleigh bells tinkling and snow just starting to fall, all women looked beautiful.

He handed her up into the seat, which was surprisingly comfortable. He arranged the rugs across her lap, gave one last tug to secure her muffler, and then he came around the front, offering the horse a friendly pat, and climbed into his own position beside her at the reins.

She didn't ask where they were going. She didn't care. It was enough merely to exist in this moment of extraordinary beauty. The heavy sky was like a silver silk canopy over their heads, and the frost-sparkling trees swept by like candles. The night was intensely quiet, broken only by the whoosh of the runners over the icy snow, the crunch of the horse's dancing hooves, and the clear crystal ringing of sleigh bells.

It was cold, so cold that the air streamed white from the horse's nostrils, and her cheeks burned under the frigid fingers of the wind. But it was glorious, and she never wanted it to end.

Finally, though, she saw a building, a low-slung wooden cabin surrounded by trucks. Lucky's Lounge, the neon sign out front read, at least sometimes. Occasionally the first *L* sizzled and disappeared, making it look like "ucky's Lounge."

Sarah looked at Parker, a question in her eyes.

"I know," he said, one corner of his mouth tucked into his cheek. "It looks awful. But it's got some of the best pizza in town, and, most importantly, there's a barn where I can stable the horse while we're eating."

She waited for him, reluctant to enter the lounge ahead of him. *Someone* had driven all those trucks here, and where she came from it wasn't always safe for a woman to enter a roughneck bar alone.

Besides, she liked watching him handle the horse, whose name was Dusty, it seemed. Parker murmured and stroked "—That's right, Dusty. You're a fine girl, sweetheart—" as he unhooked the harness and released the sleigh. Dusty nuzzled Parker's shoulder, blowing a soft snort, as if she understood and wanted to answer.

Finally Parker made sure Dusty could reach the hay. He arranged a blanket over the horse's back and turned to Sarah. "Okay. Now it's our turn."

The lounge was exactly what Sarah expected— smoky and low-lit, brimming with very large, unshaven

men in flannel shirts who seemed able to simultaneously watch a football game on television, play pool
and sing along with the country-western song on the
jukebox.

Parker knew them all. He backslapped or was
slapped by almost every man he passed. But somehow
he maneuvered Sarah to a booth in the back corner,
where the smoke was a fraction less dense and the
sportscaster's excited voice was almost inaudible.

They had just barely placed their order—one large
pizza, no anchovies; one beer, one bottled water—when
a giant of a man came by with his hand out.

"You in?"

To Sarah's surprise, Parker pulled a five-dollar bill
out of his pocket and laid it in the other man's huge
palm. "Ninety-seven," Parker said.

The giant turned to Sarah. "You in?"

She looked at Parker for guidance. Obviously they
were betting on something, but what were the rules?
Should she, as an outsider, say yes or no? He was
smiling, and he nodded subtly. She dug around in her
pockets and found a five. "Okay," she said, depositing
it in the man's hand.

"How many?"

"I beg your pardon?"

"How many yards?"

She glanced at Parker again, but his grin was so amused
that she made up her mind to bluff this out on her own.

"A hundred and eleven," she said briskly. The giant
nodded, made a note on a napkin and moved on.

Parker burst out laughing. "Do you have any idea
what you just bet on?"

"Yards," she said, raising her chin. "And since he

didn't look like a landscape designer or a dressmaker, I assume it must have something to do with the football game. Your guess of ninety-seven was too high for a spread. So I figured yards running. Yards passing. Something like that."

Parker's eyes glinted in the light from the neon beer sign on the wall next to them. "Darn. You're good. Where did you learn all that?"

She raised her eyebrows in polite disdain as she unfolded her napkin. "I have had my share of sweaty, muscle-bound boyfriends, sir." She chuckled. "Besides, I teach high school, remember? My kids don't know what I'm talking about unless I express myself in sports metaphors."

He laughed.

"But isn't betting illegal? Aren't they worried about doing it in front of The Law?"

"Technically, we're not betting. We're paying to watch the football game on television. The chance to win the pot is just, and I quote, a fringe benefit of paying the TV tax."

When she looked incredulous, he smiled and shrugged. "Believe me, this has been through the local judicial system. Judge Bridwell ruled that if it's a fee for the television, it's not betting. Presto-chango, it's legal."

It was beyond Sarah's comprehension, but she let it go. Joining the pool must have been the right move, because from that moment on she was one of the gang. Dozens of men came over to say hello, often bringing their wives and girlfriends.

When their pizza was finished, one of the guys at the bar bought her a new bottled water, having discovered that she didn't drink. Later a bearded man in a hat that said *Lumberjacks Do It Till You Fall Over* came by and gave her a dollar for the jukebox.

She was the only optimist who had guessed over a hundred, and when the quarterback threw his final touchdown, putting the total at one-o-seven, the whole bar erupted in a rich, throaty cheer. "Sarah, Sarah, Sarah," they chanted until she felt herself blushing.

She won five hundred dollars. With a huge, congratulatory grin, the giant dumped it in her lap, a hundred five-dollar bills, all crumpled and stained, some so worn they were held together with Scotch tape.

Embarrassed, she did the only thing she could think of. She bought a round for the whole bar. And the chorus went up again, this time even louder. "Sarah, Sarah, Sarah!"

All in all, it was wonderful—as cozy and welcoming as any group she'd ever tried to infiltrate. But, even so, she was glad when Parker tilted his head toward the door, indicating that it was time to make their escape.

"What nice people," she murmured, half-sleepy now that she was tucked into the rugs again. Parker was clicking Dusty along at a slow walk that set the sleigh into a rhythmic motion almost like the rocking of a cradle. She and Parker were fitted so close she could feel his body heat warming her from shoulder to thigh.

The clouds had moved off while they were in the bar, and the world looked just born, white and new and hushed. The sky had lifted, revealing a silent explosion of stars.

"Yes, they are," Parker agreed. He glanced at her. "And they certainly approved of you. They don't approve of everybody."

She smiled drowsily. "I'll bet they approve of anyone who buys them a round of beer."

"Well, maybe." He rode in silence for a minute. "Actually, I was thinking of my ex-wife. Once, when she came home with me for a visit, I took her to Lucky's. God, what a disaster. Tina sat there looking like someone had put a steel rod in her back, like she was afraid she'd catch something if she moved. And she had this bad-smell pucker on her face. After about ten minutes, not a soul in the place would speak to us." He shook his head at the memory. "Tina wasn't a fan of small towns."

Sarah looked over at him curiously. "What *was* she a fan of?"

"Our life in D.C. It was the perfect town for her. Tina was a fan of power. Money. Excitement. She breathed glamour like other people breathe air."

Sarah touched his arm with her gloved hand. "And *you*. After all, she married you. She must have been a pretty big fan of yours."

"Only when I was part of the power package." He shrugged. "When she heard that I wanted to leave D.C. and come back here, she permanently resigned her membership in the Parker Tremaine fan club."

"She divorced you because she didn't want to live in a small town?" Sarah squeezed his arm, thinking what a fool Tina Tremaine sounded like. "That must have been very difficult for you."

Parker shook his head. "Not really. Receiving those divorce papers was like getting a pardon from the governor. For both of us. Our marriage was the difficult part. For both of us. It was a terrible mistake, almost from the beginning."

So Parker had moved away, leaving his ex-wife behind. Sarah felt a stirring of sympathy for Tina, which she knew was absurd, given what she'd heard about the woman. But Sarah had been left behind, too, and she knew how it felt. Was it possible that Ed and Parker had more in common than she had thought?

She shivered suddenly. Assuming the wind was bothering her, Parker reached over comfortably and wrapped his arm around her shoulders, pulling her more tightly against the solid warmth of his body.

No, she thought with an intense, instinctive defiance. Ed and Parker were nothing alike. Parker would have brought his wife, if only she'd been willing to come. Ed had made it clear that Sarah was not invited.

Gradually the streets they traversed became more and more populated, until they were in the thick of town. Parker slowed Dusty down even further, offering Sarah time to enjoy the view.

And what a view it was, especially for a little Southern schoolteacher who had never even seen snow before. Firefly Glen was like an enchanted village, with its snow-laden roofs, its smoke-plumed chimneys, its old-fashioned streetlights floating like neat rows of glowing golden orbs.

"Look over there." Parker suddenly drew Dusty to a standstill. "The Spring House—look!"

Sarah followed Parker's gloved finger, which was pointing toward a storybook Victorian mansion, all pink and white and dove-gray, with fanciful gables and ornate gingerbread woodwork. A huge porch wrapped around the entire house.

"Yes," she said, transfixed by the extraordinary feminine charm of the house. "My uncle showed me all four Season Houses when I came here years ago. It's even more beautiful than I remembered."

"But look," Parker said softly. "Up on the porch."

Sarah looked more carefully. And then she saw what he saw. Up on the wide verandah, pressing their noses against the honeyed warmth of a lighted window, were two large brown deer.

"They're cold," Parker whispered. "They want to go in where it's warm."

Sarah realized she was holding her breath. "They don't look real. Will they be all right?"

"Sure." Parker clicked his tongue softly, and Dusty began again to walk sedately down the tree-lined street. "The yard may be missing a few plants by tomorrow morning, but the deer will be fine."

Sarah watched the deer over her shoulder until she and Parker were too far away to make out the dark, still silhouettes against the golden windowpane. Then she settled back into the warm circle of Parker's arm.

"Did your uncle ever tell you how we got our Season Houses?"

Sarah thought back. "No. He just told me that Firefly Glen had begun as a tiny settlement of loggers and trappers, but that some millionaires from New York City discovered it around the end of the nineteenth century." She snuggled down into the rugs happily. "Why? Is it a good story?"

"It's a little unusual," he said. "Do you remember the Summer House?"

Sarah thought back. "Yes, I think so. A huge Italian villa? Seems to be deteriorating? Some crumbling mosaics, big empty swimming pool, long colonnades filled with leaves. I remember thinking it looked haunted."

"That's the one. Well, that was the first mansion built here—almost a hundred years ago by Dr. and Mrs. Mark

Granville, the darlings of New York society. Mark, they say, was tall, funny and kind. Moira, the story goes, was tiny and elegant and sweet. Anyhow, everybody wanted to do whatever the Granvilles did, so within a couple of years several other rich young couples had moved here, too. They built the Spring House, the Autumn House—"

"I remember that one, too," Sarah said eagerly. "Huge, out in the woods. Wood and glass and stone, kind of a ranch house."

"Yep." Parker grinned. "You have a good memory."

"The houses are fairly spectacular," she said. "And of course since my uncle lived in one of the Season Houses, I was extra curious about the other three."

"That makes sense. Anyhow, the Winter House was the last one built by the Granvilles' friends. After the Winter House, no new mansions were built here for thirty years."

Sarah turned to look at him. "Why on earth not?"

"That's where the story gets good. I guess a lot of women were jealous of Moira Granville. And suspicious, too. They didn't know anything about her family, about where she came from. In a small town, that's important. They investigated the heck out of her, and eventually they discovered something shocking. Apparently Dr. Granville had met his sublime young wife in a brothel in Boston."

At Sarah's raised eyebrows, Parker chuckled. "Yes, a brothel, where, by the way, an hour of her company had undoubtedly cost him considerably less than it did *after* the wedding."

Sarah caught her breath. "Oh, no," she said.

"Oh, yes. The judgmental old witches were furious.

Jealousy happily switched to hatred, and Moira Granville was immediately ostracized."

"How awful," Sarah said sadly. "How cruel."

"It's always struck me that way, too. But the women meant business. Have you ever noticed that half-painted ceiling in your uncle's house?"

Sarah sat up excitedly. "Yes! Of course. But when I was here at thirteen, he said I was too young to hear the story of why it was never finished."

Parker smiled. "You *were.* Apparently the original Winter House wife came bursting into the parlor, frightening the poor artist half to death, demanding that he cease painting immediately. She was, by heaven, not going to live next door to a *whore.* She moved out the next day, and for thirty years the Granvilles lived in the Summer House alone, with only loggers and trappers and three empty mansions for neighbors."

Sarah shook her head helplessly, almost unable to believe the story wasn't exaggerated, as legends often are. How unforgiving everyone had been! It felt almost shameful to be descended, however distantly, from such a judgmental woman. Sarah could only imagine the humiliation and loneliness the lovely Moira must have endured.

"Later, new, less finicky millionaires moved in—eventually even a descendent of that original outraged Mrs. Winters came back. There hasn't been a shortage of millionaires since." Parker laughed. "Now, as your uncle points out, the only problem is keeping them away."

But suddenly Sarah didn't feel like joining Parker's laughter. This was the other side of the small-town experience, the side she'd been forgetting. The narrow-mindedness, the prying eyes, the power to punish its members for sins real or imagined.

And how different was it in Firefly Glen today? Sarah had been here only a few weeks, but already she knew that the Glen was still essentially a small town, with both the small-town virtues—and the small-town vices.

Her uncle was open-minded and tolerant. But he was an acknowledged eccentric. What about the others? What about Theo Burke at the café, and the fussy, flowery Madeline Alexander? What about the mothers of the Firefly Girls, and the Daughters of the Revolution? What about the Junior League and the Altar Guild and the Garden Club?

What would happen when they found out that the newcomer, Sarah Lennox, was unmarried and pregnant and daring to date their darling favorite son, Sheriff Tremaine?

And at that moment, Sarah realized that she had been dreaming a dangerous dream. She had been dreaming that perhaps she could stay here, under the protective roof of her liberal-minded uncle, forever. She had been dreaming that this storybook town might embrace her, become her home.

And her child's home.

How ridiculous. She knew better. You couldn't hide from your problems forever, not even in Firefly Glen. She had to snap out of this daydream before it was too late.

Sensing that the rocking motion of the sleigh had ceased, Sarah looked up, trying to clear her mind. But her eyes were misty, as if the cold had stung them to tears.

"Sarah." Parker leaned over her, touching her face

with soft leather-covered fingers. "You're awfully quiet. Are you all right?"

"I'm fine," she said, nodding firmly. But the motion caused the stinging tear to run down her cheek, where it instantly froze. "I'm fine. I'm just cold. It's getting colder, don't you think?"

"Maybe." Leaning across her, he pulled the largest, softest rug up, tucking it under her chin. He arranged her muffler so that it reached almost to her lower lip. Then he tugged down her white woolen hat, gently easing it so low on her forehead that her eyelashes brushed it when she blinked.

"Better?" he asked.

She nodded, watching him from her soft cocoon. His eyes were dark and soft, like moonlight. Yet deep in his gaze lay something else—something powerful but, for the moment, tightly leashed. It made her breath come shallow and fast to look at him.

"You're all eyes now," he said, slowly tracing the edges of her woolen hat, the rim of her muffler, with one gloved forefinger. Drawing a tingling line across the arch of her brow. "And they're so beautiful. All green-and-gold fire. I could lose myself in your eyes, Sarah."

She wondered if that were true, that her eyes were full of fire. She could feel something like that, deep in the pit of her stomach, something hot and sweet, like too much brandy.

"If you don't want me to kiss you, maybe you'd better say something now." He half smiled, but it had a ragged edge, as if it had been torn from something darker.

She was silent, except for her heart, which seemed to be drumming high in her throat. He drew closer. "Or now," he whispered, and his breath feathered out to brush against her cheek.

But she didn't say anything. And so, gently, he kissed her.

It should have been enough. That much would have been safe, or almost so. When her time in this enchanted village ended, she could take this one soft kiss with her as a reminder. A treasure pocketed against the poverty to come.

But let the kiss begin to burn—let it press and harden and catch fire—and it would no longer be mere memory. She would carry it forever as a scar.

She knew all that, and still she didn't stop him. She let him take her into his arms, enfolding her with more rising, pulsing warmth than a thousand rugs of the finest wool. He groaned, low and hungry, and she answered with a small sound that would have been his name, except that, like a fire, he consumed the syllables before they could reach the air.

Oh, she was a fool, the worst kind of fool. But she no longer even wanted to resist. The magic of this winter night had crept inside her, filling her with hot, pointed stars and melting ice crystals of bliss.

Tomorrow, she thought hazily as she sank into the sweet heat of his lips. She would regret this tomorrow.

But tomorrow was on the other side of the stars, and it had no power here.

CHAPTER TEN

"SO WHAT DOES WARD THINK about you helping with the festival?" Madeline Alexander bit off the end of her white thread and started threading it expertly through the eye of her sharp silver needle. "Is he very angry with me for drafting you into the enemy camp?"

Sarah smiled. "He hasn't said much about it. He just commented once that it was a shame we were doing so much work for nothing, since there wasn't going to be any festival. He hasn't mentioned it since."

Sarah dug around on the sewing table, which was frothing with about fifty yards of white netting, fourteen bolts of cotton lace and nine spools of sequined ribbon. With any kind of luck, in three weeks this chaos would have become a dozen snowflake costumes for the Firefly Girls.

Right now, though, it was the hopeless mess in which she'd lost her scissors.

"Well, then I wonder why he hasn't come down to say hello?" Madeline cast another glance toward the staircase, which she'd been doing with increasing frequency over the past hour. "Are you *sure* he's not mad at me?"

Sarah was beginning to regret having agreed to let the troop leaders meet at Winter House. Madeline was doing very little sewing and a whole lot of mooning over Ward.

"I'm sure he'll be down later," she lied. Ward had told her he'd rather walk a tightrope naked over a crocodile pit than put one foot down those stairs while the Firefly Girl leaders were in the house. At least three of them, he said, had plans to chloroform him and drag him to an underground altar.

Finally having found her scissors, Sarah sat back and scanned the other women, wondering which three he meant. Madeline, of course. And maybe Bridget O'Malley, little Eileen O'Malley's grandmother—one of the most gorgeous sixty-year-old women Sarah had ever seen. She was about five-eleven and had eyes as green as shamrocks, dyed fire-red hair and a temper to match.

The third was probably Jocelyn Waitely, the hotel-owner's wife, though of course she'd have to divorce Bourke first. That little detail wouldn't stop her. Jocelyn was small and blond and smart enough to be darn dangerous. After knowing her only an hour, Sarah had decided she definitely wouldn't want to be standing between Jocelyn Waitely and whatever she wanted.

"Tell me, Madeline," Jocelyn said mildly, without looking up from the portable Singer she had set up on the parlor table. "Have you decided who you're going to vote for in March—Harry or Parker?"

Sarah's needle slipped, digging into the pad of her index finger. She whisked the finger away, popping it into her mouth before she could bleed on the white lace.

Looking up, she caught Jocelyn's sharp gaze on her, and she cursed her own clumsiness. Was she really so far gone that the mere mention of his name could make her twitch? Oh, brother. She was going to have to do better than this.

Madeline frowned over at her friend. "Parker, of course. Aren't you? It doesn't seem quite cricket, does it, for a man to run against his own brother-in-law?"

"I heard he may not still *be* his brother-in-law come March," Jocelyn said. Her tone was bland, but Sarah could see that her eyes were alight with an avid, rather unpleasant, curiosity. "He and Emma have split. I heard he moved out."

"That's just a temporary tiff, Jocelyn," Bridget O'Malley put in sternly. She had opinions as large and solid as she was herself. "Harry Dunbar and Emma Tremaine belong together, and they'll get over this. Everybody knows that."

This was news to Sarah. She and Emma and Heather had lunched together just two days ago, and, though Emma had seemed subdued, she hadn't mentioned anything as dramatic as a separation.

Of course, as much as Sarah liked Emma, she hardly qualified as an intimate of hers. Emma might well not talk of personal things around an outsider.

And Sarah was definitely still an outsider. She hadn't even known about the upcoming election. She wondered how Parker felt about it. He seemed so comfortable as sheriff, such a natural fit for the job. What would he do if Harry took that little gold star away from him?

"What does Parker think about it, Sarah?" Jocelyn's probing gaze was still on her. "Last night, when you two went to Lucky's, did he mention the election?"

Sarah stared stupidly. How did Jocelyn know that already? The Glen gossips obviously didn't work with anything as old-fashioned as grapevines. They must send their tidbits by fax.

She bent over her work, trimming a fluffy white-net skirt with silver sequins, cravenly glad to have something to look at other than Jocelyn's fox-sharp features.

"No," she said honestly. "He didn't."

"Oh." Jocelyn smiled. "I thought maybe he might have. After all, a sleigh ride is so cozy, isn't it? There's lots of time to talk…and so forth."

The other women must not have checked their fax machines this morning for the latest from the Glen Gossip Gazette. They seemed surprised. They closed in around her, or at least it felt that way, though no one actually moved. They peppered her with questions, determined to drag out every detail about anything as romantic as a sleigh ride.

For the next ten minutes, Sarah dodged questions that ranged from innocently curious to rudely speculative. She prayed she wouldn't blush. It was too soon to have to face such a grilling. She needed more time—time to think through what last night had really meant…to her, or to Parker.

And she definitely needed time to forget the feel of Parker's hot hands against her skin.

But somehow she managed to keep the details boringly generic enough: it had been quite cold; the pizza had been very good. Eventually the interest died down. Even Jocelyn seemed ready to move on to more fertile ground.

And then the doorbell rang.

Knowing that Ward would never let a mere doorbell lure him into the crocodile pit, Sarah got up to answer it. To her intense pleasure, followed by sinking dismay, it was Parker.

He looked wonderful. He was in civilian clothes, dark corduroy jeans and a black turtleneck that made his eyes blaze like blue fire. She felt herself flushing, weak-kneed all over again. Please, she prayed, don't let Jocelyn Waitely see her now. The gossip would race around and around the Glen, doubling over on itself, growing and swelling until it became a full-fledged scandal.

"Hi," she said, feeling ridiculously nervous. She hadn't slept with the man, for heaven's sake. She had just kissed him a few times after a pleasant evening out. They had been amazing kisses, yes. The kind that turned your legs to water and your mind to mush. But, as the song said, even a hot, mind-shattering kiss is just a kiss.

"Hi." He smiled.

The smile was enough to liquefy her bones all over again. It was full of an intimate delight, as if they shared an intensely private and miraculous secret. Her insides did a tight, thrilling swoop under that look. She felt weightless and tingling, as if they had just joined hands and jumped off a very high diving board together.

As she fought to steady herself, she realized sadly that Ed had never looked at her that way. Not even after they had first made love. Not even when he had asked her to marry him. Not ever.

"Sarah," Parker said huskily, still smiling. "Kiss me."

She took a deep breath and fought the impulse to move toward him, mindlessly obeying both his words and her own body's primitive urgings.

"Don't be silly," she said in a half whisper, shaking her head firmly. "The house is full of people. The Firefly Girls troop leaders. They're probably all pressed against the parlor window right now, waiting to see what we do."

"So?" He tilted his head. The sun was bright today, and it caught one side of his face, illuminating his glossy black hair and sparkling on the clear blue of his eyes. "Kiss me. Let's give them something to talk about."

"They're already talking."

He didn't look impressed. "That's what bored old gossips do, Sarah. Let them." He took a step toward her. "I've waited twelve long hours to kiss you again, and I don't give a damn who sees me do it."

She resisted the urge to back up. "Perhaps not. But *I* do."

He stopped. "Oh." A muscle twitched in his jaw. "I see."

"Parker, I'm sorry. But I did tell you that I…" She lowered her voice. "I'm not ready to take on any emotional complications right now. I'm not ready to get involved with anyone. You knew that. Maybe I shouldn't have said yes to any date at all. But I thought you understood that it would just be as friends. Just for fun. Nothing…well, nothing serious. A few kisses can't change any of that."

While she talked, his smile had been sneaking back, one fraction of an inch at a time. "You sound as if you're working pretty hard to convince somebody of all that. Who, Sarah? Me? Or yourself?"

She forced herself to stand firm. "Both of us," she said with painful honesty. "I know we hadn't planned to end up…the way we ended up. I think it was just that everything had been so—oh, you know. The whole night had this strange kind of magic…. I know you didn't plan it that way."

He laughed. "Are you so sure? Maybe that's where I take all the dates I intend to seduce. Maybe after a romantic evening watching football at the Ucky Lounge, women are just putty in my hands."

Finally she had to smile, too. "I didn't mean Lucky's. I meant the whole package. The sleigh bells, the snow. The stars. The deer at the window. Even the way the sleigh rocked was…"

"Sexy?"

"Designed to throw us together." She shook her head, feeling again the searing awareness of his thigh sliding almost imperceptibly against hers as Dusty trotted unevenly down the fairy-lighted streets.

"It was like a conspiracy," she said. "On another night, with different weather, in a normal car, things would have been easier to control."

"Think so?" He grinned, as if she had provided the perfect opening. "Okay, we'll test that theory. As soon as I get back."

"Back?" The question didn't sound as casual as it should have. "Are you going somewhere?"

"That's what I came to tell you. I have to go to D.C. for four days. My ex-wife is having some legal problems, and she needs some advice."

Four days? That was a *lot* of advice. Somehow Sarah fought back the illogical twinge of jealousy she felt. Hadn't she just reminded Parker that she wasn't interested in him that way, that even last night's kisses had merely been the accidental by-product of a lethal concoction of sleigh bells and starlight?

So what difference did it make whether he spent four minutes or four days or four years with his ex-wife? None at all.

"That's nice of you," she said politely. "I hope it goes well."

"Me, too. But I'll be back on Friday, Sarah." He looked at her that way again, the way that made her weightless and falling, falling, falling.

"And Saturday night I'll take you on the most boring, completely unromantic date in the history of dating."

Still smiling, he leaned in and kissed her on the temple. He slid his lips lightly down to the flushing ridge of her cheekbone. For one, aching moment, his breath blew a soft warmth against her ear, sending white flashes of starlight through her veins.

"And then we'll see what happens."

"I DON'T FEEL LIKE being a Gravity Gladiator today," Emma whined as she looked over the menu at the Candlelight Café. "I feel like being a Calorie Coward. I say, open the floodgates! I'm going to have double-battered fish and French fries and a hot-fudge sundae. With *two* cherries."

Sarah and Heather exchanged a smile. Emma did this every time they got together. She always threatened to eat the most artery-clogging items on the menu, but when the moment of truth came, she ordered a salad. Heather said Emma was just letting off steam, so they never bothered to argue with her.

Today, though, she shocked them. When Theo came to their table, Emma ordered the fish and chips, extra tartar sauce, super-sized sundae on the side. Theo didn't bat an eyelash. She knew that in five-star restaurants the customer's choice was always the right choice.

But Heather had no such inhibitions. "That's about ten thousand calories, you know," she said when Theo had taken their menus and departed. "And about ten months off your expected life span."

Emma made a face. "Living forever is highly over-rated, especially if you can't have hot-fudge sundaes."

Heather's frown deepened. "Emma," she said quietly. "This won't help."

"Of course it will. I'll be in a carbo coma all afternoon, which will definitely help."

It was an uncomfortable moment. Obviously the two were communicating in some subtext that Sarah wasn't supposed to understand. Emma looked over at her guiltily, then seemed to come to a decision.

"Sorry, Sarah. We didn't mean to talk around you. It's just one of those boring personal problems, and I didn't want to monopolize lunch with it."

Sarah shook her head. "That's okay," she began.

"No, really. I want to tell you. You probably will hear about it before long, anyhow. The concept of privacy isn't recognized in the Glen."

Heather put her hand over Emma's supportively. Sarah could see that Emma's eyes were glittering, but she took a deep breath and when she spoke her voice was steady.

"Harry and I are going through a rough patch right now," she explained tersely. "So rough, in fact, that he moved out last week."

Sarah took Emma's other hand. "I'm so sorry," she said, aware of how useless the words were. "I'll bet he won't stay gone for long, though."

"Of course he won't." Heather looked fierce, and Sarah could tell how much she cared about her friend's happiness. "Harry can be a bullheaded mule sometimes, but he's not dumb. He'll be back." She lifted one eyebrow. "Unless, of course, you eat ten thousand calories at *every* meal."

Emma, flanked by support, seemed to gather strength. She gave a squeeze to her two hand-holders, then extricated herself and took a swig of white wine. "Okay, ladies. This self-pity party is officially over. I don't want to talk about me. I want to talk about Sarah and Parker."

Sarah froze, her water glass halfway to her mouth.

Emma grinned. "Yes, my friend, the rumors are flying, but I don't know which ones to believe. Some people say you and Parker spent the night in the barn when you returned the horse to the Autumn House. Others say you just parked the sleigh in front of the Spring House for a couple of hours and did some heavy duty getting acquainted."

Sarah sighed. But Emma wasn't finished.

She wiggled her eyebrows. "Another rumor says you won five hundred dollars at Lucky's lap-dancing with the loggers before Parker got jealous and beat a bunch of them up." She turned to Heather. "I don't believe that one, do you? Parker would get jealous long before that."

Sarah covered her eyes with her hand. "This is crazy," she said. "One date. Just one innocent date. How can people read so much into so little?"

"It comes from living in the frozen North," Heather put in wryly. "All those long winters with nothing to do, no one to talk to, nothing to think about. Survival favors people with overactive imaginations."

"Well, that's what's happening here," Sarah said emphatically. "We had one date. It was very nice, but it was nothing worth gossiping about. We're friends, that's all. Chances are we won't even go out together again."

"Oh, yes, you will," Emma said. "Parker is already talking about it. Although I have to warn you, it doesn't sound that great. He was pumping me for ideas, and he wanted to know what some of my very worst-ever dates had been."

Theo arrived with the food, and Sarah busied herself tossing her chicken-breast salad carefully, cutting up her meat into tiny chunks. She hoped Emma would be distracted by her own high-calorie feast, which, Sarah had to admit, looked fabulous.

But of course she couldn't be that lucky. Emma went right back to the conversation, like a homing pigeon.

"So I said to him, are you sure you wouldn't rather hear about my *best* dates? But he said, no, he was putting together the all-time most terrible date."

Heather was scowling at the greasy food, so Emma stuffed a huge French fry into her mouth defiantly. She wrinkled her nose at Heather before turning back to Sarah. "The worst date ever? What gives with that?"

"He's just pulling your leg," Sarah said. "It's just this…this dumb joke."

"Well, I figured maybe he was kind of testing you a little. Or maybe testing his own feelings. You know what I mean? I told you how hung up he is on finding the perfect woman. Well, maybe he's trying to be sure he's not reacting to the date itself, you know? Trying to be sure you're the perfect woman even if all the other conditions are awful."

Heather made a scoffing sound. "Of all the convoluted ideas you've ever come up with, Em, that may be the weirdest."

But Sarah was amazed at how close to the truth Emma had actually come. She put down her fork.

"If that is what he's doing," she said, "I could save him some time. I'm *not* the perfect woman. The perfect woman doesn't live a thousand miles away, for one thing. The perfect woman doesn't come with a lot of baggage, like an ugly engagement ended only weeks ago. The perfect woman doesn't come with…"

She caught Heather's eye across the table. But Heather had on her most professional face, and Sarah couldn't extract any guidance from her expression. She let her sentence disappear into a swallow of water.

Emma looked thoughtful. "I don't know about all that," she said. "The perfect man wouldn't be, as Heather so vividly put it, a bullheaded mule. The perfect man wouldn't be trying to steal your brother's job. The perfect man wouldn't pack his bags and move to a motel when the going gets rough. And yet Harry is definitely the perfect mule—I mean *man*—for me."

Sarah stared at her friend. "This is different," she said helplessly.

"Maybe." Emma smiled. "But Parker doesn't think so."

PARKER PULLED HIS Jeep off the road, put the gear in neutral, yanked on the emergency brake and killed the engine.

"Here we are," he said, turning to Sarah with a poker face. "I hope you are good with a wheelbarrow."

Sarah wasn't quite sure how to react. The empty lot in front of them looked like the ruins of a bombed-out building. Several heavily bundled people were walking back and forth, doing something that looked a lot like dismantling the edifice.

"Our date is *here?*"

Parker surveyed the scene with a hint of smug satisfaction. "Right. I asked around and, working with details from several different sources, I put together a composite of the world's worst date."

She waited. He was enjoying himself thoroughly, and she found his amusement ridiculously cute.

"Here's how it goes. First, I make you do something only *I* care about—fix me dinner, clean out my garage, carry my golf clubs while I play eighteen holes, stuff like that. In this particular edition of The Date From Hell, I've brought you to the site where we usually put the ice castle for the festival. This year, we'd just begun to build the frame when the property owner decided to withdraw his permission to use the land."

Oh, dear. Her instincts told her this involved Ward. She squeezed her eyes shut, hoping she was wrong. "My uncle?"

"You guessed it. Anyhow, now we have seventy-two hours to clear our mess off his land. You get to help. But that's only part of our horrible date."

She raised her eyebrows. "There's more?"

"Yep. While you're getting bored and tired and dirty on my behalf, I spend most of my time talking to my friends, ignoring you. If I do talk to you, I talk only about myself. I drink too much and completely forget to feed you anything. Then I take you home and maul you like an animal, blindly assuming you've had as much fun as I have."

She had to laugh. She'd had a couple of dates like that in her time. They were always first dates. And last.

"Okay," she said. "That should definitely kill the magic."

But it didn't.

The Date From Hell turned out to be even more fun than their first.

She loved his friends, who ranged from seventeen to seventy and who were unfailingly polite and welcoming to her. She loved hearing him talk to them, and she loved hearing him talk about himself. She learned more about Parker Tremaine in three hours out here than she had in the entire three weeks she'd been in Firefly Glen.

And she liked everything she learned. He was witty, self-effacing, hardworking and well liked. He gave credit to others, took very little for himself. He was quick, well-informed and tolerant. He didn't get annoyed when people around him messed up. He laughed off small mistakes, and he pitched in to help remedy big ones.

She couldn't have found a more striking contrast to Ed, with his petty, tyrannical perfectionism and his limitless ego.

She worked hard, but she didn't mind that. It was fun being part of a team, and everyone was eager to show her how to pull out nails safely, or how to stack broken boards so they wouldn't topple over. The hours flew by, and though she definitely got dirty, she couldn't say she ever got bored.

According to the bad-date rules, Parker couldn't feed her, but when the sun started to fall on the horizon, he quietly instructed someone else to bring her a thermos of soup and a mug of hot chocolate.

Plain food…but delicious. It was warm and salty, rich and nourishing.

She sat on a large red cooler, watching Parker over the rim of her steaming mug. He had taken off his jacket, hard work providing its own heat as he muscled a large plank of wood onto someone's truck.

He caught her watching him and, brushing his tousled hair back from his damp brow, he smiled.

Oh, that smile, she thought with a sinking sense of doom. He didn't need romance and music and starlight, did he? He had that smile, and it warmed her from head to toe, in spite of the snow that had just begun to fall around them.

A few minutes later, he came over and sat down on the cooler next to her, a thermos of coffee in his hand. "We're going to have to call it a day soon," he said, gazing up into the darkening sky. "Because of the snow."

He tugged off his work gloves with his teeth, then turned to her. "You okay?"

She sipped her chocolate to hold back a grin. "Hey. That's against the rules. You're not supposed to care."

He shook his head helplessly, then he reached out and pulled free a strand of hair that had been caught on her cheek. "Maybe not," he said softly, tucking the hair behind her ear. "But I'll be damned if I can stop myself."

She opened her mouth, ready to offer a flip rejoinder, but she found herself without words. Gazing into his tired, dirty face, she realized that Parker Tremaine was a far greater threat than she had ever imagined.

Oh, she had known from the start that his sex appeal was nearly lethal. She had expected resisting him to be a challenge. Later, when they were alone, the sparks between them might flare up again, creating a fire that would be difficult to douse.

That would have been trouble enough. For a woman in her condition, falling in lust with this man, with *anyone,* would be vulgar and stupid. Unthinkable.

So she had given herself an ultimatum. Resist him, or tell him it's over. If she succumbed to even one of those dangerous kisses, she would end it here, tonight.

But suddenly, as if she had been running through a field that abruptly ended, just beyond the tips of her toes, in a sheer free fall down an open cliff, she saw the much greater danger.

And she knew she had to end it anyhow.

Falling in lust was the least of her worries.

She was in danger of falling in *love*.

CHAPTER ELEVEN

AS PARKER DROVE toward Winter House, he wondered whether maybe he'd gone a little too far with this Date From Hell business.

Although Sarah had entered into the day with a willing tongue-in-cheek enthusiasm, for the past hour or so she had been polite but stilted, growing more and more subdued. Hell, ever since they got in the car, she'd been practically mute.

He backtracked over the afternoon, wondering when the change had hit her. Had someone offended her? Had he said something stupid?

Maybe she was just tired. She had worked too hard. She couldn't be used to that kind of bruising labor, especially at these altitudes.

He glanced at her out of the corner of his eye as he steered his Jeep toward her uncle's house. She did look pale, with smudges of exhaustion under her eyes. He was reminded suddenly of how weak and vulnerable she had looked that first day, on the mountaintop, leaning up against a tree, as if she needed its strength to help her stand.

For a dreadful moment, he wondered if she might be sick. Really sick. But Ward would have told him, wouldn't he? And most of the time she was so glowing and sensual, he couldn't take the idea of illness very seriously.

Probably, like a fool, he had just let her wear herself out.

He pulled into the driveway of Winter House and stopped the car. Sarah looked so far away over there in her bucket seat, with the gearshift sticking up between them like some chrome-plated techno-chaperone.

Suddenly he wished he had the damn sleigh back. He clearly had been too cocky, believing he could make magic for her without any romantic bells and whistles. Sarah didn't look like a woman caught in anybody's magic spell tonight. She looked tired and remote and— just his luck—still so desirable he could hardly breathe.

He would have given every penny in his pocket for one lousy trickle of starlight.

He reached over and gently tugged a wood shaving from her hair. He ran the back of his finger along her cheek. "Tired?"

"A little," she said quietly. "I guess I should go in."

He wanted so much to take her in his arms. Damn these intrusive gearshifts. Who had invented them? The Society for the Protection of American Virgins?

"Sarah," he said, letting his finger touch the corner of her mouth. "Sarah, look at me."

"I have to go in," she said, still in an exhausted monotone. "Maybe we should wait and talk tomorrow."

He leaned over, ignoring the bite of the gearshift into his side. He put his finger under her chin and turned her face toward him. She did look sick, he thought suddenly. She was in some kind of trouble, some kind of pain.

"Sarah. Sweetheart. Tell me what's wrong."

"Nothing's wrong," she said, and for a minute she rallied. She turned the corners of her mouth up, as if she were a puppet controlled by strings. It was sweet, but it damn sure didn't feel real. He preferred no smile at all to that saccharine pretense.

"Honestly, nothing is wrong. It's just that I…" She swallowed and started over, doing a little better with the smile this time. "I had a lovely time today, Parker. I always have fun when I'm with you. But, even so, I think we should stop seeing each—"

She never finished the sentence. From the direction of Winter House, a loud, smashing noise exploded into the quiet evening air. It was the sound of glass shattering. And it was followed by the rapid pounding of someone's footsteps running across the hard snow of the estate's grounds.

"Oh, my God!"

Though Sarah looked immediately toward the house, Parker's gaze flew instinctively toward the running footsteps, just in time to see a hooded figure fleeing into the dark stand of trees.

"My uncle!" With one hand, Sarah was shoving open the car door, the other pulling frantically to release her seat belt. Parker reached over, flipped her belt open, then addressed his own.

Reluctantly he abandoned any thought of chasing the hooded figure. He couldn't let Sarah go up to the house alone, not knowing what she would find inside. What if the fleeing man hadn't been the only one here?

So the two of them raced up to the big front door alone. Parker was dialing 911 on his cell phone. Sarah already had her key out and, in spite of her obvious anxiety, her fingers didn't fumble. As the door swung open, she was already calling, "Uncle Ward! Uncle Ward! Where are you? Are you all right?"

They found him in the library, which was growing very cold as the evening wind blew snow in through the large, star-shaped hole in the beautiful stained-glass window. A small white layer of powder already dusted the dark green leather top of the library table.

Parker scanned the scene quickly. Ward lay in a tangle on the carpet, pieces of gold and red glass rayed out around him. A deep, ugly cut on his forehead was oozing blood that had reached the floor and was mingling with the intricate flowers of the Oriental rug.

Frosty sat by his shoulder, obeying his guard dog instincts, but the frightened puppy in him was whimpering softly and shaking all over.

When he saw Sarah, Frosty ran to her, ears flopping. She scooped him up, murmuring comfort, and held him tightly as she rushed to her uncle's side.

It didn't take long for Parker to size up what had happened. Just beyond Ward's head, a large rock lay near the carved leg of the table. It had clods of frozen dirt stuck to it, obviously having been dug recently, probably from the Winter House grounds. It was roughly the size and shape of a football, though distorted with sharp, jagged edges. A piece of paper had been tied around the rock with a rubber band, and big black letters had been scrawled on the paper.

"Butt out, Grinch. Leave our festival alone," it said.

Parker wasn't surprised. He had been afraid something like this might happen if Ward persisted in his sabotage of the festival.

It probably hadn't been intended as a physical attack, but with horrible, blind accuracy, and the world's worst luck, whoever had lobbed this rock through the stained-glass window had hit Ward Winters on the head, hit him hard enough to knock him from the chair where he'd been reading.

Parker bent over Ward, checking his pulse. *Thank God.* It was faint but steady. Sarah had set Frosty down and was kneeling on the other side of her uncle, brushing away enough blood to get a good look at the size of the cut. Parker heard her abrupt inhale, and he knew it must be deep.

She cradled her uncle's head in her lap, elevating it to slow the bleeding. She turned dark eyes toward Parker. "Can you get me a clean cloth from the kitchen? Something I can hold against this? Please. I don't want to leave him."

Parker was on his feet before she finished her question. "I'll be right back," he said. "I've already called the medics, so if you hear someone at the door, don't worry. I'll let them in."

He was almost certain no one else was in the house. The hole in the window was too jagged and awkwardly placed for anyone to have entered there, and all other points of entry seemed secure. Plus, his instincts told him this was merely a threat. It was a coward's trick, that nasty little note wrapped around an anonymous missile. The imbecile who had thrown it was undoubtedly the same punk Parker had seen scuttling into the woods.

Still he quickly checked rooms as he passed on the way to the kitchen. Everything looked normal.

By the time he got back with the cloth, he heard two very welcome sounds—the crunch of the ambulance pulling up the driveway, and the loud, fussy rumble of

Ward's voice complaining that he was perfectly fine, leave him alone, for God's sake.

Parker pulled open the door, motioning the medics to come in, and then he led the way to the library, where Ward was now sitting up in the upholstered armchair nearest to the table. Blood was dripping down over his eye, but that didn't keep him from looking as energetically bad tempered as usual.

He glared at Parker and the medical technicians as they entered the library.

"Damn it, it's just a little nick. Who the hell called in the army?"

Sarah put her hand on her uncle's shoulder. "Uncle Ward, calm down. They're just going to take you to the hospital—"

"The hell they are!" Ward lunged forward, but was held in place by Sarah's restraining hand and, probably, his own discomfort. "I'm not going anywhere."

Parker handed the clean cloth to the older man.

"You know, Ward," he observed placidly. "I think your brains may have fallen out of that gash on your head. You're talking like an idiot."

Ward chuckled, then grimaced as the motion clearly caused pain. "Insult me all you like, Sheriff. This is my home, and I'm not going to be driven out of it by any rock-tossing jackass."

The arguments took forever. The debate was far from balanced, with Parker, Sarah and the two medics on one side, and Ward alone on the other. But in the end they compromised—as Parker could have predicted they would—by letting Ward win. He would not be going to the hospital.

He did agree to let a doctor come to the house and stitch him up. Parker arranged that, and while he was out of the room, he also called Harry. He told the deputy what had happened, then gave him a few fairly simple instructions: catch the vandal, and catch him tonight.

Two hours later, the doctor finally had Ward back in one piece, though it had taken eleven stitches to do it. Ward also had several bruises, and a sprained elbow, which he'd fallen on as he tumbled from the chair. Somehow, using all her persuasive skills, Sarah had coaxed her uncle into bed, though he had expressed a strong desire to storm out into the night, find the stone-throwing jerk and teach him a lesson.

But Sarah had deposited Frosty on the bedspread beside her uncle, and that had done the trick. Ward was a fool for the puppy already, and Sarah had warned Parker that Frosty probably wouldn't be moving out of Winter House any time soon. Which was fine with Parker. One puppy was enough to handle.

And anyhow, it was starting to look as if Ward might be better off with a dog in the house.

While Sarah had been tending Ward, Parker had cleaned up the broken glass. He found some large pieces of heavy cardboard and taped them over the hole in the library window. He wondered if the moron who threw that rock realized how expensive a stained-glass window like this was to replace. This wasn't like scrawling something rude on a bathroom stall, which could be erased or painted over. This was big-time vandalism, and there would be hell to pay.

"He's asleep." Sarah's voice came from behind him. She sounded exhausted.

With a sigh, she plopped onto the library sofa. She had bloodstains on her white sweater, and blue circles under her eyes. She looked even more tired than she sounded.

"Thank you, Parker," she said, smiling over at him with obvious effort. "I don't know what I would have done without you here."

"I'm glad I was." Parker set the tape down on the refectory table and came over to join her on the sofa. He unbuttoned her sweater, helped her ease it off and, folding it up so that the bloody stains didn't show, tossed it aside.

He gathered her into his arms and held her close, rubbing his hands along her arms to keep her warm. The library was still half-freezing.

"You should go to bed now, too," he said.

"I can't." It was a clue as to how exhausted she was that she didn't try to pull away from his embrace. He was well aware she had decided to put an end to whatever had been developing between them. "I have to check on him every two hours. The doctor suspects a concussion."

"You sleep. I'll do the checking," Parker said, resting his cheek against her hair. The motion pressed her head onto his chest. She didn't resist that, either. "I'm planning to stay down here tonight, anyhow. Just in case the fool who did this gets any more dumb ideas."

She shook her head, but there was almost no force behind it. "I can't let you do that. You've done too much already."

"It's my job," he said softly. "Protect and defend, all that stuff. Besides, I want to. He may be your uncle, but he's my friend, too."

"What about Snowball? He's been alone all day."

"No, he hasn't. While you were up with Ward, I called Emma. She's going to take him home with her. She adores him. I think she'd secretly like to steal him from me anyhow."

He felt her lips curve up in a smile, though she didn't move a muscle. "We'll do it together, then," she said. "I'll stay down here, too, and we'll take turns."

He shook his head. "It's too cold for you, with the window broken. Too uncomfortable. You'll get sick."

"I never get sick," she said sleepily. "It'll be fine. It'll be like camping out. I could light a fire."

Yes, he thought, looking down at her graceful curves, folded like a butterfly up against him. She certainly could.

But he resisted the urge to follow that train of thought. He looked around the room. The sofa near the fireplace was roomy, overstuffed and covered with pillows and soft satin throws. He might be able to make it comfortable enough.

He sighed and gave up. It was too tempting to resist.

"All right. But I will take the first shift. That's not negotiable."

She nodded, her head moving softly against his shirt. "Yes, Sheriff."

"And you have to promise me that you'll get some sleep."

But there was no answer to that. He felt the butterfly softness of her body go limp, relaxing against him in utter innocence.

She was already asleep.

SARAH WOKE SLOWLY, registering where she was with her senses rather than with her mind.

The sweet-ash smell of wood burning. She was close to a fire, so close she could see its amber shadows dancing against her eyelids. So close she could hear the hiss and simmer of the logs as tongues of fire licked them.

She was in the library. But why, and why was it so

chilly? She burrowed deeper into the warm comfort of satin wrapped tightly around her body. It was warm in here, but out there, beyond the satin, it was not. Her cheeks and ears were tight with cold.

She opened her eyes, peeking at the fire between her lashes, wondering if the heater was broken.

And then she remembered. Her uncle. The smashed window. Parker.

She sat up, holding the comforter around her shoulders. The fire provided the only light in the room, but it was enough. She found Parker easily. He was dozing on the Queen Anne armchair, his feet stretched out, long and graceful and utterly still, toward the fire.

She rubbed her eyes hard, wondering how long she had been asleep. Had she missed her turn to check on Ward? Carefully, so that she wouldn't disturb Parker, she eased out of the tangled comforter and stood, hoping her socks would muffle her footsteps. He must need sleep desperately. She certainly had.

But Parker wasn't sleeping. As soon as she moved toward the door, he opened his eyes. "It's all right," he said quietly. "I checked on him an hour ago."

She stopped beside him. "Is he okay? Did you wake him? The doctor said we have to make sure he's coherent, and that his eyes are focusing correctly."

Parker raised his eyebrows without lifting his head. "Oh, I woke him, all right. The first two times he was almost civil. This last time, he suggested—perfectly coherently—that I should pay a visit to the devil."

He shut his eyes again. "By the way, he said if we wake him one more time tonight, he's going to shoot us."

Sarah chuckled. "He probably won't, though."

"No," Parker agreed, smiling. "Probably not."

Sarah checked her watch, squinting at it in the volatile orange firelight. To her surprise it was almost five in the morning. It would be dawn soon.

"I must have missed my turn more than once," she said guiltily. "I'm sorry about that."

"I'm not." Parker opened his eyes and looked at her appraisingly. "You look much better now. You needed the sleep."

That probably was true. The drama of the evening had been exhausting, and Heather had warned her that the baby might sap her strength a little, leaving her more easily tired than usual.

She put her hand to her stomach instinctively.

But Parker was watching her, his eyes unreadable in the strange, shifting light from the fire. Suddenly self-conscious, Sarah tugged her shirt a little farther down over her jeans, as if it might be possible for someone else to recognize the slight swell of her waistline.

It wasn't possible, of course. Not yet. She couldn't even see it herself, not by looking in the mirror. It was only when she ran her hand over her stomach that she sensed something different. Something new.

Still she felt vulnerable. She crossed her arms against the sudden cold that slipped through Parker's cardboard shield.

"It will be light soon," she said. "No one is going to come back and cause trouble now. Why don't you go on home and get some real sleep?"

The fidgety restlessness that had come over her didn't seem to have affected him at all. He sat in complete repose. He hadn't taken his eyes away from her.

"Is that what you want?" He spoke without pressure,

as if whatever she answered would be all right. "Do you want me to leave?"

It seemed ungrateful to say yes, after all he had done for her. How could she explain that his presence here, in the notoriously weak willed hours before dawn, felt somehow dangerous?

"It's just that I want you to get some sleep," she equivocated. "And trying to sleep here doesn't seem very…"

"I won't be able to sleep at home, either," he said gently. "Either place, I'm just going to lie awake. I'm just going to lie there thinking how much I want to make love to you."

She turned her head away. "Parker. Don't."

"Why not?" He reached his hand out and captured hers. Gently he tugged her toward the armchair, until her thighs were pressed against the upholstered arm.

She tried to pull away, but he held her easily. Slowly he fingered the palm of her hand in a subtle massage. He tilted his head, as if reading her response to the touch.

"Why are you fighting this so hard, Sarah? You know you feel it, too. Would it be so awful if we just let it happen?"

She breathed hard, concentrating on ignoring his clever fingers. "I told you. I can't get involved right now. Just a month ago I—"

"I know. You were engaged to another man. You might be on the rebound. The timing is terrible. Okay, let's say all that is true. What should you do, lock yourself in a deep freeze until the appropriate amount of time has passed? What is the acceptable mourning period for a bad engagement, anyhow? Two months? Six months? A year?"

He shook his head. "I can't wait a year, Sarah. I won't."

"It's not just the engagement," she said, knowing that he wasn't going to give up this time, not until he pushed her all the way, right to the final, fatal admission. "It's much, much more complicated than that."

"What?" Narrowing his eyes, he sat up a little straighter. "You're not still in love with—what was his name, anyhow? You never told me his name."

"Ed." She half swallowed the syllable. "His name is Ed McCutcheon."

"Ed." He repeated the word with clipped distaste. "Okay. You're not still in love with Ed, are you? You can't be. The way you kissed me…"

"No." She looked down at their hands. She was holding on so tightly, as if he were the only thing that kept her grounded. She realized how easy it would be to come to count on that hand. To believe it really could save her from danger. It couldn't, of course. Because *he* was the danger.

"No," she repeated numbly. "I'm not in love with Ed anymore. I'm not sure I ever was. Not really."

He took a deep breath. "Okay. Good. Then whatever it is, we can get through it." He leaned toward her, running his other hand along her arm, up to the elbow. The touch sent shivers through her from shoulder to toe.

"We can make this work, Sarah. I know we can. You just have to give it a chance."

"You don't understand. That's still not all." She continued to stare at their hands, at his strong fingers wrapped around her fragile wrist. "I never loved Ed. But I *made love* to him, Parker."

He made a low, furious sound. "Do you think I give a damn about that?"

"Yes. I think you will. Because I may not love Ed McCutcheon, but I am going to have his child."

She finally looked up at him, at his blank and staring eyes. "It's true, Parker," she said softly. "I'm pregnant."

CHAPTER TWELVE

SARAH HAD NEVER SEEN a living hand so still. Not even her uncle's hand earlier tonight, when he had lain unconscious and bleeding on the floor. Parker's hand was more like that of a painted statue. Even the fitful firelight couldn't give it the illusion of life.

She pulled her own hand free of the frozen fingers and turned away. She wasn't disappointed, not really. Because she had always known it would be like this. She had always known that Parker's interest in her couldn't survive the truth. She hadn't ever allowed herself to hope.

Not really.

"So now you see why I've been trying to avoid any new complications." Rather than look at his stunned, expressionless face, she busied herself folding up the satin comforter that had cocooned her just moments ago.

She plumped and settled the pillows, until no one could have guessed she had ever been there. "Obviously I can't even think about starting a new relationship right now. I have to concentrate on the baby, on getting my life back in order."

And, as she said the words, she realized that they were absolutely true. She needed a new plan. A new, detailed life plan, to replace the one that had been tossed in the trash can, along with all the little pink x's.

Yes, a new plan right away: that was the answer. Without a plan, she had been like a ship without a rudder, and any wind had been able to blow her off course. This one had blown her into Parker Tremaine's path, and straight toward a collision of the heart.

"But why didn't you tell me about this sooner?" Parker's voice was strangely rough. "God, Sarah. Why didn't you tell me right away?"

Was he angry? Surely he wouldn't dare. What right did he have to be angry? It was he who had pushed this relationship. She had always hung back, insisting that it must not, could not, be.

She turned and looked at him. "Because I wasn't ready to talk about it to anyone," she said stiffly. "Because it wasn't any of your business."

He frowned hard, a straight line driving like a gash between his brows. "It wasn't," he repeated slowly, "any of my business?"

She stood very straight. "No. It wasn't."

They stared at each other across the cold room, the silence somehow just as unpleasant as a quarrel would have been. Perversely, part of her wanted to quarrel. At least then she could release some of this emotion pressing against her chest. It was such an unbearable weight, as if the burden of losing him were something physical she would now have to carry from place to place, like a rock.

But that was ridiculous. *Losing* him? How could you lose something you never had?

"I'm going to check on my uncle now," she said, picking up her bloodstained sweater. She didn't even remember taking it off. "I do thank you for all your help tonight, Parker. You know the way out, so—"

Suddenly there was a rapping on the front door. Sarah's breath stalled, and she realized that she must be even more unnerved by the night's events than she had understood.

And why shouldn't she be? Her uncle had enemies out there, hiding in the freezing black shadows.

All at once, she was intensely aware of how odd this mansion was, how isolated and deep an Adirondack winter could be. And she realized that, if Parker hadn't been in the room with her, she might have felt true fear.

Ashamed of what seemed a foolish weakness, she tried to mask her thoughts. She didn't want him to think her a coward. She *wasn't* a coward.

She lifted her chin and made a motion toward the hall. But Parker was already standing.

"I'll answer it," he said firmly. "You stay here in the library."

She obeyed, but she followed him as far as the doorway. She needed to see who it was.

It was Parker's deputy sheriff, Harry Dunbar. And he was holding someone else by the scruff of the neck. A teenage boy, it seemed. Sarah edged forward. Yes, a nice-looking teenage kid. Dressed all in black, but red faced and miserable.

"Here's your criminal," Harry Dunbar was saying. He sounded disgusted. "Although why I should have to drag my ass out of bed in the middle of the night to track down a stupid punk like this…"

Parker was shaking his head. "Mike? I can't believe it. Of all the people I expected to see—"

"God, Sheriff. I'm sorry." The kid's voice was terrified. He ran his hands through his dark hair over and over, as if he wanted to pull it straight out of his head.

"I'm so sorry. I didn't mean to hurt anybody, honest I didn't. I did it for Justine. For her father. I was just supposed to send the message—"

"Shut up, Frome." Parker sounded as tough as nails, completely unmoved by the misery before him. "I don't want to hear any excuses out of you. There is no excuse. Blaming other people isn't going to help. You're in more trouble than you have ever seen in your whole sorry life, buster."

"What do you want me to do with him?" Harry still had hold of Mike Frome's jacket collar, which forced the kid to bend over at a strange, tangled-puppet angle.

"I'll take him," Parker said tersely.

He looked back at Sarah, who was still standing in the doorway, wondering how on earth this apparently nice, normal teenage boy could have done so much damage here tonight, and why?

"I have to go back to the department," Parker said. "We'll have to sort this out—talk to Mike's parents, for starters." The kid groaned, but Parker didn't so much as blink in reaction. "It'll take a while. Will you be all right?"

She nodded. "We're fine," she said carefully.

He paused, and she could tell that he wanted to say more but was constrained by the presence of Harry and the boy Mike.

"I'll call you later," Parker said finally. "About how Ward is doing. And about—that other matter."

That other matter. She shook her head. "No, that's not necessary. You'll be busy. And I think we've really discussed it pretty thoroughly."

"No, we haven't," Parker said grimly as he grabbed the boy's arm and steered him toward the waiting car. "Not even close."

HE DIDN'T CALL THAT DAY, or the next.

At least not to talk to her. He talked to Ward several times, updating him on the investigation into poor, red-faced Mike Frome. But he never asked to speak to Sarah, and of course she wouldn't have dreamed of asking to speak to him.

What would have been the point?

Mostly, Sarah tried not to think about it. And for the most part she was successful. She was busy, and that helped. The news about her uncle had gone out with the speed of a microchip, and as soon as the sun was fully up, Madeline Alexander had come bustling into the Winter House, eager to play Florence Nightingale. Ward was a terrible patient, crotchety and demanding. It took both of them to keep him placated and in bed.

And then there was the matter of replacing the broken window, which required hiring glaziers to put in a tempo-rary glass, and a dozen calls to artisans around the country, requesting bids for a new design. The estimated price was in the thousands, and in spite of herself Sarah felt sorry for the teenager who had made such a costly mistake.

On the third day, she found a flyer shoved through the Winter House mail slot, alerting everyone to an emergency session of the Firefly Glen City Council, that night at seven o'clock. Final Festival Vote: Cancel or Continue? it read. No further details were provided.

Sarah didn't show it to her uncle until almost seven o'clock, fearing that he would insist on attending. The doctor had told him to keep calm and close to home for at least a week. But to her surprise, Ward merely snorted when he read the flyer, crumpled it into a ball and lobbed it into the nearest trash can.

"Let them meet until they're blue in the face," he said, turning his attention back to the chessboard, which Sarah had transplanted to Ward's bedroom. "Those morons at City Hall can't regulate Ward Winters into submission."

He looked up and grinned as he captured one of Sarah's pawns. Frosty, who sat next to him on the bed, grinned, too, his tongue hanging out cheerfully.

"I am far too clever and devious for them." Ward puffed out his chest and leaned back against his pillows. "I am an outlaw now, my child. I live by a different code. Like Zorro."

Sarah responded by taking her uncle's bishop. "And what code would that be? Do we find it in the *Mischief Maker's Manual? The Gray Panther Guerilla Guidebook?*"

He frowned, then leaned forward to study the board grumpily. "We don't find it in *Make Anyone Do Anything—A Primer of Persuasion,* that's for sure."

Sarah looked up, startled.

"Didn't know I knew about that, did you?" Ward looked extremely self-satisfied. His bandage, which angled over his right eye from his hairline to his temple, merely intensified his rogue charm. "I guess you and your beloved sheriff aren't quite as clever as you think, isn't that right, Short Stuff?"

Sarah almost fell for it. She almost jumped in with a denial. *He's not my beloved sheriff.* But she caught herself in the nick of time. Ward was just fishing for an excuse to open that topic again. She wasn't going to give it to him.

"That's right," she agreed evenly, moving her queen two spaces to the right. "But you may not be, either. I think that's check, Mr. Zorro, sir."

Ward didn't like to lose, so after that he concentrated harder on the game. He had finally escaped her clutches, regrouped and managed to turn the tables when Madeline, who had been downstairs puttering around in the kitchen, suddenly showed up in the doorway.

"Parker is here to see you, Ward," she said. Though she was dressed as cheerfully as ever in a pattern of fluffy pink peonies, she looked nervous. She twisted a blue dish towel tightly between her hands. "He says he has news from the meeting. Shall I show him up?"

Sarah glanced at her uncle. He appeared completely serene, pulling slowly and rhythmically on Frosty's ears, sending the puppy into a trance of joy.

He moved his knight. "Sure. We're through here." He gave Sarah a smug smile. "Checkmate."

When Sarah made a motion to stand, Ward stopped her. "I might need you," he said with a plaintive tone that Sarah recognized as one hundred percent fraudulent. He touched his bandage pitifully. "In case I feel faint."

Sarah gave him a dirty look, but she sat back down. She could hear Parker's footsteps in the hall. It was already too late to escape.

Ward apparently needed only one glimpse of Parker's face to guess the outcome of the meeting.

"They're going ahead with it, aren't they?" With a low curse, he collapsed back against the carved headboard of his bed. The drapes of the canopy cast his face in shadows, but the annoyance in his voice was crystal clear.

Parker nodded. He seemed unfazed by such an unconventional greeting. "Hi, Sarah," he said politely. Then he turned toward the older man. "Of course they are, Ward. The vote was unanimous."

"Those greedy morons." Ward growled. Frosty looked up at him quizzically, thumping his tail. "I can't believe it."

"Why not?" Without waiting for an invitation, Parker sat on one of the armchairs near the fireplace. "You didn't think a few pranks could destroy a tradition that's almost a hundred years old, did you? They held the festival the year spring came early, melting the ice castle faster than they could build it. They held it right after the blizzard of '33 killed more than thirty Glenners. They held it during the Depression. They held it during the war." He smiled gently. "Did you really think you could stop it?"

Ward was silent a moment, his fingers fidgeting irritably with the fine Egyptian cotton bedclothes. "Where are they going to put the castle?"

"In the square. It will have to be smaller, of course. Medford is going to draw up new plans tonight."

"The decorated sleigh parade?"

"Those who have privately owned sleighs will use those. The rest will make do. Cars, sleds, trucks. Whatever."

"What about Bourke Waitely?"

Parker hesitated for the first time. "Reservations at the hotel are down by fifty percent. Not much the city council could do about that. Looks as if he's going to lose a lot of money."

Ward laughed. "Well. At least there's that."

"Yep. There's that. You annoyed the heck out of Bourke, Ward. Congratulations. And it only cost you… what? Ten grand and a busted head?"

"It was worth it," Ward said acidly. "Meddling old bastard."

Sighing, as if he gave up on the whole thing, Parker stood. "I need to get going. Sarah, any chance I could talk to you for a minute?"

She looked at her uncle, who didn't seem as distressed as she had expected by Parker's news. Had he known all along that the festival would survive his attacks? Or did he have something else up his sleeve?

"Didn't you hear the sheriff, Sarah?" Amazingly, Ward's voice was as mischievous as ever. "He wants to talk to you."

"I'd better not leave you," she said sweetly. She touched her forehead. "You know. In case you feel faint."

"I'm much better now," Ward said irritably, pulling Frosty closer and stroking him, as if to say that at least *someone* in the room was sweet and agreeable. "Parker, take Sarah away. Clumsy, ungrateful sarcasm makes my stitches hurt."

PARKER LET SARAH LEAD the way. On the surface, she appeared completely composed. She walked smoothly down the wide staircase in front of him, her slim hand pale but steady on the banister. Her hair was tied back neatly with a green ribbon that matched perfectly the green wool dress she wore.

But he knew she was edgy. He could see it in the tight set of her jaw.

It was ironic, wasn't it, that he could read her so well after such a short acquaintance? Ironic, too, that he found the simple, tailored green dress on Sarah sexier than the skimpiest lingerie would be on any other woman?

Yes, it was ironic, all right. In a hundred ways she seemed to be the perfect woman. The one he'd been looking for, dreaming of, ever since the fiasco with Tina.

They could still hear Madeline in the kitchen, so Sarah turned left. She avoided the library, too, though they passed right by it. Instead she took him to Ward's personal den, a small room with an alcove formed by the square front bay window.

During the day, Parker knew, that alcove was brilliant with a gold and green light, which streamed in through the stained glass panes. At night, though, the windows were black, and the only illumination in the room came from several small Tiffany-style reading lamps.

He knew she had chosen this room for privacy, and because it was as close to the front door as she could get without actually throwing him out of the house. He felt her tension growing by the second. This was going to be a tricky conversation. He hoped he could find the right words to say what he needed to say.

"My uncle tells me that he isn't going to press charges against the boy who broke the window." Sarah had started talking even before they were fully in the room, obviously rushing into a topic that would keep the conversation safely impersonal. "I'm not sure I understand why."

"I'm not sure I do, either. Mike Frome could use a good scare. He says he threw that rock because he thought it would impress his girlfriend, Justine. She's Mayor Millner's daughter. The mayor's whole family is furious that Ward has tried to sabotage the festival. I guess they like the idea of ruling an ever-expanding kingdom."

Sarah frowned. "So Mike thought what? That a little vandalism would enhance his stock with this Justine?"

"Apparently. And the worst part is, I think maybe he was right."

"Sounds as if Mike could use a different girlfriend."

"Definitely." Parker sighed. "Or a couple of days in court. Ward likes Mike, though. We all do. Maybe that's part of the problem. We've always cut the kid a lot of slack." He shrugged. "So anyhow, Ward is going to make Mike work off the window, but otherwise his record will still be clean."

She nodded. She stood awkwardly in front of Ward's big floor globe. Parker thought he could safely assume that she'd rather be anywhere on that globe right now than here in this room with him.

She seemed to be out of small talk. She looked at him, and she swallowed, squaring her jaw even further.

"Listen, Parker, maybe I should start. I want you to know that you don't need to feel uncomfortable around me. I know you're not interested in getting mixed up in anything this complicated. I never expected you to. You're a very nice man, but please, don't worry about how you're going to explain it to me. I already understand." She smiled. "And it's really okay."

He looked at her, helplessly caught in an inner debate. He ought to just nod his head and walk out of here. He'd spent two whole days trying to persuade himself to do exactly that.

Because Sarah Lennox was *not* the perfect woman. Not even close.

And he knew from experience how miserable two badly matched people could make each other. He knew that once the initial fog of sexual chemistry burned off, all the molehill flaws in the relationship stood out like mountains.

He wasn't going to do that again. He'd rather be single forever. That was a simple, unchangeable fact.

And yet he couldn't walk out of here right now.

That was a fact, too.

He couldn't explain it, but something in Sarah spoke to him. Maybe her beautiful face, or her gorgeous body. Maybe her passionate empathy for the underdog, or her stubborn loyalty to her uncle. Maybe the way she made friends everywhere, whether it was with boozing loggers, gossiping matrons or his own insufferable sister. Maybe her Madonna grace when she cradled a sleepy puppy, or her circus-clown clumsiness when she crawled, laughing and unashamed, toward him across the ice.

Which was all probably just another way of saying that Sarah Lennox was full of love, and full of life. Was it any wonder that her amazing vitality had found a physical expression? Could he really be surprised that someone so brimming with life was in the process of creating life, as well?

"I need to ask you two questions," he said. "If you don't want to answer them, you don't have to. But I have to ask."

She looked at him, a question in her hazel eyes. "All right," she said.

"Do you still love the father of this child?"

She lifted her chin. "No. I already told you. No."

He took a deep breath. "Okay. One more. Do you think that, even without love, there's any chance you and he will get back together? For the sake of the baby?"

He hated to ask. He could see the hurt flicker behind her eyes. "No," she said quietly. "Not because I wouldn't try. I might. I might try anything to make a good life for my child. But Ed isn't interested. He made that perfectly clear."

Parker tried not to be relieved. He tried not to put his own personal desires ahead of needs of this innocent life. But he *was* relieved. He had been so afraid she would say yes.

"Then I can't give up," he said. "I can't stop wanting to see you."

She looked at him. "But Parker, we—"

"I know it doesn't make any sense," he interrupted. He didn't want to hear her answer yet. Not before he had made his case. "But I can't just give up on us. Not without at least trying. Not without doing everything we can to see if we can make it work."

She shook her head. "We can't."

"You don't know that." He took a step closer to her. She backed up, but she hit Ward's armchair, and there was nowhere else to go. "There's something happening between us. Something powerful."

She was still shaking her head. "Yes, it's called sex. We're attracted to each other, Parker. It would be nice if I could stop being a woman just because I'm becoming a mother, but apparently I can't. When you kiss me, I…" She looked away. "It's just sex."

"You're wrong. It's sex, all right. But it's not *just* sex. Believe me, I've been there. This is different. This is more."

She couldn't put any distance between them, but her head was tilted away from him, and the dragonfly light from the Tiffany lamp spilled across her hair, onto her cheek. She was breathing raggedly under that soft green wool.

"You want the perfect woman, the perfect family," she said, her voice roughly trembling. "And why shouldn't you? I wanted that, too. Everyone does. But that's not what I am, Parker. I'm definitely not the perfect woman."

"Then I don't want her anymore, whoever she is. I want you, Sarah. I need you." He touched her cheek. "Give me a chance to see if I can be what *you* need."

She turned toward him. Her eyes were bright, as luminous and trembling as dragonfly wings.

"I'm not sure I can trust my own feelings right now," she said. "My body—my emotions—what if I'm just feeling unbearably vulnerable? What if I'm just a coward? What if I'm trying to trap someone into helping me, into being a substitute father for this baby?"

He smiled. "You're not a coward."

"I am." Her eyes widened. "I'm scared, Parker. Sometimes I'm so scared I can hardly breathe."

"I think that's normal," he said, feeling his heartbeat quicken with the need to comfort her. "But you are certainly not trying to trap anyone. Look at yourself. For weeks now, you've been trying desperately to keep me at arm's length. And yet you can't, not quite. Doesn't that tell you something, Sarah?"

"Yes." She took a ragged breath. "It tells me I'm in danger. It tells me I could get hurt."

"We both could," he said simply. He put his hands on her shoulders and met her gaze with a straightforward honesty, trying not to think of what he would do if she gave the wrong answer.

"It's a risk. A big risk, one I probably haven't got any right to ask you to take. But I am asking, Sarah. I don't know what lies ahead for us. I don't know if what we feel is—enough. But I want to find out. I want to keep seeing you, even knowing that one of us, or both of us, could get hurt. Will you take that risk with me?"

She stared without speaking. He could see the questions hanging between them like a cloud. He couldn't answer them. He didn't have the answers yet. So, almost without breathing, he waited.

She studied his face. Finally she nodded slowly.

"Yes," she said, lifting her chin in that way so like her uncle's. "I will."

CHAPTER THIRTEEN

AT THE CITY COUNCIL MEETING, the citizens of Firefly Glen had taken a solemn vow to create an ice festival, no matter what dragons stood in their way. And so, beginning the very next day, they went about keeping that vow with a vengeance.

The streets were suddenly full of bustling purpose. Signs advertising the event hung in every window. Ballot boxes for King Frosty and his Snow Queen stood in every store. That contest quickly eclipsed the Parker-Harry showdown as the most entertaining election in town.

And, overnight, everything turned white. White garlands replaced the green ones from Christmas, looped between streetlights, across storefronts, around the central town square. Frog's Folly Children's Fashions displayed an enchanted window of white velvet dresses and suits, ivory hats and alabaster muffs, amid a flurry of silver snowflakes.

With the costume ball only two weeks away, the fabric store had a run on white satins and silks. The craft store ran out of silver glitter, opalescent sequins and seed pearls. Sewing machines hummed as everyone rushed to create snowmen, snowflakes, snow queens, ice fairies and polar bears.

And behind it all, from sunup to dusk, and sometimes late into the night by spotlight, the hammers pounded as workmen hurried to build the frame for King Frosty's magnificent ice palace.

Though Ward still refused to admit he had lost, Sarah had to agree with Parker. Nothing could stop this festival from coming.

Meanwhile, Sarah and Parker had their own vow to keep, the vow to give this relationship, whatever it was, whatever it might become, a chance. During these two weeks, they honored their vow, too. It was as if somehow, that night, they had stumbled onto the magical phrase that caused the wall of resistance between them to blink and vanish. They hesitated…they smiled…they touched, and then they abandoned themselves completely to the sheer joy of being together.

For the whole fourteen days, she didn't sleep much, and neither did he, as if they resented any hours apart. They lunched at the Candlelight Café, holding hands. They borrowed the green sleigh from the Autumn House and took it into the woods in search of wide-eyed deer. They played chess with Ward, but even two against one they always lost because they couldn't concentrate on anything but each other.

One snowy afternoon, Parker taught her how to eat thick, sweet icicles cut from the Winter House cornices. They fell laughing onto the snow and made angels.

Parker even tried to teach her to skate, though after a few minutes he realized it was hopeless and decided he'd rather sit on the bench and kiss her until the heat they generated nearly melted the three feet of lake ice down to nothing.

And they talked. They talked about everything— work and family, friendship and food, politics and pirates and porcupines. But they didn't talk about tomorrow. She had a ticket on her dresser back at Winter House, a seat on an airplane that left the day after the ice festival ended, winging its way back to Florida, where it was already eighty degrees and sweltering. Parker knew about the ticket. She knew he knew. But neither of them mentioned it.

For the first time in her life, Sarah didn't try to look ahead. Instead, she accepted each day as if it were an ice crystal, a thing of beauty shot through with deep rainbows, but so fragile she had to cup it carefully in both hands and speak softly in its presence.

Even at such a glorious time, Parker did occasionally have to work. And then, slightly guilty, Sarah would finally attend one of the Gravity Gladiator meetings. These were rarely held at the exercise class anymore. It was too cold, and everyone felt too torpid, lulled into a semi-hibernation by the weather.

More often, the women met for lunch at the Candle-light Café and seriously considered changing their name to Emma's earlier suggestion: the Calorie Cowards.

"Well, what an honor!" Emma grinned as Sarah sat down that Thursday, the last day before the festival officially opened. She picked up Sarah's left hand. "Why, Heather, look. It's a miracle! They were able to surgically remove Parker's hand from Sarah's!"

Heather chuckled. "Leave the woman alone, Emma. We were just saying how nice it was to see *someone's* romance working out, remember?" She raised her water glass in a welcoming salute. "I'm glad you were able to come, Sarah. We've missed you."

Nice to see someone's romance working out? That didn't sound promising. Sarah squeezed Emma's hand before she let it go. Then, as she unfolded her napkin, she quickly scanned the other woman's face. Emma looked thinner, and the sparkle in her blue Tremaine eyes had all but disappeared.

"I guess that means Harry hasn't come back," Sarah said softly.

Emma shook her head. "He's the stubbornest man alive. I've just about decided to kidnap him from that stupid motel room and tie him up in our cellar until he comes to his senses."

Theo came by, and Sarah placed her usual order. When they were alone again, she turned to Emma. "I know it's not really any of my business, but…is there anything I can do?"

"No." Emma's voice was uncharacteristically harsh, and she toyed with her wineglass in a way that suggested it might not be her first today.

"No," she said again. She sighed from the bottom of her diaphragm and turned her tense, drawn face toward Sarah. "Not unless you can convince dumb Harry Dunbar that a woman marries a *man*. She doesn't marry a goddamn sperm count."

Heather's eyes widened. "Well, okay." She dragged the word out in a wry drawl. "I guess that got right to the point. But now let's see if we can employ some civilized euphemisms here, Em. Just for the sake of the other customers, who might be trying to eat."

Sarah kept her eyes on Emma. "You mean you and Harry can't have a baby? Is that what you're saying?"

"I'm saying *Harry* can't. As he's forever pointing out, *I* could, with someone else." She closed her eyes and tilted her head back, breathing deeply. "Only problem is, I don't *want* to. Not with someone else."

Sarah didn't know what to say. This problem was bigger than she had imagined, and far beyond the reach of mere friendly advice.

However, the irony of their two dilemmas didn't escape her. Here Sarah sat, struggling to cope with the fact that she would be a mother much too soon. And next to her, Emma, who was trying to cope with the possibility that she might never be a mother at all.

Mute with distress, Sarah met Heather's gentle, understanding gaze across the table. And she knew that the irony had occurred to her, too. Heather shook her head once, solemnly, and raised her shoulders, as if to say, *Life!*

"Okay, no more wine for you." Heather slid the glass toward the center of the table. "Don't get drunk, Em. Get mad. Go kidnap that handsome husband of yours, like you said. And when you've got him all trussed up in the basement, just keep saying one word to him, over and over."

"Oh, yeah? What word is that? *Homicide?*"

"No." Heather smiled. *"Adoption."*

Emma shook her head. "I've said that word a million times. Frankly, I like *homicide* better."

"Hello, ladies. Sorry to interrupt, especially just when the conversation was getting interesting. Who are you going to kill?"

Sarah looked up, a little sunburst of warmth spreading through her as she saw Parker. She hadn't noticed him come in, though he must have taken a while winding his way through the crowded café to their table at the back.

"Oh, good grief." Emma tossed up her hands, looking thoroughly disgusted. "I thought we finally got rid of you."

"I'll just be a minute." He didn't even look at his sister. He kept his eyes fixed on Sarah. "I think I may have left something here," he said, smiling.

"Well, what? Get it and go. We're having some quality girl time."

"What did you leave?" Sarah tilted her head.

"This." Parker leaned over and kissed her, a soft touch of heat that made its way through her veins like slow white wine.

"Oh, give me a *break!* Heather, have you ever seen anything so sappy as my idiot brother?"

But Parker just kissed Sarah again, waving Emma to silence with one hand. Sarah heard her two friends begin to chuckle, but she couldn't help herself. She hadn't kissed Parker in hours, and she simply couldn't resist.

"Damn it, Sheriff," a man's voice broke in suddenly. "I've been looking for you. What the heck is this? Aren't you supposed to be on duty?"

Parker let go of Sarah reluctantly. As he straightened and turned, she could see the man who had come up so rudely behind them. He was short and snub-nosed, probably in his early seventies, with a few sparse white strands of hair combed desperately over a large pink scalp. He reminded Sarah of a Pekinese dog. His eyes were black and shiny and small, and he was obviously so mad his face was holly-berry red.

"Hello, Bourke," Parker said mildly. "As you can see, I'm at lunch right now. If you've got an emergency, take it to Dunbar."

So this was Bourke Waitely. Sarah had been wondering about the man behind the name—a name her uncle couldn't even utter without a growl of fury. Parker had told her that the two old men had been feuding for so long no one could quite remember why. Something to do with Roberta, he thought.

And suddenly she remembered where she had seen this man before. On her first day in Firefly Glen, in the coat store, talking to Parker. Warning him to get Ward Winters under control.

"I'm talking to *you*, Tremaine. I want you to do something about Winters once and for all. It's criminal, the trouble he's causing. And all to spite me. You know what's really wrong with the old coot, don't you?"

Parker looked impassive. "Why don't you tell me, Bourke?"

"This is his first festival without Roberta, that's what. He can't stand the thought of it. He can't stand it because he's eaten up with guilt. He knows he killed her."

Sarah half rose, nearly knocking over her water. *"What?"*

Parker put his hand on her shoulder. "What the hell are you talking about, Bourke? Roberta Winters died of pneumonia. You know that."

The little man's face was so dark it looked downright dangerous. Sarah wondered if he might be going to have a stroke.

"I know that's what the death certificate says. But Ward is responsible, you can be sure of that. If he hadn't driven their car into a ditch that night, she wouldn't have broken her hip. And if she hadn't broken her hip…"

He took a few deep breaths, as if he had to push back the emotion a little before he could go on. "He killed her, all right. And I told him so."

"When?"

"Over Christmas. He got to talking all big about how much she had loved him, and…well, anyhow, he's been after me ever since. That's what this festival thing's all about. I told him the truth, and now he hates me for it."

Sarah was on her feet.

"Let me get this straight." Parker's voice was darkly controlled. "You told Ward Winters that he killed his wife?"

Bourke nodded, pulling out his handkerchief and wiping his half-bald head, which was covered in perspiration. "Yes, sir," he said belligerently. "I damn sure did."

Parker and Sarah exchanged glances.

She picked up her purse blindly, touching Parker's arm with her other hand.

"It's okay," she said. "I'll go to him."

HER UNCLE WAS STANDING at the upstairs oriel window, staring out onto the undulating white landscape below. It had begun to snow again, light but fast. The chaotic flakes flew crazily past the window, in all directions at once.

Sarah came in behind him quietly. On the ride home, she'd been trying to come up with something useful to say.

He heard her, but he didn't turn around. "Hi, Short Stuff," he said. "You finally finished fraternizing with the enemy?"

She put down her purse on the marble-topped table. "I was having lunch with Emma and Heather," she said. She paused. "But while I was there, Bourke Waitely came by."

Her uncle's head half turned, but then he stopped

himself and continued gazing out the window. "I guess that was enough to ruin your appetite."

"He seemed pretty upset. He said some…some ridiculous things."

Ward snorted. "Well, that could have been predicted. Every time Bourke Waitely opens his mouth, something ridiculous comes out."

She moved up behind him, and put her hand on his arm. "You know what I mean," she said. "He was talking about Aunt Roberta. And you."

His arm was as tight as a brick. "You know, I think I'll sue the bastard for slander." He nodded firmly. "Yeah. I'll sue him for every penny he has. That would be amusing."

Sarah's heart twisted. "You don't need to do that," she said quietly. "Everyone knows he's talking crazy." She put her head on the back of Ward's shoulder. "Parker says Bourke was in love with Roberta once, too. But she married *you*. So the things he's saying now— everyone knows they're just a bunch of bitter, jealous lies."

Ward was silent for a moment. Then, still without turning around, he reached over and patted Sarah's hand. "He *was* jealous, poor devil. It made him just about crazy to lose her." He shook his head slightly. "I can't blame him for that. I would have gone crazy, too, if she'd chosen him."

"But she didn't." Sarah tightened her grip on his arm. "She chose you. And she never regretted that choice. Never."

"No, I really don't think she did, Short Stuff. I think she was happy with me." He inhaled raggedly. "But does that make it any better, if I killed her at the end?

If she died because I made a stupid mistake at the wheel?"

Sarah felt her heart wrenching. So much pain lay behind that question. And what could she say that would help? She hardly even knew the details of the accident. It had been last winter, the final night of the festival, and Ward had been at the wheel. That was all she'd ever heard. But winter driving was always tricky....

"Well, what did *she* say?" Sarah wished her uncle would turn around. She wanted to judge from his eyes the depth of his guilt. "Did she blame you?"

He laughed harshly. "Of course not. It wasn't in your aunt to be cruel. She never said one word about it."

"Right." Sarah smiled, remembering her aunt's warm, perceptive concern for everyone she met, including her little thirteen-year-old great-niece, who was so morose and unlikable that summer. "And if she didn't want you to be unhappy, if she didn't want you to feel guilty, don't you think you owe it to her to be happy? In a way, haven't you dishonored her memory by suffering over it so much?"

He turned, then. His shaggy eyebrows were thrust down hard over his intelligent eyes. "That's a pretty low blow, Short Stuff. Tell me. Are you trying to manipulate this pitiful old man into something here?"

She grinned at him. "Chapter Twelve of *Make Anyone Do Anything*. How to get your great-uncle to drop that heavy load of unnecessary guilt and get on with being happy. As happy as his wife would have wanted him to be. As happy as she spent her whole life trying to make him."

To her shock, Ward's eyes suddenly were moist and gleaming. She held her breath, disbelieving. Never, never had she seen her uncle shed a tear.

And apparently today wasn't going to be the first time. He cleared his throat and scowled at her in the old, familiar way. He seemed to have forced the moisture back in place with a sheer, stubborn will.

"I knew it. Throw that ridiculous book away, Short Stuff. I told you it was garbage."

She met his gaze and, with relief, she recognized the old-time twinkle. "Yes, sir, " she agreed meekly, holding back her smile. "Yes, I suppose you're right."

He grumbled under his breath, but the words didn't matter. She knew it was going to be all right. She gave him a quick kiss.

"I'd better get back to work," she said. "I've still got two snowflake costumes to finish."

He nodded absently. She was almost out the door before he spoke again.

"Hey, Short Stuff," he said gruffly.

She paused. "What?"

"I've been thinking. Why don't you stay?" He asked the question casually, as if it were as unimportant as a query about the weather. "Why don't you just tell them down in Florida to take that teaching job and shove it? Have your baby here. At Winter House. We could use a little life up here in this frozen hole we call a town."

Sarah was strangely paralyzed. Everything she considered as an answer seemed to lodge in her throat like pebbles clogging a stream. She looked at him, trying not to let the ache in her chest reach her face, where it would become visible, and he would know how much she wanted to say yes.

"So why not?" He shrugged. "I mean, what do you need to go back for? So you can find another constipated jerk like Ed? Hell, no. You fit better here, Short Stuff. Can't you feel it?"

"Here?" The word sounded tight and thin, as if it came from someone else's mouth. "In Firefly Glen?"

"Right." His brusque, no-nonsense tone helped her to stay in control. "It's small, and it's colder than God's basement, but it's never boring. You could live here with me. Winter House is a creaky, weird old mansion, but it's seen a lot of love in its day. I'm going to leave it to you eventually anyhow, so why wait till I'm dead? As far as I'm concerned, it's your home now, Sarah. And the baby's. If you want it."

Home.

She fought back a strangled sound. Did he know, she wondered, what mystical, aching power that word held for her? Did he know how many years she had longed to find a place that could deserve that hallowed name?

All those terrible childhood years. As her mother had tugged her from one house to another, from one stepfather and stepfamily to another, she had searched in vain for "home." That paradise other people seemed to take for granted.

But "home," she had discovered, was more than a bed, a warm meal, an address. It was even, to her surprise, something more than love.

It was a complicated concept built on a foundation of the completely unconditional, the wholly reliable, the intangible, unchangeable something you knew you could always trust, no matter what.

She looked at her uncle. Was it possible that finally, after all these years, she was standing on ground firm enough to support such a concept?

"Well, come on, Short Stuff. What do you say? Will you think about it, at least?"

"Thank you, but I—"

She stopped.

"I—"

She swallowed back the jagged pebbles and took another risk.

"All right," she said. "I'll think about it."

THE SNOW STOPPED FALLING at eight in the morning the first day of the festival, as if under orders from the Firefly Glen City Council. The weather held its breath at a crisp, clear, blue-skied and perfect twenty-eight degrees.

Bravely Sarah offered to stay at home with her uncle, but he shooed her out of the house, saying Parker would never let him hear the end of it if he allowed Sarah to miss a single event.

She couldn't remember ever having so much fun. On Friday, she cheered as Parker's team won the hockey game, and the sleigh from Autumn House won the decorated sleigh rally, in spite of stiff competition from Theo Burke's Candlelight Camaro.

And she got her first look at the finished ice palace. It was simple but beautiful, a square building with a tower at each end. Its pure, translucent walls caught the sunlight and fractured it into a million prisms, so that the entire structure seemed to sparkle.

But Saturday was the most important day of the festival. Sarah woke that morning with a bubble of excitement that nothing could pop, not even knowing that her efforts on behalf of the Firefly Girls had prevented her from creating a costume of her own for tonight's ball.

When her uncle joined her at breakfast, Frosty trotting at his heels, he carried a large, flat box with him. "From your aunt," he said tersely, setting it down beside Sarah, then turning his attention to his cereal and his newspaper.

Sarah opened it slowly. Inside, shimmering like a sheet of ice crystals, was the most beautiful dress she'd ever seen. A simple, ankle-length sheath, with a fur-trimmed ballerina neckline and long, fitted sleeves, it was made of white velvet encrusted with seed pearls and clear glass beads.

Sarah was speechless.

"She wore it years ago, when she wasn't much older than you," her uncle said without looking up from the sports page. "It's supposed to be an ice angel. It should fit." He sneaked a sly glance at her. "Of course, *she* wasn't pregnant at the time."

Sarah laughed, holding it up against her breast with a deep, inarticulate joy. It was exquisite. She could imagine how beautiful her aunt had looked in it. And how her uncle's eyes would have glittered with pride when he looked at her.

She kissed her uncle softly. "Thank you," she said. "It's perfect."

He fidgeted, as if the kiss annoyed him. "There's a white fur coat in the upstairs closet. I had it cleaned. And she did this thing with her hair—" He waved his hands around his head hazily. "You know, powdered it, or glittered it or—" He frowned, realizing that this wasn't "men's" talk. "Hell, I haven't got a clue how women do that. Your aunt looked great, that's all I know."

From then on, Sarah counted the dragging minutes

until nine o'clock, when Parker was going to take her
to King Frosty's ball. It was the highlight of the entire
festival, with music and dancing inside the ice castle,
which would be lit by dozens of swirling multicolored
spotlights.

She got through the day somehow. She walked with
the Firefly Girls in the children's costume parade, and
then she manned the giant snow slide for several hours,
until her ears were ringing from the high-pitched
squeals of delight and terror.

Finally darkness fell. Still buoyed by that bubble of
anticipation, she went home, bathed and dressed. She
was glad to discover that the slight thickening of her
waistline didn't prevent her from wearing the ice angel
costume. Finally she rummaged through the scraps
from the snowflake costumes to find tiny silver sequins
to arrange on her softly powdered hair.

Her uncle stopped in his tracks when he saw her. "I
wouldn't say you're more beautiful than Roberta." He
cleared his throat roughly. "But you're a close second,
Short Stuff. A mighty close second."

If she still had any doubts, Parker's reaction told her
all she needed to know. It wasn't what she expected. He
didn't smile with misty pride and compliment her effu-
sively. Instead, as he looked at her, his mouth tightened
to a fierce hardness. His eyes glinted, and suddenly his
face looked intensely male, and hungry.

"I'm not letting you out of my sight all night," he said
as he helped her into the car. "You look so gorgeous it's
damn dangerous."

She smiled. He looked fairly amazing tonight
himself, though he wasn't technically wearing a
costume. Emma had warned her that most of the men

compromised by pretending to go as lumberjacks, which meant they could use their everyday clothes.

Parker wore a thick, white Irish wool sweater over black slacks. And he looked as sexy as any man she'd ever seen.

"You may have to let me out of your sight," Sarah said. "What if you're elected king? You'll have to sit on the throne beside your queen. And I'll be left to dance with whoever takes pity on me."

Growling, he took her in his arms. "You won't dance with anyone but me."

"But I've heard people talking. They think you'll be elected king, and then you—"

He shook his head. "I won't be."

"How can you be—"

He put his finger over her lips. "Trust me. I won't be. And if I were, I'd give up my throne. I won't leave you, Sarah. How could I ever leave you?"

He was so close his breath misted white against her mouth before he kissed her. She felt herself melting as his arms closed around her, and his chest pressed hard against hers. The temperature might have fallen to nineteen degrees outside the car, but in here her body was practically on fire.

But they were expected downtown in a very few minutes, so somehow they pried themselves apart, and Parker started the car.

They arrived just in time for the ritual storming of the palace by the new king and his army, a mock battle that included fireworks and a homemade cannon that fired snowballs at the castle walls.

Hundreds of spectators, many of them visitors from neighboring towns, had gathered to watch. Emma rushed up to join them just as Mayor Millner prepared to announce the royal ice court. "Found you," she said triumphantly.

Emma had told Sarah she was coming dressed as the moon queen, and her silver-and-blue costume couldn't have been more lovely.

"Hey! I thought you weren't going to have a costume," Emma said as she hugged Sarah warmly. "Darn. That was the only hope I had of outshining you." She knocked Parker on the chest. "Hi, bro," she said playfully. "Love *your* costume!"

Parker shushed her. "They're about to announce the queen. Show some respect."

"Sorry," Emma said, making a face. "No can do. Wrong queen."

The name was announced over the microphone with a flourish. *Justine Millner.* Emma growled as the blond, smiling mayor's daughter accepted her crown from her father with a graceful, but not entirely convincing, display of surprised humility.

Justine was beautiful, Sarah thought, but she looked like trouble. Poor Mike Frome. He was going to get his heart broken, she suspected.

The king was next. *Harry Dunbar.* Sarah applauded vigorously, surprised but delighted. She looked over at Emma, who was clapping harder than anyone.

In contrast to Justine, Harry looked utterly stunned. He glanced around him at the others, as if to say there must have been a mistake. But the crown was placed upon his head, his people cheered, and he was told to give the order to storm the castle.

Sarah looked at Parker, wondering if he minded losing, especially to Harry. But Parker was studying

Emma, who was watching her estranged husband with a proud, protective, bittersweet smile.

"You knew," Sarah whispered. "You knew it was going to be Harry."

Emma turned to Sarah with damp, happy eyes. "It's called stuffing the ballot box, my friend. It's a time-honored tradition in Firefly Glen." She rested her head on her brother's shoulder briefly. "Besides, Parker actually would have won, and he wouldn't have accepted the crown, so…"

She looked up at Parker. "Thanks, bro," she said.

"No problem, sis," he responded lightly. "Now how about you scram? I'm trying to have a date here."

With Emma gone, Parker put his arm around Sarah and drew her close, warming her as they watched the mock battle raging in front of the ice palace.

This was the first time Sarah had seen the palace at night. She hadn't thought it could be any more beautiful than it was in the daylight, with the sun setting it on fire. But tonight it was like something out of a dream.

Its icy profile seen by moonlight was infinitely romantic, deeply mysterious. Its two towers rose into the starry night like knives of flashing crystal. Its clear, frozen walls undulated with color from the constantly turning spotlights.

When the fireworks exploded overhead, signaling the victory by the king, the crowd roared its pleasure. King Harry led his men inside the gates, and hundreds of fairies and princesses followed, each escorted by a rugged lumberjack or a white-velvet prince. The costume ball was officially underway.

Sarah and Parker danced for hours, under silver

streamers and pearly white balloons. As he had promised, he never left her side, not even once. They talked to friends, sampled the delicious buffet, drank wine and admired the elaborate ice sculptures, but they didn't ever allow more than an inch of distance between them.

As the night grew late, Sarah gradually began to realize Parker was seducing her with the music, with the movement, with his warm, strong body.

He held her more tightly with each song. His cheek brushed hers softly, came away, and then dipped to hers again. His hand drifted low, his fingers finding the sensitive hollows of her back. She moaned, but he didn't let up. He tightened his hands. He kissed her ear, her bare neck, her shoulder. And all the while he moved, subtly, to the music she only barely heard.

Soon she was a live ember in his hands, glowing for him, aching for him. Her skin felt too tight to hold all the glittering desire she had inside. She could hardly lift her head from his shoulder.

What if he made it happen right here, out on the dance floor? What if this shimmering thrill she felt inside simply exploded like a silent, internal firework? Would everyone know? Would he hold her up, intact? Or would she fracture like a spray of silver confetti and collapse in his arms?

"Sarah," he whispered. "It's time."

She had to breathe deeply to find enough air to speak. "Time? I don't know what you—"

"Yes, you do." He tilted back and smiled into her eyes. That smile alone was almost enough to undo her. She clutched his arms and tried to find her legs, which had suddenly begun to tremble.

"You see, Sarah? Your body is telling you, too. We've waited as long as we can, sweetheart. It's time to take another risk."

CHAPTER FOURTEEN

THEY RETRIEVED Sarah's coat and walked to the Jeep without saying much. The temperature must still be dropping, she thought, trying to shrink inside her coat. She was like someone with a fever. Burning up and shivering at the same time.

Every parking space was filled, and cars lined the road, nose to bumper as far as the eye could see. Many had license plates from as far away as Pennsylvania and Quebec. It would take an hour to get out of here.

But Parker obviously wasn't in the mood to be patient. When he found his exit blocked, he cut across the snow, the Jeep bumping over the curb and across the corner of the square. Finally he reached the road again, and his way was clear.

He took Sarah's hand and held it tightly on the seat between them, his finger stroking her palm with a slow, deliberate warmth. She closed her eyes and let the rhythm move through her.

They had been driving several minutes, apparently following the moonlit curve of the lake, before she said anything.

Finally she spoke. "Where are we going?"

"I thought I'd take you home," he said. "My home." He glanced at her, his eyes flashing in the darkness. "Would you like that?"

"Yes," she said simply.

He had never suggested taking her to his house before. They had needed time to get to know each other better before they rushed into anything serious. But they also knew their willpower had limits, so they had forced prudence on themselves by staying out in the open, in crowds, in public. Even at Winter House, someone had always been just around the corner, preventing them from taking this one final, oh-so-dangerous risk.

The house was silent and mostly dark as they came up the driveway, but Sarah fell in love with it instantly. It was a large, two-story modern Adirondack cabin that hugged the western shore of Llewellyn's Lake. It was made of smooth, symmetrical red-pine logs and rose from the surrounding woodlands with a comfortable sense of belonging.

One golden light shone above the gleaming wood porch, and in one of the upstairs windows another light burnished the curtains with a welcoming glow.

It was so quiet out here that Sarah could hear the wind moving through ice-covered pine needles with that haunting, glassy tinkle of wind chimes. It was a sound she'd hear in her dreams forever, she thought. Whenever she dreamed of Parker.

He opened the door and flicked on the interior lights. The entire first floor seemed to be one room, one rich, red-pine room with cool green accents: a hunter-green leather sofa pulled up to a huge, river-rock fireplace, a green-and-red Oriental carpet spread across the floor; a glossy green philodendron cascading from a built-in bookshelf.

"It's wonderful," she said. She thought it might be the most peaceful room she'd ever seen. "You can forget, living at Winter House, that simplicity like this still exists in the world."

He smiled as he draped her coat over a wooden tree, then moved toward the fireplace. The logs were already arranged and ready. He simply drew a long, thick match from a box and struck it against one of the stones.

The kindling caught immediately, and a sweet, smoky smell wafted into the cool, clean room.

"Well, if I had your uncle's income to hire a house-keeping staff, I might buy more knickknacks," he said, tossing the spent match onto the logs. "On a sheriff's salary, I prefer to keep things low maintenance."

She shook her head. "This wasn't done on a sheriff's salary," she said. She had just noticed that the eastern wall was entirely windows, two-stories tall, and they overlooked the lake.

"You'd be surprised how well Firefly Glen pays its employees," he countered lightly. "These millionaires have forgotten how to think in terms of minimum wage. But actually, you're right. I was a lawyer for several years, and I worked in Washington for a while, too, so I was able to save some. Plus, I was very lucky. I inher-ited enough money to live comfortably."

That made sense, looking at this sophisticated room. Its delicate balance of ease and elegance had been achieved by a trained eye, by someone accustomed to living around quality and beauty.

"And yet you work so hard. Why?" She thought of the grief he put up with from the querulous Glenners, the long hours, the freezing nights squaring off against coyotes in people's kitchens. "Why work at all?"

He shrugged. "I work because my folks believed in it. I guess I believe in it, too." He smiled. "And besides,

I'm no good at crossword puzzles, and I hate to fish. What would I do with my time?"

They had been talking to ease the tension, to lower the temperature that had risen so dangerously between them while they danced. But suddenly, with that innocent question, the flame shot once again into brilliant life.

He came over to her. "Of course, now that I've found you, I can think of a few things."

He put his fingers under her chin and tilted her mouth toward his. A silver sequin tumbled from her hair, sparkling as it fell.

"Maybe I should let Harry have the job. He wants it bad enough. And suddenly I can imagine spending all day, every day, doing nothing." He smiled. "Nothing but touching you. And looking at you."

She let her eyes drift shut, the sound of his voice like warm water washing through her.

"And making love to you," he said softly. He took a long breath. "God, Sarah. I'm falling in love with you. Do you know that?"

She opened her eyes and looked into his. "Yes," she said. "I know that."

"And you are falling in love with me. Do you know that, too?"

She nodded carefully. Her whole body felt as if it were dropping into some terrifying, bottomless space, and yet she knew she hadn't moved an inch.

"Yes," she said. "Yes, I know that, too."

"Then this isn't wrong," he said, his voice suddenly fierce. "It's right, damn it. It's so amazingly right, and it's going to be beautiful. I want you to believe that. I want you to stop being afraid."

"I'll try," she said around the swollen beating of her heart. "I'll try."

He unzipped her costume with one hand, still holding her chin with the other. She felt the velvet fall apart from her shoulders to her thighs, exposing her naked back to the cold moonlight that streamed in through the windows.

He slid his hand around, the movement pulling the dress from her shoulders. Silver sequins caught the firelight as the velvet slithered over her skin and fell to the floor.

She wore almost nothing beneath, and she suddenly felt more vulnerable, more insecure, than ever before in her life. She didn't really know her own body anymore. The pregnancy had finally begun to change her, subtly still, but unmistakably.

She wondered if the new contours would make her less desirable to him.

But his face was as tense, as focused and hungry as ever. He finished undressing her, and then he lay her on the carpet, close enough to the fire that she could hear it crackling and feel its fingers of heat reaching out to stroke her.

The rug was thick, scratching softly at her back. Closing her eyes, she wrapped one hand across her stomach, the other across the unaccustomed fullness of her breasts.

She heard him remove his own clothes, but she couldn't watch. It seemed impossible, but she already felt the deep, warning clenches of climax moving through her, like the early readings of an earthquake. She was afraid that, if she saw him now, she might not be able to wait.

And then, with a slow animal grace, he stretched himself out beside her. Finally she looked at him, at the bronze, ribboned muscles, the glowing satin skin. She followed the line of firelight and found the beautiful, shadowed power of his erection. Her whole body spasmed once, in unbearable anticipation.

He unwrapped her hands carefully, one at a time. "You have nothing to hide," he said, bending over to touch his lips to her tingling breast. "Every inch of you is perfect, Sarah. I have never wanted a woman more than I want you now."

He ran the palm of his hand across the small, hard swell of her stomach, learning it. Loving it. He trailed gentle kisses from one side to the other, and she groaned, fighting off the waves of climax that threatened to crash over her. It was too soon, too soon. She wanted this to come slowly and last forever.

He paused, obviously registering the tension that rippled through her limbs. "Look at me, sweetheart. What's the matter? Are you still afraid?"

"Not of you," she said, trying to smile. "I'm a little afraid I'm about to spoil everything. I'm—" She found that her lungs were moving so shallowly she could hardly speak and breathe at the same time. "Things are happening pretty fast. I may not be able to wait for you…for you to…"

He laughed softly. "Then don't wait," he whispered, bringing his lips to her aching breast once again. "Just let it happen."

She could hardly think now. He had let his hand drift down, and she was spinning in a private darkness that disoriented her. And the waves kept coming closer. "But I…we…"

"We will. I promise." He slipped his fingers inside her, and she felt herself tighten helplessly around him as the tide completely overtook her. "It's only the first time you'll feel like this tonight, sweetheart, not the last."

THE DAWN WAS PEACHES AND HONEY. It had spilled onto the pillow, mingling with the tangled gold strands of Sarah's hair. And reluctantly Parker had wakened her with a kiss.

He had to take her back to Winter House, though the idea of having her more than an arm's reach away from him was almost unbearable. He didn't ever want to open his eyes again, and not see her lying beside him. He didn't ever want to breathe and not find the small flower of her perfume in the air.

But she had to go home. Her uncle would worry. And, though he didn't give a damn what the gossips said, something told him that Sarah wasn't ready for what would happen when the town found out about the change in their relationship.

She had never lived in a small town. She couldn't imagine how intensely connected everyone felt, how entwined their lives, how useless any attempt to keep a secret.

But he knew. He'd lived here too long to delude himself about the gossip that was coming. As his grandfather used to say, Glenners would gossip the tread right off their lips.

When they learned that Sarah was his lover, they would start. And when they learned that she was already pregnant by another man...

Well, even Parker couldn't quite imagine what would happen then. He simply knew that he didn't care. Sarah had brought happiness back into his life, and a sweetness he had stopped believing in years ago. He hadn't ever thought to see it again.

He wanted that sweetness. He wanted Sarah Lennox in his life. In his bed. And as soon as she was ready, he was willing to stand on the top of the Congregational Church steeple and announce it to the world.

But it wasn't that easy. Her life was in Florida, and she still had an airline ticket for tomorrow morning to prove it.

Tomorrow.

The realization hit him like an electric shock. She planned to go away tomorrow.

What a fool he was. For the past two weeks, they had been living in a fantasy. Their own secret ice kingdom, where the real world didn't intrude. But it was time to come out now. He couldn't dawdle in this haze of smug sexual satisfaction. It was time for discussions and decisions.

Big ones.

"Sarah, we need to talk," he said. They were almost at Winter House now, though he had driven as slowly as the Jeep would go.

She nodded sleepily, stirring from her drowsy nest against his shoulder.

"I know," she said, rubbing her eyes. "But not right now. I need to see my uncle. I need to let him know I'm all right. He might be awake, and he might have been worrying."

"He knew you were with me, Sarah. He hasn't forgotten that much about being young."

She smiled. "Still." She ran her fingers through her hair, sending one last rain of sequins onto the black leather of the seat. "I need a nap. I want a bath. And I want some time to think. Last night was…"

"Amazing."

"Yes." She rubbed her arm, as if the mere mention of last night had raised goose bumps. He knew, because he felt the same way. "But it was also confusing. Sex can cloud your thinking, Parker. We need a few hours to clear our heads before we talk about anything serious."

"Sex *is* serious," he said. "That kind of sex is, anyhow."

She smiled over at him placatingly. "Six hours? Just until noon? I promise we will talk then."

He couldn't deny her anything when she smiled like that. Oh, hell, he couldn't deny her anything ever.

"Okay," he said, taking one last kiss as payment. He deepened the kiss and he heard her small whimper as the easy fire caught. He was glad. If he had to suffer, she should suffer, too.

"Just wait," he said, pulling away, "until you see how long six hours can be."

BUT IT WAS ONLY TWO HOURS, really.

Two hours until everything blew up in his face, as if fate had planted one of last night's ice festival fireworks squarely in the middle of his naive little portfolio of happily-ever-after blueprints.

Parker had picked up his puppy from Suzie, who had agreed to keep him while Parker was on twenty-four-hour call for the festival. Then he had come home, showered, redressed and finally passed out on the sofa.

The phone had probably rung a dozen times before he heard it. The puppy was sitting next to the sofa, whimpering to get his attention. Parker put one hand on the puppy's head and reached over his shoulder with the other one, fumbling for the receiver.

It was Sarah.

"Hi," she said too brightly. "I'm sorry to wake you up. I just wanted to let you know there's been a little hitch. I won't be able to meet you right at noon."

He shouldn't ever try to sleep during the day. It left him muddy headed. At first he didn't even have the sense to be alarmed.

"Why not?" He raised himself to a half-sitting position. "Is everything all right?"

She hesitated. And in that tiny silence, Parker's internal alarms finally began to go off. No. The answer was no. Everything was *not* all right.

"Sure," she said, though her tone was a neon sign that announced she was lying. She was a terrible liar. "It's just that…"

Another pause.

"I've heard from Ed," she said in a tense, unhappy voice. "He's here. He wants to see me. He wants to talk about the baby."

CHAPTER FIFTEEN

"DAMN IT, GRIFFIN. Can't you be a little more convincing?" Emma broke off her kiss and scowled at the sinfully handsome man sitting next to her in the window seat of The Paper House. "Surely they wouldn't call you Playboy Cahill if you couldn't seduce a woman better than this."

Griffin Cahill's elegant, tanned face looked wounded. "I'm not accustomed to *pretending* to seduce women, Emma. Apparently I'm not at my best unless my feelings are sincere."

She rolled her eyes. "Hogwash. You haven't had a sincere interaction with a female in ten years. Just pretend I'm one of the bimbos you date every weekend."

"The bimbos I date aren't *married* bimbos," he pointed out reasonably. "And we aren't actively trying to get their husbands worked into a dangerous lather." He glanced out the window. "Are you sure this is, at heart, a particularly intelligent plan? As I recall, your husband carries a weapon."

Emma sighed. "What, you're afraid of a little gun?"

"Well, yes, Emma, as a matter of fact, I am. I forgot to wear my bullet-proof codpiece this morning."

She had to laugh. She *was* asking a lot, but Griffin,

with his blond hair, blue eyes and shockingly white teeth, was the best-looking man in town. One of the richest, too. Harry had always secretly been a little jealous of him, all the way back to high school. Emma intended to exploit that as much as possible. This was war, and she needed every advantage she could get.

So it had to be Griffin.

"Look. He's not going to shoot you, damn it," she said. "He might throw a punch or two, but—"

"Emma." Griffin held up one long, graceful hand. "If we're going to do this, let's just do it. You said he'll be here at noon, so unless you want him to walk in on us arguing—"

"No. You're right." Emma positioned herself to be thoroughly romanced. "Let's go."

This time Griffin was significantly more effective. Emma's disappointment was almost intolerable, therefore, when the next person to open the door was not Harry, but Jocelyn Waitely.

At the sight of Emma Dunbar in Griffin Cahill's arms, the prissy woman looked shocked to her dyed-blond roots.

"Oh!" Apparently she was shocked speechless, which was a first for Jocelyn, Emma thought waspishly. "Oh, dear."

Emma exhaled irritably. "We're closed, Jocelyn," she said. "I forgot to turn the sign."

Jocelyn's eyes had begun to glitter unpleasantly, and Emma noticed that she didn't have to be asked twice to leave. She could hardly wait to get out and start spreading the dirty word.

Sighing, Griffin watched her go. "Not that I'm complaining, Emma, but how many takes do you expect our little scene to require?"

"One more. I promise. Just one more." She hoped that was true. Maybe Jocelyn's appearance had been a blessing in disguise. If blessings *could* come disguised as witchy old bats with filthy minds.

But maybe, if for some reason Theo had forgotten to send Harry to The Paper House at noon as planned, Jocelyn would do it for her. She was probably making a beeline for the sheriff's office right now.

Five minutes later the door opened again. Griffin must have great ears, Emma thought, because he swept her into his arms just in the nick of time and began kissing her so passionately she thought her eyelashes would catch on fire.

Wow, she thought. And then again, stupidly. *Wow.*

From there, things began to happen quickly. The door slammed, someone cursed fiercely. And suddenly Griffin was thrown to the side. When Emma caught her balance, Harry was standing between them, his whole body tense and threatening.

"Get the hell off my wife, you bastard." He whipped his furious face around to Emma. "What in hell do you think you're doing?"

"You know what I'm doing," she said calmly. "I'm doing exactly what you told me to do."

"The hell I did."

Griffin was standing now, and he looked superbly in control, just smug enough to goad Harry into a real temper. Emma was glad she'd picked somebody smart, because her pre-scripted dialogue would only go so far. Sooner or later Griffin would have to improvise.

"Listen, Dunbar. Maybe you'd better not talk to your wife that way."

Harry made fists. "And maybe you'd better not say

one more goddamn thing about how I should handle my wife." He jammed a forefinger into Griffin's expensive silk-and-cotton shirt. "*My* wife. Hear that? *My wife.*"

"Well, maybe you should start treating her like your wife, then. In my experience, and I've had plenty, well-tended wives don't go around looking for other men."

Emma could have kissed him all over again. That was the perfect thing to say. Harry would never be able to endure having Griffin Cahill suspect he might be a lousy lover. It was pure locker-room mentality, but weren't all men boys at heart? Especially her foolish, darling Harry?

"Get out, Griffin," Harry said between clenched teeth. "I need to talk to my wife. Alone."

Griffin looked toward Emma. The man deserved an Oscar. Though she knew he could hardly wait to be tossed safely out of this ridiculous situation, he managed to look reluctant, tenderly protective.

"Emma? What do *you* say? Does he have the right to tell me to go?"

She thought for a minute. Then she turned slowly to face Harry, her hands on her hips. She had worn a new dress for the occasion, and she knew she looked great. Plus, her hair was probably all tumbled, and her lipstick smeared, so she probably looked pretty sexy, too. Harry had that look, as if it was driving him crazy to see her like this.

Thanks, Griffin, she said silently, mentally blowing him a kiss. He was such a terrific kisser, it probably would be a mistake to ever try that again.

"I don't know. Do you have the right, Harry? A husband who loves his wife, who is *living with* his wife, has the right to tell her she can't kiss other men. A husband who is living at the Firefly Suites doesn't have any rights at all."

She paused. "At least that's the way I see it. What do you think, Griffin?"

"Seems eminently logical to me," Griffin said conversationally. "Though I might also say—"

"Shut up, Cahill." Harry was looking at Emma with an expression she recognized. He might, just might, have begun to see through her charade, she thought. But maybe it didn't matter. He still knew he hadn't liked seeing her kiss Griffin. And he knew he wouldn't ever want to see it again. "I'm going to tell you one more time. Get out."

Griffin, bless his chivalrous heart, still hesitated. "Emma?"

She smiled up at her husband. She was glad she had worn her prettiest slip, because she had a feeling this was going to be her lucky day.

"Go ahead, Griffin," she said without taking her eyes from Harry. "And lock the door on the way out, would you, please? Harry and I don't want to be disturbed."

IT TOOK SARAH ten minutes to find a parking space. Though this was the last day of the festival, plenty of activities were still going on. The judges were handing ribbons to the winners of the ice sculpture contest, the broomball tournament was in full swing, and the polar bear dip for charity would begin in another hour or so. The town square was teeming with people, and the streets were clogged with traffic.

So, by the time she got out of the car and began walking the length of Main Street back to the Firefly Suites, she was already late. And she hadn't forgotten how Ed hated for anyone to be tardy. She felt a tightening in her chest. She was dreading this encounter more than she could ever have imagined.

"Sarah. Sarah, wait." Out of the dense crowd, Parker appeared at her side. His breathing was slightly irregular, as if he'd been running to catch her. Maybe he had seen her from the sheriff's department windows, which overlooked the municipal parking lot.

"Come." He took her elbow and steered her toward the secluded walkway between Theo's café and Griswold's Five and Dime next door. "I need to talk to you."

She glanced at her watch. "Parker, I'm late." Fifteen minutes late, in fact. Ed would be livid.

"I know." Parker looked drawn, as if his sleepless night had cost him. She wondered if she looked equally exhausted. "I called Winter House, but Ward said you'd already left. I wanted to tell you…" He shook his head. "Damn it, Sarah. Don't go."

She frowned. "You know I can't—"

"Why should you meet him? What right does he have to come back now, asking to see you?" His mouth was tight and grim. "I don't want you to go."

His frustration was so intense it was like a physical presence between them. She tried to smile, hoping she could defuse his tension by being relaxed, by acting as if this were not the end of the world.

"I have to," she said as calmly as possible. "You know what right he has, Parker. He is the baby's father. I can't ignore that fact just because I don't like it. Or because you don't."

"Yes, you can." Parker's hand on her arm tightened. "He did."

"I have to go," she repeated numbly. "Try to understand. This is Ed's baby, too. I tried to run away from that fact, but I can't keep running forever. Reality has to be faced."

"Then let me come with you. I'll explain it to him. I'll tell him that you and I…"

She shook her head. If Ed met Parker, he would be illogically jealous, no matter how little he wanted Sarah himself. He was like that, petty and insecure, and vindictive. No telling what he would do if he thought another man was sniffing at the crumbs he'd left behind.

"It's better if I go alone. Really."

Parker backed away two steps, holding up his hands. "So what do you want me to do, Sarah? Be noble? Stand back politely while this bastard comes in and stomps all over our future? Last night we—" He stopped. Cleared his throat. "We made love, and—"

"I know," she broke in softly. "But the fact that you've become my lover does not make you the baby's father. You know that. He has rights, Parker. Legal rights. Moral rights. Biological rights. I can't wish them away so that you and I can make love happily ever after."

He was silent. With a sinking heart, she watched the struggle in his face. Oh, how he hated this, as she had always known he would. He hated not being the first, the real, the only.

She realized then that he hadn't ever honestly faced the messy truths about her pregnancy. He had simply created a light, manageable scenario in which, because he loved her and loved the baby, he could step in cleanly and, by virtue of his higher moral ground, essentially *become* the baby's father.

Ed's reappearance was his wake-up call. This was the moment when Parker had to accept that his fairy tale could not survive even one strong blast of reality. That standing on high moral ground didn't, in the end, protect you from much of anything.

Even worse, this was the moment she had been dreading ever since she had first kissed him. The moment when he realized that loving her, loving a woman who was about to bear another man's child, was simply too messy and painful and complicated.

It was simply too hard.

"Do you know what I really think, Sarah? I think you want this meeting with Ed." Parker's tone was rough, suddenly, and his eyes had darkened until no blue remained. Sarah flinched, though with some part of her mind she understood that this was just his jealous misery scraping the smooth surfaces from the dialogue. "You *want* to see him."

He didn't mean that. He didn't believe that.

"In a way, I guess I do," she said carefully. "I want to face him, because he must be faced. That's all. I want to know what I'm up against as I try to piece together my new life."

"He'll want you back. He'll want his child." Parker shook his head, a deep line of anger slashing the skin between his brows. "What man wouldn't?"

She smiled at his innocence, at the profound goodness he possessed that made him believe such things. "This man didn't, Parker. His first reaction was to tell me to get rid of it."

"But he's had time to think. Time to come to his senses. He'll want his child." He wiped his hand over his eyes, as if he could wipe away his visions. "And you'll say yes, won't you, Sarah? For the baby's sake, if not your own. You'll say yes, and then the three of you will be the perfect little family."

Oh, God. Parker, don't.

She felt her throat close up as she turned away from him.

"The perfect family is *your* fantasy, Parker. Not mine."

THE MINUTE SARAH SAW ED, standing next to the bar, his body rigid with annoyance that she had dared to keep him waiting, everything about this terrible meeting suddenly became shockingly simple.

She didn't have to struggle with the moral dilemma of what to do if he had, as Parker feared, come to try to win her back. She didn't have to wrestle with her conscience, didn't have to weigh her own selfish desires against her deep commitment to provide the best possible life for her baby.

She didn't have to search her soul, trying to determine whether she was, by rejecting Ed, making her child pay the price for the mother's sins.

There was no struggle to find an answer, because there was no question.

She could never go back to Ed. And it wasn't because she had fallen in love with a more-rugged face, a sweeter nature, a sexier body. Even if she had never met Parker Tremaine, she could never have returned to the miserable, one-sided relationship she'd endured with Ed.

She had changed, in these few weeks. She had grown. She had learned a lot about herself, and a lot about love.

She didn't love Ed, and a family without love was the worst life any mother could offer a child. And Ed, petty, vain, tyrannical Ed, would be the worst father, much worse than no father at all.

So it simply didn't matter what he had come to say. She would never, ever go back to him.

With at least that much of the burden lifted from her shoulders, she found herself able to walk up to him serenely.

"Hi," she said politely. "I'm sorry I'm late."

"Damn, Sarah." Ed stared at his watch, as if he simply couldn't believe what the hands were telling him. "I've got a plane to catch. Won't you ever learn how to get anywhere on time?"

She looked at him evenly. "If you're short of time for this meeting, Ed, maybe you shouldn't waste any more of it complaining about how late I am."

He did a small double take. She had never talked like that to him before. But he covered it quickly. She could almost watch the progression of thoughts across his handsome features. He wanted to be indignant, but he realized it wasn't prudent.

So that must mean he wanted something. He obviously didn't feel that he occupied the power position in whatever discussion he'd come here to have. Selfish need was the only thing that ever forced him to moderate his temper.

"Sorry," he said with an obvious but not very successful attempt at being gracious. He gestured to one of the lounge tables. "Shall we sit down?"

She accepted the chair he held out for her. But he didn't sit right away himself. She thought he might be staring at her waistline. The dress she wore had, over the past few weeks, grown a little bit too tight. Soon she would have to buy maternity clothes.

But he wasn't. She followed his gaze, and she saw that he was clearly eyeing her noticeably larger breasts.

She found herself flushing with anger. She hated having his gaze on her. How had she ever tolerated his hands? Her stomach tightened, and she felt a brief, vicious return of the morning sickness she thought she'd left behind.

When he realized that she had caught him staring, he glanced away. "You look well," he said awkwardly. "Are you?"

"Yes," she said, setting aside her annoyance. "The morning sickness only lasted a few weeks. I'm fine now. I've seen a doctor up here. The baby is fine, too."

He didn't respond. He just shifted in his seat and looked anywhere but at her, as if any mention of the baby made him uncomfortable. But she didn't allow herself the luxury of hating him, of despising his cold, selfish denial of this helpless child he had fathered.

She couldn't afford to think about that. She was determined to keep this civil. He had a right to know the basic details.

"I may have miscalculated the due date at first. The doctor up here says I'm about five months pregnant now. The baby will probably be born in June."

He toyed with his napkin.

"Really," he said, obviously struggling to say the right thing, strike the right attitude. "That's good. I guess." He looked up, his eyes tense. "I'm sorry, but I still think you were wrong, deciding to go through with it. It would have been so much simpler if you would just have—"

"Not for me," she said with enough unyielding emphasis to make him look away again.

She leaned back in her chair and gazed at him steadily, amazed at how angry the suggestion could still make her.

He had no concept of how real this baby had become to her, did he? To him, it was still a *problem,* a *thing.*

"Ed, let's get to the point. Why are you here? You do know, don't you, that it's far too late now to be hoping I'll agree to any procedure."

"Of course I know that." He offered her his best half-profile, his most wounded expression. "God, Sarah. I'm not really a monster, you know."

She let her silence speak for itself.

He flushed. "You've really turned into a bitch, haven't you? I saw this change starting in you even before we broke up. Once, at the beginning, you were such a sweet woman, Sarah. So easy to get along with."

Once, at the beginning, she had been such a fool. So easy to push around. So grateful that a strong, steady man wanted to make a strong, steady life with her. So relieved that she was not going to end up like her mother, bouncing from one weak, faithless man to another like a marble in a pinball machine.

Ed had liked that needy, insecure woman just fine. What bully wouldn't?

But she didn't say any of that to him. What was the point in needling each other? She just wanted to get this over with. It was giving her a headache.

"You know, I had hoped that when we met again you wouldn't be bitter, Sarah. I had hoped you might have taken time to see this from my perspective. To see how I've suffered, too, because of what's happened." He tugged on his cuffs, sniffing slightly to show his disappointment. "But apparently I overestimated you."

"No, I think you overestimated *yourself,* Ed. And your so-called suffering."

He bristled, offended. He set his chiseled lips into

an unforgiving line. Touching her aching temple with her fingers, Sarah sighed, sorry that she had risen to the bait yet again.

"Look," she said quietly. "This is pointless. Why don't you just tell me why you've come to Firefly Glen?"

He tossed his napkin onto the table in a weary gesture of resignation. "Okay. Here's why. I want to know what it will take—" he paused "—to keep this quiet."

She had been prepared for many things, but not this. She couldn't even be sure what he was talking about.

"To keep what quiet?" She narrowed her eyes, trying to figure it out. "I don't see how I can keep people from learning that I'm having a baby. A baby has a way of making itself known, especially after it's born."

"No." He tightened his mouth. "I mean my involvement. My involvement in your problem."

She tilted her head. "I think you'd better be more specific," she said carefully.

"All right." He folded his hands on the table, the picture of rational male patience face-to-face with unreasonable female emotion. "What I want to know, Sarah, is exactly how much money it's going to take to make this problem go away for me. How much you are asking for your silence."

She didn't trust herself to speak. She just looked at him, feeling a strange pity for the woman she used to be, all those light-years ago. How could she ever have been so weak as to think this man was strong?

He fumbled in his pocket and pulled out a long, narrow brown envelope. "I've had the papers drawn up. All that's left is to fill in the numbers and write the check."

He finally noticed the look of quiet disgust on her

face. Alarmed, he pulled out his most-reliable weapon. His charming, wheedling tone, the one she'd heard him use so many times with difficult parents.

"The truth is, I'm hoping to get married soon, Sarah," he said with a boyish candor. "I've fallen in love. She's the most wonderful woman. But she's very young. Very innocent. She's the daughter of the chairman of the board. It's a terrific chance for me. If he—I mean, *she*— ever found out about you and me..."

He spread his hands, as if surely she could appreciate the dilemma. "It's a very high profile family. If they find out that I have a pregnant ex-girlfriend who could show up at any moment, making headlines, causing trouble—"

Sarah almost laughed, but with effort she controlled herself. Did Ed have delusions of grandeur now—did he really think that their tawdry affair and illegitimate baby would make "headlines" anywhere in the world? They wouldn't even make headlines here in Firefly Glen.

"What is this wonderful woman's name?"

"Melissa," he said cautiously. She noticed that he carefully omitted the last name. "Why do you ask?"

Without answering, Sarah took the envelope from his hands. She opened it and scanned the brief legal document that lay, in triplicate, within. It was almost obscenely simple. For *X* amount, Sarah Lennox absolved Ed McCutcheon of any responsibility for the child they had conceived.

Probably, she thought, she ought to turn it over to a lawyer. Most people would say that she was a fool. Here was her chance to take him for every cent she could get. Just scrawl in a few nice, round zeros after her favorite number and...

But she didn't want anything from Ed.

Except her freedom.

For extra convenience, the envelope even held a pen. She pulled it out, clicked it open and boldly wrote "One dollar" on the empty line. Then she signed her name, pulled off a copy for herself and handed the document back into Ed's limp, disbelieving hands.

He looked at the papers, then at her, with a kind of bewildered anxiety in his eyes, as if he suspected a trap.

"One dollar?"

"That's right." She stood. "Don't just sit there with your mouth open, Ed. You're free. Put the dollar on the table. We'll leave it as a tip for the waitress. And then go on back to California."

He kept frowning at the contract, turning it over again and again, as if he thought she might have used disappearing ink to scribble in some diabolical trick.

She began to walk away.

"Sarah, wait." He caught her arm, stalling her. "Are you planning something? Why did you want to know Melissa's name?"

She looked down at his blunt-fingered hand, so alien now against her skin.

"Because," she said, a cold distaste turning her voice to sheer ice. "I'll be mentioning the poor child in my prayers tonight. If she's really going to marry you, Ed, she's going to need all the help she can get."

CHAPTER SIXTEEN

IN THE CLEAR DELFT-BLUE SKY overhead, the winter sun looked as pale and thin as a white dinner mint. But its appearance was deceptive. As the afternoon wore on, that anemic-looking sun managed to muscle the temperature up to almost fifty degrees.

The tourists took off their sweaters and tied them around their waists. Worried officials inspected the ice palace, checking for weak spots. The ice sculptors huddled in anxious clusters, fretting that their creations would not last the day.

The only people who welcomed the heat wave were the Firefly Glen United Charities volunteers, who stood shivering, waiting to make their heroic dip into the freezing water of Llewellyn's Lake.

Sarah didn't care about the weather at all. For the past hour, ever since she left her meeting with Ed, she had been wandering through the exhibits at the ice sculpture contest, only half seeing anything, just hoping to buy enough time to sort out her muddled thoughts.

The theme this year was "People We Love." And the sixty-five entrants had, as usual, interpreted the theme in sixty-five different ways. One artist had chosen Scooby-Doo, another had carved a bust of Shakespeare, and a third had, in a fit of amusing candor, sculpted a six-foot replica of himself.

Sarah was standing in front of an anatomically correct sculpture of Marilyn Monroe when she spotted Harry and Emma walking by. They seemed so contentedly absorbed in each other, she almost didn't speak. Harry's arm was around Emma's shoulders, and her fingers were hooked casually over the edge of his back pocket. It completed a simple, magical circle.

Sarah would have let them pass. But they saw her first.

"Sarah!" Emma dragged Harry over, though he clearly would rather have been alone with his wife on a planet all their own. "How are you?"

Sarah dug through the ashes of her mood and salvaged one real smile for Emma's joy. "Great," she said. "I guess I don't have to ask how *you* are."

Emma grinned. "It shows, huh?"

Sarah caught Harry's eye. "A little. You're pretty much glowing like a lightbulb, Emma."

"Well, here's my special secret. A rip-roaring fight does wonders for the circulation." Emma grinned. "And making up afterward is good exercise, too."

Harry was flushing, so Sarah took pity on him and changed the subject. "How's Mike Frome doing? My uncle says he donated some of Mike's restitution hours to the city. Has he started working yet?"

Harry nodded. "He's been painting Parker's office. Nothing too hard, but we'll keep him busy, I guess. We considered the chain gang, busting rocks, but then we thought, no, the kid can't be trusted with rocks."

His brown eyes twinkled, and finally Sarah could see why Emma was so crazy about her husband. He had a lot of laughter in those eyes.

"But Mike's worst punishment," he went on, still smiling, "is having to put up with Suzie. She's our clerk, and she's a pistol. She never shuts up. She rags Mike about Justine Millner so bad the kid's going to get a complex. But he's getting his eyes opened about Justine, so maybe it's worth it."

Emma snorted. "I don't know how you get to be eighteen whole years old without already having your eyes opened about Justine Millner, but hey, maybe the kid's slow." She glanced wryly at the Marilyn Monroe ice sculpture. "Or maybe—" She jerked a thumb toward the amazing translucent breasts, which hadn't melted an inch, even in all this heat. "You know."

Sarah laughed. Emma looked around, as if noticing for the first time that Sarah was alone. "Hey. Where's Parker?"

"Parker? I'm not sure," Sarah answered, as normally as she could.

"You're not sure? You two have been breathing the same square inch of air for two weeks straight. And now you're not sure where he is?"

Sarah shrugged casually. "I think maybe he had to work."

Harry shook his head. "No, we put a temp on call today so that everyone could…"

But Emma had caught on. She glared at Harry, who finally got the message, too.

"I don't know, though," he amended awkwardly. "Maybe he had to go in."

Sarah smiled. "Maybe," she agreed. Harry was a very nice man.

Emma touched her arm. "Hey, we were going to go get a hot chocolate over at the elementary school. Want to come?"

"No. I'm fine." Sarah nodded firmly. "Really. You go ahead."

"Well, okay." Emma looked worried. Then she grinned. "But remember what I said, girlfriend. Sometimes a good argument is the sexiest thing you can do for a relationship."

Sarah shook her head and waved Emma away with a laughing smile.

But when they were gone, her smile faded away quickly. She moved on down the rows of sculptures numbly. She had the strangest feeling of needing to see everything today, needing to commit to memory all the special sights and sounds of Firefly Glen.

The snow banked up against the buildings, like piles of glittering white sequins. The laughter of children, carrying clear across the crisp air. The tattered brown lace of bare tree limbs, waving against a powder blue horizon. The ice palace, wetly gleaming, already dissolving by microscopic degrees under the rays of that powerful white disc in the sky.

It was as if she knew her hours here were numbered. And she wanted strong, clear memories to take with her, to pack and unwrap at home.

She tried to keep her spirits from sinking too far. She would survive. And somehow, someway, she would create a home for her baby. That was the only thing that really mattered.

In fact, it was actually much better that Parker had been forced to face the problems now. No real harm had been done in these two weeks of romantic fantasy. They had made love once, and the rest had been achingly innocent. They had been like children, willfully oblivious and naive but not wicked.

Just children. Playing house in the mouth of the volcano.

But they had been lucky. They could walk away now, and know that they had not permanently damaged anyone. How much worse it would have been if he had found out later, found out two, three, four years from now that he simply couldn't stay the course.

Later his defection would have been truly terrible. Later, when her child knew him. Depended on him. Loved him, just as Sarah had so foolishly allowed herself to do.

She tried to tell herself that she was lucky she hadn't made another terrible mistake. Lucky that these risks she'd foolishly taken hadn't led to real disaster.

She took a deep breath. She knew now what she needed to do. Once she got home, once she got past the worst of this, she would sit down and make a new plan. She would map out a safe life for herself and her baby, down to the minute, if possible. She would think it through carefully. She would accept only complete control, total security. She would depend on no one but herself. She would, if she could, eliminate all risks.

She was almost at the end of the last row of sculptures. Only one exhibit remained ahead of her. Her car was in the other direction, but she decided to go look at it. At least she could truly say she had seen them all.

And then she would go back to Winter House, and tell her uncle her decision. She would be flying back to Florida tomorrow.

It wasn't the biggest sculpture she'd seen today. Or the showiest. But it was, perhaps, the most beautiful. Only about two feet tall, it was a magical butterfly carved in the act of rising from a rose, its icy wings catching rainbows in the brilliant winter sunlight.

It had been carved with great delicacy, and it was unusually thin, almost mystically transparent. In today's unseasonable temperatures, the tips of the wings had already begun to melt.

The artist, who was sitting on a folding chair beside his creation, didn't seem at all disturbed by the fact that his sculpture was doomed. Sarah watched his peaceful face, turned up to catch the rays of the sun as if he were a surfer in Malibu, with no thought but enjoying the warmth.

"Hi," she said impulsively. "I just wanted to tell you that I love your butterfly. It's very beautiful."

He opened his eyes without straightening up. His eyes were beautiful, too, ringed with thick black lashes. Extremely sensitive eyes. And extremely intelligent.

He smiled broadly. "Hey, man, thanks. I liked that one, too."

She noticed that he was already referring to it in the past tense. She watched helplessly as one shining teardrop of water dripped from the butterfly's wing. It made her feel, absurdly, like crying. She wanted to catch the drop and hold it, put it back, make it stay. She wanted to stop this dying by degrees.

"Don't you mind?" She knew she ought to just move on, but she couldn't. She wanted to understand where he found this serenity, this amazing acceptance of the inevitable. "Don't you feel..." She searched for a word. "Cheated? Cheated to have worked so hard on something so ephemeral? Something that simply can't last?"

He glanced over at his butterfly. "Not really," he said pleasantly. "It's the rules of the game, you know?"

"No. I'm not sure I understand."

"Well." He scratched his two-day growth of beard. "I don't know. It's just that all the best things in life don't last very long, right? Thunderstorms. Rainbows. Bird songs. The perfect hamburger. Great sex."

He grinned. "They kind of streak through, and if you're lucky enough to be in the right place at the right time, you reach out and touch 'em. But you can't hold on. It ruins stuff like that if you try to hold on."

Sarah was temporarily unable to think of a sensible response.

"But, hey." He raised his brows. "I guess you know all about that, huh?"

How did he know that? She wondered if her heartache was as clear on her face as Emma's joy had been on hers. "What do you mean?"

He gestured toward her stomach. "I mean, well, excuse me for getting personal, but you're going to have a baby, right?"

She hesitated, shocked to discover that her "secret" could be visible to a discerning stranger. But suddenly she realized that she was glad—that it felt lovely and healthy to discuss her baby openly. A baby now. Not a secret.

She nodded. "Yes, I am."

"So what can be more ephemeral than that? The baby will be like your very best ice sculpture, but it won't be yours for long. You'll make it, and you'll take care of it, and then, when the times comes, you'll have to let it go."

Sarah swallowed hard. And then she gasped softly. She put her hand on her stomach, feeling for the first time a tiny quiver inside her, like the sleepy beat of butterfly wings.

He grinned again, and then he leaned back, closing his eyes, returning to his mindless basking in the sun.

"So yeah," he murmured absently. "Beautiful things are like that."

SHE COULDN'T FIND PARKER, though she practically ran from one end of the square to the other. She went to the Sheriff's Department, the café, even back to the Firefly Suites, in case he had been looking for her there.

She checked everywhere, asked everyone. But no one knew where Parker had gone.

Finally, almost exhausted, she drove back to Winter House. She would rest a little, then renew her search by telephone.

As she pulled into the driveway, she saw his Jeep. Her heart stumbled. It felt a little like a miracle, and she had been afraid she was out of miracles.

But he was here. He had been here, at Winter House, all along.

He was coming down the steps from the house, his hands jammed into his jacket pockets, heading toward his car. He still looked tired, she thought. His hair was tousled and his head was bent as he walked in the face of the wind.

She yanked hard to engage the emergency brake and scrambled out of her car as fast as she could release the seat belt. He looked up when he heard her. "Sarah?"

She began to run. His face changed, and then he was running, too. They met somewhere between the two cars, colliding awkwardly, all desperation and no grace.

"Sarah!" He pulled her into his arms, kissing any part of her his lips could reach—her hair, her chin, her eyes, her mouth. "Oh, my God, Sarah. Tell me you didn't go back to him."

She spoke against his lips, the words half-distinct. "I didn't go back to him."

He let out a low groan. "Thank God." He tilted her

head so that he could look into her face. "Sarah. I'm so sorry. Can you ever forgive me?"

She could hardly speak. She had run only a few yards, but her heart was racing as if the distance had been a marathon.

"No," she said. "I mean yes, oh, God, you know there is nothing to forgive. Parker, I was such a fool—"

"No, *I* was." He closed his eyes on a deep, ragged breath. "I was terrified, Sarah. I was so afraid that I was going to lose you. You must have loved him once, and I was so afraid that if you...if he—"

He couldn't finish. Infinitely touched, she reached up and pushed a strand of his dark, silky hair out of his eyes. "I told you I never loved him. That was true. Until I met you, I didn't even know what love was."

He looked at her with a gaze that was equal parts hope and fear. His eyes were so blue, she thought. They were as blue as the sky above them right now. She felt a sudden, distinctly maternal urge to take every fleck of fear or pain out of those wonderful, beautiful eyes. She wanted to leave only the hope. And the love.

"Can you forgive me, Sarah? You had every right to meet him today. I understand that. I always did understand it. I was just so damn scared."

"I know," she said. "I know."

"I want you to know that I understand he's going to be a part of your life forever. I can't promise to like it. But I *can* promise to stop being such a possessive, jealous jackass."

"Oh, really? You can promise that?" She smiled. "What if Ed and I need to confer daily about the baby?"

He hesitated. "On the phone?"

She laughed softly. "I was thinking over lunch."

He gritted his teeth, but he managed to nod. "Even then. I don't want to share you. But if I have to, I will. I meant it, Sarah. I *will* stop being such a possessive, jealous jackass."

She squinted thoughtfully. "What if Ed needs to spend the night occasionally, to help see the baby through an attack of colic?"

But now he knew she was teasing. He tightened his grip around her waist. "The man can move into the downstairs bedroom and play tiddlywinks on my dining room table, for all I care." His voice was husky with emotion. "Just as long as you're in the upstairs bedroom with me."

"Liar." She rested her cheek against the soft warmth of his leather jacket. Her breath misted against the gold star.

"But you don't have to promise me anything," she said. "That's what I wanted to tell you. You don't have to promise me anything at all."

He had begun to stroke her hair. It was as if, after their desperate race to touch, to speak, to explain, they had found their way to the other side and entered a place of profound peace. "I don't?"

She shook her head, a tiny movement that he probably barely felt. "No, you don't. It's enough that you love me today, that you want me today. I've never understood that before. But I do now. I have learned a lot in the past few weeks, Parker. From this odd, wonderful little town. From the baby. And from you."

He didn't jump in to contradict her. He obviously sensed that she was saying something that mattered a great deal to her. And he was listening. She loved him more than ever, just for that sensitive silence.

"I've spent so much of my life trying to control the future," she said. "From the time I was a little girl, I've been practically obsessed with it. I've made elaborate, detailed plans that somehow gave me the illusion of safety. I think I wanted to believe that I could take a pencil and paper and plan away any risk of failure or pain."

He tightened his grip and put a kiss on the crown of her head.

"But I've finally realized that trying to control the future is absurd. And arrogant. Because if you think you can decide what the future *will* be, that means you think you know exactly what the future *should* be. And no one ever knows that."

She closed her eyes against a sudden sting of tears. "This baby, for instance. I didn't plan this baby, and yet it's one of the most wonderful things that ever happened to me."

She lifted her face to his, though she knew her eyes were moist and aching with love. "And you. I could never have planned you."

"I didn't plan you, either." He gazed at her with eyes warm with kisses to come. "Although I think I might, on one of my loneliest winter nights, have *dreamed* you."

Somehow she managed not to kiss him. She had just one more thing to say.

"So here's my promise to you." She put her hands on the lapels of his supple jacket. "I promise to stop trying to plan the future. I'll let it unfold in its own way, in all its terrifying, wonderful mystery. Things could go wrong. Someday you may find that you can't really love a woman who carries another man's child. But that doesn't mean we can't have today."

"Sarah—"

"I promise it, Parker. No more plans. Just today. I promise to cherish the way you feel about me today, without asking whether it will last forever."

He smiled. "I guess we both think we sound like very reasonable, mature adults, don't we? But let's see if I've got this right. I'll try to live with my fear that you might stop loving me. And you'll try to live with *your* fear that I'll stop loving *you*."

She looked at him. It did sound a little ridiculous, put that way.

"Essentially, yes. We'll both accept a level of fear and insecurity we were never willing to accept before."

He put his hand under her chin.

"Or maybe this would be easier," he suggested. "How about if we just go inside, tear up your plane ticket, tell your uncle we're getting married next week, and then drive back to my house and make love to each other until we can't breathe, or talk or even think? Until there's no room in our hearts for anything as foolish as fear."

She felt her pulse begin to race. Her eyes filled with sweet, fiery tears.

"Now that," she said softly, "is a plan."

EPILOGUE

THEY WERE MARRIED two weeks later, on election day.

Parker said he felt he owed the town something exciting to do that day, since he had denied them the thrill of a dramatic, family-feud race for sheriff.

To everyone's surprise—except maybe Emma, who guessed, and Sarah, who had been in Parker's arms when the decision was made—Parker announced that he would not seek a second term in office, leaving Harry to run unopposed.

Shortly thereafter, Parker told his closest friends that he planned to set up his own law practice, in the big brick professional building at the opposite end of Main. He said he was pretty sure he could make a decent living defending Ward Winters from defamation lawsuits alone.

The gossips in town were almost sick from all the delicious, gooey news, like children let loose in a bakery. Emma Dunbar had been seen kissing Griffin Cahill. Harry Dunbar had nearly killed Griffin with his bare hands. Inexplicably, Emma and Harry were living together again. Parker Tremaine was going to marry Sarah. Sarah was going to have a baby. *And, oh, my heavens, have you heard, Parker's not the father!*

Sarah knew that Parker made sure she never heard the worst of it. And by the time the wedding came around, it was all fairly old news. Glenners liked Parker Tremaine, that was the bottom line. And if Parker could live with the mystery baby, they supposed they could, too.

And besides, they did love a wedding.

Winter House, filled with flowers and music and hundreds of smiling, weeping people, had never looked more beautiful. Its eccentric, Gothic-monastery charm, Ward explained wryly, was the perfect stage for anachronistic tribal rituals of high drama.

Sarah remembered very little of the ceremony, which had passed in a blur of confused joy and trepidation. She remembered best the steady feel of Ward's arm under her fingers as she walked down the aisle, and then the familiar, comforting thrill of Parker's hand in hers.

But she knew that she would never, never, forget the reception.

Everyone was there.

Madeline Alexander had stayed up every night for two weeks, sewing Sarah a wedding dress, so of course she was there, coming by every few minutes to adjust a pearl button or tug at a ruche of lace.

Harry and Emma came, too, of course. Emma was the matron of honor, beautiful in blue, and Harry wore his shiny new star with a rather endearing, grateful pride.

Eileen O'Malley had been the flower girl, and as she stood beside Sarah, so serious in her blue velvet, her red hair a fire of curls around her pudgy shoulders, Sarah had caught her first, breathtaking glimpse of the beauty to come.

Heather Delaney came, too, though she wore her pager and had to leave halfway through the reception to deliver a baby. She and Sarah exchanged glances as

the beeper went off, and Sarah knew they were both
thinking the same thing. Someday that little electronic
sound would call her to Sarah's side, to bring her child
into the world. Heather kissed Sarah as she left and
hugged her, too, something the ultra-contained young
doctor rarely did.

Theo catered the food, which was served in the dining
hall by candlelight, of course. No wedding feast had ever
been more visually enticing, or more delicious, and yet
Theo had stayed in a constant agony of embarrassment,
sure that she hadn't lived up to her own standards.

Even Mike Frome was there, working off some restitution hours by serving hors d'oeuvres to the guests.
Sarah winked at him as he went by, handsome in his
tuxedo. He'd worked off about one square foot of a fif-
ty-foot window so far. Poor Mike, Sarah thought. He was
going to be working for the Winters family for years.

Actually, everything started well. Sarah and Parker
danced the first dance, posed for pictures, shared champagne and cut the cake.

And then the trouble began.

Justine Millner walked by, wearing a bright red gown
made out of approximately three-quarters of a yard of
silk. Watching her, Mike Frome tripped on something—
Parker later suggested it might have been his tongue—
and sent a plate of hors d'oeuvres flying into the library
window, which broke.

Ward, who simply couldn't believe it, yelled something rude, to which Mike's grandfather, Granville, took
offense. The two old men began shoving each other, and
several of the younger men started circling them, trying
to find a safe way into the fray.

Madeline Alexander began to cry, wailing that surely

her beloved Ward was going to die. And at that Bridget O'Malley reared up like the warrior queen she had been born to be, and announced that Madeline had better stop acting as if she had dibs on Ward Winters, which she didn't.

Jocelyn Waitely, who had knocked back too much champagne, joined in the debate, announcing loudly that *she* was the one Ward liked the best, which caused her husband Bourke to dash his drink into the fireplace, causing a semi-spectacular explosion that sent the rest of the guests screaming for the exits.

Sarah watched in mesmerized horror as her lovely reception turned into a scene from an Irwin Allen movie. Somehow, just as the chaos reached its peak, Parker came to her rescue.

He took her hand, pulled her into the one remaining quiet corner and, looking deeply into her eyes, asked huskily, "So, Mrs. Tremaine. This is what you've married. Want an annulment yet?"

She settled into his arms. "Nope," she said. "How about you?"

"Well, no," he answered, kissing her nose. "But, then, this was my town already."

"And now it's mine." She put her hands on either side of his face. "I love Firefly Glen, Parker Tremaine. And I love you."

He grinned. "As much as Madeline Alexander loves your uncle?"

She considered it carefully. "I don't know," she admitted. "I still wouldn't set myself on fire for you."

"Then come with me," he said, pulling her to her feet. "Let's get out of this insane asylum and go home. Perhaps I can start that fire myself."

Dear Reader,

I'll admit it right up front. I love babies. I'm a hopeless cornball on the subject. Madison Avenue must love me. I'll buy anything if a freckle-faced little boy asks me to. I'm even worse about my own children. Avoid going to lunch with me unless you want to hear every precious word my son uttered this morning. Don't come over unless you're dying to watch the blurry video of my daughter's school play. But here's my other confession. I don't love babies *because* I had two of my own. I love them *in spite* of that.

If you made a list of the pros and cons of having babies, the cons would fill a notebook. They are expensive and exhausting. They're terrible conversationalists. They have shocking table manners. And let's be honest. Sometimes they don't smell quite right. The pros... Well, there's just one, really. One big, wonderful pro. Babies make the world new again.

They put the magic back in the merry-go-round, the sparkle back in snow. They make you believe in fairies and flying elephants and Forever. They cleanse the past of pain and fill the future with promise. Best of all, they remind you that happiness is not complicated.

Griffin and Heather, the hero and heroine of *Babies in Arms*, knew all this once upon a time. But ten years ago they bitterly ended their engagement, and the world hasn't held much magic since. Until the babies come to stay...

I hope you enjoy their story. And if your son said anything precious this morning, remember I'm one of the few cornballs who would really like to hear about it.

Warmly,

Kathleen O'Brien

BABES IN ARMS

To Mikey, because I'm crazy 'bout you.

CHAPTER ONE

FOR ONE CONFUSED and horrible split second when he first woke up that Monday morning, Griffin Cahill felt—

He couldn't even say it. He stuffed his aching head under his silk-covered pillow to make the word go away. But there it was, darting around his brain like a sniper, eluding every attempt to capture and evict.

Old.

Griffin Cahill felt old.

It didn't last long, of course. Because it was ridiculous. Griffin was only thirty-four. He was mystifyingly healthy, considering how little attention he paid the issue. He was active and fit and, by some lucky combination of mix-and-match genes, the first Cahill since the *Mayflower* who didn't look like a horse.

Definitely not old.

The sniper receded.

Still, if he wasn't old, Griffin wondered as he emerged from the pillow and slid his feet over the edge of the bed, why did he ache all over? He hadn't played tennis yesterday. He hadn't been out fishing yet this year. He hadn't—

And then he remembered. *Miranda.* He was achy because he'd spent the night with Marvelous Miranda, who got her blue eyes from Bausch & Lomb, her blond hair from L'Oréal, and her high spirits from a bottle of Chivas Regal. But she got her body, and her flair for using it creatively, straight from God.

Griffin ran his fingers through his tangled hair. That proved it, then. Women like Miranda damn sure didn't think he was old. They thought he was a state-of-the-art roller coaster, and one ride was never enough.

So there. *Goodbye, sniper. And good riddance.*

Griffin's housekeeper didn't come until noon on Mondays, so Griffin gathered the sheets off the bed and dropped them into the laundry chute himself. He disliked an unmade bed—especially if it still held a whiff of last night's perfume.

As he always did, he plotted his day while he showered. Coffee and toast, a couple of hours in the darkroom, two interviews with candidates for this year's photography scholarship. Then, at five, that damn city council meeting.

Griffin made a mental note. Never, ever again allow anyone to talk him into sitting on the city council. That was probably why he'd woken up feeling so rotten this morning. The politics of Firefly Glen could make a grumpy old man out of Peter Pan himself.

If they weren't planning to vote on Heather Delaney's rezoning request today, he might have skipped the meeting altogether. Heather needed his vote, though of course she hadn't asked him for help. Griffin was well aware that she'd cut out her tongue with a pair of nail scissors before she'd ask him for anything.

Still, he'd go, and he'd vote for her rezoning. Not to do Heather a favor, but merely because it was fair.

He had finished the *Glen Gazette* and started on the

Wall Street Journal when the doorbell rang. He was tempted not to answer. It might be Miranda, who had a tendency to think the Griffin Cahill amusement park was open twenty-four hours a day, which it wasn't.

But he put his mug on the butcher-block table and crossed his sunny, two-story great room to reach the door. He knew how to get rid of Miranda, or any other uninvited female. And he knew how to do it with a smile.

He opened the door, letting his eyes and his body language send the required rebuff—what a shame, it would have been delightful, but this simply isn't a good time.

Unfortunately, it wasn't Miranda. It was someone else, someone who didn't give a damn about Griffin's body language. It was Griffin's little brother, Jared.

And in his arms Jared was holding his twin eight-month-old sons, Stewart and Robert.

Jared lived on Long Island. Hours away. Griffin hadn't seen him in months. Jared was a corporate lawyer, a hotshot. He hated small towns, Firefly Glen in particular. And where was Katie, Jared's wife—the one who was officially in charge of those squirming creatures?

For several seconds, Griffin was too surprised to do anything but stare at the babies stupidly. They stared back, frowning in openmouthed curiosity at this man they probably didn't recognize, though he had met them several times, and each time had brought ridiculously expensive gifts.

"Jared?" Griffin wasn't doing very well verbally, either. He squinted into the spring sun, trying to read his brother's face. "What— Is anything wrong?"

"No. Well, yes." Jared shifted the boys higher on

his arms, to balance the burden. "Damn it, Griff. Let me in."

Reluctantly Griffin moved out of the doorway, and Jared lurched in, bumping clumsily into everything with the huge blue-plaid plastic cases he had slung over each shoulder.

Griffin's early detection radar was sending out a signal. This didn't look right. He mustered a smile for the boys, who were starting to get on his nerves. They kept staring with those wide, unblinking eyes. And their little pink pudgy lips were drooling something suspiciously milky in hue.

He managed not to make a sound when Jared jostled the Chihuly bowl that stood on a pedestal by the door. The large green glass rocked precariously. Griffin's heart waited politely, watching Jared steady the bowl with one hip, before resuming its regular beat.

Jared didn't even look alarmed, much less apologetic. He merely scowled at the museum-quality piece and shook his head. "That will have to go."

"Really?" Griffin raised his eyebrows. "And why is that?"

"Because glass is dangerous." Jared scanned the large, simple room with a critical eye. "God, Griffin, why do you have so much glass around here?"

"I like it." Griffin let his voice get chilly. "Frankly, I hadn't noticed it being particularly dangerous. Most of the time it just sits there."

"Well, when you have kids around, it can be lethal."

"Perhaps. But you may remember I don't have children."

Griffin saw the discomfort dig furrows into his brother's face. Jared was obviously miserable. Griffin glanced at the boys, at their overflowing bags of supplies. Then he glanced back at Jared.

"Or do I?" he asked mildly.

Jared sighed, a heavy, helpless sound that came from the depths of his diaphragm. He plopped down onto the large beige sectional sofa, his boys still safely in each arm.

"I'm sorry, Griff," he said. "If there were any other way. If there were anyone else we could ask…" He groaned, obviously reading Griffin's face correctly. "It's only for a few weeks, Griffin. I'll be back in just over three weeks."

Three weeks? Jared must be out of his mind. Griffin subdued a weird impulse to start talking very loudly and very fast, using his hands, like an Italian grandmother, like someone in a panic. Nonsense. Griffin never panicked. Not even at a moment like this.

"There must be someone else, Jared," he said slowly and rationally. "Where's Katie?"

"With her mother in Toledo. Remember her mother is having a hysterectomy? She'll be there for at least three weeks. She just can't handle the boys and her mom, too, so I promised I'd keep them while she was gone."

"If you *promised,* why are you—"

"I can't help it." One of the boys had grabbed Jared's nose, so his answer had a strangely adenoidal quality. "I've got to go to London. Tomorrow. Remember how we thought the Bailey merger had fallen through? No, of course you don't, I probably never even mentioned it. It's on again, and I have to be there for the negotiations."

"But why does it have to be you? Can't you send—"

"No. I can't send anyone. I have to be there, or it won't happen. It's worth millions, Griff. I have to be there."

Jared was beginning to sound a little desperate. Even worse, his tension seemed to communicate itself to the children. One of the babies...the one in red. Griffin couldn't ever remember which one wore red. Robert, maybe? Anyway, one of the boys screwed up his face, as if preparing to let loose a sympathetic wail.

Griffin began mentally scanning the possibilities. There had to be a way to fix this. He had learned in his early years as a photographer that even the trickiest problems had answers, if you just kept trying new ideas. Some small adjustment to an f-stop or the lighting, or the angle or the lens—and suddenly the "impossible" picture was yours for the taking.

"Didn't you have a nanny? An au pair or something?"

"Just for the first six months. She's with a different family now. Griff, relax. It won't be so hard. They're easy kids, really—"

"Doesn't Katie have a sister? I thought I remembered a sister."

Jared frowned at him. "Katie's an only child."

"Then who do you use for a baby-sitter the rest of the time?"

"Teenagers. That's fine for an hour here and there, but Katie would kill me if I left the boys with someone like that for three weeks." Jared leaned his cheek against the downy head of one of the babies. "She's going to kill me anyhow. She's always saying I spend too much time at work. This is just going to prove it."

He lifted his head, and Griffin was shocked by the raw desperation he saw in his brother's face. "Griffin, you've got to help me. You're the only person she'll trust. If it's anyone else, she'll really never forgive me."

Griffin tilted his head. "Come on, Jared. Katie doesn't even like me."

"Yes, she does. Well, she *trusts* you. You knew we'd named you as guardian in our wills. And besides, she's said several times that you'd make a great father."

Griffin merely raised one brow skeptically and waited. His little brother wasn't much of a liar.

"Well, okay, she said something kind of like that. She said it was too bad you were so allergic to commitment because fatherhood would probably be the saving of you." Jared looked sheepish. "But she thinks you're smart, and she knows you're reliable—except with women, of course."

Griffin half smiled. "Of course."

"And most important, she knows you'd never let anything bad happen to your own nephews, your own flesh and blood." Jared's voice deepened. "Griffin, you've got to do this. You've got to help me."

Griffin knew that look, that sad wrinkling of the high, Cahill brow, that twitch under one eye, that pulse just above the jaw. It was the "don't tell Mother I got suspended for fighting" look, the "don't tell Dad I wrecked the car" look. It was the "you're my big brother, and you can fix anything" look. Griffin was helpless against it. He always had been.

"Damn it, Jared," he said softly. "You're a serious pain in the ass, did you know that?"

But apparently Jared knew Griffin's looks, too. He grinned, obviously aware that he had won. "I knew it! I knew you'd say yes."

"I'll bet you did," Griffin said cynically. "I'll bet

your car is filled with the tacky, plastic paraphernalia of parenthood. Toys and bottles and—" he closed his eyes "—and a hundred other items too personal to imagine."

"Diapers, bro. Zillions of 'em. I even brought you one of those diaper pail deodorizers."

"How thoughtful," Griffin drawled, trying not to imagine the situations that would make such an item necessary. "You know, Jared, maybe this isn't such—"

But Jared was already on his feet. He handed one of the babies to Griffin—the one in red. Was it Robert? Griffin dimly suspected that he ought to find out before Jared drove away.

Jared took the other one—the one in blue—with him to the car. Griffin eyed his red-clad baby much as he might watch a ticking bomb, waiting for him to start bawling because Daddy had disappeared.

But Robert—or was it Stewart?—showed no signs of distress. He studied his uncle for a few seconds, then, apparently finding him boring, transferred his gaze to Griffin's crisply laundered shirt. He reached out a handful of fat fingers and, as slowly and carefully as the arm of an orbiting space shuttle might lock around a satellite, took hold of Griffin's top button.

The baby crowed softly, pleased at the success, his damp, toothless mouth beaming. Then, without warning and certainly without permission, he bent his wet face into Griffin's chest and began trying to gum the button right off the shirt.

Oh, great. It didn't take a Ph.D. in parenting to know that little hard plastic discs, like buttons, could be swallowed and were therefore *dangerous*. Like bleach and stairs and light sockets. And sea-green Chihuly art glass.

"I'm afraid not, champ," Griffin said softly, prying the button free before any damage could be done. Any damage to the baby, anyhow. His once-pristine shirt was soggy with little bubbles of milk that would undoubtedly dry into nasty, smelly stains.

Jared kept bustling back and forth, bringing in more blue plastic stuff than one car should have been able to hold. A portable playpen, two car seats, five boxes of diapers, a diaper pail, a crate of baby food, dozens of plastic bottles, a mechanical swing, a small plastic circle on wheels that Griffin couldn't figure out to save his life, and more.

And more and more and more. Griffin watched, stupefied, as his sleek, minimalist decor became as junky and cluttered as a carnival midway. God—could it possibly take this much gear to sustain two babies for three weeks? He had photographed whole armies setting out to war with less artillery than this.

"Don't look so shell-shocked." Jared, who was still holding one of his sons while deftly erecting the playpen with one hand and one knee, looked over at Griffin with a smile that struck Griffin as completely patronizing. "You'll get used to it. And maybe you can get someone to help you. Do any of your girlfriends have a secret hankering to be a mommy?"

"I certainly hope not." Griffin shuddered. "It would mean that my screening process was profoundly flawed."

Jared laughed. "You'll never change, will you, Griff?"

"Well, I'm definitely going to have to change my shirt."

"Don't bother. Not until they're asleep for the night, anyhow."

With that ominous warning, Jared finished with the playpen, then began digging one-handed through an overstuffed suitcase. He emerged with a pair of small stuffed toys. He handed one to the baby he still held, and then brought the other over to Griffin.

With a bubbling cry of obvious delight, Griffin's baby lurched eagerly toward the toy, a multicolored caterpillar whose eyes had clearly been removed. Griffin had to react quickly to hang on to the boy.

"Say hello to Mr. Giggles, Stewart," Jared said, waving the rather nasty toy in front of his son's face.

Ahh. Stewart, then, Griffin noted carefully. This one, the one in red, was Stewart.

Stewart clasped the toy blissfully toward his face, then immediately and, Griffin felt sure, deliberately, dropped it on the floor.

Patiently Griffin retrieved the caterpillar and handed it back to the boy.

"Yes, Stewart," he said. "Say hello to Mr. Giggles." He looked impassively over the boy's head at the shambles that once had been his elegant home. "And goodbye to life as we know it."

HEATHER DELANEY was so happy it almost frightened her.

As she stood by the fanciful front door to Spring House, she touched her fingers softly to the exquisite cut-glass doorknob. Then she ran them slowly along the cool edge of the beveled rainbow glass.

So lovely. And it all belonged to her. Well, to her and the Firefly Glen Mountain Savings and Trust Company.

She closed her eyes, absorbing through her other senses the happy camaraderie of the workers around her, half-a-dozen men who were whistling, wallpapering, painting, sanding, hammering and laughing.

They thought they were doing an ordinary remodeling job, just a routine cut-and-paste, as the architect had called it. They had no idea they were putting the finishing touches on a dream.

A deep thrill beat fast in her chest, and she took a long breath to slow its pace. But she couldn't help herself. She loved Spring House, this pink-and-white gingerbread Victorian mansion that was one of the Glen's four premiere "season" houses. Really loved it. She always had. She had dreamed of living here, working here, creating a family here, as long as she could remember.

And now, or at least as soon as the city council put their official seal of approval on her zoning variance this afternoon, the dream would come true. The remodeling was almost complete. Next Monday, Tuesday at the latest, she would be able to close up her little office over on Main Street and move her fledgling obstetrical practice here, to the first floor of Spring House.

She rested her forehead against the glass of the door, marveling that she had actually had the courage—or was it the foolishness?—to invest so much, both emotionally and financially, in one grand, outrageous, beautiful plan.

One dream.

Because frankly her track record with dreams was fairly abysmal.

She was thirty-three years old, and in all those years she had allowed herself to want—really, truly, desperately want—only three things. She had wanted to know her mother, who had died when she was three. Much later, she had wanted her father to win his war with cancer. And she had wanted Griffin Cahill to love her.

Yep. Heather Delaney was batting zero in the dream department.

Until today.

"Heather, have you fallen into a trance? We're going to be late. And where's your umbrella? It's raining buckets out there."

Heather smiled at Mary Brady, her bossy young receptionist and good friend. Mary was five years younger than Heather, but she had raised four brothers, and she hadn't been on the job ten minutes before she had begun running Heather's life, too.

"Maybe I *have* fallen into a trance," Heather said softly, transferring her gaze to the window, where she could see one of the dedicated workers kneeling in the mud, trying to get the last of the pansies planted before the rain drove him inside.

"Oh, yeah? Well, snap out of it."

Heather didn't respond. She touched the fine Irish lace curtain that fell like a soft white mist alongside the window. She could hardly bring herself to leave. She wanted to be here to see every minute of the transformation.

She took a deep breath, and the air was full of wonderful smells—wood chips and fresh paint and clean, sweet rain.

"I keep thinking I'm going to wake up and discover that none of this is really happening."

Mary had dug a second umbrella out of the hall stand, and she nudged it against the back of Heather's hand.

"Oh, it's happening all right. But it's going to be happening without you if you don't hurry. It's ten to five already."

Heather took the umbrella and began to open it. Mary was right. She needed to be there when the council took up her request. They might have questions.

With a low cry, Mary leaped to stop her. "Good grief, Doc, what's the matter with you? Do you want to jinx this vote before we ever get to city hall?"

Heather shook her head. "Mary, you know I don't believe in—"

"Well, I do. We've already got the rain. That's bad luck right there. You don't want to go opening any umbrellas indoors, not on a day as important as this."

Heather began to protest again, but somewhere in the back rooms of Spring House a loud bang sounded. A worker cursed, and then something shattered, something heavy and glass and probably dreadfully expensive.

Heather winced, thinking of her tight budget, but a look of true horror spread across Mary Brady's tanned and lovely face.

"Oh, no," she said; wide-eyed. "You don't think that was a mirror, do you?"

"Mary," Heather said sternly. "Stop pretending you're some old-country Irish fishwife. You know perfectly well that superstitions are pure nonsense. The city council has already given tentative approval to this zoning variance. Mayor Millner himself told me to go ahead with the construction. Nothing can happen now to spoil things. Not at this late date. Not even a broken mirror."

Mary returned the glare haughtily. "Tempting fate.

Overconfidence. That's as bad as a broken mirror any day."

Groaning, Heather stepped out onto the wide verandah and opened her umbrella. She didn't care what Mary said. She didn't care about rain or mirrors or anything else.

This was her day, the day Dr. Heather Delaney finally caught a dream by the tail and reeled it in. She intended to enjoy every minute of it.

"NO. NO BABIES. NO."

Griffin stared at his housekeeper, wondering what had ever possessed him to hire such a bad-tempered old bat. It was just one hour of babysitting. No big deal. You'd think he had asked her to dance naked in the middle of the town square.

"It's just an hour or two. I have to get to the council meeting. I have to go right now, Mrs. Waller. I'm already late. It started five minutes ago."

She folded her arms over her apron and stared at him. "No babies. I took this job, I never said babies."

Griffin cast a desperate glance out the half-open door. It was a monsoon out there. The five-minute ride to city hall would probably take fifteen in this weather. He tried to remember how many other things were on the agenda before Heather's zoning variance came up. Enough, he thought. Enough that he still could get there in time.

If Mrs. Waller would just listen to reason.

"Look, Mrs. Waller, they're both asleep, and I'll be back very soon."

"They'll wake up," she said darkly.

The sad truth was, she was probably right. They

hadn't slept more than ten minutes at a time since they'd arrived this morning. But still, this was important. Why couldn't she see that?

"Damn it, Mrs. Waller—"

She scowled fiercely, the lines in her sharp face deepening into troughs of displeasure. "No cursing. No babies, and no cursing."

God. Griffin was ready to tear his hair out. But the twins had been working on that all day, and his scalp was already sore. What, he wondered, was the diabolical fascination babies had for grabbing things and trying to stick them in their mouths?

As if he didn't have enough to contend with, the telephone took that moment to ring. He picked it up, growling "What?" in a voice that could have etched glass.

"Where the hell are you, Cahill? You need to get down here."

It was Hickory Baxter, one of the other four councilmen. Griffin frowned, wondering why Hickory sounded so tense. He'd been late for meetings before himself. In fact, Hickory had been known to skip a meeting altogether now and then.

"Why? What's going on?"

Hickory lowered his voice to a whisper. "I'm not sure. But I don't like it. Somebody has been stirring things up on the zoning."

Griffin wasn't sure he had heard correctly. "Zoning? You mean Heather's request for a zoning variance?"

"I tell you, I smell something rotten. It may be Millner. You'd better get down here, Cahill. And you'd better hurry, or she may take a fall on this one."

With that cryptic warning, the old man hung up.

Griffin replaced the receiver slowly, trying to make sense of it all. How could anything have gone wrong with Heather's zoning variance? The council had given its tentative okay two months ago. The Planning and Zoning Commission committee had unanimously recommended approval. So had the Firefly Glen Chamber of Commerce and the Home Owners' Association.

Heather was no doubt deep in construction on Spring House already.

But Griffin recognized that urgent note in Hickory Baxter's voice. Hickory had been old Doc Delaney's best friend, and he loved Heather like a daughter. He might be mistaken, but Hickory obviously believed that someone was about to hurt Heather.

That meant Griffin couldn't play power games with Mrs. Waller any longer. He knew how to reach her, so he went straight for the kill.

"An extra hundred dollars," he said bluntly. "For one hour. An extra hundred dollars in this week's check."

He saw her eyes light up, and he knew he had hit on the right amount. Though she worked like a Trojan cleaning houses every day of her life, Griffin suspected that Mrs. Waller was probably richer than he was. She loved money, would do almost anything if you offered her enough cash. And, as far as Griffin knew, she had never been seen spending a single cent.

"A hundred and twenty," she said slowly, her narrowed eyes appraising him, estimating the depth of his desperation. "No. One-fifty. Because they will wake up."

He could get her down to one twenty-five, but he didn't have time to haggle. "Done," he said, pulling on his raincoat. "Those boys had better be damn happy when I get back."

"They will be as happy as kings," Mrs. Waller said, smiling for the first time since he had dared to suggest that she might serve as a babysitter. She followed him to the door, helping him with his coat, oddly expansive now that she had secured her cash bonus.

She handed him his umbrella. "So, Mr. Cahill. A beautiful woman is making you rush like this and be crazy? This is all because of a woman?"

Griffin paused at the threshold, turning his collar up against the driving rain. He considered trying to explain that, while Mrs. Waller might think he was a good-for-nothing dilettante, he was actually a city councilman, that it was his duty to attend all city council meetings.

But would he really have spent a hundred and fifty dollars, abandoned his innocent nephews and tramped through this rain just to cast a vote on some anonymous businessman's zoning request?

He sighed. Of course not.

"Yeah," he said, glancing back at her sharp, clever face with a rueful smile. "This is all because of a woman."

CHAPTER TWO

HEATHER HAD TO ADMIT, as backstabbing betrayals went, this one was going to be a doozie.

There she was, settled in the front row of the Firefly Glen City Council chambers like the proverbial sitting duck. She had arrived so innocently, in her nice dress, all smiles and eagerness, like a child who is unable to see that she is climbing the stairs to her own execution.

How could she have been such a fool? She should have realized something was wrong in the first five minutes, when the council took up the matter of her zoning variance first, ignoring the printed agenda.

Zoning variance. It sounded like officious bureaucracy and moldy red tape—not real human beings and their hopes and dreams. But it would certainly be easier to cast a no vote against a "zoning variance" than to tell Heather Delaney, the daughter of Tim Delaney, who had been Firefly Glen's obstetrician for six decades, that she couldn't work and live under the same roof. That she would probably eventually have to sell her dream house just to make ends meet.

And no was exactly what it appeared they were going to say.

Like an idiot, she hadn't suspected anything. It wasn't until Mayor Millner had begun talking morosely of "complications," mentioning anonymous "complaints" about the prospect of having a medical clinic in the neighborhood, that she had begun to feel true fear.

Finally, when two other councilmen began to echo the mayor's comments, even Heather, who had been half-blind with excited anticipation, could see what was happening.

She had been set up. When they had given her tentative approval at the last meeting, she had believed them, as trusting as a baby. She had put a team of men to work and spent a fortune. She had, in essence, placed her own head on the block, sparing them the trouble.

Now she was about to get it chopped off.

Her heart had begun to pound again, this time in an extremely disagreeable way. Fight or flight—as a doctor she recognized quite clearly that she was having a primitive reaction to danger.

But she'd be darned if she'd let them see it. She lifted her chin and stared unwaveringly at the four councilmen sitting on the dais, four men who held the executioner's ax in their well-manicured hands.

"Heather." Mary, who was sitting next to her, cast a worried side glance. "What on earth is going on here? This was a done deal. You've already spent thousands—"

Heather didn't take her eyes off the councilmen. "Someone appears to have undone it," she murmured acidly.

And she had a pretty good idea who that "someone" was. Mayor Alton Millner, who even now was smiling down at her from the podium with a smarmy pretense of sympathy.

"It would trouble this council to reverse its position. We are well aware that we granted tentative approval to this zoning variance. But, although we sympathize with Dr. Delaney's dilemma, I believe we cannot in good conscience ignore the concerns of her neighbors. I'm sure Dr. Delaney will understand."

He smiled right at her, the arrogant hypocrite. She knew that smile. Confident, smug. Triumphant.

Her racing heart paused for a blinding moment of painful clarity. Her Spring House clinic was doomed.

And all because she had offended Alton Millner. All because she had dared to give him advice about his daughter Justine. She had known he was offended, had seen it immediately in his arrogant little black-marble eyes. But she had never, ever considered the possibility that he would retaliate by trying to sabotage her here, in the council chambers.

He would never abuse his public powers, she'd thought. Naively, she had assumed that kind of thing might happen in New York or Los Angeles…but certainly not in Firefly Glen.

How stupid of her! Corruption was human nature, not a product of city living. Vindictive, amoral people like Alton Millner probably existed in villages even *National Geographic* hadn't discovered yet.

She felt like getting up and stalking out right now, right in the middle of the vote, just to show them how disgusted she was. But she wouldn't give them the satisfaction. She sat utterly still as they went through the farce of roll call and vote.

Hickory Baxter.

"Yes." The white-haired old man, who had been Heather's father's best friend, smiled down at her apologetically, as if he knew his one little vote wouldn't make much difference. She smiled back, assuring him that it did. At least her rejection wouldn't be unanimous.

Sylvester Brooks. "Yes."

Heather was surprised. She wouldn't have thought Sylvester had the courage to defy the mayor. But the young man winked over at her and shrugged. The shrug said it all.

Bart Miglin. "Opposed."

Stuart Leith. "Opposed."

So it was a tie.

Mary was twisting her purse strap into knots. She leaned over and whispered furiously. "Where the hell is Griffin Cahill? He didn't even show up? The *coward*."

But Heather didn't think it was cowardice that had kept Griffin, the fifth councilman, away from today's meeting. He wasn't afraid of Alton Millner or anyone else. It was far more likely to be a woman.

Or sheer, lazy, self-absorbed indifference.

"My God, this is disgusting! I can't *believe* it." Mary was so agitated it was like sitting next to boiling water. "I mean, Cahill may be a spoiled, rich brat, but still. I just can't *believe* he'd let you down like this."

But Heather wasn't one bit surprised. Playboy Cahill's record of disappointing her went back approximately twenty years.

He'd been her teenage sweetheart, her first lover, the man she'd planned to marry. But from the beginning she had known that her spoiled, gorgeous fiancé was frivolous and unreliable. For years—through high school, into college and even into the arduous years of medical school—Heather had been too in love to object to the endless string of forgotten promises, careless mistakes, thoughtless betrayals. Some were small and easily overlooked, but eventually they grew profound and painful. By the end, taken together, they had finally been enough to destroy even Heather's blind adoration.

So why should today be any different? He was probably still asleep. Or else he'd seen the rain from the big picture window in his ultramodern bachelor pad and decided it wasn't worth getting his beloved BMW muddy.

She stopped herself, ashamed of this sudden, sharp bitterness. She had thought that her feelings toward Griffin had mellowed.

But she was human, wasn't she? Griffin's vote could have saved her. The variance would have passed three to two. Mayor Millner's scheme would have been thwarted, all by one lazy yes cast by the Glen's golden boy.

If only he'd been able to drag himself out of bed.

Now it was tied, two to two, which was probably just what Alton Millner had been hoping for. In case of a tie, the mayor cast the deciding vote.

"I'm afraid I must vote opposed. The vote is three to two," the mayor intoned gravely. "The variance is denied."

And, just like that, her dream was dead.

"No." Mary made fists in her lap and growled fiercely under her breath. *"No."*

Heather didn't say anything. She felt frozen in her seat.

"My God." Mary's voice was shaking. "Can they do that? Just waltz in here and destroy everything? Just like that?"

Heather nodded. "Yes. Just like that."

"But—" Mary was temporarily incoherent. "But—"

She looked at Heather. "Does he have any idea how much money you've already spent?"

Heather watched the mayor pompously shaking hands with his council. "Of course he knows. He loves it."

Mary turned and watched him, too. *"Bastard,"* she hissed heatedly. "Do you think this is all because of Justine? Because of what you said?"

Heather nodded. Her jaw felt so tight she wasn't sure she could speak whole sentences. "Probably."

"Son of a—" Mary held herself back with an obvious effort. "I knew it. I have to tell you, I was afraid something like this would happen. He's a petty bastard, isn't he?"

Heather nodded. She was beginning to feel a little numb, a little distant. Maybe that was a good thing.

"Well, can we sue?"

"I don't know," Heather answered tersely. "We'll look into it."

She was so consumed by her own distress that when her pager went off, just a small vibration at her waist, she felt as if it were a summons from another planet.

She looked down, read the short sentence her service had typed in. Mrs. Mizell wanted an emergency after-hours visit. In less than thirty minutes.

So life went on. Heather automatically pressed in the number for yes.

People needed her. She was going to have to pull out of this quicksand of disappointment somehow and go back to work. Maybe that was a blessing in disguise.

Up on the dais, the meeting was breaking up. Heather didn't think her poise could hold much longer, especially if Alton came over to gloat.

She picked up her raincoat, which was still damp. "Come on. Let's go."

But they were too late. At the front door of city hall, where the rain was beating the newly blooming tulips into the mud, the mayor intercepted their path. He had arranged his round, fleshy face in a show of concern.

"Heather. My dear. I just wanted to say I'm so sorry things didn't work out for your clinic. I would have liked to help. But unfortunately, as I mentioned in the meeting, we received several complaints from your neighbors and…" He shrugged sadly. "We just couldn't ignore their concerns about their property values."

Heather stared coldly into his lying face. He knew darn well there had been no complaints. Long before she had even bought the place, Heather had consulted each and every one of the Spring House neighbors, exploring their feelings about her idea to turn the first floor of the lovely old Victorian gingerbread house into a clinic. Not one of them had been opposed.

Including Mayor Millner, who lived four houses down from Spring House.

But she wasn't going to brawl with him about it now, not out here on the City Hall steps, where everyone could see them.

Mary obviously had no such inhibitions. She would have wrestled the mayor to the mud if Heather hadn't put a restraining hand on her arm.

She settled for scowling at him under her rain hood. "Tell me, Mayor," Mary said acidly. "Why was no one concerned about their property values when *your wife* turned your carriage house into an antique shop?"

Mayor Millner's lips tightened. "That was quite different."

"Oh, yeah? How? And what about Ginger Jackson's preschool? Or Parker Tremaine's new law offices? Or Mrs. Bry—"

"Mary." Heather glanced quellingly at her friend. The list could have gone on forever. Spring House was on Old Pine Barren Road, which was so close to the center of town that most of the fine old houses there had already been converted to retail or professional uses.

In typical Firefly Glen fashion, rather than rezoning the entire street—which would have felt sweeping and impersonal—they granted the zoning variances one at a time.

Still, no one had ever been turned down. Until today.

"Mary," she said again.

"What?" Mary looked over at Heather mutinously. She wasn't the type to give up without a fight. "It's true. You know it is. This is so unfair."

Heather turned her even gaze toward the mayor. "There's really no need to explain, Alton," she said calmly. "I fully understand your motives."

He flushed, narrowing his beady eyes, but Heather found an extra measure of strength from somewhere, and she didn't allow the ugly expression to ruffle her. She smiled slightly, raising her eyebrows in polite inquiry. "By the way. How is Justine?"

The mayor's face purpled, and Heather wondered whether someday soon his nasty temper was going to give him a stroke. As a doctor, she cared. But as a woman, and as the victim of his latest dirty trick, she thought maybe he had it coming.

"Dr. Delaney," he said darkly, with a sarcastic emphasis on the "doctor" part. "My daughter is no longer your patient. Maybe you should keep your nose out of my family's private business."

"I'd be glad to," she said smoothly, fastening the top button of her raincoat with steady fingers. "If you'd stay out of mine."

She snapped open her dark green umbrella so quickly that he had to duck to avoid being hit by the spokes. Beside her, Mary opened her own, the sound echoing hers like a crisp salute.

Without bothering to say goodbye to the silently fuming mayor, Heather turned toward the parking lot. Mary was right behind her, their footsteps splashing in unison down the City Hall steps and across the sodden green. Cold mud sprayed up against Heather's hem and worked its way inside her shoes.

God, she hated April.

Mary had driven separately, so when they reached her little sedan she waved a quick goodbye without standing to chat. Heather understood. The disappointment was too fresh, the blow too stunning. There would be plenty of time tomorrow to rehash and analyze the council's ambush—and to decide how to respond. Right now Heather wanted a warm shower and a hot bowl of soup more than anything on earth, even more than she wanted justice.

Or revenge.

Of course, she couldn't have either one. She had to go back to the office, and she had to calm Anna Mizell down one more time.

She huddled at her car door, her small umbrella propped on her shoulder and funneling rain onto her head, then down the back of her coat, while she fumbled through her purse, looking for her keys.

Suddenly, above the rain, she heard a new sound. She lifted her head to see a small, gleaming ice-blue BMW come purring into the empty space next to her.

No. She shut her eyes, refusing to believe her luck could be this bad. It couldn't be.

But it was. The BMW's tinted window hummed down, revealing Griffin Cahill.

The sight of him, handsome as sin, as beautifully tailored as if he'd just stepped out of a magazine, brought all her repressed anger suddenly surging to the surface.

It was unfair, she knew that. It wasn't his fault he looked so glamorous when she looked so soggy, that he looked so confident when she felt so defeated.

This was just pure, everyday Playboy Cahill. The last time she'd seen a single golden strand of hair out of place on his elegant head, he had been seventeen years old. Just seventeen—sexy, sweaty, tousled and panting…and locked in her trembling arms.

She blinked away the image, as she had done a million times through the years. It wasn't his fault she couldn't forget.

But it was his fault she'd lost the vote today.

"Heather?" He peered up at her through the window. "Oh, hell. I haven't missed the meeting, have I?"

She knew how she must look, with her hair soaked to the scalp, and rain dripping off her chin. She used her hand to wipe her cheeks, just in case mascara had begun to run. But it was hopeless. Her fingers were as wet as her face.

"Yes," she said succinctly. "You missed it."

"What's wrong, Heather?" But before she could answer, his eyes tightened. "You lost, didn't you?"

For the first time, she felt the threat of tears. She didn't want to talk to him about this. She didn't want to talk to anyone. Not yet.

"Yes," she said. "I lost."

He said something then, but the rain was drumming loudly on the fabric of her umbrella, and she couldn't make out the words.

"What?"

"Nothing." He shook his head. "I just said I'm sorry I didn't get here in time. I could have helped."

She held herself stiffly, hoping the dignity she'd clung to since the vote wouldn't desert her now. But it was true, and she couldn't help feeling bitter. He could have changed everything. And not just with his vote. He could conceivably have talked the others into supporting her, too.

Everyone in town listened to Griffin, though Heather wasn't exactly sure why. He was frivolous and sardonic, lazy and self-absorbed. But he was also young and handsome, smart and rich and fiercely admired, by women who wanted to bed him, and by men who wanted to be him.

If Griffin had been there, if he had argued passionately for her case, perhaps he could have swayed the other councilmen, and thwarted the mayor completely.

Their fear of Alton Millner's bludgeoning anger was strong. But perhaps their desire for Griffin Cahill's lazy approval was even stronger.

It was possible.

But who was she kidding? Griffin never argued passionately for anything or anybody. He simply couldn't be bothered. Just look at him now. He hadn't even been able to bestir himself to get to the meeting on time.

"Heather." He leaned over and shoved open the passenger door. "You're drenched. Get in and tell me exactly what happened. Maybe I can think of some way to fix it."

She looked into the little car, at the rain spattering against its silver leather seats. The seats hadn't been leather, back when Griffin was a teenager. They had been nubby, tattered black cloth that scratched her shoulders and left small red burns against her bare skin.

"No," she said, pushing the door shut quickly, so that the rain wouldn't ruin those expensive seats. "I mean, thanks anyway. But I don't need your help. And I have to get back to work."

"Heather, we should talk—"

But the afternoon's disappointments had finally gotten the better of her. She let loose a jagged laugh.

"Don't be absurd, Griffin. We haven't talked in ten years, and I don't intend to start now. If you had anything to say, you should have said it in there. With your *vote*."

He took her anger with a small smile, as he took everything. He was impenetrable, she thought, watching the corners of his mouth turn up in that old, familiar way. Nothing ever hurt him, did it?

Because nothing mattered to him.

"I really did mean to be there, Heather," he said softly. "Something important came up."

She looked at him, unable to form a reply. Did he even remember how often, in their long, lost past, he had come to her with those very words? *Something came up.* But some*thing* always turned out to be some*one*. A blonde, a brunette, whatever. Any great body and empty head that wanted to party instead of study, idolize instead of criticize. Any girl who wouldn't require him to be more than he wanted to bother being.

But of course he didn't remember. It was such a

long time ago. If she were half as smart as she claimed to be, she'd forget all about it, too.

"Come on, Heather." Looking at her from this angle, through the sports car window, required him to tilt those blue eyes up, against those thick dark lashes. He probably thought she would find him irresistible. "You can't really intend to slay this dragon alone. Millner is an ugly enemy. You need help."

"I know I need help, Griffin," she said, pressing the button that zipped open her door locks. As she lowered her umbrella, she met his warm, teasing smile with a piercingly frigid one of her own.

"I just don't need *yours*."

CHAPTER THREE

FIREFLY GLEN, according to the brochures, had everything.

Nestled in a soft valley in the Adirondacks, it was a charming township of approximately 2,938 people.

It had quaint old houses and elegant shopping. It had hushed white winters, colored Easter-egg springs, smiling green summers, and red-gold, breathtaking autumns. It had Llewellyn's Lake, which ran thick with trout; Silver Kiss Falls, which spilled like tinsel down John's Cliff; and the Lost Logger Trail, which wound silently through dark, steepled pines.

The only thing it *didn't* have was a nanny service.

Not one single professional babysitting service in the whole damn town.

Disgusted, Griffin tossed the telephone book onto the end table, knocking the small metal lamp up against the wall with a clatter. He cringed at the sound, looking nervously toward the door to his office, which had become a temporary nursery.

Please God. Don't let them wake up.

They'd been in their cribs less than an hour, but Jared had warned him that Stewart, the one in red, was a light sleeper. A bird chirping, a telephone ringing, heavy rain on the roof, a shaft of sunlight touching his eyelid…that was all it took.

Oh, great. It was spring in the Adirondacks. It was nothing *but* birds and rain.

Griffin had been about ninety-nine percent joking when he suggested maybe Stewart needed a thimble of brandy in his baby formula. But Jared hadn't seemed amused. Parenthood obviously did a number on your sense of humor.

Or maybe it was the sleep deprivation that did it. Over the past seventy-two hours, Griffin had learned a lot about the exhaustion that came with having twins in the house.

Was it too much to ask them to sleep at the same time? Just this morning, he had caught himself begging an eight-month-old baby—he thought it was Stewart— to please, please, *please* go back to sleep.

The kid had just looked at him as if he was crazy. Which he was. Babies *made* you crazy. They cried for no reason, sometimes for hours. They never slept, at least not at the same time. They tried to eat everything, especially nonorganic oddities they found in strange places. If Griffin had lost a penny in 1980, these babies would find it like radar and try to swallow it whole. You were scared to take your eyes off them for a split second.

Anyhow, the lamp clatter must not have been loud enough to penetrate the closed door. The small white baby monitor remained blessedly silent.

But he couldn't go on much longer without some real sleep. He reluctantly admitted that, though he hated asking anyone for a favor, he was going to have to get some help.

He'd already tried his friends. But they had careers, families, obligations. Emma Dunbar owed him a favor, but she was in Hawaii, enjoying a second honeymoon.

Mrs. Waller had refused to be bribed a second time, though Griffin had, in his desperation, raised his bid into four digits. She had simply folded her substantial arms again and scowled, repeating her mantra of rejection.

No. No babies. No.

That left only one hope. Though it was against his basic life philosophy to encourage any woman to think simultaneously of Griffin Cahill and babies, he had no choice. He had reached the point that he didn't trust himself to take care of the boys properly. He had caught himself dozing off this morning, while Stewart crawled toward the kitchen sink.

It was irresponsible not to get some help, wherever he could get it.

Blinking hard to force his eyes to stay open, he picked up his little black book and began to flip the pages.

TWO HOURS LATER, when Miranda rang Griffin's doorbell, he thought it was perhaps the most beautiful sound he had ever heard, better than Beethoven by moonlight, better than rippling brooks in the rain forest, better than the ching of three cherries lining up in Vegas.

It was the sound of salvation.

"Come on in. It's open."

He hoped she could hear him. He didn't dare go to the door. He was in the kitchen, parked in front of the twin high chairs, up to his elbows in smashed bananas.

In theory, he was feeding the boys. But like all theories, this one was flawed. Maybe a spoonful or two had gone into their stubborn mouths, but the rest of it was smeared across their faces and their clothes, and spattered on every surface within flinging distance.

Griffin heard the light slap of sandals across the hardwood floors. And then Miranda appeared in the doorway.

"Griffin, where is everything? Where's the Chihuly? Oh!" Her lovely mouth hung open as she took in the sight of the three banana-coated males. "Oh, my God. Griffin, what happened?"

Griffin tried to smile, but he was so tired his facial muscles weren't cooperating very well.

"I'm not sure," he said. "A couple of days ago everything was under control. And then…this."

Robert, whose blue playsuit was sticky with yellow mush, decided to greet Miranda with his favorite new joke. He spit a mouthful of bananas in her direction as forcefully as his chubby cheeks would allow, and then dissolved in a fit of giggles so strenuous it knocked him sideways in his high chair.

Miranda, who had excellent reflexes, backed out of the way just in time. She looked over at Griffin in bewildered horror.

"He thinks it's funny," Griffin explained unnecessarily. "He had a long nap, and he's in excellent spirits."

Stewart, who had dropped his spoon for the tenth time in the past ten minutes, began to cry. He rubbed his eyes, and when he took his fists away his lashes were glued into clumps with banana goo.

"Stewart, on the other hand, is now tired." Griffin sighed. "He and his brother have thoughtfully adopted a schedule of alternating naps, apparently to ensure that I'm never lonely."

Griffin watched Miranda struggle with the dilemma. Her instincts apparently were telling her to run, and run fast. She was a professional beauty, not a nanny. And certainly not a *mother.* The idea of getting smashed bananas in her hair clearly made her dizzy with revulsion.

But obviously she also knew an opportunity when she saw one. When Griffin had telephoned her, she had sounded stunned, thrilled to hear from him again so soon. His unwritten but until now unbroken rule was that women were luxuries he indulged in only on the weekends—and he never indulged in the same treat two weekends in a row.

So obviously Miranda understood that this was a rare chance. If Griffin had suddenly developed paternal instincts, she would be a fool not to adapt. She might not like babies, but she most definitely liked Griffin. A lot.

Enough to swallow down her disgust and give Robert a sickly smile.

"You are a cutie, aren't you?" Her performance was pretty good. If Griffin hadn't seen that first instinctive recoil, he might have believed that Miranda adored sticky baby boys.

She turned to Griffin. "Oh, Griffin, you just look exhausted." She came closer, a triumph of will over aversion. She ran her fingers through his hair tenderly, though Griffin noticed she did so carefully. "Honey, how long has it been since you've slept?"

"I lost track. I may be in triple digits."

"Well, I'm going to fix that right now." She took the plastic spoon out of his hand and set it on the kitchen table. "You go get a shower and climb in bed. I'm going to finish feeding these little cuties, and then they're going to get baths, too."

He looked at her dubiously, suddenly wondering whether calling her had been such a good idea after all.

It was a shame he didn't have Heather Delaney's number in his little black book anymore. She was probably the only woman Griffin had ever dated who had a single solitary maternal instinct written into her DNA. Even as a teenager, Heather had loved children. Everywhere they went, she had always stopped to smile at toddlers, babble to babies. It hadn't surprised anyone in Firefly Glen when Heather had become an obstetrician like her father.

But Heather's name hadn't been in Griffin's book for years. And after what had happened at the city council meeting the other day, she probably wouldn't throw him a rope if he were drowning in Llewellyn's Lake right in front of her eyes.

So instead he had names like Miranda Bradner. And what good did that do him now? Miranda had no experience—no children, no nieces or nephews. She didn't even have a younger sibling. She might not know about pennies that inexplicably appeared in forgotten corners. She might not realize how quickly a baby could crawl out of sight, slip into the bathwater, roll toward the edge of the table…

Really, it was damn terrifying all the ways infants could get hurt. For the life of him, Griffin couldn't imagine why anyone dared to have them in the first place. Except that, when they smiled, you got this strange warm feeling, as if someone had turned on a sunlamp…

His thoughts must have been written across his face like neon on a billboard. Miranda, who wasn't ordinarily the most perceptive woman in the world, understood immediately.

"Don't worry, sweetheart," she said, still using that

cooing-Madonna tone. "I did about a million hours of babysitting when I was a teenager. I'm actually very good with children."

Somehow he doubted that. But she couldn't be any worse than he'd be if he didn't get some sleep. He'd probably drop one of the boys from sheer exhaustion.

"Griffin." Miranda bent down and put her lovely, liquid eyes on level with his. "I'm here for you, honey. Let me help you."

It was such an obvious charade. But he couldn't fight it any longer. He couldn't even keep his eyes open. And at least he could count on her eagerness to impress him. She had come here to show what a valuable partner she could be, the perfect woman to have around in a crisis. She would meet this challenge if it killed her.

"Thanks, Miranda," he said wearily, standing up. "I owe you one." He patted Stewart's gooey head as he made his way toward the door. "So long, guys. Be good for the pretty lady, okay?"

"Of course they will. They are such little darlings, Griffin. We'll be fine."

He almost laughed at that, thinking of the past seventy-two hours. But he was too exhausted to laugh, and it wasn't very funny, really. She'd find out the truth soon enough. He just hoped that, before they drove her stark, raving mad, he could manage to steal at least one blissful hour of sleep.

Actually, he got nearly two. He sat up suddenly, alerted by something…some noise he couldn't identify. Groggily he noticed that it must be well past noon. The afternoon sun lay in soft yellow stripes against his white sheets.

He glanced toward his bedroom door. Miranda stood

there, looking strangely different. Her hair was a mess, and her belt was twisted sideways.

"Griffin?" Her voice had lost that gentle Madonna tone sometime during the past two hours. Now it sounded ever so slightly shrewish. "I'm afraid we have a problem."

ANNA MIZELL LAY on the examination table, listening to her baby's heartbeat with her eyes shut, an expression of concentrated rapture on her face.

Heather had already spent an extra ten minutes with Anna, and she had other patients waiting. Her nurse, Tawny, was subtly giving her the finger-across-the-throat sign that meant *cut it short.* Time's wasting.

But Heather held the microphone against Anna's stomach a little longer. The thirty-five-year-old woman had miscarried four times in the past ten years. This was the first baby she had carried long enough to have any hope of ever holding in her arms.

Now eight months pregnant, Anna had started to come in about four times a week, each time with a new imaginary crisis. Strange twinges, spotting, headaches, swollen ankles. Everything frightened Anna, and though Heather sometimes had to struggle to squeeze her into the schedule, she never really minded. She could easily imagine the dread that haunted Anna's dreams—the dread that this baby, too, would vanish in a cloud of blood and pain.

"He sounds perfect, Anna," Heather said softly, finally taking the microphone away and setting it on top of the monitor. "In fact, everything looks great. So far, so good."

Anna opened her eyes slowly, returning to the real

world reluctantly. When Tawny had wiped the lotion away and pulled down her shirt, Anna put both hands over her stomach, as if she could literally hold the baby in place. Heather had rarely seen Anna in any other posture.

"Thanks, Dr. Delaney," Anna said as she wriggled to a sitting position. She looked over at Heather, her eyes misty. "You have really worked a miracle, you know. I couldn't have made it this far without you."

Heather touched Anna's shoulder. "Sure you could," she said gently. "I'm not in the miracle business. Your own body does that. I'm just here to keep notes and hold the microphone."

"But the other times—" Anna swallowed, and Heather felt her shoulder tremble slightly. "Sometimes I'm so afraid—"

Heather sat down and took the woman's hand in hers. "This baby is strong, Anna. You're already eight months along. Even if he decided to come today— which I hope he won't, because I have a waiting room full of pregnant women, who aren't exactly famous for their patience…"

Anna smiled, as Heather had hoped she would.

"Even if he comes today, he'll be fine," she assured her. "He's big enough and strong enough to make it on his own. The next four weeks are more or less icing."

Tawny cleared her throat loudly. "Speaking of that waiting room full of irritable pregnant women…"

"I'm sorry!" Anna slid off the table to a standing position, still holding her stomach. "I'll try not to bother you again this week, Dr. Delaney."

Heather smiled from the doorway. "Come any time you're worried," she said, handing Anna's chart to Tawny. "That's why I'm here."

In the hall, she scanned the exam rooms, with their color-coded markers over the doors, designating the status of the occupants. Every one was full.

She took a deep breath. It wasn't even two o'clock, but they were already way behind schedule. She really was going to have to interview some candidates for a partner. She'd been putting it off for weeks, hoping she could wait until they had moved to Spring House. But now...

She mustn't think about Spring House. She hadn't managed to fully shake off her disappointment yet, and she couldn't afford to be distracted today.

She turned to Tawny. "Room Four next?" She held out her hand for a chart. "Who is it?"

Tawny grinned. "No chart on this one. This one is—" She raised her eyebrows. "Interesting."

"Interesting?" Heather glanced at the closed door to number four. "I'm not in the mood for 'interesting.' I need ordinary. I need easy. I'm a half hour behind already."

"Well, sorry, Doc." Tawny hadn't stopped smiling. "Interesting is what you've got here. A double dose of interesting, you might say."

With that mysterious comment, Tawny bustled off to deliver Anna Mizell's chart to Mary at the front desk. For one self-indulgent second, Heather stared at Room Four wearily, wishing she could maybe have just one simple, unchallenging day. Just one.

She loved her job. She had gone into medicine because she liked helping people, was stimulated by the constant kaleidoscope of challenges. Still...just one day of humdrum predictability now and then would be restful.

But a second was all she had to spare. And then she put a welcoming, professional smile on her face and briskly opened the door.

She wasn't sure exactly what she had been expecting. But she definitely hadn't been expecting this. No wonder Tawny had preferred to let her be surprised. The whole office was probably out there buzzing with the gossip.

Griffin Cahill lay on the examination table.

He was stretched out on his side, his head propped up against the knuckles of one hand. His six-foot-three body was much too long for the table, and much too male. His dark denim designer jeans covered long, powerful legs, which hung carelessly over the edge of the table. His sport shirt rippled along upper body muscles so tight and perfectly proportioned they hardly looked real.

All in all, his extreme masculinity was a serious shock in this place that specialized in estrogen. The strangest sight, though, was his utterly flat stomach. Heather hadn't realized how accustomed she was to swollen, distended moms-to-be—until she encountered the fit, sexy planes of Griffin Cahill.

For a moment she had to hold on to the edge of the door, just to keep her balance.

He obviously hadn't noticed that she'd opened the door. He was smiling, looking down, dangling one hand toward some large thing, some kind of—she squinted, disbelieving.

A *stroller*. It was undeniably a stroller, an expensive two-seater baby carriage. But what was Griffin doing with a stroller? Dimly she registered a strange clicking sound. She looked up, then realized that he was shaking a large ring of multicolored plastic keys.

Finally, after an absurd number of seconds had passed, she became aware of the other occupants of the room. The blue stroller, it seemed, was loaded with two absolutely beautiful baby boys dressed in blue rompers and tiny white socks.

Twins, she realized with a tremor of shock. Twin boys, both reaching happily for the plastic keys Griffin was dangling, burbling their pleasure at the game.

But whose twins? Griffin didn't have any children. Did he?

She forced herself to move into the room.

"Griffin?" She wrapped her hands lightly around the two ends of her stethoscope, a classic pose of professional detachment. Besides, it kept her from having to shake hands, or reach out and touch him in any way. "What on earth are you doing here?"

He sat up quickly, swinging those long legs over the side of the table. "Heather." His smile was so bright the room seemed suddenly lighter. "Thank God you're here. I was running out of ideas. You can only keep them interested in keys for so long, you know."

It seemed that Griffin was right. One of the little boys was already whimpering, leaning over to try to extricate himself, pushing at the front bar of the stroller so hard his face began to turn red. The other boy watched quietly, but his smile had faded, so Heather suspected it wouldn't be long before he was trying to escape as well.

She bent down. "Hi," she said mildly, so that she wouldn't frighten them. "Who are you?"

"Oh, sorry." Griffin took a deep breath. "These are my nephews. You remember Jared? Well, he and Katie got married a couple of years ago, and these are their twin boys. Stewart and Robert. I'm babysitting for a few weeks."

She remembered Jared well. Just three years

younger than Griffin, he had idolized his older brother and had stuck to him like glue, determined to go everywhere, do everything that Griffin did. Heather and Griffin had frequently resorted to some fairly elaborate tricks in order to elude him.

"Oh, how wonderful for Jared," she said, letting the quiet one take her stethoscope in his fat little fist. She smiled at the other one, so that he wouldn't feel left out. "Which one is which?"

Silence.

She twisted her head to look at Griffin. "Which one is Stewart?"

Smiling, he cocked one eyebrow sheepishly. "Funny you should ask. Actually, that's why we're here."

She stood, carefully peeling the baby's fingers from her stethoscope. When he realized he was losing his toy, he began to whine softly and wriggle in his seat.

She looked at Griffin squarely. The expression on his face was just about as embarrassed as she'd ever seen it be. "Griffin? What do you mean?"

And he looked tired, too, she thought. Not the way other people looked tired—not wan or bloodshot or disheveled. It was just that his blue eyes were a shade less brilliant, and oddly appealing dusty shadows had formed beneath them.

"I mean I honestly don't know which one is Stewart," he said, running his hand through his blond hair roughly. "They look exactly alike. I mean *exactly.*"

"They're twins," she pointed out reasonably.

"Yeah, but I never noticed that they looked *exactly* alike, you know? They are always dressed in different colors. Stewart's red. Robert's blue. I never had to try to tell them apart. I just always went by the colors."

She glanced back down at the babies, who were rapidly going from fussy to furious now that they weren't getting any attention. They were straining at their halters, pushing at the bars. They wanted out, and pretty soon they were going to get vocal about it.

But they were definitely both dressed in identical blue rompers.

"I know, I know," Griffin said when she returned her quizzical gaze to his. "Both blue. It was a serious miscalculation."

"*Your* miscalculation?" She couldn't imagine Griffin doing anything this stupid.

"Not exactly." He sighed. "Well, yes, I suppose it was, in a way. I miscalculated by letting someone else bathe them while I took a nap."

"Who?"

Was he flushing? Surely not. But he wasn't eager to tell her, either. "A friend of mine," he said.

She started to ask who again, but she stopped herself. She knew who. His bimbo of the moment, no doubt. Rumor had it he was dating three different women, and if you added all their IQs together you'd still be on the low end of the charts.

She looked away, not wanting him to see the disapproval in her eyes. She had no right to judge him. But God, what an unbelievably dumb move!

The babies had progressed from whimpering to outright crying. Griffin reached down and tried shaking the plastic keys again, but the boys weren't buying it.

Heather spoke louder, to be heard over the din. "You still haven't explained why you're here."

Griffin hopped off the table and bent down, extricating the louder baby from the stroller and hoisting him into his arms. Heather felt a slight knock of her pulse. Playboy Cahill holding a baby was a sight she hadn't ever expected to see.

"I was hoping you might have some idea. Some trick for identifying them."

She stared at him. "You're joking, right?"

He frowned. "No. Of course I'm not joking. I have to know which one is which. I can't keep calling them 'champ' for three weeks."

The baby left behind began to howl at the injustice of it all. Griffin shut his eyes briefly, then bent again, wrestling the second boy free of his halter awkwardly, while balancing the other one on his shoulder.

Finally he rose again, this time with a baby on each shoulder. Heather felt speechless with amazement as the boys instantly sniffed back their tears and rested their fat, downy cheeks against Griffin's rigid chest muscles.

Tears still pooled around their eyes, but they began sucking their thumbs, obviously content with the safety of their new perches.

He looked at her hard, as if daring her to laugh. She didn't.

"There must be some way. Aren't there footprints on file somewhere or something? What about blood tests?"

She smiled in spite of herself. "Well, I guess we could do a DNA analysis."

"Great." Nodding eagerly, Griffin shifted one of the boys higher. "Go ahead. Hurry."

"I was kidding, Griffin." She watched his face fall. Amazing—he was so sophisticated about some things, and yet so dumb about everything to do with babies. He'd obviously avoided the subject like the plague.

"Honestly, Griffin. I don't have any tricks for telling babies apart. There's nothing I can do for you. Maybe you should just call your brother and ask him."

Griffin shook his head emphatically, his golden hair catching the light from the overhead fixture. "No, ma'am. I'm not admitting to this, not if I can help it. Katie wouldn't ever let me hear the end of it."

"Well, then, I guess you're stuck with the situation," she said. She looked at the babies, who had closed their eyes and appeared to be falling asleep, as if Griffin's hard pectoral muscles were the softest goose-feather pillows.

The sight was oddly touching. And, even more shocking, she also found that it was disturbingly sexy. It made her strangely angry to discover that she still went a little weak in the knees at the sight of him. After everything he'd done to her, that must mean she was a little weak in the head, too.

She turned around, forcing herself to stop looking. She had a room full of pregnant women waiting for her, remember? She had no time for his foolish predicament. He'd brought it on himself. Now he had to live with it.

"Good luck, Griffin. I'm sorry I couldn't help."

"Heather, wait."

"I'm busy," she said curtly. "I have patients."

"Please."

But she didn't have time to wait, she really didn't. And she didn't have the strength to be in this small, intimate room with Griffin much longer. She'd come a long way in ten years. But she obviously hadn't come far enough.

She had her hand on the door when he said her name again. The sound was low and urgent. "Heather. Please."

"What?" She turned reluctantly. "I told you. I can't help you."

He looked at her over the babies' heads. "Yes, you can."

"How?"

He took a deep breath, but he met her gaze squarely. "Spend the next three weeks with me. Help me take care of the boys."

She frowned, wondering once again if he might be joking. The idea was so utterly preposterous.

"Don't be ridiculous, Griffin. I can't do that."

"Why can't you? You're good with kids. You're responsible and kind. You have medical training, and you're absolutely perfect."

Though she heard the exhaustion in his voice, though she sensed real need, she steeled herself to resist it. She reminded herself of the dozens of times he had not been there when she needed him. Including last Monday, at the city council meeting.

She hardened her voice, so that he would know she was strong enough to resist him. And the babies. The whole absurd package.

"What on earth makes you think I'd say yes to such an outrageous proposition? Why should I feel the slightest obligation to help you? For old times' sake? Hardly." She didn't hide the bitterness she felt. "Or perhaps as thanks for all the help you gave me over the zoning variance?"

He shook his head. "I can still help you with that," he said. "I can get Alton to call for another vote."

"I can get him to call for another vote, too," she responded curtly. "I'm consulting a lawyer next week."

"Lawyers are expensive."

"I'll manage."

"Wait. I know," he said suddenly, looking up at her with a new light in his eyes. "I have something you want. A lot."

She shook her head. "I doubt that," she said tightly.

"But I do." He smiled, tired but more relaxed now, as if he was sure he had her. "I have your love letters."

She didn't speak, didn't even breathe for a long, empty moment. The only sound in the room was the soft snuffle of the babies' little stuffed noses.

Finally she found her voice. "All of them?"

"All of them."

She swallowed hard. "Even the one you promised to burn? The one about Silver Kiss Falls?"

He nodded slowly. "*All* of them," he said again, and his voice told her he hadn't forgotten a word that was in those letters. Those stupid, stupid letters.

She couldn't think what to say. He had promised to burn them. But then, he had promised so many things. And he had never done any of them.

She would hate it if those letters ever fell into anyone else's hands. They had been the foolish, naive ravings of a teenager newly in love, newly awake to the joys of sex. Having anyone else in the world read them would be desperately embarrassing.

She didn't really believe that Griffin would ever let the letters go public. Not at their ugliest moments had she ever thought him capable of that level of cruelty. But even if he did, she could take it. A little embarrassment wouldn't kill her.

"I'll give them back to you, Heather. All of them."

"I don't want them." She smiled at him coldly. "They're ancient history, Griffin. I wouldn't give you a minute of my life for them, much less three weeks."

He was surprised, she could tell. Staring at her blankly, he leaned back against the examination table as if he were suddenly too tired to stand on his own. One of the babies began to wriggle and fuss, but Griffin rested his chin against the crown of his head gently, and he quickly settled down.

He looked at her over the baby's head. His face was devoid of its earlier rogue charm. He just looked tired and worried and desperate. Ironically, it made him look more attractive than ever. More real, somehow. More human.

"Oh, hell, I'm going about this all wrong. Look, I'm sorry I brought up the letters, Heather. You can have them any time you want them. No strings attached."

"I told you. I don't want them."

"Okay. But hear me out. Please. I need your help. I don't have anything to offer in return. And I don't deserve it, I admit that freely. But you have always been generous, ready to help anyone who needed it. Well, now I need it."

She hesitated. She had to set her shoulders against some stupid protective instinct that made her want to walk over and take one of the boys from his arms. Some insane impulse to lighten the burden of exhaustion she heard in his voice.

The baby began to whimper again. Absently Griffin rubbed the baby's cheek with his knuckle, and the little boy rooted sleepily toward the touch. He clamped his little rosebud mouth around Griffin's knuckle, and, sucking softly, went back to sleep.

Watching, Heather felt her stomach do something strange.

But Griffin seemed unaware of the entire episode. He had acted out of instinct, his mind entirely concentrated on her.

"I know it's an imposition, Heather. But I'm at the end of my rope. I haven't slept in three days. I'm afraid something will happen to them, something worse than two blue outfits. Please help me take care of them."

She closed her eyes, blocking out the sight of those pink, trusting lips locked around Griffin's hard, tanned finger. But when she opened them, the urge to say yes was as strong as ever.

She was a fool. No good could come of this.

She walked over and looked down at the sleeping babies. Lifting her hand slowly, she grazed the back of it across one curved, downy cheek. It was as soft and dewy as the clover that spread along the banks of Llewellyn's Lake in the spring.

"Three weeks," she said gruffly. "Not a day longer."

He nodded carefully. "Three weeks."

He paused. "Thanks, Heather," he said tentatively, as if he didn't trust his luck to hold.

She didn't meet his eyes. "I'm not doing it for you."

"I know."

"I'm doing it for them."

"I know."

"I mean, already you've got the poor boys mixed up. God knows what you'd do next."

"God knows," he agreed meekly.

Finally she looked up, and she saw the gentle smile in those blue eyes that she had once loved better than life itself. And at that moment she finally realized what a dangerous decision she'd just made.

She might be able to protect the babies from Griffin and his foolish mistakes.

But who was going to protect her?

CHAPTER FOUR

OKAY, BENJAMIN BRADY, listen up. You're nineteen now—old enough to know there are no secrets in Firefly Glen. I found out when you set the boys' bathroom on fire, and I found out when you knocked out Digger Jackson's front teeth. Did you think I wouldn't find out that Sheriff Dunbar caught you doing ninety through Vanity Gap? I—

The purr of an expensive sports car pulling into the front driveway of Spring House interrupted Mary Brady's train of thought. But that was okay. She could write this particular *Listen Up* lecture, aimed at her youngest brother, in her sleep. In fact, maybe she should check her portfolio of old *Listen Up* letters. She probably still had the one she wrote when Dooley got his first speeding ticket. She could save herself some time by recycling that one.

And she was going to need all the time she could get, now that Heather had gone and made this stupid arrangement with Playboy Cahill, which was going to create tons more work for everybody.

Come to think of it, maybe the person who needed a *Listen Up* lecture right now was Heather. *Honestly!* What kind of fool agreed to let a heartbreaker ex-boyfriend and his two suspicious infants move in for the express purpose of obtaining free babysitting?

Couldn't Heather see what was going on here? Or was she still a little blinded by those cocky blue eyes? It just went to show you, didn't it? Even smart women made dumb decisions. Mary could already feel the beginnings of a lecture. *Okay, my dear Dr. Delaney. Listen up.*

A car door slammed. Putting down her pen, Mary cast one last look around the hastily assembled Spring House "nursery." Everything was ready. She sighed. Like it or not, Griffin Cahill had arrived. Time to play welcoming committee.

As she trotted down the curving staircase, she could see Griffin through the beveled glass that framed the front door. He had his backside to her, bending over to retrieve the babies from their car seat.

It stopped her in her tracks. Normally, Mary didn't go all breathless and poetic about the male body. Growing up with four brothers had cured her of that. But, even so, she had to admit that, from this angle, Griffin Cahill had a rather nifty little backside.

Too bad he was such an ass.

She grinned, enjoying the play on words. She stood there watching, chuckling, until Griffin began to climb the steps toward the porch, a sleeping baby in each arm. Then she finally took the rest of the stairs and opened the door.

"Need any help?" She made no move toward him, and the tone of her voice made it clear that only one answer would be acceptable.

"No, thanks," he said politely, obviously getting the message. Nobody had ever accused Griffin of being stupid. Not even Mary.

Shifting the baby in his left arm slightly, he flicked a glance into the foyer behind her. "Where's Heather?"

"She's working."

"Working?" He looked genuinely surprised. He probably had expected Heather to be waiting by the door with bells on.

Mary smiled. "Yes, working. It's a darling little idea they've invented. You go to an office, and you spend a few hours being useful. Afterward, they pay you."

"How clever," Griffin said, all admiration. "I should try it sometime." He raised one eyebrow. "Oops. That was probably supposed to be your line, wasn't it?"

Maddeningly, Mary couldn't think of a witty reply. So she didn't try. She just stepped aside grimly, letting Griffin stride into the house, which he did as if he owned it, the cheeky bastard. He'd probably walk into heaven itself with that same cocky stride.

But a few feet inside the door, he stopped cold. Whistling just under his breath, he scanned the large hall slowly, obviously stunned by the restored beauty around him.

Mary waited. She had wanted him to be impressed, and yet now she was strangely annoyed by his surprise. Of course Spring House was beautiful. Why wouldn't it be? From the moment Heather Delaney had bought it, she had pampered this sad old relic like a baby. She had spent her entire inheritance renovating it.

Thanks to Heather, sunlight poured in through the beveled glass side lights, tossing quivering rainbows onto the polished honey-wood floors. An elegant gold-and-green patterned carpet rose up the graceful curve of stairs toward the upper stories. Sparkling mirrors bracketed by gleaming brass sconces offered glimpses into other rooms of equal beauty.

You never would have guessed that only two years ago Spring House had been a dark, creaky, moldering old mess, good only for haunting or tearing down.

Griffin turned back to Mary, a ridge forming between his brows. "I thought Heather was turning it into her offices. Into a clinic."

"Not this part," Mary explained impatiently. "Just the back, where the old kitchen and pantries and servants rooms used to be. She was very careful to keep the clinic from spoiling the rest of the house. She even put the parking at the back, so the cars wouldn't annoy the neighbors."

Griffin nodded thoughtfully. "Still. It's incredible."

"I don't see why you're so shocked, Griffin. Heather presented the plans to the city council when she applied for the zoning variance. Didn't you even bother to look at the blueprints?"

Griffin glanced over at her, his chin brushing the forehead of a sleeping baby. "I didn't see any need to. I knew I was going to vote yes."

"Really." Mary narrowed her eyes. "Then it's too bad you didn't."

"Oh, I see." He tilted his head quizzically. "Is that what's eating you, Mary? The vote? Is that why you were standing at the door doing that over-my-dead-body routine?"

"You bet it is." Mary saw no reason to beat around the bush. "Well, that's part of it, anyway."

As if sensing the animosity around him, one of the babies began to stir and whimper. Griffin bent his lips to the little half-bald head and whispered something. The baby nuzzled his chest drowsily for a minute, then subsided with a powdery sigh and fell back asleep.

Griffin was still looking at Mary. "Okay. The vote is part of it. What's the rest of it?"

"The rest of it could fill a book," she said irritably, annoyed with the baby now, too. Even a baby should know better than to fall for this jerk's whispered promises. "But in a nutshell, the rest of it is that I like Heather Delaney. I think she's a damn fine person. I think she deserves to be happy."

"Me, too." Griffin shrugged. "I'm only going to be here for a couple of weeks, you know. I don't intend to interfere with anybody's long-term happiness."

Mary kicked her heel against the wood floor, though she knew someone would have to polish out the scuff mark. "Yeah, well, you may not intend to, but you always seem to have a way of doing it anyhow."

"Really? How?"

"Just by being around, damn it. Just by being you."

He grinned. "Gosh. You make me sound pretty powerful."

"Don't kid yourself, blondie. You're not powerful— you're just Trouble. Like the time you stole Eddie's prom date and had sex with her out behind the gym."

Griffin laughed softly. "Come on, Mary. That was more than fifteen years ago. And we didn't actually have sex."

"They found her corsage in your underwear."

He laughed out loud, startling the babies, who jerked in their sleep. Silencing himself quickly, he winked at her. "That's nothing but an urban legend, and you know it."

"Okay, how about the time you and Dooley went joyriding in Hickory Baxter's Cadillac?"

"Twenty years ago," he said. "Even Hickory has forgiven us by now. Come on, Mary. You can't still be this ticked off about a bunch of teenage nonsense. Other than missing the city council meeting, which, by the way, was not my fault, what sins have I committed lately?"

She looked him straight in the eye. "Well, there was that charming episode with Emma Dunbar. That was just a couple of months ago. Recent enough for you?"

Mary was pleased to see that Griffin finally looked uncomfortable. As well he should. Emma and her husband, Firefly Glen's Sheriff Harry Dunbar, were getting along fine now, but a couple of months ago their marriage had been in real trouble.

And the trouble was spelled "Griffin Cahill."

"Been listening to gossip, Mary?"

"It isn't just gossip," she retorted. And it wasn't. Harry himself had caught Griffin with Emma, kissing her, and God only knows what else. The two men had squared off in Emma's pretty little Paper Shop on Main Street, with half the town watching through the plate glass window.

"Are you so sure?"

"Darn right I am." She lifted her chin, daring him to downplay the situation. "I knew you were a tomcat, Cahill. But I honestly thought you drew the line at married women."

For a long minute he didn't answer her. He just idly stroked the pink cheek of one of the sleeping babies with the tips of his fingers.

It made Mary madder than ever. "Well? Haven't you got any explanation at all?"

He smiled. "As a matter of fact, I do."

Mary snorted. "And?"

"And, in spite of your obvious curiosity, I don't feel any particular need to share it."

God, he would never change, would he? He'd always been too handsome, too rich, too bloody full of himself. Too…she felt her vocabulary stuttering with annoyance. Too blond.

Maybe he was the one who ought to get her next *Listen Up* lecture. But what a waste of good ink and paper that would be. He wasn't the type to listen up to anyone.

"Besides," he added, eyeing her with a glimmer of real curiosity, "I'm not sure you have a dog in this race, do you, Mary? You're not Emma's guardian. Or mine."

"No, I'm not," she admitted. "But here's fair warning, blondie. Starting right now, I'm Heather's."

OH, YOU FOOL. You idiot. You complete and utter moron.

No, worse than moron. Much worse. Heather wished she had a thesaurus. There must be a bigger word, a word with five-inch fangs. An absolute ogre of a word for people like her, people who were dumber than dumb.

But she couldn't think of one. She could hardly think at all. For five solid minutes, she had been standing in the front hall, her briefcase in one hand and her keys in the other, frozen in place by the sounds that floated down to her from the upstairs bathroom.

Thumping. Splashing. Giggling. Laughter. A baby's exuberant soprano. A man's calm baritone.

Fairly normal sounds, really. Just the noises any mother might hear when she got home from work. The noises of a happy young family at bath time.

The only difference was that she wasn't a mother.

And this wasn't her family.

Oh, how could she have been so stupid? She let her

briefcase slide out of her fingers with a soft leather plop
and stared at herself in the hall mirror. Why hadn't she
just offered to take the babies and let Griffin go his merry
way? She could have handled them alone somehow.
Even if it had meant doing completely without sleep for
three weeks. It would have been worth it.

Anything would have been preferable to this—to
Griffin Cahill living in Spring House. With her.

It had seemed so sensible yesterday. Obviously, if
they were going to be a team, they'd have to sleep under
the same roof—but setting up camp at Griffin's
bachelor den was out of the question. She'd been there
once, at a party she couldn't avoid. He collected ridiculously expensive art glass, for heaven's sake. And all
those metallic angles, all those highly polished
hardwood floors, that modern, free-floating staircase…

Ultra-elegant, no doubt. But a nightmare for infants.

Besides, to be brutally honest, she had simply
wanted the home field advantage. She'd wanted him
to be the "guest," the one who had to make all the ad-
justments, the one who had to politely request every
glass of water he drank.

But, in all her strategizing, she hadn't realized one
simple thing. She hadn't realized how…how difficult
it would be to come home and find him here.

Suddenly a prickle of unease broke into her
thoughts. Tuning into the bath time sounds, she realized
that the squealing laughter had changed. As in a complicated piece of music, a new note had been intro-
duced. Under the laughter, a wail of frustration. Maybe
even distress.

Finally, thankfully, Heather's paralysis lifted.
Dropping the keys in the cut-glass rose bowl, and

shedding her ridiculous case of nerves at the same time, she hurried up the stairs, ready for anything. She didn't dash, but she covered the steps with quick efficiency, her lab coat ruffling out behind her. Yes, this was more like it. She was a doctor, after all. Not a silly, dithering, hand-wringing ninny.

She didn't slow down until she reached the threshold to the bathroom—but then she stopped dead, stunned by the chaos in front of her.

Water was everywhere. A hurricane of droplets dappled the mirror over the sink and pooled in the cracks between the floor tiles. Griffin had obviously caught the worst of it. His T-shirt stuck to his chest, and the soaked front of his jeans lay dark and heavy against his thighs. His blond hair tumbled over his forehead, wetly tickling his eyebrows.

One of the babies was trying to crawl out of a large white plastic tub that had been placed on the counter next to the sink. Drenched and shining, wriggling and giggling, he looked for all the world like a baby pig.

The other boy was in a small playpen, naked and red faced, holding on to the rails of his prison and screaming his indignation at being left out of the fun.

Griffin stood between the two, contorted into an almost impossible position. He was leaning sharply forward, holding on to the baby in the tub, but he had one hand desperately extended behind his back, shaking the multicolored ring of plastic keys at the baby in the playpen, who couldn't have been less interested.

"I kid you not, Stewbert. You've gotta give me a break here, pal." Griffin's baritone was raspy with frustration. He jiggled the plastic keys behind his back feverishly. "Your dad said this damn thing was your favorite toy, remember?"

Heather didn't wait for Griffin to notice her. She just kicked off her work shoes and waded, stocking-footed, into the fray. She leaned over the playpen and gathered the naked, wailing little boy into her arms. He stopped crying instantly, and smiled up at her through his tears, as if to say it had all been a grand joke.

"Yes! Attaboy, Stewbert," Griffin said without turning around, still jiggling the noisy ring of plastic keys frenetically. "That's it, pal. Just give your Uncle Griffin sixty seconds of peace and quiet, and maybe he won't go stark, raving crazy after all."

Heather reached out and covered the clacking keys with her free hand. "I don't know," she said mildly. "It may be too late."

"Heather?" Griffin swiveled his head without letting go of the baby in the tub. The expression on his face was ten percent embarrassment and ninety percent pure, unabashed relief.

"Thank God," he said simply. He dropped the keys on the floor and, using both hands, gave the baby in the tub one good rinse, then plucked him out. Ignoring the boy's immediate squeals of protest, Griffin flicked a towel from the rack and draped it across the wet, wriggling little body.

Then he turned around and gave Heather a smile that caught a glistening drop of water in one dimpled corner.

"Hi," he said sheepishly. "It may be hard to believe, but the Stewberts and I actually had decided that being all cleaned up would make a great first impression when you got home." He blinked away a damp strand of hair that had caught on his lashes. "I'm willing to admit I may have miscalculated just a little."

She looked around the soggy room. "Just a *little?*"

He grinned and began rubbing the baby dry with the soft blue terry towel. "I know. But remember…you didn't see what the Stewberts looked like *before* their baths. Maybe I shouldn't brag on my own nephews, but I have to say they do things with pureed peas that are really quite creative."

She chuckled. She couldn't help it. For no apparent reason, the baby she was holding had decided it might be fun to look at the world upside down. He had dropped his head and was now leaning so far back his little belly button was pointing at the ceiling.

She righted him with effort, but he flopped back immediately, determined to slither headfirst out of her arms. It was like trying to hold on to a wet eel.

"The Stewberts?" She looked at Griffin over the writhing little boy. "That's what you're calling them?"

"Well, I had to split the difference," he explained reasonably. "'Stew' for Stewart and 'Bert' for Robert. I tried other combinations, but 'Bert-wart' sounded almost vulgar."

She laughed, which caught her baby's attention. He stopped twisting abruptly, pulled himself erect, and stared at her. Frowning, he reached out and pressed his tiny forefinger against her teeth curiously.

She planted a small kiss on the exploring hand. "Still," she said, "you're going to have to fess up sooner or later." She glanced at Griffin, who was sharing the towel with his nephew, alternately rubbing the baby's wet face, then his own. He had spoken to Jared several times, assuring him that the boys were all right and letting him know about the temporary move to Heather's house. But he'd never mentioned the mix-up in names. "Why don't you just call Jared and ask him what the secret is to telling them apart?"

"I can't. I still have my pride, you know." Griffin took one step and landed with a piercing, falsetto squeak on a yellow rubber duckie. "Well, some of it, anyway."

Heather didn't know an awful lot about babies—at least not once they were born and turned over to the local pediatrician. But she did know that it was probably courting disaster to postpone the diaper process much longer. "How about if I help you get these guys dressed?"

Griffin smiled. "That would be great. Thanks."

She turned toward the large dressing room, which she had hastily converted into a makeshift nursery late last night. It was conveniently located between the spacious his-and-her bedrooms so common in Victorian floor plans. Griffin would sleep on one side, Heather on the other. Both of them would be within earshot of the boys.

"Heather." Griffin's voice came from behind her.

She turned around. "What?"

"I really mean it," he said softly. "Thanks. For everything."

He sounded sincere. She felt herself start to melt a little around the edges, just looking at the sweet picture of man and baby, both damp and tousled, both staring solemnly at her with blue eyes so clear and open their souls seemed to shine through.

It was so strange. It made her feel a little light-headed. She'd seen him just like this in dreams, a thousand times. Her husband. Her baby. She remembered waking up and hugging her pillow, not wanting to let the dream go. Of course, that had been a long time ago. At seventeen, she had still had complete faith that the dream would one day come true.

"Heather, I—" He let out a slow breath, as if he weren't sure where to begin. He stroked the baby's back idly. "Listen, I've always wanted a chance to tell you that I—"

Suddenly his expression changed. He looked down.

"What the—?" Holding the smiling baby at arm's length, he cursed, sharp and hard. "God damn it, Stewbert, couldn't you have waited one more lousy minute?"

Heather looked at Griffin's shirt. It had always been wet, so she couldn't discern anything new, but obviously he could. He was glaring at his nephew, and the horrified shock on his face couldn't have been any greater if the baby had just shot him with a popgun.

She began to laugh, sorry for Griffin, but relieved that the weirdly intimate moment had passed safely. She wasn't up to exchanging confidences with him now. It was too late for that. Years and years too late.

"It's not funny," he said, transferring his glare to her.

"Yes, it is. You should see yourself."

"It could be you next," he growled. "I hope it is, you heartless—"

She grinned. This was a whole new side of the ordinarily suave and glossy Playboy Cahill. This man was disheveled. Clearly perplexed. Practically inept.

He came shockingly close, in fact, to being human.

Still smiling, Heather turned toward the nursery. Griffin followed quickly, still holding the baby out with stiff arms, as if he were an unstable time bomb.

"Well," he observed wryly as they paraded down the

hall, "it's nice to know that you find my predicament so amusing."

Heather crossed the room, picked up two diapers from the changing table and handed him one politely.

"Yes," she agreed, her smile broadening as she watched him try to open the diaper and lay it on the table without letting the baby within striking range. "In fact, I'm starting to think these next couple of weeks might just be extremely entertaining."

CHAPTER FIVE

TEN O'CLOCK AT LUCKY'S LOUNGE. Typical Friday night full house, lots of noise and smoke. A hot, greasy pizza waiting back at the booth. A well-chalked cue in his hand and a Knicks game on the overhead television. The twelve ball sinking into the corner pocket just as the go-ahead shot sinks into the TV basket, nothing but net either place.

And best of all, not a baby in sight.

It was, Griffin decided as he racked his cue and joined Parker Tremaine at their corner booth, about as close to heaven as the average guy ever gets.

Well, a beer might have nudged him an inch or two closer, but for the time being alcohol was off-limits. Still a field general in disguise, Heather had posted a complicated rotation of responsibilities. According to her typewritten schedule, Griffin had Daddy Duty in just over two hours.

Setting his jaw, he picked up his diet soda and tried not to smell Parker's Michelob from across the table.

"So. Tell me the God's truth, Griff." Parker leaned back and wiped the foam from his upper lip. "How tough is it?"

Griffin shrugged and stalled by taking a swallow of his cola. He couldn't exactly tell Parker the truth.

Parker's wife, Sarah, was going to have a baby this summer, and Parker was clearly scared to death.

So he couldn't say, *It's hell, pal. Run for your life.* But he wasn't going to lie, either.

"It's weird," he said, grimacing as the cola went down. *God.* This stuff could ruin a good pizza. "I mean, they're cute. Sometimes they're so damn adorable you just can't believe it. But they're after you all the time, you know what I mean? They need something every fifteen seconds. I've never been so tired in my life."

Parker blinked, then took a fortifying swig of beer. Griffin looked away. It was strange. He used to scoff at his friends who seemed so emasculated by the arrival of a new baby. Weaklings, he had thought them, with their shadowed, tired eyes, their fretful double-checking of their watches, their frequent calls home to check out mystery fevers and erupting teeth.

And what happened to their conversation was a crime. Brilliant men could deliver twenty-minute monologues about burping, and CEOs would discuss projectile vomiting until you practically lost your lunch.

Yeah, he had thought they were pretty pathetic. And now here he was, in the same boat. For the past hour, all through the first half of a damn good Knicks game, he'd been fighting an urge to call Heather to find out if Stewbert was still refusing to eat.

"You in?" Micky Milligan, the seven-foot bartender who had been collecting the "TV tax" at Lucky's ever since Griffin was a teenager, came by with his hand out. Everyone at Lucky's knew that the TV tax was just a clever ruse to get around the prohibition against gambling.

Tonight they were betting on the point spread in the

basketball game. When he handed over his five-dollar bill, Parker called for the Knicks by two. Griffin felt wilder. He guessed the Knicks would blow it out by twenty.

Parker laughed. "Haven't you even been watching the game? The Knicks are down by six, with only five minutes left." When Griffin just shrugged, Parker narrowed his eyes curiously. "You didn't have a clue what the score was, did you? What's with you tonight? Is anything wrong?"

Griffin shook his head. Was anything wrong? Besides the fact that his brother had just saddled him with two babies who never slept, which meant he didn't sleep, either? Besides the fact that he had to drink swill with his pizza?

He downed the last watery dregs of his cola. "Nothing's wrong. I just believe in the Knicks." He smiled at Parker. "I notice you handed over your hard-earned cash without a second thought. Sarah doesn't mind your gambling away the baby's college tuition?"

Parker smiled that goofy smile he always got when he talked about Sarah. The man was so in love it was funny. "She'd mind if I didn't. The first time she came here, she won the whole pot, so she thinks it's good luck."

Parker drained his beer. "Besides, you know Sarah. She's not the judgmental type."

That was true. Parker was a lucky son of a gun. He had a wife who was beautiful and smart and gentle—and one of the most easygoing women Griffin had ever met. She was that rare female who loved her man just as he was. She had no interest in changing him, holding out hoops for him to jump through, setting up hurdles for him to clear before he could be considered worthy of her.

Not, to put it bluntly, at all like General Heather Delaney.

Griffin tried to imagine himself married to Heather, with a baby on the way. The sex would be fine. In fact, it would be fantastic. He remembered that, all right. But hell. What was he thinking? They probably would have stopped making love within two weeks of the wedding. The first time Griffin came home late, or looked at another woman walking by…

God, he hadn't thought about all this in years—and he'd be better off if he didn't think about it now. He had no idea what marriage to Heather would be like, but he was fairly sure it wouldn't involve beer at Lucky's and betting on the Knicks game.

"Stop daydreaming, Cahill. Shove over and make a little room. And while you're at it, pour your long-lost friend a beer."

Griffin looked up, shocked by the sound of the familiar voice.

"Troy?" He shook his head, disbelieving. But it was definitely Troy, his friend and sometimes partner, the writer who provided the copy to go with his pictures. Troy, complete with his movie-star tan, his shaggy Beatles haircut, and his compulsively buffed body, all of which worked hard at disguising the fact that Troy Madison was standing on the other side of what he called "the great divide"—his fortieth birthday.

"What the hell are you doing in Firefly Glen, Madison? I thought you were in Acapulco, interviewing that actress."

"Naw. I cut that short. She turned out to be completely plastic." He grinned at Griffin's raised eyebrow. "Her personality, you filthy-minded animal. I wouldn't know about the rest of her. I'm a married man, remember?" He slid into the spot Griffin had created. "For the moment, anyhow."

Griffin didn't take the bait. Troy was a gifted writer, but a lousy family man. He had been complaining about his rotten marriage for the past ten years. Every time Griffin worked with him on an assignment, Troy would swear that a divorce was imminent. But after a decade of grousing, the man was still wearing that little gold ring.

"You remember Parker Tremaine, don't you, Troy?"

Troy brushed his brown hair out of his eyes and extended a hand across the table. "Of course. Good to see you, Sheriff."

"Not the sheriff anymore," Parker explained. "I traded in my badge for a shingle. I set up my own law practice in town a few months ago."

Troy grinned. "Maybe I could use you. Do you do divorces, Counselor?"

"I haven't done any yet. Haven't done much of anything yet, actually. A couple of wills, a couple of trust funds, nothing too exciting."

"That's what you get for living in Firefly Glen, where when they want a real thrill millionaires dress up like loggers so they can spend Friday nights in dumps like this." Troy looked around, exhaling a sigh full of pity. "God, what a yawner. You probably couldn't even get a good fight going in this town unless you insulted somebody's mutual fund."

Parker smiled. "Or dinged their BMW."

"Hey." Griffin tilted his empty glass toward Parker threateningly. "You leave my BMW out of this."

Troy groaned. "Rich people have got to be the most

boring people on earth." Reaching over, he shamelessly poached a slice of pizza from Griffin's plate. "But don't worry, my small-town friend. I've come to take you away from all this."

Griffin watched him eat half the pizza in one bite. "You don't say."

"I do say. I've got a proposition you'd be a fool to refuse. And you're no fool." Troy scowled at the table. "Hey, where's the beer?"

"Griffin isn't drinking tonight, Troy," Parker put in, a mischievous glint in his eye. "He's got to go home soon. He's got a curfew. He's got to take care of the babies."

Troy froze, his mouth half-open, which wasn't a pretty sight. "The what?"

Parker's grin was splitting his face. "The babies."

"Shut up, Parker." Griffin gritted his teeth. "It's not like that. I don't have any babies. I mean, I have babies, but—"

"Later. You can tell me the baby story later." Troy held up both hands. "Right now just listen. Forget the babies, whoever they are. Forget everything. I've got an assignment for us."

"But I can't—"

"Just listen, I said. This is special, Griffin. This is the one we've been talking about, the one we've been waiting for. It's Nepal."

"Nepal?" In spite of himself, Griffin's heartbeat revved a little. This really was special.

"Nepal. And that's not all. Get this. It's *National Geographic,* man." Troy nodded his head, his tan glowing almost copper with rising excitement. "It's the one and only *National Geo*-Chance-Of-A-Lifetime-*graphic.*"

Griffin's mouth wasn't working right. He couldn't seem to get it to form the word "no." He just looked at Troy, whose eyes were shining. Then he looked at Parker, whose eyes were not. Parker's kind blue eyes were dark, and somber.

Parker understood.

"Well?" Troy sounded indignant. "What are we waiting for? Go home and get packing. If we leave tonight we'll have a couple of weeks to play around before the shoot officially begins."

"Troy," Griffin began slowly. "I think maybe I'd better tell you the baby story now."

"Oh, come on, Griff—" Troy paused. As he looked around, he finally seemed to register the grim expressions on the faces of the other men. "Damn, Griffin. You haven't done something really stupid, have you? They aren't yours?"

"No. They're not mine." Griffin took a deep breath. "But for the next three weeks they might as well be."

"Well, if they're not yours, then what difference does—"

"If you'll listen, God damn it, I'll tell you."

Troy tugged on his shaggy hair irritably, grabbed another piece of pizza and settled back with a grunt.

"Okay," he said flatly. "But I'm warning you. I'm not taking no for an answer."

MARY HAD STRAIGHTENED up only about half the magazines in the waiting room when somebody began knocking at the front door.

"We're closed," she muttered under her breath, bending over to retrieve an issue of *Fortune* somebody had kicked under a chair. It was Saturday, for Pete's sake. Even Heather Delaney, guardian angel of the entire hopelessly dependent female population of Firefly Glen, deserved to close up shop on Saturday.

But apparently whoever was out there didn't agree. The knocking continued.

Mary growled and walked over to the glass doors, prepared to shoo the pest away. To her surprise, though, it wasn't a pregnant female. It was a male. A very male male.

He looked to be in his late thirties or early forties, and he was aiming a fairly charming smile at her through the glass. Not charming enough to get her to open that door, though. Saturday afternoon was her only time for writing, and her writing was much more important than any pair of nicely tanned, rather broad shoulders.

She pointed at her watch, then pointed at the door, where the office hours were clearly stenciled. "We're *closed*," she mouthed broadly, so he couldn't mistake her meaning. But she smiled. He might come back on Monday, and she'd like him to remember her warmly.

"Am rucknggh pr Gffarn Chll," he mouthed back, returning the smile. He tilted his head, laced his fingers together in supplication and managed to make one word come through clearly. "Please?"

Oh, heck. Mary reached up and twisted the dead bolt.

"The doctor isn't here," she said firmly. "We're closed."

"Actually, I'm not looking for the doctor," he explained politely. "I'm Troy Madison. I work with Griffin Cahill. I was wondering if he might be here."

He *worked* with Griffin Cahill? That was a joke. Cahill hadn't worked in his whole spoiled life. But she felt a small drag of disappointment. She should have known that this man, with his major-league good looks and his cheerful assumption that any door he knocked on should miraculously fall open, would be buddies with Playboy Cahill.

"Well, he's not." She let the door narrow an inch. "Listen, I hate to be rude, but I'm pretty busy here."

Troy, or whatever his name was, quickly adopted an apologetic expression. "I know. I am sorry. It's just that Mrs. Burke at the café said she thought Griff was coming here, to see Dr. Delaney. And I really need to talk to him. It's important."

She tried not to fall for it, but he was awfully good. She liked it that he had bothered to find out Theo's name at the Candlelight Café. And she liked it that he called Heather "Dr. Delaney." That showed respect.

"You see," he went on, as if he sensed a chink in the fortress, "it's about a job. It's rather exciting, really, and a decision has to be made quickly. Otherwise, I wouldn't have dreamed of bothering you when you're closed."

He even sounded sincere. And he had an open face. He really did look excited about something.

"A job? You're a photographer, too?"

He laughed, as if that were very funny. "Gosh, no. Even at Christmas I mostly end up taking pictures of my thumb." He pantomimed fumbling absurdly with an imaginary camera. "Actually, I'm a writer. That's why Griff and I make a good team. I come up with the words, and he provides the pictures."

"Really? You're a writer?" Mary hoped she didn't sound like an ingénue. But she didn't meet many writers, buried here in Firefly Glen. Most of the men she met were either loggers, like her brothers, or millionaires, like Griffin, who didn't do anything but play with their stock tickers. "For a living?"

"Yes, I am. I mostly do travel pieces. But of course I'm working on a novel that I may even finish someday, if I live long enough."

She looked at him, fascinated by the blasé way he made that announcement, as if everyone understood about writing novels, as if everyone probably had one half-completed in a drawer at home.

She had to bite the inside of her cheek to keep from telling him about the box full of stories she kept under her bed, stories she had written to amuse her little brothers after their mother died. The stories weren't much good—strictly amateur, family stuff. But sometimes she dreamed she'd polish them up a bit, send them to an editor and see what happened.

It wasn't a fact she usually felt like broadcasting. Not anymore. She'd made the mistake of telling Dooley about it one day, and he'd laughed so hard lemonade had come running out his nose. He'd been showing off that trick at parties ever since.

That was her world. The world everyone thought she "belonged" to. But someday, she'd vowed that afternoon, as she tossed her paper napkin to Dooley, someday she'd show them all how wrong they were.

She wondered if this man, this Troy Madison, had ever felt the need to show anyone anything. Probably not. He looked as if his parents had been called Scott and Zelda, and read each other poetry after dinner. He looked as if he'd been born in a thirty-room country house that had a library lined with a hundred thousand books.

She, on the other hand, had been born with only a dog-eared library card. In spite of that discrepancy, she felt a strangely powerful kinship with him now.

"So what is this exciting assignment you mentioned? Is it a travel story?"

He beamed. "Yes. It's in Nepal. I've been sending the idea around for years, and somebody finally bit on it. And not just 'somebody.' *National Geographic.*"

He looked absolutely adorable, with that proud, happy grin. And why shouldn't he be proud? *Nepal.* She liked the exotic sound of it. And she definitely liked the idea of Griffin Cahill in Nepal.

"Actually, Griffin was here about twenty minutes ago," she said, suddenly deciding it would be a good idea to cooperate. She could tell Troy was surprised by her abrupt change of topic, but he nodded attentively. "He did come to see Heather. He was planning to take the babies to the park."

"And what? He wanted her to go, too?"

"I guess so. He didn't exactly ask her, but why else would he have come here? He doesn't have to clear all his movements with her."

"And did she go?"

"Followed him within five minutes. Like he had her on a string."

Probably, Mary figured, she shouldn't be so obvious about her displeasure. But Heather had shocked the heck out of her this afternoon. Heather didn't believe in wasting time. She always spent Saturday afternoons, when she had no patients, going over medical records. She never just went to the park, for no good reason. Never.

Not until Griffin Cahill and his two pudgy bundles

of joy—drooling all over their identical blue rompers—had strolled in here today.

"I think she was concerned that he couldn't handle them alone." At least that was the explanation Mary preferred.

Troy looked thoughtful. "Oh, man, if there's a female involved…" He shook his head, as if to himself. "No. A doctor would be too serious. Not his type. And we're talking *Nepal* here." He scratched his ear and frowned at Mary. "You don't think that he…that she…"

She recognized the concern in his face quite easily. It was a mirror image of her own.

He started again. "I mean, you don't think that they—"

"Not if you get there fast enough," she said. Smiling, she strode over to the front counter and tore a blank sheet from the sign-in clipboard. "Here. I'll draw you a map."

WHEN HEATHER REACHED THE PARK, she wished for the first time in her life that she could take photographs the way Griffin could. She would have liked to have a picture of this day, to look at when she was cold, when the sky was low and gray, when it was winter again.

It was one of those magical early May days, when everything was washed in gold. It wouldn't last. Soon spring would gather a vigorous green strength. But today—maybe only today—the blue-gold sky rose clear for miles; the emerald-gold grass was tender underfoot. The sable-gold trunks of budding oaks grew alongside white-gold birches, and daffodils shone like cups of honeyed champagne.

Add to that the peachy-gold cheeks of the laughing Stewberts, and Griffin's golden hair—and you had a scene that begged to be captured, and kept forever.

But Heather had no camera. So she just stepped into the picture and became a part of it.

The boys already sat in a pair of baby swings, fully harnessed, and Griffin stood centered behind them, gently pushing one with each hand. The Stewberts clearly loved it. With each rhythmic arc, they crowed delightedly and kicked their tiny legs like baby frogs trying to swim through the air.

Griffin must have been very sure she would follow him, Heather thought wryly. He couldn't have heard her coming up behind him, but he turned his head and smiled at her over his shoulder, unsurprised.

"Hi," he said. "You must have ESP. I was just wishing I had another pair of hands."

She stepped into place in time to catch one of the Stewberts on the downswing and give his padded bottom a push. "Really? I thought you seemed to have things remarkably well under control."

"An illusion," he assured her. "They're trying to lull me into a false sense of security, and then they'll hit me with it."

"With what?"

"Whatever. Crying. Screaming. A tumble. A pinched finger. A runny nose. A leaky diaper." He grimaced. "Projectile vomiting."

She laughed, which was a mistake, because it caused Stewbert to writhe in his harness, trying to get a look at her. She caught the swing. "It's just me, sweetie," she said, kissing him on the top of his head.

He smiled at her broadly, his two white front teeth

gleaming in the spring sunlight, and he let go of the chain, reaching out for her with a low gurgle of recognition.

She felt a small, sweet pinch somewhere in her chest. But she fought the urge to pick him up. Taking his little fist and planting it back on the chain, she twisted him face-forward and gave him a new push. His feet began to kick contentedly again.

She glanced over at Griffin, who had been watching her with a strangely admiring half smile on his face. She felt herself flushing, but she squelched it somehow, concentrating on pushing the swing. *You've seen this before,* she reminded herself. *It's just that old, cheap Cahill charm.*

"You know what, Dr. Delaney?" Griffin spoke softly. "I think maybe you're a natural."

She eyed him coolly. "And I think maybe *you're* full of—"

"Cahill? Cahill! Can I borrow you for a moment?"

They both looked toward the edge of the square, where the sidewalk traced the perimeter of the park. Alton Millner stood there among the daffodils, waving awkwardly, looking stiff and overdressed for a mild Saturday afternoon in a dark suit and tie. But then he always overdressed. He probably thought it made him look mayoral.

Griffin waved back politely, but without enthusiasm. He sighed and turned to Heather. "Sorry. Are you okay alone here for a minute?"

She nodded and watched as Griffin loped off toward the other man, his corduroy pants and light brown bomber jacket gilded by the April sun. His movements were light and graceful, she thought.

After Griffin reached the mayor, Heather looked away.

She wasn't going to try to guess what they were talking about. She kept her attention on the Stewberts, pushing them back and forth, back and forth, like clockwork.

Griffin was gone a good bit more than a minute, which could have been predicted, considering what a talker Mayor Millner was. The babies began to tire of their game. One of them started to whimper.

Heather had already discovered that whenever one of the twins switched moods, the other wasn't far behind. She circled round to the front and began un-hitching the first baby. The harness was a diabolical contraption, though. It would take a civil engineer to ex-tricate Stewbert from its clutches, especially while the little boy was wriggling and twisting like this.

Her fingers flew, but the latch wouldn't give. The baby seemed to sense that he was trapped. She heard the first ominous sputters, the short grunts that signaled the onset of a full-blown tantrum.

"Oh, Stewbert, please," she begged in a whisper, tugging at the straps. "Not yet. Not now."

But it was too late. Stewbert sucked in a deep breath, tilted back his head and let loose the most bloodcur-dling scream Heather had ever heard. The other baby frowned, openmouthed with shock, and then decided to join in vigorously, for no apparent reason except that he refused to be outdone by his brother.

It was like being the star of a nightmare. Parents all around the park turned and watched in horror. A pair of terrified starlings shot out of the treetops. Even the squirrels seemed to freeze, mid-acorn, and stare.

Of course Griffin chose that moment to return. He squinted at the god-awful noise, then squatted down beside Heather and put his hands over hers.

"Here. Let me," he said. "I already figured it out once."

Gladly. She pulled her shaking fingers away and let him work. Within seconds he had the baby loose. He handed the screaming boy to Heather, then went to work on the other swing.

In less than a minute, both babies were free, and, miraculously, silence had returned to the golden spring day, except for their small, watery hiccuping and the terrified pounding of Heather's heart.

Griffin smiled. "I take it back," he said, patting his baby's damp head. "I guess you're not a natural after all."

She shuddered. "There was *nothing* natural about that sound," she said. With one last hiccup, Stewbert lifted his head and smiled at her, all dewy innocence. She shook her head. "You can't fool me," she told the baby soberly. "There's a demon inside you, and that's a fact."

Griffin chuckled. "At least now you see that it really does take two people to handle this."

"Three or four might be even better." But the little demon had placed his cheek against her collarbone, put his thumb in his mouth and closed his eyes, soggy lashes brushing pink satin cheeks. It was amazingly difficult, she realized, to stay out of sorts with any creature this soft and warm and trusting.

Which must be the way Nature planned it. Otherwise, who would dare to have children at all?

The other baby had shut his eyes, too, so by mutual, unspoken agreement Griffin and Heather began walking slowly back toward her office. It wasn't far—nothing was far from anything else on the quaint little streets of downtown Firefly Glen. Besides, Heather's shift was next, and they'd make the transfer there.

"I'm sorry to have left you alone so long," Griffin said, speaking quietly so that he didn't get the twins stirred up again. "But Alton is such a windbag."

"What did he want?"

Griffin hesitated. "He wanted to offer one of his daughters as a nanny—just in case the arrangement I made with you wasn't working out."

She felt a surge of irritation, but she kept her voice low somehow. "One of his daughters? Who? Mina? She's only fifteen, for heaven's sake! And she's the most ditzy teenager in town."

Griffin nodded. "I know."

"I mean, *really* ditzy. She had to quit the cheerleading squad because she couldn't remember the cheers." Heather stroked Stewbert's back protectively, hoping he wouldn't sense the quietly furious pumping of her heart. "Honestly, how absurd! He can't really believe that Mina could possibly handle it. Her judgment is terrible and—"

"Hey." Griffin put his hand on her arm. "Relax. It's okay. I told him no."

Heather looked at him blankly. His smile was slightly quizzical, and he looked both amused and curious. She took a breath, suddenly aware that she must have been overreacting.

She resumed walking. "I mean, it's not that I wouldn't be delighted if you could find someone else to help you out. I've got my practice to think about, and I hardly have the time to moonlight as a nanny. I just think it ought to be someone mature. Someone responsible."

"I agree completely," he said politely. "Much better for it to be an older woman, like you."

She looked at him hard, but his smile was so open and infectious that she couldn't help smiling back.

"Besides," he added thoughtfully, "I think Alton knew I wouldn't go for it. He was just clutching at straws. I think it shocked him to see us working together on this. Or anything."

"It has probably shocked a lot of people." She side-stepped around Theo Burke's cat, who had found a sunny spot in the middle of the sidewalk outside the Candlelight Café and claimed it. "Frankly, it even shocked me a little."

Griffin smiled. "Me, too, for that matter. But I think it particularly confuses Alton because he was counting on our somewhat—" he seemed to choose his next word carefully "—*complicated* history to keep us at odds. He apparently assumed that just because we used to be engaged we must be enemies."

"Imagine that," she said, allowing herself the slight-est hint of sarcasm. "Of course, the fact that we live in the same small town but hardly ever even speak to each other might have contributed to that notion."

"Might have," Griffin agreed easily. "Anyhow, I think he had been assuming I was on his side of this zoning battle. Apparently he was taking it for granted that I would be only too happy to vote against you the other day."

Heather didn't say anything. She concentrated on walking softly, rhythmically, lulling Stewbert to sleep. The sunshine blinked in and out of newly leafed maples and pale green oaks like a golden strobe.

But she knew Griffin was looking at her, waiting for her response.

"Heather," he said finally. "You do know that, if I had been able to get there on time, I would have voted for your variance."

She still didn't answer. What was there to say?

"Heather. Tell me you know that. Tell me you know I would have voted yes."

She turned, then, and leveled her gaze at him. "Actually, I don't ever spend much time thinking about what 'would have' happened in life," she said. "It doesn't really get you anywhere, does it? He managed to kill the zoning variance. That's the reality I have to deal with. And I am dealing with it."

They had finally reached his car, which was parked in front of her office. That elegant little whip of a vehicle, always so streamlined and racy, looked strangely alien today, she thought. And then she saw why. The top was down, and the soft leather seats were filled with large plastic baby restraints.

She had hardly absorbed the incongruous sight when Griffin turned to her abruptly.

"Damn it," he said roughly. "The son of a bitch isn't going to get away with it."

"With what?" She put her hand over Stewbert's head instinctively, as if to protect him from Griffin's sudden vehemence.

"With vetoing the variance. I told you I'd get him to change his mind, and I meant it. You'll get your variance, Heather. I promise."

She tensed. She wasn't quite sure how to react to this Griffin, who was so uncharacteristically earnest. And besides, he had promised her things before. So many broken promises littered the past that no one could safely stroll down Memory Lane anymore.

"I didn't ask for your help," she said carefully. "I never asked for anyth—"

"God, Heather, do you have to be so stiff-necked? I

asked you for a favor, didn't I? Can't you ask me for one in return?"

"No," she said, civilly but firmly. "I can't."

His face darkened. He looked angry for a moment, but almost as soon as the expression appeared it vanished. He stared at her blankly for the second it took him to adjust, and then his old, sardonic smile slowly returned.

He tilted his head, catching the afternoon sunlight in his hair.

"All right, then, I won't do it for you. I'll do it for Lady Justice. Like any good superhero, I'll stop the bad guy in the name of fair play."

She raised her brows. "So you're a superhero now?"

He grinned. "Superuncle, they call me." He looked down at the baby, who still slept in his arms. "That's right, Stewbert. I'd love to stay and change your diapers, but I have to be going. Your Uncle Griffin is off to fight for truth, justice, and the Firefly Glen way."

CHAPTER SIX

WHEN THE PHONE RANG that rainy Sunday afternoon, Heather was working in her office at Spring House, going over the results of Mrs. Mizell's most recent blood tests.

She didn't bother to answer it. Griffin was officially on duty until six o'clock, and they had agreed that whoever was in charge of the babies was also in charge of the house. That way, whoever was *off* duty could get some real relief—could actually sleep or work or just relax.

Surprisingly, the schedule she'd designed was working fairly well. Even so, she had to admit she hadn't been this exhausted since medical school. She knew Griffin was tired, too, though he dismissed the notion with his usual insouciance. But once, when she reported for her shift, she'd found him sprawled out on the floor of the nursery, sound asleep next to the cribs.

It was an oddly appealing sight, his golden head pillowed by a stuffed caterpillar, his feet bare, a cloth ABC book lying forgotten on his chest. She had hardly been able to bring herself to wake him.

Who would have thought he'd be so good at this daddy thing? She had been listening to the three of them upstairs while she worked. She caught muffled notes of music—the Stewberts loved music—and once or twice some laughter, then the mysterious sound of something scraping across the floor.

Maybe Griffin was down on all fours, playing roaring tiger games, the way he had been last night. Or maybe he was moving the crib closer to the window, so that Stewbert could watch the rain.

It was strange, she thought, laying aside Mrs. Mizell's Rh readings for the moment. Griffin and his nephews had been at Spring House not quite a week. And yet, somehow, it seemed as if they had always been here.

In fact, when she tried to remember life before the Stewberts, she sometimes had difficulty remembering exactly what she had done with all her free time.

"Sorry to interrupt, but I think I may have bad news."

Griffin was standing in the doorway, looking so crisp and fresh it was hard to believe he'd just been wrestling with a pair of twin infants.

"What is it?" She put her pen down carefully. "Are the boys all right?"

"They're fine. They're asleep. But Missy Stoppard just called. She's still twenty miles outside of town. Her car broke down, and she doesn't know when she'll be able to get home."

"Oh, no. Missy's childbirth class meets here this afternoon. It starts in—" She looked at her watch and groaned. "Two minutes."

He smiled ruefully. "I guess that explains why three minivans have just pulled up in your back driveway."

"Oh, heck." She began closing files and stacking them in the desk drawer. "They're here already?"

But the soft chime of the office door opening answered her question before Griffin could. A babble of happy voices filled the waiting room, which was, thank heaven, pristine and ready. Here at the Spring House office, every room was always pristine, always ready and waiting. The rooms had never been used and—if Alton Millner had his way—never would be.

Except for Missy Stoppard's childbirth classes, which were sponsored by the local hospital and thus somehow got around the zoning problems.

"Do you want me to tell them Missy's not coming?" Griffin had automatically begun helping her with the files. "Want me to send them home?"

"No. I always fill in for her when she can't make it. Before she came to the Glen last year, I used to teach these classes."

"Really?" Griffin paused, obviously surprised. "I didn't know that."

Heather looked at him. If the parents-to-be weren't already out there waiting, she might have succumbed to the temptation to tell him just how many, many things he didn't know about her.

He'd been gone a long time—he'd peeled out of Firefly Glen the day she handed him back his diamond ring, and he'd spent the next eight years traveling. He had returned only about a year ago, surprising everyone, especially Heather.

And during that year, they had hardly spoken beyond a civilized "hello" if they passed on Main Street. So, actually, Griffin Cahill knew as little about Heather's present life as, say, newcomer Missy Stoppard did.

But the parents-to-be *were* waiting. And what was the point in bringing all that up anyhow?

So she settled for saying, "You weren't here then."

She walked to the door and headed briskly toward the reception area. She didn't even know whether he followed her or took the other way out, back to the residential part of the house.

The waiting room was full. Five couples had enrolled in Missy's class this time, and the women were sitting on the floor, chatting companionably with each other. The men had begun to shove chairs out of the way, making room for everyone to practice.

This was the fourth of six sessions. Clearly they were already pros.

Heather smiled. "Hi, everybody. No, no," she said, waving her hand playfully, "you needn't get up!"

A chorus of chuckles swept the room. Most of the women were round and bulky, somewhere near their eighth month of pregnancy, and needed help climbing to their feet anyhow.

"Sorry, ladies and gentlemen, but Missy's not able to make it tonight," Heather announced. "So you're stuck with me."

She didn't expect anyone to be particularly upset. All the women were Heather's patients anyhow, so it wasn't exactly like asking them to work with a stranger.

But Sarah Tremaine let out a low, disappointed groan. "Oh, darn, Heather, I was hoping you'd be my partner tonight."

Heather looked toward Sarah, noticing with surprise that her friend was alone. Parker Tremaine and his petite, honey-blond bride had been almost inseparable since their wedding last winter. Parker caught a lot of ribbing about it, but actually the newlyweds were one of the Glen's favorite love stories.

"Why? Where's Parker?" Heather couldn't believe

the doting bridegroom had picked such an important time to go missing.

"He's sick, poor guy," Sarah said, and so much worried tenderness crept into her voice that it made the other couples grin. "He wanted to come anyhow, but I told him he couldn't risk giving germs to everyone else."

"Yeah, I'd heard he was sick," Joey Stillerman put in mischievously. "Lovesick, that is. I didn't know it was contagious."

Aleen Stillerman hit her husband over the head with the pillow they'd brought along. "Too bad it isn't," she said. "I wouldn't mind if you caught a little of what Parker's got."

"Oh, yeah?" Joey reached over and tickled his wife, and the two of them ended up in a rolling heap on the floor.

Sarah folded her hands over her stomach and sighed. "If you've got to teach tonight, Heather, who am I going to work with?"

Heather thought it through. Maybe, if she worked it right, she could do the teaching, and spend at least a little time coaching Sarah, too. But it would mean juggling the—

"How about me?"

It was Griffin. Heather turned, surprised. Apparently he had followed her after all.

He certainly knew how to command the attention of an entire room. Everyone stared at him in silence. Even Joey and Aleen stopped wrestling and sat up straight.

One of the dads—it might have been Boomer Bigwell—made a low, whistling sound. "Pinch, me, Betty. I'm dreaming. I thought I saw Playboy Cahill standing in a room full of pregnant women."

Heather spoke under her breath. "Don't be silly, Griffin. What about the babies?"

He shrugged. "For once, they're both sleeping. I have the portable monitor in my pocket."

She felt herself fumbling, but she needed a polite way to send Griffin away. Surely, given the stories she'd been hearing about Griffin and Emma Dunbar, who was Parker Tremaine's adored little sister, this wasn't a good idea. Sarah herself was probably horrified, but too kind to hurt Griffin's feelings.

"I'm serious, Sarah," Griffin said. "If you tell me what to do, I'll be glad to pitch in."

Joey Stillerton grinned. "I don't know, Cahill. If you spend the next two hours with your hands on Sarah's belly, Parker just might rise up off his sickbed and kick your—"

"I'd love it," Sarah broke in. Her voice was firm. The smile she aimed toward Griffin was both grateful and welcoming. "Thanks, Griffin. You're a lifesaver."

Heather cast Sarah a quick, questioning glance. But Sarah nodded subtly, assuring her that everything was fine. Heather caught the determined look in Sarah's eyes and decided not to interfere.

She settled for aiming a cautionary glare at Griffin as he passed. She caught his arm. "This class is serious, Griffin," she whispered. "It's not an excuse for a flirtation. And Sarah is a friend of mine, so—"

"Hey, lighten up, Doc." Griffin's smile was wry, but it didn't quite make it to his eyes. He put his hand over hers, hard. "I'm pretty sure I can control my animal instincts for an hour or two."

Warned by the taut quality of his voice, she pulled her hand away and turned to the others. "Okay, then.

Partners, get into position. Let's review the first breathing technique."

She watched as Griffin took his place on the floor beside Sarah. Heather didn't like this arrangement—maybe just because she suspected Parker wouldn't like it—but she couldn't prevent it. Though Sarah might look fragile, she was actually a very strong woman. If she'd decided to work with Griffin, that was exactly what she'd do.

"Okay, ladies, take a deep, cleansing breath. And…*contraction begins*."

Heather roamed the room, checking on each of the couples, making sure they were using proper technique, occasionally cheering excellent teamwork. But all the while, out of the corner of her eye, she was watching Griffin and Sarah.

He clearly hadn't ever done anything like this before. Sarah had to fill him in on each step. But by the end of the class, Heather had to admit that, to her complete surprise, Griffin made a terrific partner.

He had good instincts, a soothing voice and gentle, deft hands. He read Sarah's body like a pro. He saw where she was still tense, where she needed to relax more. During the simulated "contractions" they communicated as easily as any couple in the room.

And unfailingly, when he massaged Sarah's stomach, or her back, he touched her like a brother. He was warm, confident, comforting, focused—without any inappropriate sensuality. His professional calm eliminated any hint of the wolfish liberties Heather had feared.

In fact, she felt a little foolish for having let herself think such things. She knew that Griffin had been angry.

Perhaps he had been justified. He wasn't an animal, was he? She stared as he bent over Sarah, their gazes locked for focus, his gentle hands tracing light circles across her swollen stomach.

No, not an animal. Far from it.

Miraculously, the Stewberts continued to sleep through the entire class. Their first wriggling, snuffling noises had just begun to sneak through the baby monitor while Heather was congratulating and officially dismissing the class.

Griffin helped Sarah to her feet with a smile. "Terrific job, Mrs. Tremaine," he said, smiling down at her. "You were pretty darn impressive."

"I couldn't have done it without you," Sarah answered. And then she raised herself on her tiptoes, took his lean, tanned, handsome face in her hands and kissed him on the cheek. "Thank you, Griffin."

Heather looked away. She hated to discover that the only inappropriate sensuality in this room was in her own mind. She hated it, but it was true. The sight of Griffin's hands on a woman's body, however brotherly the touch, made her heart skip a little too fast.

She knew how those hands felt. She thought she had forgotten. Her brain probably had forgotten. But her skin remembered, and it tingled now with a primitive awareness. As meaningless as a sneeze, or a shiver—but just as uncontrollable.

"Mmmm…bamagadada," the monitor sang suddenly.

The Stewberts were awake. Almost instantly a second voice joined in fretfully. "Bagagada. Damamadada. Geep."

The babbling was so ridiculous—and yet so adorable—that everyone had to laugh.

"Uh-oh, stud," Joey Stillerman said, slapping Griffin on the shoulder. "Looks like somebody is paging his papa."

"Playboy Cahill," Boomer Bigwell called out with an irreverent grin. "That's what that 'goo-goo' stuff really means. It means, 'Playboy Cahill, please report for stinky-diaper duty.'"

"For heaven's sake, guys," Sarah said, frowning. "Stop teasing him."

"It's okay," Griffin assured her with a smile. "They'll be standing in my shoes one day soon."

He turned, raising the monitor in a playful goodbye salute to the other men. "But by then, gentlemen, I'll be in Tahiti, sipping drinks from coconut shells. You see, I've only got two weeks left in my sentence. You, my friends, are in it for life."

I'VE ONLY GOT two weeks left in my sentence.

You're in it for life.

The sardonic phrases played in Heather's head, over and over, as she and Griffin bathed and fed the babies. His shift had ended at six o'clock, but during the six-to-seven hour each night, they worked together. Then Heather took over for her shift, which would run till midnight.

The routine was complicated. But she had thought it was all working fairly smoothly. She had even, occasionally, thought perhaps Griffin was enjoying himself, just a little. She hadn't been dumb enough to think he would suddenly fall in love with the idea of home and hearth and dirty diapers, but sometimes when he smiled at Stewbert, or made those silly lion roars...

She'd been a fool, that was all. He couldn't have

made his position any more clear, could he? *Two weeks left in my sentence.* This enforced domesticity was like a prison term to him, and he was counting the days until his parole.

Well, so was she. She also had a life to get back to.

In the long, bronze shadows of sunset, she sat on the nursery chair, rocking Stewbert, who, after a big meal of mashed lamb and rice, and a sudsy, warm bath, was fighting the need for sleep. He lay in her arms, sucking on his bottle and gazing up at her with softly unfocused blue eyes.

He had wrapped his fat fingers in the long ponytail that draped over her shoulder. Now and then he would tug lightly on it, as if to reassure himself that she was still there. But he was losing his battle with sleep. His eyes were almost completely shut.

Griffin was slowly pacing the room, with the other baby cuddled up against his chest. That Stewbert wasn't ever as easy to get to sleep.

Though at first Heather had thought the babies were identical, she knew them apart quite easily now. There were a hundred tiny signs. One had a dimple in his left cheek. The other had a cowlick forming in his pale, feathery bangs. One talked much more than the other. One kicked his leg like a metronome when he was drinking from his bottle. One ate pureed peas like candy—the other would scream at the sight of them.

If only she knew which was Robert, and which was Stewart. If she could put names to them now, she thought, she'd never get them mixed up again.

She placed the sleeping baby in his crib, glancing over at Griffin, who was still working on the other Stewbert. She held out her arms, asking silently if he'd like to turn over the job. He shook his head almost imperceptibly, so that he wouldn't disrupt Stewbert's descent into dreamland, and kept walking.

Heather could only wait.

The twilight was turning from bronze to the deep red of ripe grapes. The doors to the sleeping porch were open, so Heather strolled out there, drawn by the trill of a nightingale in the nearby quaking aspen, which was white with spring bloom. The air smelled of the violets she had planted last year.

God, she loved spring in Firefly Glen. She breathed deeply, taking its mild sweetness into the bottom of her lungs. It was hard to believe that, up on Lost Logger Trail, patches of snow still lingered.

She always rushed the season. One year, she'd lost every single flower to a mid-March frost, because she had planted far too soon. But sometimes, she thought, sometimes you couldn't stop yourself. Sometimes you wanted the new, fresh birth of spring so much that you simply closed your eyes and pretended there was no such thing as winter.

She felt oddly like crying, which was absurd, especially on such a beautiful evening. She hoped that Griffin would be gone when she returned to the nursery. She didn't feel up to trying to hide her fragile edginess from him any longer.

Oh, what was wrong with her tonight?

It had all started during the childbirth class. But why? She had taught that class a hundred times, and never let it bother her. She had never let herself yearn to trade places with her patients, to be heavy with pregnancy, to be cherished and protected by a husband, to be initiated into the deepest mysteries of love and life.

She had never, ever, let it become personal. So why today? Why had it been so different today?

She recoiled from the answer her heart offered up. *No,* she said. Not Griffin. *No, no, no.*

She heard movement behind her. Griffin had come out onto the porch, too. He didn't speak, but she knew. She could tell by the small, cool current of air that opened and eddied, accepting his presence, and by the faint scent of baby powder that joined the smell of violets.

"Heather?" He was only inches away. His warmth touched her shoulder blades and trickled down to the small of her back. "Is anything wrong?"

"No," she lied. "I'm fine."

"Are you sure? You seem tense."

"I'm fine." But she didn't turn around. She *was* tense. She had been tense since the day he moved into her house. She would be tense until the day he moved out.

"I don't believe it." He touched her shoulder. "God, you're positively humming with tension."

"I'm not," she said tightly. "Honestly, Griffin. I'm just tired."

"All right, then, prove it. Let me check."

Still standing behind her, he reached his right arm across her body and took hold of her left arm. He gripped her by the elbow, shaking her very gently, to see if her wrist would flop.

It was one of the moves she taught in the childbirth classes. He learned fast, she thought. He learned well.

And of course her body betrayed her. Her arm was stiff, though she fought to relax it, the way she had always told her students to relax. But how could she? How could she be calm with him standing so close?

"Relax, Heather," he said softly. "Just let go."

She tried, but this was harder than it looked, this isolation of certain muscle groups, this total focus and control. Her arm remained awkward, inflexible. God, what had she been thinking—all this time, teaching things she knew nothing about?

She inhaled shakily.

"That's right," he whispered. "Breathe. Take a deep, cleansing breath, all the way in."

But she could hardly breathe at all. His cheek was against her cheek, warmth to warmth. She hadn't been in Griffin's arms in so long. How could it be so strange, so erotic—and yet so terrifyingly familiar?

Her heart was like something caught in her chest, bumping into things in its panic.

"Breathe in through your nose. Come on, deeper."

She couldn't. It was hopeless. Her lungs just wouldn't cooperate. She made a small move to get away. But his fingers on her elbow and the light band of his arm across her chest were enough to stop her.

She realized that she was strangely powerless, desperately frightened. And shamefully excited.

"Shh," he whispered, the way he might have done to the baby, or to a lover about to climax. "Don't fight. Just breathe."

And then, pressing himself against her from behind, he put both hands on her stomach. She gasped, but he ignored her. He began to move his fingers in slow, sure circles.

"Remember what you said—it's like a wave. Just ride it." He put his lips against her neck. "Come on, breathe deeper. That's right. Just like a wave."

Like a wave. Damn him. Those were her words, the words of her class. The words of the delivery room. In her years as a doctor, she'd heard a hundred ashen-faced men whisper them to their brave, terrified wives.

They were words of struggle, of pain, of survival, miracles, birth.

Not words of shallow seduction and sex.

But because shallow emotions were all he knew, he couldn't possibly understand. He knew nothing. *Nothing.* He was taking her words and twisting them, distorting them. Cheapening them.

And even worse—she was falling for it, melting under the spring sun like the last lacy edges of ice.

In her disgust—with him, with herself—she found enough breath to speak. She pulled away.

She stared at him.

"I knew you'd do it," she said between clenched teeth. "I knew you'd abuse what you learned there today. I knew you'd turn it into a joke."

His face was hard to read in the deepening shadows. "I'm not laughing, Heather," he said softly. "And neither are you."

"No," she agreed. "Because it isn't funny. It's pathetic. Pathetic that you would take something as profound as that and turn it into a cheap pickup line."

He hesitated, standing very still. "Is that what you thought I was doing?"

"You bet it is," she said tautly. "But you can save the performance for some other woman, Griffin. I'm not interested."

"Heather," he began gruffly. "Damn it, Heather, I—"

"I said I'm not interested." She lifted her chin. "But don't be too disappointed, Griffin. You'll get out of jail soon. You only have two weeks left in your sentence, remember?"

CHAPTER SEVEN

*ALL RIGHT, TUCKER BRADY, listen up. You may think tat-
tooing a fire-breathing dragon on your bicep will make
you look like Killer RockHard ThugMan, but it won't.
It will just make you look like a puny little goofus who
dreams about being tough. Face it, Tuckie. You weigh
about one-twenty dripping wet. If you've got fifty bucks
to burn, burn 'em at the gym.*

Mary was composing her latest *Listen Up* letter as
she climbed into her car. *That idiot Tucker.* She growled
as she searched for her key, which had fallen to the
bottom of her purse. *Fire-breathing dragon, my foot.*

Actually, she might need to soften this letter up a
little before she sent it to Tucker, who was only
eighteen, pimply and painfully insecure. But right now
she didn't feel like sugarcoating anything.

It had been a long, frustrating Monday. Nothing had
gone right. Every patient had been late, or early, or
grumpy, or too chatty, or ready to argue about the bill.
Test results had been late or wrong or misfiled. The new
girl in the office had lost the prescription pads and
dropped a delivery of test tubes.

Worst of all, Mrs. Mizell had shown up again, convinced that her backache meant she was about to
miscarry. Calming her down had taken Heather nearly

an hour and had blown the afternoon schedule to bits. Then, leaving the office in turmoil behind her, Heather had gone racing home right at six, eager to play nanny to Griffin Cahill's drooling twin blobs.

But, thank God, the workday was finally over. Mary was going to go home and sleep for a month.

She put the key into the ignition and turned. Nothing. She glared at the car, a 1957 Thunderbird that Dooley had bought and restored for her last year. She hadn't wanted the darn thing. Dooley had just used her as an excuse to buy it, because he thought it was cool.

Well, you couldn't prove it by her. She hadn't ever thought a car was cool. As far as she was concerned, they were just transporting machines. And this one was a damn sorry transporter. It rarely went more than fifty miles without breaking down.

She turned the key again. "Listen up, you rusty bucket of bolts," she said fiercely. "Start, or you're headed straight for the junkyard."

But no matter how hard she whipped it, the motor just whined and struggled, coughed, shuddered, and finally passed out with a rather ominous *thunk*.

"I'm going to kill you, Dooley," she muttered, her knuckles white on the steering wheel. "And then Tucker. And then the rest of you, one by one, until I feel better."

"Hi." Troy Madison's ridiculously cheerful voice floated in through the window. He bent down and smiled at her. "Wow. What a car—'57, right? Look at those fabulous fins!"

She narrowed her eyes. "I'm going to pretend you didn't say that."

"Why?"

"Because otherwise I'd have to kill you."

She tossed the key back into her purse, where it would undoubtedly get lost again, and reached over to shove open her door. Troy, who thankfully was a pretty smart guy, backed out of the way quickly. She climbed out, slammed the door shut behind her, then kicked the fabulous fins for good measure.

"Oh." Troy glanced at the Thunderbird, then at her face, which undoubtedly looked a little scary. "Car trouble?"

"You might say that. For the price of a bus token, I'm selling it to the first person who walks by. Well, gosh. That would be you, wouldn't it?" She held out her hand. "A buck fifty."

He chuckled. "How about if I just give you a ride home? I've got a rental car down the street." He tilted his head charmingly. "Of course you'll have to promise not to kill me."

She felt her irritation subsiding. He really was kind of a cutie, even if he was Griffin Cahill's friend.

"You're probably pretty safe," she said, almost smiling. "You're at the end of a very long list."

She locked up the Thunderbird—though frankly if anyone could steal the useless thing, that was fine with her—and then they walked to his car, which was at the other end of Main, down by the City Hall.

It was a little chilly, one of those May days that were really more kin to April. Now, with sunset coming on, the sky was a frosty purple over the rolling black humps of the mountaintops.

She shivered—in her fury, she had left her sweater in the back seat.

Troy took off his camel-hair jacket and held it out. "Here. This might help."

She thought about refusing it, but a gust of icy wind puffed around the corner of the Candlelight Café and changed her mind.

"Thanks," she said, pulling it together in the front, enjoying the way it was still warm from his body. She slanted a sideways glance at his face, hoping he knew this wasn't flirting. She really was cold.

But he didn't have that smug blowfish look guys usually got when they thought they were going to get lucky, so she relaxed. They walked the rest of the way without saying much, just an occasional pleasantry to shopkeepers closing up for the night.

His car, when they reached it, was a no-nonsense, generic sedan, the kind she would have bought if Dooley had let her pick out her own. Newish, boring, reliable. She loved it on sight.

Of course, it started perfectly. She gave him general directions to her house, then leaned back and let herself go limp for the first time all day.

He was amazingly good company. He was one of the few men she'd ever met who knew when to shut up. They were almost at her house before he spoke.

"So," he said playfully, "who is ahead of me on this hit list of yours?"

She opened her eyes and tilted her face to look at him without lifting her head. "Let's see. All four of my fool brothers. That useless mechanic. The shyster who sold us the car in the first place."

She pointed to the half-hidden turnoff that would lead them to her road. "That way. Oh, yeah, and if I have time, Griffin Cahill, too."

Troy glanced over at her briefly, though he needed to concentrate to maneuver his way safely down the pocked road. "Why? What has Griffin done?"

"Nothing," she said, making a small scoffing noise. "That's Griffin's specialty. He does a whole lot of nothing, while Heather works herself half to death trying to keep up with his bratty nephews."

Troy smiled. "You sure don't think much of Griff, do you?"

"Sorry. I know he's your friend, but—"

"No, it's okay. It's actually kind of refreshing. You may be the first woman I've ever met who wasn't drooling over him."

"Yeah, well, I hate useless people." She pointed to a small dirt track between the pines. "Go through there. The house is at the end of that path."

"Useless?" Troy sounded perplexed. "Sorry, I've got to disagree. Griff's a lot of things, but he's not useless."

"Are you kidding? The man wouldn't dream of really working at anything. It might muss his hair. I based every single detail of Prince Dudley Do-nothing on Griffin Cahill, right down to his curly eyelashes and his nifty velvet pants."

"What?" In spite of himself, Troy was laughing. "Prince who?"

"Prince Dudley Do-nothing. He's—" She shook her head, suddenly embarrassed to have mentioned those silly stories to a real writer. "Oh, he's nothing. Just a character in some stories I wrote to keep my younger brothers out of trouble. They thought Griffin was the ultimate, and I had to find some way to keep them from imitating everything he did." She grinned. "Or didn't do, as the case might be."

They had arrived at her big, rambling country farmhouse, home to the whole Brady clan, including all
four brothers, two wives, two babies and Mary.

She had expected to feel self-conscious. She appreciated its history and its unpretentious charm, but she
could imagine how weird and ramshackle it must look
to a world traveler like Troy.

Strangely, he didn't even seem to notice it. He had
parked the car and turned toward her, his eyes lit with
curiosity.

"I didn't know you wrote," he said eagerly. "That's
terrific."

"I don't. Not like you do, I mean. Not real writing.
It's just dumb stuff. Kid stuff." She bit her lip to stop
her inane babbling. Why was she being so stupid about
this? She was a rather astringent woman of almost
thirty, not a stammering ninny. And her stories weren't
anything to be ashamed of. The boys had loved them.

"All writing is 'real' writing," Troy said firmly. He
moved his arm, which had been resting across the back
of the bench seat, and touched her shoulder. "I'd love
to see some of your work, if you'd feel comfortable
showing it to me."

It was almost dark, which frustrated her. She wanted
to see his face, wanted to see whether he looked sincere.
Probably he was just trying to flatter her, hoping he
could butter her up until she just slid right into bed with
him.

"That's nice of you," she said, carefully noncommit-
tal. "But not tonight. I'm tired and hungry. It's been a
rough day."

He made a disappointed sound. "Wait. I know. I
could take you out for dinner, so you wouldn't have to

cook. You could bring a few of your stories along, and we could talk about them."

Well, at least he hadn't offered to fix her a quiet dinner at his place. Or, even worse, to come in and fix dinner for her here. But he could probably tell from all the other cars in the driveway—many of them "collectibles" like the Thunderbird—that no one could expect any privacy in this house.

As she sat there trying to gauge his motives, the screen door of the farmhouse slammed, and a young, gawky bundle of bones came loping out toward one of the cars. Oh, heck. Tucker was probably on his way to the tattoo parlor, and she hadn't had time to finish his *Listen Up* letter.

She rolled down the window. "Hold it right there, Tucker Brady. You're not going anywhere tonight."

The poor boy froze like a cartoon character and squinted guiltily through the dusk, trying to identify the unfamiliar car.

Mary turned back to Troy with a smile.

"Thanks, anyway," she said. "I hope you'll give me a rain check, but I really am tired. And I have to see a man about a tattoo."

GRIFFIN STARED at the mishmash of cards in his hand and sighed. A three, a five, two deuces and a king. And the way his luck was going tonight, there was no point drawing for an inside straight.

"I'm out." He folded his cards and set them down. "Damn it, Troy, if you're not going to deal me anything better than this, I might as well go read a book."

Troy rubbed his hands together gleefully, then made a conspicuous display of raking in the pot. "Maybe you should just go to bed, like Mommy told you to," he suggested helpfully, cocking his head toward the baby duty schedule Heather had printed out and taped to the kitchen wall. "See? Eight to midnight, Heather on duty. Little Griffie takes a nap."

Griffin ignored him, concentrating on shuffling the cards. Troy had been teasing him about that stupid schedule ever since he'd arrived an hour ago. It was annoying as hell. But Griffin's theory was that if Troy didn't get a rise out of him, he'd eventually get tired of the game and move on to another topic.

But apparently he wasn't bored yet.

"Does anybody really do that?" Troy grinned. "Sleep from eight to midnight?"

God, he was like a dog gnawing a bone. Griffin dealt new hands without answering.

"Playboy Cahill doesn't, that's for sure," Troy said. "I mean, does this lady *know* you, Griff?"

"She knows me. Pick up your cards."

"Okay, okay. Listen, Griff. I gotta be honest with you, buddy." Troy popped a potato chip into his mouth and arranged his cards while he chewed. "At first I was afraid you might have a thing for this doctor lady. I mean, you guys are living together, and she is gorgeous, right? The package might be wrapped a little too tight, if you know what I mean, but she's still a knockout."

Griffin didn't look up from his cards. "So what if I did? Since when do you worry about which women I 'have a thing' for?"

"Since I need you to come to Nepal with me, that's since when. What do you think I'm hanging around for? If you're really just babysitting your nephews, I'll talk you into the trip sooner or later. But if you're actually in the middle of a hot thing with this doctor lady…"

Griffin tightened his grip on his cards, which were rotten, of course. "Troy, you're missing the mark in so many ways I hardly know where to begin. First off, I'm not in the middle of any hot thing."

"I know," Troy assured him, grabbing another fistful of chips. "Believe me, the minute I saw that schedule on the wall, I knew I was wrong about you two. I mean, it's like being in prison, isn't it? With her as the warden."

Griffin was strangely torn. He had this instinctive urge to jump to Heather's defense. How dare Troy criticize her? What did Troy really know about her, anyhow? He'd only met her yesterday, for about fifteen minutes.

On the other hand, deep inside, Griffin agreed with him. Heather was bossy, rigid and judgmental—she always had been. It had come between them ten years ago. And it would come between them now, if he were fool enough to try to start anything.

Which he wasn't. She hadn't changed a bit. She still went through life wearing a straitjacket.

Take last night, for instance. She'd gone off the deep end just because he'd tried to give her a back massage.

Hell, he should have known better. But he'd acted on impulse. Just an impulse, damn it, not an agenda. Certainly not a seduction. Frankly, when he set out to seduce a woman, he was a hell of a lot more systematic and, at the same time, more subtle.

And definitely more successful.

Last night had been different. His intentions, for once, had been ridiculously honorable. He had felt close to her. Cozy. Intimate. Like a brother. Like a friend.

Like an idiot.

Maybe it had been how young and gentle Heather had looked there in the nursery, her head bent over the drowsing Stewbert. For a minute he had seen, not the General Delaney she was today, but the teenaged Heather, the innocent Heather, the laughing girl he remembered mostly from dreams.

But actually his strange mood had begun even earlier—during the rather surreal experience of Heather's childbirth class.

If he'd made a list of the top ten places he never wanted to end up, a childbirth class would be on it. He'd only offered because he liked Sarah Tremaine. And, frankly, for the fun of shocking Heather, who obviously expected him to bolt like a scalded cat in the other direction.

And yet, gradually, as he had knelt there, working with Sarah, he had begun to feel something very strange, something that felt a lot like…envy.

Not envy of Sarah herself. No, nothing that simple. He'd felt envious of something he couldn't even name. An elusive truth he had glimpsed in the face of every woman in that room.

The women glowed, there was no other word for it— as if they were lit by some source Griffin had never seen. And the smiles they turned upon their husbands held such courage and faith and joy and promise that when the men smiled back their eyes were full of tears.

Those smiles had made Griffin feel strangely hollow. As if all these people—even dense, affable Boomer Bigwell—knew something he didn't know. Something exciting. Something about happiness.

Something about love.

Oh, hell, he'd been back in Firefly Glen too long. Tucked away in this sheltered little valley, you could forget that the world was chaotic and cruel, that love mostly went sour in less time than it took to make a baby, and that, out there, nobody really lived happily ever after. Nobody.

Maybe he ought to go to Nepal with Troy after all. Coping with foreign languages, strange currency, mysterious foods and unpaved roads would be much simpler than coping with General Heather Delaney.

"Hello? You going to bet or what? This isn't a game of chess, you know."

Griffin threw in a couple of blue chips, though he knew he would lose them. "Too bad," he said. "I could beat you at chess."

That was when the tapping started. Light, but insistent, like pebbles at the window.

Griffin frowned. "What the hell—?"

But Troy was already on his feet, smiling and heading for the kitchen door. "Hot damn," he said happily. "I bet it's the girls."

Griffin felt frozen in his seat. This did not sound good. "The girls?"

"Yeah. The girls from Lucky's. Margie and Barb. Or Barbie and Marge. I forget which." He scratched his cheek. "Whoops. Did I forget to tell you I invited them to stop by here after they ate?"

"It must have slipped your mind," Griffin commented dryly. "Not that your mind was involved in the decision, I suspect."

"Damn. You're starting to worry me, Griff. Look, just repeat after me—I am a consenting adult. Those babies upstairs are not really mine. I am allowed to have fun." He scowled at Griffin's pointed silence. "Okay, don't repeat after me. But you'd better put a smile on your sour puss, buddy, because I promised these ladies some laughs."

BP 155/90. THAT WAS TOO HIGH for Anna Mizell, even during a panic attack. How high had it been last time?

Distracted and slightly anxious, Heather walked down the back staircase carefully. She held on to the banister with one hand and tried to flip Anna's chart with the other, while, with any kind of luck, she'd avoid dropping the pair of empty baby bottles she had tucked under one arm.

The Stewberts were going to wake up soon. She could tell by the restless shifting in their sleep. She wanted to be ready, with fresh, warm bottles in hand.

Let's see...Only 130/85 last time. Nearly normal. But still...Can't risk preeclampsia at this point. What about weight gain?

Still squinting at the chart, searching for clues, she moved though the darkened dining room, the quickest route to the kitchen. The baby monitor swayed heavily in the pocket of her robe. No noise from the babies yet—if she hurried, she'd make it back before they began to cry.

As she shouldered open the swinging door to the kitchen, the unexpected sound of laughter stopped her in her tracks. Who on earth was in the breakfast nook at this hour? It was nearly eleven. She had thought she was alone in the house.

There it was again. It wasn't really laughter, not exactly. It was giggling. Girlish giggling. And from more than one girl.

She had a mindless impulse to back out again before she was seen. But her foot caught in her robe, and she stumbled, dropping the baby bottles on the bare tile floor with a loud plastic clatter.

Glasses clinked, chairs scraped back, voices whispered…and then four faces emerged from the breakfast nook. Troy Madison held a handful of cards, and was red faced, transparently guilty, like a little boy caught licking the icing off the cake.

He stood awkwardly between two young—very young—women. Improbable blondes, they were smacking gum like a synchronized act and staring anxiously at Heather as if she were their Mother Superior from high school—a very recent memory for them, no doubt.

Of the four, only Griffin looked completely unfazed by Heather's appearance. But blasé was, of course, Griffin's natural state, and it would take more than getting caught playing poker with a couple of wide-eyed convent girls to embarrass him.

Ten years ago, when she'd caught him in the shower with her college roommate, not a single inch of his fully exposed body had so much as blushed. He'd even combed his hair and nicely knotted a towel around his waist before coming out to explain that Nicolette's arrival under the pulsing jet head had been a shock to him, too.

He strolled over now and retrieved the bottles for her. "Everything okay upstairs?" he asked pleasantly.

"Just fine," she answered, equally pleasant. "Hello, Troy. Hi, everyone," she added to the young women. "Don't mind me. I'm just getting a couple of new bottles ready for when the boys wake up. I'll be out of here in a flash."

Troy's color was returning to normal, and even Griffin's smile looked a little more natural. Returning the smile sweetly, she edged around him and went to the refrigerator, where they kept the prepared bottles.

She felt him watching her. But she went about her business, ignoring him. If he thought she was going to start ranting and throwing crockery just because he'd invited a couple of girls over, he was mistaken. She'd quit losing her temper about his sex life ten years ago, when she quit giving a damn what he did. She supposed, in a way, she had Nicolette to thank for that.

She popped the bottles into the microwave—fifteen seconds, she'd learned, was perfect. When it beeped, she pulled them out and, tucking them back under her arm, exited the kitchen with casual goodbyes all around.

She had reached the bottom tread of the staircase when she heard Griffin's voice.

"Heather."

She turned around.

"You forgot this." He held out Anna Mizell's chart.

"Thanks," she said politely, taking it. She smiled again and turned back toward the stairs.

"Heather. Wait."

She looked at him impassively. "Yes?"

"I just wanted you to know…Troy invited those women over here, not me. Troy and I were playing poker, and all of a sudden they were just there."

She smiled, remembering the drenched and defiant Nicolette. "Poor Griffin," she said. "That happens to you a lot, doesn't it? But don't worry. It's not a problem."

"Well, I didn't want you to think that I—I mean, it is your house, after all. I would have checked with you first."

That had occurred to her, too. Ordinarily she would have considered it fairly cheeky for a man to host a coed poker party in her kitchen without her permission. But she had to remember that she'd forced Griffin to spend the three weeks here at Spring House. His preference clearly had been to do the babysitting at his place. Now she could see why.

"It's really no problem," she assured him. "But shouldn't you go back? They're probably waiting for you, don't you think?"

Griffin grinned. "I have a feeling Troy is enjoying himself just fine without me."

"Yes, I imagine you're right." She finally felt a prickle of the irritation Griffin had been expecting. "You know, now that you mention your friend Troy..."

"Yes?" Griffin looked curious.

"I guess it's none of my business, but something you said made me think that...well, isn't he—isn't he married?"

Griffin shrugged. "Apparently he's actually filed for divorce this time. Honestly, I never thought he'd do it, though he's been threatening to for years."

"Still." She tightened her hold on the warm bottles. "Filing for divorce and actually *being* divorced aren't exactly the same thing, though, are they?"

Griffin raised one eyebrow. "No, they aren't. But playing cards with a woman and committing adultery aren't exactly the same thing, either."

She felt herself flushing. She knew what that flat, amused tone meant. It meant that he found her to be insufferably uptight, a bourgeois bore who wasn't capable of understanding the sophisticated, elastic morality of jet-setters like Griffin and Troy.

"I couldn't care less what the state of Troy Madison's marriage is—or what his intentions are with regard to his fellow card players. My only concern is that he seems to have developed an interest in Mary Brady, and apparently he forgot to tell her that he's married." She stared at him unwaveringly. "Mary is a very special person. I don't want to see her get hurt."

Griffin looked surprised, but after a second he began to chuckle.

"Nuts. There may be a man somewhere in this world who could seduce Mary Brady, but I promise you Troy is not that man. He's not subtle enough. If he tried to make a pass at her, she'd chop him into little pieces and feed him to her brothers for lunch."

"He may be more subtle than you think. Mary called me just a while ago. I don't think I've ever heard her so excited. Troy gave her a ride home tonight, and when they got talking, he expressed an interest in her writing. He wants to look at some of her stories. You know how much she's always wanted a future as a writer, Griffin. She's positively breathless at the prospect."

Griffin made a silent *oh* with his lips.

"That is different," he said. "And a hell of a lot more perceptive than I'd have given Troy credit for being." He chewed his lip thoughtfully. "You know, I'm actually not sure he *was* being clever. He might just really be interested."

"He might be." She let her skepticism show in her voice. "Or he might just see it as the perfect pickup line. In which case it's doubly unkind. He will end up dashing her hopes twice. Once about him, and again about her writing."

Griffin looked as if he might be going to argue, but

he apparently decided against it. "Okay," he said slowly. "I get it. I'll talk to him."

A burst of high-pitched laughter exploded from the kitchen. Griffin smiled. "See? I told you they'd be fine without me." He hesitated for a brief moment, then went on. "You know, I could come up with you now and help you feed them. I wasn't exactly dying to play cards. I had meant to get some sleep. It's just that Troy came over, and I—"

"You really don't need to explain anything to me," she said, but she said it without any sting. She felt rather mellow toward him, actually—at least for now. He had taken her criticism of Troy well, and now he was almost as good as admitting he'd rather be upstairs with the Stewberts than down here with the bimbos.

Which she'd suspected anyhow. They weren't his type.

"You do whatever you want with your free time, Griffin. If you want to rest, fine. If you'd rather play cards, or shoot pool at Lucky's, or go skinny-dipping on Mars, that's fine, too."

His eyes twinkled in the crystal light from the stairwell chandelier. "Skinny-dipping on Mars... Now there's an interesting i—"

"Whatever." She pointed one of the bottles at him in mock severity. "Just make darn sure you present yourself at that nursery door at midnight. Or I'm sending in the baby brigade to break things up down here."

Grinning, he straightened himself to stand at full attention, then raised his palm in a crisp salute. She couldn't help smiling back. She had forgotten just how devastatingly attractive he could be when he let that facade of sardonic cynicism slip for even a minute.

"Yes ma'am, General Delaney, ma'am," he said. "Any further instructions?"

"Just one thing," she said as she turned to go back up the stairs. "I've seen you play poker. Don't keep drawing to an inside straight."

CHAPTER EIGHT

THE CANDLELIGHT CAFÉ WAS so crowded Tuesday morning that Griffin, Troy and the Stewberts had to squeeze themselves into one of the tiny back booths. The chaos actually worked to their advantage, because all the noise and movement fascinated the little boys, who sat happily in their baby seats without making a peep.

Breakfast was always a bustle at the café. Theo Burke, the owner, made blueberry pancakes so light they flew into your mouth. But that wasn't what had drawn the crowd today.

Today the chamber of commerce was meeting to discuss the possibility of starting a new Firefly Glen tradition: a Carnival of Spring.

Granville Frome, who owned most of the downtown buildings and didn't ever let anyone forget it, was the chamber president this year. He didn't let anyone forget that, either.

He had set up a computer presentation tracking tourism figures, and he was talking the group through past years with painstakingly detailed slides and graphs and pie charts.

He had made it as far as 1937 when Bourke Waitely finally stood and shook his elephant-tusk cane in the air.

"For God's sake, Frome, shut up! Who cares about all that? The only real question is whether Ward Winters will *let* us have a spring festival. You know how the meddling old fool acted during the Ice Festival last winter!"

"Now, Bourke, you just calm down," Granville said, though he didn't look very calm himself. Granville's temper was legendary in Firefly Glen. Griffin nudged Troy, alerting him to the potential for a good geriatric fistfight. Frome's face was red under his silver hair, which was one of the signs he was about to come unglued.

"Ward Winters doesn't call the shots around here." Granville puffed out his chest. "I do!"

"Well, now, I don't know about that," Alton Millner said, standing up from the back of the room. "As the mayor of Firefly Glen, I think I can honestly say I call the shots around here."

"Sit down, Alton," Hickory Baxter chimed in, his mouth full of pancakes. "Don't be such a jackass—"

"Well said, Hickory," Griffin whispered to Troy, grinning. Both Stewberts grinned, too.

Troy clearly didn't see the humor. "Griffin, pal, you've got to get out of this town. You can't really know—or care—which of these bad-tempered old coots runs this backwater burg." He gulped his coffee, scalded himself and grimaced. "Can you?"

"The real question," Hickory went on, wiping his mouth with his linen napkin, "is how in hell we could possibly persuade tourists to come here in the spring. Summer, sure, they'll come boating and hiking and whatnot. Fall's kind of pretty. And winter, we've got the best powder in three states. But spring? Hell, gentlemen, it rains every goddamn day until June. We could offer nude mud wrestling, I guess, but short of that—"

"You volunteering, Hickory?"

"I'll buy a ticket to that!"

A few wolf whistles passed through the room, followed by a lot of laughter, including a couple of whoops from the Stewberts. Then there was just the clinking of silverware against plates as the chamber members returned to their pancakes.

Finally accepting that no one was going to pay attention to him, Granville huffily flicked off his computer and sat down with a grunt.

"Aw, too bad," Griffin said, disappointed, tickling one Stewbert's chin playfully. "Hickory has defused another bomb. And here I was, hoping to show you we're not such a sleepy little town after all. Those old boys really know how to mix it up."

"I'd have thrown them all out on their thick heads," Theo Burke said as she carefully set the pancakes in front of them. "Men! Bunch of thugs, that's what."

"Not all of us, Theo." Griffin picked up her thin, heavily veined hand and kissed it with a flourish. He knew she loved that kind of thing.

The angular spinster scowled at him, growling, but she couldn't hold out. "Oh, yes, you are," she said gruffly. "Some of you just come gift wrapped." Clucking, she reached over and tousled his hair as if he were ten years old.

As she walked away, Troy stared at Griffin, his brown eyes wide with horror. "Cahill, let me get you out of here. Right now, before the soles of your shoes grow roots."

Griffin tossed his hair back into place and picked

up his fork. "Can't. You know that. Not yet. Isn't that right, Stewbert?"

"Come on. You need to start working again. When was the last time you took a picture?"

Griffin smiled. "I just agreed to take some for the new chamber brochure."

Troy rolled his eyes. "I'm telling you, buddy, I can see it happening. If you stay here, it'll get hold of you. One day you'll wake up and you won't know where your life went. Or your hair."

Griffin held out his forkful of pancakes, steaming and aromatic. "There are worse things that could happen," he suggested.

"Name one."

Griffin looked at him. "I could wake up one day and discover that I didn't really like my wife or know my kids. I might realize that I hadn't been home in six months. That I didn't, in fact, even really have a home."

"That's low, Griff." Troy ducked his head and began fiercely carving up his pancakes. "Anita's having an affair, damn it. You make it sound as if it's my fault for being gone so much."

"Well? Isn't that possible? Seems kind of naive to think any relationship is going to succeed without a little hands-on effort."

Troy drew his brows together hard and stabbed a triangle of pancake. "Oh, so now you're the expert on relationships?"

"I'm the expert on how to ruin them," Griffin responded easily. "And believe me, ignoring a woman is the second most effective way to lose her. Comes in just behind the old tried-and-true, number one method—cheating on her."

He leaned back, dangling his fingers for Stewbert to play with. "And kids. Well, I'm just a beginner at this part, but from what I see, kids need you every damn second of every damn day." He smiled down at the baby. "And don't you dare go home and make 'damn' your first word."

For a minute, Griffin thought Troy might be so angry he couldn't speak. He stared into his coffee cup, his jaw tightening until a pulse pounded in his neck. But then, finally, Troy looked up, and Griffin could see that his friend was actually fighting back tears.

"Yeah, well, when they're little, they do need you," Troy said, staring hard at his Stewbert, who made a low, cooing sound and smiled, appreciating the attention. "That's the good part, when they are so small and helpless, and they look at you, and you feel—"

Troy cleared his throat roughly and took another breath. "Hell, Griffin, everybody likes babies. But then they start to grow up, and they don't need you so much anymore. Nobody does. And if you have to work, you have to be gone a lot, and they get used to you not being there."

"Troy, you know they don't—"

"Yes, they do. They get used to it, and they start to like it. Vicky is fifteen, Griff. You can't imagine the looks she gives me if I ask her to get off the phone so I can use it. And Mark is fourteen. He won't even talk to me. It's all grunts and rolling eyes, or silence."

Griffin hardly knew what to say. "Maybe it's just that they're teenagers. I remember being kind of—"

"They talk to their mother. It's not their age. Anita feels the same way. I'm just an inconvenience when I'm there. They never come right out and say so, but they wish I'd hurry up and leave again so they can go back to being normal. All they want from me is my signature on the mortgage check."

Griffin drank his coffee, then adjusted Stewbert's sock, stalling for time. How could he argue with anything Troy was saying? He knew it was possible—perhaps even likely—for a marriage to deteriorate into just such a hell. He'd seen it a million times.

The first time he'd seen it had been in his own home.

Against his will, he could suddenly hear again the ugly arguments that had so often filled the air in the Cahill house, poisoning it until the little boy Griffin had found it difficult to breathe.

"You frigid bitch," his father had said one memorable night, his ironic, well-modulated voice as sharp as a diamond cutter. Griffin's father never yelled. He was much too well-bred, too *intelligent* to raise his voice. Trashy people yelled, he explained. Stupid people yelled.

"You frigid bitch. If you could think of a way to get hold of my bank account without ever having to see me, or talk to me, or, God forbid, *touch* me, that would make you happy, wouldn't it?"

And his mother's voice had come back, acid with elegant cruelty, "Blissfully happy, Edgar. Do you suppose it could be arranged?"

Griffin felt a little dizzy. He put down his coffee cup and stared numbly at Stewbert. Where had his brother Jared found the courage to marry at all? Katie was great, but…didn't he remember their own parents? Didn't he read the papers? Didn't he know how heavily the odds were stacked against a successful marriage?

And how would anyone dare to create these helpless

beings, innocents who would ultimately suffer the most when their parents began slicing each other into pieces?

"You know, you're right," he said suddenly, transferring his gaze to Troy.

Troy blinked. "I am? About what?"

"About how my advice is worth absolutely zip. I don't know the first thing about marriage, thank God, except that it seems to be the most deadly battleground on earth. So I say if that lawyer can get you free, Troy, go for it."

HEATHER LOOKED AT the empty plastic pocket on the door to Room Four.

She turned back toward the central common area, where the office staff were working. "Where's the chart for four?" she asked, trying not to be impatient. But this was such a beginner's mistake. She didn't have time for mistakes today. They were already running behind schedule, and it wasn't ten o'clock yet.

The nurses looked at one another and shrugged.

"Don't know," Tawny said without looking up, carefully touching a swab to a strep test strip. "Maybe there's not really anyone in there."

The coded flags above the door indicated otherwise. But one mistake was no more likely than the other, so Heather opened the door to find out.

To her surprise, the person sitting on the examination table, fully dressed, hands folded in her lap, was Mary Brady.

For one tense moment she wondered whether Mary really was a patient. Could she need…? Could she be…? No. She couldn't be… *not Mary.*

This had to be some kind of joke. And unfortunately, Heather didn't have time for jokes today, either.

She folded her arms, pressing her stethoscope against her chest and raised her eyebrows. "Yes?"

"Don't look like that," Mary said firmly. "I made an appointment. I knew I'd never get ten minutes to talk to you otherwise."

Heather frowned. "Don't be silly," she said. "You can talk to me anytime."

"No, I can't. I really can't. Haven't you noticed how overworked you are?"

"Mary." Heather sighed. "If you're going to complain about Griffin and the Stewberts again, I just don't know what to tell you. I promised I'd help and—"

"It's not Griffin." Mary held up her hands, protesting her innocence. "I've already told you how I feel about that, and I'm not going to nag. Well, not much, anyhow. And not now. Now I want to talk to you about business. About this office."

She took a deep breath, as if she needed it for courage. "I want to talk to you about how you absolutely, positively, *must* start looking for a partner."

Heather backed up a step. "Nonsense," she said. "We're just going through a busy spell. It'll calm down. It always does."

"No, it won't." Mary looked as stubborn as a mule, her brown eyes narrowed, her delicate jaw squared. "I just took three new patient appointments today. All pregnant. We're double-booking, Heather, just to get them all in. You always said you didn't want to do that."

"I don't." Heather put her hands in her lab coat pockets and toyed with the otoscope she kept there. "There must be something we can do to avoid that. Would it help if I took evening appointments? Or maybe if we stopped closing early on Saturdays for a while…"

"Oh, great. Then when will you have time for a real life? Your personal situation is already pretty pathetic, if you ask me, Doc. You haven't had a date in four months. And, believe me, a midnight rendezvous in the nursery for a strained-bananas cocktail with Playboy Cahill does not count."

Heather stiffened. "Mary, you run my medical office. You are not my social secretary. When I feel the need to spice up my personal life, I'll deal with it myself."

They stared at each other in silence for a long second.

Mary blinked first.

"Okay, boss, you asked for it."

Mary stood up, the stiff examination table paper crinkling as she moved. "Here's the truth, plain and simple. If you aren't interested in having any fun, so be it. But the rest of us *are*."

What? But as the message sank in, Heather felt herself flush, washed by a sudden sense of shame at having been so selfish.

"Look," Mary said, softening instantly. "We love you. We love working for you. But we don't want to work all day and all night, too. We don't want to work Saturdays. Nobody does."

She picked up a stack of manila folders from the shining stainless steel countertop. She held them out formally to Heather, both hands extended, like a butler offering a tray filled with cut-crystal decanters.

"So here's a bunch of résumés you've already received in the mail, just unsolicited inquiries from doctors who are curious about the possibility of coming to work in Firefly Glen."

Heather took the stack reluctantly. "You're kidding. All these people have already contacted us?"

"Right." Mary patted the top folder. "So here's the deal, Doc. You can hire a whole new office staff, assuming you can even find a crew of robots out there who want to work twenty-four-seven."

"Mary," Heather murmured. "I'm so sorry—"

Mary smiled. "Or—and I vastly prefer this idea—look through these applications. Find a doctor you like. And then, for God's sake, *hire him*."

GRIFFIN PUSHED THE STROLLER through the double doors of City Hall, well aware of the stir he was going to create. But he didn't have any choice. It was his shift. Where he went, the Stewberts went.

And he had postponed this particular errand long enough.

Luckily the Stewberts were in good moods this morning. They babbled happily to each other as he moved through the walnut-paneled corridors, making his way to the mayor's inner sanctum. Along the way, he passed about a dozen city employees, all of whom had to stop and admire the babies—and rib Griffin.

"Why, I never thought I'd see the day!" "Will wonders never cease!" "Can this be true? Griffin Cahill pushing a baby carriage?" Griffin began to lament the Glen's lack of imagination. Did everyone have to say the same damn thing?

But then he ran into Suzie Strickland, a high school junior who worked part-time at the sheriff's office next door. Suzie sported orange-tipped black hair, heavy black Buddy Holly glasses, a green eyebrow ring and a neon-purple backpack, quite a statement here in Firefly Glen, where most teenagers wouldn't be caught dead in anything but Polo khakis and Hilfiger pullovers.

Suzie, thank God, could usually be counted on to see things a little differently.

"Hi, Suzie." Griffin paused, giving her plenty of time to take her best shot. She was sitting Indian-style on the floor, eating wheat germ straight out of the bottle, which put her nearly at eye level with the Stewberts.

The babies were, for once, completely silent. Suzie studied them phlegmatically.

"Gross," she pronounced finally, tilting herself another mouthful of wheat germ. "They look just like Cahills already."

Griffin grinned. Thank God for Suzie. "Yeah," he agreed. "We ordered them that way. We thought about asking for the Kennedy look, but we decided no. Great hair, but a little too much tooth, don't you think?"

"Totally." She crunched on her wheat germ a while. "So do they always do that?"

"Do what? Drool? I'm afraid so."

"No." In spite of herself, Suzie smiled. "No, I mean do they always look like whoever their father is?"

"Not always." Griffin wondered what had prompted this odd curiosity. "But they might, so you probably would want to take that into consideration when you're deciding who should get the job."

"God, not me." Suzie shuddered dramatically. She eyed Griffin, obviously deciding how much she ought to say. "No, I'm just hoping that when Justine Millner comes back to town with her baby, it looks just like whatever dumb jock fathered it."

Griffin's curiosity deepened, especially since he thought he'd detected a break in Suzie's voice at the end there, on the word *fathered*.

"Why?" He kept his voice level. "What difference does it make?"

She glared at him with suspiciously shining eyes. "Because Mike Frome thinks it might be his, that's why. She told him it wasn't, but he keeps thinking maybe, and it's eating him alive. That's why."

So that was it. Griffin had heard that Mike Frome, who was a pretty nice kid on the whole, had gotten mixed up with that minx Justine, but he hadn't really followed the local soap operas very carefully.

Watching Suzie now, he realized there was a far more interesting subplot. Shocking Suzie had a crush on Conventional Mike, who unfortunately was still at the age when he'd rather be bored to death by a girl with big breasts than intellectually stimulated by a girl with a big brain.

"That's tough for Mike," he said carefully, not sure how to proceed. Suzie wasn't ordinarily the weepy type, but if she started crying here, that would probably get the Stewberts going, and then all hell would break loose.

"Yeah, well, he brought it on himself, the big idiot." She scowled, and the shining had disappeared from her black-lined raccoon eyes. "Maybe it'll teach him not to stick his finger in any old light socket, if you know what I mean."

Griffin, who considered himself a fairly sophisticated fellow, was momentarily speechless.

Luckily, at that instant, Alton Millner stuck his head out of his office. The front receptionist had obviously alerted him that Griffin was on his way back.

"Cahill? Are you coming in or not? I've got a meeting in twenty minutes."

"Yeah. Sorry," Griffin said, starting up his stroller. "So long, Suzie."

"Bye," she mumbled, her mouth full again. She cast one last look at the babies and shook her head. "God. Totally gross."

Alton shut his door firmly. "That girl is damn strange," he said to Griffin. "And the way she dresses! I wish Harry would get rid of her."

"Really? I like her," Griffin said. "She may be one of the few kids around here who actually knows how to think."

"Justine knows her. Justine says she's a freak."

Griffin smiled. "That's a coincidence. I think Suzie has a word for Justine, too."

"Don't you dare repeat it," Alton said loudly.

Griffin held back a chuckle. He enjoyed watching Alton's eyes bug out, as if he were going to pop with indignation. He knew which word had come immediately to the man's mind. It was a word no father should associate so quickly with his own child.

"Actually, I think she referred to Justine as a 'live wire.'" He propped himself against Alton's desk, nudging the stroller back and forth with his foot. "Something like that, anyhow."

Alton had retreated to his big leather desk chair, and was trying to collect himself by shuffling papers into pointless piles. "Did you have something to talk to me about, Cahill?"

"Yes, I did. I want you to bring Heather Delaney's zoning variance request up for a new vote at the next council meeting."

"What?" Alton made a sputtering sound. "Why the hell would I do that?"

"Oh, I don't know," Griffin said, picking up Alton's paperweight shaped like a gavel and toying with it. "Maybe because it's the only fair thing to do?"

"The hell it is."

Griffin gazed calmly at the mayor. "Or maybe because, if you don't, I'm going to lodge a formal ethics complaint against you."

"What?" Alton stood furiously, his chair rolling back so hard it hit the wall. "Are you crazy? On what grounds?"

"On the grounds that you engineered the defeat of that variance because you harbor a personal grudge against Heather Delaney."

"That's—" Alton slammed his fist against the desk. "That's slander."

"No, it isn't." Griffin smiled. "You're such an ostrich, Alton. You think no one knows about the day Justine brought Heather Delaney home with her, because she was afraid to face you alone? You think no one knows how you went nuts because Heather dared to defy you, suggesting that Justine be allowed to remain in Firefly Glen, allowed to have her baby at home, surrounded by friends and family? In a town like this, Alton, everyone knows everything. They probably knew Justine was pregnant before she knew it herself. They *undoubtedly* knew it before you did."

Alton was purple with fury.

"You'll never make a charge like that stick. Not in this town. Nobody threatens Alton Millner!"

"This is not a threat," Griffin said quietly. The Stewberts didn't like angry voices. Griffin had already learned that. So he wasn't surprised when they began to whimper. "It's a simple statement of cause and effect. Did you ever take Logic? *If this, then that.* If you don't bring it up for a vote, then I will file an ethics charge. And whether it sticks or not, it will keep the whole town buzzing for weeks."

"This was that woman's idea, wasn't it? I knew she was cooking something up." Alton tugged on his tie, as if it were choking him. "Don't listen to anything she says, Cahill. Cahill? You know she's just—"

Millner probably said other things, too, but Griffin couldn't hear him. He was already halfway out the door, and besides, the Stewberts, who might be only babies but obviously knew a bad guy when they saw one, completely drowned him out.

CHAPTER NINE

SWEET APPLES, the farmer's market at the edge of town, opened early on Sunday mornings, so Heather began dressing the Stewberts as soon as they woke up. She wanted to get there before all the best vegetables were gone.

She put the boys in something simple—soft blue sweatpants and blue-and-white-striped knit tops. At first she had been enchanted by their elaborate sailor suits and brand-name tailored rompers. But she'd quickly learned that the boys weren't dress-up dolls. They were active little people who wanted to be comfortable while they played.

Plus, what with one accident or another—at one end or another—they each went through about five changes a day. Heather had learned to judge an outfit by one standard only: how easy was it to get on and off?

One Stewbert found the dressing process highly amusing today. As he sat on the changing table, he was flailing his arms and squealing his pleasure.

"Shh," Heather said softly. "How is Uncle Griffin going to sleep if you keep making so much noise?"

"He's not," Griffin said dryly from the doorway. "Luckily, he wasn't trying." He sauntered in, cup of coffee in hand. "Need any help?"

Griffin, whose shift had just ended, looked tired, but he was wearing a jacket, and his coffee was in a to-go mug, so obviously he was telling the truth. He wasn't planning to sleep. He was going out.

"That's okay," she said, glancing down at the Stewbert who was still on the floor, waiting his turn. "They're loud, but actually they're being cooperative this morning. Besides, you had them all night. Aren't you ever going to grab some sleep?"

Griffin shook his head, bending over to hand the baby his new favorite toy, a yellow plastic car with bug eyes that wiggled rather salaciously when the wheels rolled. They had privately named it Alton.

"Not yet. I've got to take some pictures. I agreed to get some spring shots for the chamber. Granville Frome is about to have a stroke because May tourism has been declining in Firefly Glen for six-point-three straight years."

Heather wrestled Stewbert's arm into his sleeve, then kissed the fat little fingers as they emerged. "Oh, really? And is that a big problem?"

"Apparently. Granville devoted ninety minutes and seventeen full-color charts to the subject at the last chamber meeting."

She laughed. Both Stewberts looked up at her and smiled. They were always ready to share a good laugh.

"Well, let's see. Spring…" she mused, trying to finesse a sneaker onto Stewbert's foot, which was difficult because he kept mischievously curling his toes. "I know! I'm headed over to Sweet Apples, and Mary told me that their orchard is absolutely spectacular this year. Why don't you go with us?"

Even before she saw the guarded look come over his

face, she regretted making the suggestion. Of course he didn't want to go.

In fact, he had been markedly distant these past few days. The baby transfers were made with the minimum amount of interaction. When Heather arrived, Griffin didn't linger. He didn't chat, or stay for one last game of peekaboo with the Stewberts, the way he once had. He just filled her in on pertinent details, and then he left.

Probably he was just getting tired of the whole thing, and restless to get back to his normal life. But she couldn't help wondering if this new distance might be her fault. The other night, the night of the childbirth class, she had been tense and overwrought. When he made a simple gesture of concern, offering her a shoulder rub, she had stupidly overreacted.

Several times, she had considered apologizing. But his cordial distance never seemed to invite serious conversation. His laughing eyes didn't hold mockery, exactly—that would have been rude, which Griffin never was—but rather the *potential* for mockery. Somehow that was equally effective at warding off unwanted intimacies.

"How silly of me," she said, concentrating on Stewbert's shoe to cover her discomfort. She laughed lightly. "I don't know what I was thinking. Naturally, the last thing in the world you'd want during your free time is to get stuck with the babies again."

She thought quickly. "You could go to the falls instead. They're probably gorgeous right now, with the spring thaw."

He looked surprised. "You mean Silver Kiss Falls?"

"No, of course not." She took a breath. "I mean yes, you could go there if you wanted to, of course. I just meant that there are quite a few lovely falls around here, I wasn't particularly thinking of Silver Kiss."

Oh, God, she must be crazy. She was making it worse and worse. She should never have mentioned waterfalls—she should have known he'd think first of Silver Kiss, though it wasn't the showiest or best-known falls in Firefly Glen.

All young lovers had a special place. Silver Kiss Falls had been theirs. They had made love there for the first time—and the last time, too, though of course they hadn't known that then. As they stood beneath the tumbling water, surrounded by rainbows, they had still believed it would last forever.

She almost never went to Silver Kiss anymore. She could always hear things in the whispering spray. The ripple of his laughter. The splash of her tears.

Suddenly, the yellow car rolled out of Stewbert's grasp. Not good yet at judging distances, he reached over to pick it up, lost his balance and tumbled hard onto his nose. Indignant, he began to cry.

The baby on the changing table puckered up, too, his face growing hot red. Heather braced herself for an earsplitting, stereo display of frustration. But suddenly Griffin scooped the wailing baby off the floor and lifted him high onto his shoulders in one smooth swoop.

Shock silenced both Stewberts immediately.

"Wow," Heather breathed. "Great reflexes."

Griffin grinned at her from under Stewbert's fat fingers, which were plastered awkwardly across Griffin's eyebrows. Gurgling happily, the baby tilted forward, pressing his open mouth to the crown of Griffin's head.

"On second thought, I think we'd better go to Sweet

Apples together," Griffin said, shutting his eyes in silent martyrdom as Stewbert began to make soft sucking noises against his hair. "I'm not at all sure it's safe to let these little monsters outnumber you."

THE LIGHT AT THE ORCHARD was perfect. Sometimes a photographer had to use a polarizing filter to create the illusion of a sky so blue, or grass so green, but Griffin wouldn't need any such tricks today. May itself had done the work—with a little help from the April rains.

And to think he almost hadn't come. It was as if fate had given him a shove in the back, saying, hurry, go today. Yesterday the orchard could have been a degree too skimpy. By tomorrow it might have begun, ever so slightly, to droop.

But today was perfect. The apple trees, which stood in tidy lines running back from the Sweet Apples roadside stand, were as dressed-up as debutantes, showing off white gowns of a thousand frothy blossoms.

Granville would be thrilled with the pictures. Spring in Firefly Glen looked pretty darned romantic from here.

While Heather browsed the market tables, which were heaped with plump fresh vegetables, Griffin and the Stewberts gathered his equipment. He let each of the boys hold an empty plastic film case. They gnawed happily on the cylinders, while above their damp fists their bright eyes curiously watched Griffin's every move.

On impulse, he tossed a blanket across the handle of the stroller. And he slipped his waist-level viewfinder into the pack, too. If he saw a lucky picture of the boys, he wanted to be able to get a good, low angle on it without slithering around on his stomach.

By the time he joined Heather, her cloth shopping bag was filled to bursting. She expertly pinched a shiny red tomato, then slid it into the sack, somehow finding another inch of space.

"Got anything in there we could munch on?" Griffin parked the stroller off to the side of the aisle. "I thought you and the boys could picnic while I work."

She pointed to the cashier's desk, where large, softly browned homemade muffins spilled enticingly out of a grapevine basket. "I bought half a dozen of those, and a small jar of jam, too. They have free coffee over by the parking lot. We'll feast like kings."

They weren't the only ones who had come up with the picnic idea. The orchard was spotted with blankets and tablecloths. Griffin claimed a quiet spot, as far from the others as he could get.

The air was sweet back here, away from the street, and the light was a soft, Easter-egg yellow that would photograph perfectly. He moved around, taking a few easy shots, metering the light and exploring angles, while Heather fluffed open the blanket and unhooked the Stewberts from their seats.

Then she pulled out the muffins and the coffee and began arranging them on the blanket, like a little girl setting up a tea party. He smiled, the photographer in him appreciating the way the sun set off golden sparks in her auburn hair.

He slipped off a couple of pictures of her, though she didn't realize it. The waist-level viewfinder was useful that way. It allowed you to look down as you approached a shy animal, never making that conspicuous, threatening gesture of raising and pointing the camera.

She looked wonderful. The breeze blew tiny red-gold wisps of hair around her face and tickled shining strands against her slender neck. Watching her through the viewfinder, Griffin was caught unprepared by a sudden, heavy throb of desire, a tiny kick of intense arousal.

He lowered the camera and took a deep breath. God, this was familiar. How many years was it going to take to get past this knee-jerk, mindless sexual reaction? Ten obviously hadn't been enough. How about twenty?

Maybe the rotten truth was that he'd *never* be able to look at her without wanting to make love to her. He felt like some fiendish science experiment. Erotically programmed by circumstance. She'd been his first lover, and he was doomed forever to lurch helplessly at the sight of her.

He dropped his camera to his side, went over and plopped himself down beside her on the blanket.

He gestured toward the muffins. "One of those for me?"

"All you want," she replied, holding out the biggest muffin and a napkin. "The Stewberts don't like them. They just crumble them up and toss the bits around."

"Oh, but that's the sign that they *do* like them," he corrected with a smile. "Their enthusiasm can be measured by square feet of destruction."

"Oh, yeah. I forgot." Heather leaned back on her elbows, lifting her face to the sun. The Stewberts were climbing across her legs, as if she were their private jungle gym, but she obviously didn't mind.

She sighed. "How lovely it is this morning! I've been spending too much time inside lately, I think."

"It's nice, isn't it?" Griffin carefully avoided agreeing with the second part of her comment. If he chimed in, it would feel like pressure, the same pressure he'd always applied—stop working so hard, come out and have fun, enjoy the world with me.

"I just never seem to have any free time. But that may change." She reached down to stroke Stewbert's hair. "Did I tell you that I'm interviewing for a partner?"

"No." He was surprised. Very surprised. "What made you decide to do that?"

"Mary." She laughed softly. "She explained that my staff would stage a mass walkout if I didn't get some help. I think I had resisted the idea because, once I bought Spring House, money was so tight. And now if all those expensive renovations have been for nothing…"

Her voice dwindled off, as if she had lost herself in her musings. Watching her, Griffin had an intense desire to wipe that troubled look off her face. He could tell her about his visit to Alton. But he held back. Better not to get her hopes up until he was sure the mayor would do the right thing.

In a few seconds, though, she rallied on her own. How silly he'd been to think she'd need him to comfort her. She hadn't ever been the type to brood.

He'd never forget how, the day after she broke off their engagement, she had aced a chemistry final. He, on the other hand, had spent two full days in bed with a bitchy blonde and a killer hangover and a rather vicious attitude toward life in general.

"Well, anyhow," she went on, "when I thought it through logically, I realized that if there's demand for another gynecologist in town, sooner or later someone will show up." She smiled. "So, basically, the new guy can either come in as my partner or as my competition. Partner sounded better."

"Sounds like good strategy. Any real candidates yet?"

"One. He's coming up tomorrow for an interview and a look around. He works in the city, but he was born in a small town, so I'm hoping he won't be too appalled by our little dollhouse community."

"Maybe he's tired of the big city. Tired of the rat race. It can get old."

She looked at him quizzically. "Can it?"

A couple of bluebirds had lighted in the tree just beside them. Griffin began to make a quick switch to his eye-level viewfinder. "Well, sure it can," he said as he worked. "Sometimes you just have to get away for a little while. Change the scenery. Take a breather."

She didn't even blink. She didn't interrupt her steady stroking of Stewbert's hair. "Well," she said blandly, her voice perfectly even, "if he's just looking for a breather, he'd better not look here. I have no interest in taking on a *temporary* partner."

Griffin paused, his camera halfway to his eye, and looked at her carefully. Did this conversation have a subtext? What exactly was she trying to say?

He hesitated just a moment too long. The fickle birds flew away again, the apple blossoms shaking slightly in their wake. Griffin lowered the camera, wondering how he should respond.

But Heather had bent her head to the babies, who were almost asleep, leaning up against her like bookends.

"So," she said, "tell me about your photography."

Her voice expressed only a perfunctory interest. She didn't really care. She was clearly just trying to change the subject. Her primary focus seemed to be the Stewberts. She was gently combing their silky hair with her fingertips.

"What about it?"

She looked up. "Anything. I know you're helping Granville with his tourism brochure right now, but what do you have planned after this? You take mostly travel pictures, right? Anything interesting coming up?"

"A couple of things are on the table. Troy's trying to talk me into a trip he's excited about. But I may be in the mood for something different."

She laughed. "I would have thought everything you did was 'different.' I've seen some of your pictures in travel magazines, and I can't even pronounce half the names of the places you've been."

"Yeah, I pretty much wake up every morning wondering where I am." He poured himself a cup of coffee. "Until this year, anyhow."

She didn't look at him. She developed a sudden interest in the trees, which had begun to rustle in a stiffening breeze.

"And this year that you've been home," she said, still giving him her profile, "are you just taking a…a breather? I mean, I've always wondered. Why *did* you come home after all these years?"

At first, he didn't say anything. He toyed with his camera, wondering which version he should give her. The official dinner-party version, guaranteed to get a well-bred chuckle: *I work in the rain forest and the Riviera. When I want a vacation, I have to come home.* Or the teasing deflection offered to golf partners or bar buddies: *I ran out of film.* Or the polite but equally meaningless version, reserved for nice, sincere people: *I had some personal business to take care of.*

Always twenty-five comfortable words or less. No one ever got the strange, confusing truth.

Which was that he'd come home because one day he found himself sitting in the Munich airport, a ticket to Finland in his hand, listening to them call his flight. They had kept calling. *First call. All passengers. Last call*...but he hadn't moved.

He'd just sat there, like a man in a trance. And when the Finland flight had roared past the window, and finally shrunk to a speck in the twilight sky, he had stood up, approached the reservation desk, and traded in his ticket for one that read "New York."

It wasn't something he ever talked about. And he hadn't looked too far into the future. Hickory Baxter had wheedled him into sitting on the city council, which locked him in until summer. After that...

Well, he just assumed he'd stay here until one day he bought a ticket that said something else.

"I've been setting up some photography scholarships," he said, settling for a more prosaic truth. "I discovered there aren't very many of those around. I'd like to see a few gifted, underprivileged kids go to college and get some serious art training, really make something of their talent."

She chuckled softly. "Are there any underprivileged kids in Firefly Glen?"

"A few. In fact, Mary Brady's younger brother Tucker has applied for one of them, although he warned me he hasn't told Mary yet."

Heather looked pleased. "Oh, he should tell her! She'll be thrilled. Is he going to get it?"

Griffin shrugged. "Maybe. He's pretty good."

Finally Heather's smile looked genuine. "You

know…" She paused. "Establishing those scholarships was really a generous, worthy thing to do, Griffin. I had no idea you—"

"Ever did anything worthy?"

She shook her head. "No, I was going to say I had no idea you were so passionate about your career."

He didn't want to talk about this. He looked up, aware that the light had been changing as heavy clouds moved toward them, filled, no doubt, with one of their famous spring rains. Pure sunshine had a white cast, but an overcast day would photograph as slightly blue.

It might lend drama to the apple trees, which tended to be a little too anemic in their demure prettiness. But he knew that Granville would prefer bland and pretty. So he picked up his camera.

"We might be getting a storm," he said. "Mind if I take a few pictures while the light's still good?"

"Of course not. I'll pack up here."

She moved the Stewberts aside carefully, arranging the sleeping boys on the blanket without waking them. Griffin walked a little distance away. He looked at the apple trees, which were lovely. And then he looked at Heather.

Her body, as she knelt protectively over the boys, was fluid and graceful. The wind pressed her light green spring dress against her curves, her breasts, her thighs, her hips. And her face, as she freed Stewbert's little hand from an awkward position, was focused and tender—and incredibly beautiful.

So, self-indulgently, he turned his camera on her instead. To hell with Granville.

As he kept clicking, finding new secrets in her face from every angle, he lost all interest in the apple trees.

They would be here tomorrow, next week, and every spring into eternity. They were rooted in place, always accessible.

He had learned, as a nature photographer, that it was more important to seize the unexpected moment. Like a skittish deer, which will give you only one fleeting instant of heartbreaking eye contact before bolting away, Heather was a rare, elusive beauty.

After this week, Heather would never be his to photograph again.

"Hi, there, son. How about if I take a picture of the whole family for you?"

Griffin looked up. An elderly man wearing madras Bermuda shorts, a Disneyland cap and a Spending My Kid's Inheritance T-shirt was standing at his elbow. The man's wife, whose own T-shirt read 70 Is Sensational, was over near Heather, smiling eagerly.

"Yes, do let Fred take one, dear. Someone always gets left out of these family photos. You'll want at least one picture of both of you with your darling little ones!"

"Family photos?" It took Heather a second to catch on, but then she flushed and shook her head. "Oh, no, we're not—"

"That would be terrific," Griffin interrupted quickly, smiling at the elderly man. "Just let me show you how to work this camera. It's tricky."

"You go on over and put your arm around your pretty wife, son," the old man said, waving Griffin away. "I wasn't always a hundred years old, you know. I used to build skyscrapers. I think I can figure out a little old Nikon."

Griffin handed over the camera with an apologetic smile, then crossed to the blanket, where Heather was giving him a glare that would have turned him to stone if he let it.

"Isn't that nice, honey?" He knelt beside her and slipped his arm around her shoulders. "Fred is going to take our picture with our darling little ones."

"Oh, yes," she said between her teeth, smiling a broad, fake smile. "Very nice. Especially since it will be the last picture ever taken of you alive."

But he didn't really believe she was angry. A little embarrassed, perhaps, but no worse than that. He winked at her, then turned to offer the camera a grin just as Fred clicked the shutter.

Still smiling, Heather tried to pull away immediately.

"One more, one more," Fred called out. "This time, son, why don't you give your lovely wife a big, lovely kiss?"

Heather's shoulders turned rigid under Griffin's arm. "Do it," she whispered, "and you die."

"But you already told me I'm a dead man anyhow," he whispered back, taking her chin in his hand and dipping his head toward hers. "So I really have nothing to lose, do I?"

Her skin was like creamy satin under his fingers, and her green eyes were dazzling up this close. Her rosy lips were full, and her breath touched him in warm waves of cinnamon and apple blossoms.

His own breath was tight with a desire so intense it startled him. And he realized that, even if her threat had been real—even if the cost of kissing her right now *was* death—he would probably do it anyway.

"Come on, lovebirds, I'm an old man! Don't dawdle!"

"Griffin…" Heather's troubled gaze searched his, and a delicate pink stain was forming on her ivory cheeks. "Griffin, we—"

He smothered the rest of the sentence with his lips. As he found her, he felt his heart grow very still, then begin to race. Oh, yes, God help him, he remembered this. This beauty, this sweetness, this heat.

"Perfect! Damn, I'm good, if I do say so myself. You're going to love that one!"

But Fred's excited voice seemed to come from a million miles away, and Griffin ignored it. He slid his hands into Heather's hair, pulling her close, then closer. For a moment her lips were tight, but gradually, as he moved across them, they softened and fell open, releasing the tiniest of moans.

"Will you look at that! I think we started something." Fred was laughing loudly. "Boy oh boy. We may need to turn a hose on these two, Mona."

Somehow, long after he knew he had passed the bounds of good manners, Griffin found the willpower to pull away. He kept his arm around Heather's shoulders, which were trembling.

He managed to smile at Fred.

"Thanks for your help," he said. "That was a great idea."

"Certainly appeared to be." Fred handed Griffin the camera, grinning with irrepressible mischief. "I guess we can see how you two ended up with those pretty little babies."

Griffin glanced at Heather, whose head was bowed, her auburn hair falling forward over her equally auburn cheeks.

"Well, thanks again, Fred. Have a great day." He did

appreciate the old guy's help, but he very much wished that Fred would give it up now and go away.

Griffin needed to talk to Heather. Maybe he needed to apologize. Maybe he needed to kiss her again.

"Fred," Mona said, clapping her husband on the back. She seemed better at reading hints. "Come on. Let's go."

"But we just got here." Fred eyed the blanket, as if he were looking for a spot to plant himself. "I mean it, Mona, aren't those babies cute? Twins, right? What are their names, anyhow?"

Griffin smiled pleasantly. "Actually, we're not sure."

Beside him, Heather made a small, strangled sound.

Fred frowned. "What do you mean you're not—"

"You see, they're not our babies."

"What?"

Griffin fought down a chuckle, somehow keeping a straight face.

"Oh, Fred, you're such a dope," Mona said tartly, yanking on her husband's arm. "For God's sake, shut up and let's go home. Can't you see the boy wants to be alone with his wife?"

The old man harrumphed as he turned away.

"Wife? I'll bet you dimes to dollars that red-haired floozy is not his wife."

At which point even Heather couldn't handle it. She looked at Griffin, her mouth working desperately. She buried her face in his chest, her shoulders shaking.

"Floozy," he whispered. She batted him weakly with her fist, her eyes streaming with merriment. And finally the two of them collapsed in a heap onto the blanket, smothering their helpless laughter in the soft blue cotton like a couple of very naughty—but ridic-ulously happy—children.

CHAPTER TEN

OKAY, RUSSELL BRADY, listen up. I'm sure Tad Halliwell is a laugh a minute when he's knocking back shots, but the rest of the time he's a first-class fool. Tad's life is going to hell on a rocket, and you know it. You hop into that bucket of bolts with him Friday night, and you just may go with him.

Mary gnawed on the end of her pen, frustrated. She was going to have to do better than this. Russ was twenty-one now, and the number had gone to his head. Technically he didn't have to *Listen Up* to anyone, as he was fond of telling them all.

Humor was the best way to reach him, but ever since she had heard that his idiot friend Tad was setting up a Friday night drag race through Vanity Gap, she hadn't felt much like laughing.

Oh, well, it was only Monday. Maybe something would come to her.

She put her pen down on the kitchen island and, picking up the paring knife, carefully started taking the peel off a fat red plum. She was babysitting the twins for a couple of hours, while Heather attended the emergency city council meeting, which had been called just this morning.

Apparently Heather's rezoning request had been put

back onto the agenda. Mary wondered whether that might be Griffin's doing. He had promised Heather he'd help, but Mary hadn't set much store by that. Playboy Cahill had a convenient way of forgetting his promises.

Still. She wasn't an unfair woman. She'd give him credit if and when he proved he deserved it. But if he let Heather down again...

Mary traded for a larger knife and karate-chopped a banana into neat little slices. No. He wouldn't dare.

Surely Heather would come home with good news. In the meantime, Mary was going to make some plum-yummy for Robert and Stewart. It was her mother's recipe, and babies always loved it.

She had just dumped the fruit into the blender when someone knocked at the kitchen door. Wiping streams of plum juice from her hands, Mary opened it with her wrists.

It was Troy, who looked adorable this morning, in his tight blue jeans and flannel shirt. Of course, she was a sucker for a man with shaggy hair and buff biceps. It must be her earthy logger roots.

"Hi," she said, smiling. "Griffin's not here." She left the door ajar, returning to the blender. "He's at the council meeting. I thought you might have gone with him."

Troy came in and shut the door behind him. "Good God, no. Why would I do that? It's not safe. Those old men are lunatics."

Mary laughed. A couple of them were, and that was no joke. "Anyhow, Griffin will be coming back here when the meeting's over. His baby shift starts right after lunch. Want to grab a Coke and wait for him?"

"Sure." Troy got his drink, then settled on one of the kitchen bar stools, resting his elbows on the marble-topped island. He looked down at her papers, which she had foolishly left out. "What's this? Some of your writing?"

She wished she could snatch it away before he read a single word, but she had just turned on the blender, and she didn't dare leave it unattended.

"That's nothing," she said, but she knew he couldn't hear her over the pureeing plums. He had already read the half-finished *Listen Up* letter and had moved on to the pages behind it.

Oh, darn, she had forgotten about those. There were several other *Listen Up* letters, earlier lectures to Russell that she'd brought along to make sure she didn't repeat herself. And something else too, she remembered, groaning. At the bottom of the pile were a couple of her Littletown Adventures, which she'd brought over to work on in case the meeting ran late.

Troy was reading Littletown now, and he was smiling. What did that mean? Was that good or bad?

Oh, this was awful. It was as embarrassing as having him catch her naked. Worse, because frankly she didn't give a damn what he thought of her body. And for some stupid reason, she cared a lot, a whole lot, what he thought of her writing.

When the plums were finished, he was still reading. "I'm going upstairs to check on the boys," she said stiltedly. "They should be waking up any minute."

He nodded, gesturing goodbye with a preoccupied hand without lifting his gaze from the pages. She hesitated, bowls of plum-yummy in hand. She tried to read his expression, tried to guess what exact part of the story he was reading right this minute. What was making him smile like that?

Oh, what difference did it make what he thought? She stuck the bowls in the refrigerator, then exited the kitchen and stomped up the stairs, furious with herself.

Robert and Stewart were just waking up. She refused to call the poor kids the Stewberts. Typical of Cahill to think that was funny. They might be just babies, but they still deserved names of their own. She had arbitrarily dubbed the one with the cowlick Robert, though, to her eternal annoyance, neither one ever answered to anything but Stewbert.

She changed Robert's diaper first, because Stewart was always the more patient of the two.

"It doesn't matter what he thinks, does it, Robert?" She found the baby powder and shook it all over the baby's bottom. "*You* like my Littletown Adventures, don't you? You loved the one about Prince Dudley Donothing, didn't you?"

But Robert was on a mission to capture his big toe and eat it. He was folding himself in half, trying to get his foot close enough to chomp. This made diapering tricky, and Mary felt herself getting annoyed.

"Come on, Robbie, you're not even listening." She jiggled him a little. "Robert." She sighed, scowling. *"Stewbert!"*

The baby looked up, his wet, questing mouth still open, his leg still over his head. "Bee!" he said. He smiled his silly two-tooth grin. "Buck speet."

Mary had to laugh. She slid the diaper under his soft little fanny and pulled open the tape.

"Fine. I'll take that as a yes," she said. "'Five Stars,' raves famous *New York Times* book critic Stewbert Cahill. '*The Littletown Adventures* are the best children's stories to come along in decades.'"

"Aw, shucks," Troy said from the door. "He stole my line."

Mary looked over at Troy. He had clearly heard everything. She decided that she'd have to kill herself on the spot. But because the nursery had been baby-proofed, there wasn't a sharp object in sight. Just her luck.

"I love them," he said, coming toward her, holding out the sheaf of papers. "I absolutely love them. All of them."

"You don't have to say that," she said, refusing to meet his eyes. She traded Stewberts and began diapering the second one. "You don't have to say anything. I didn't leave them out so that you'd read them, you know. I didn't have any idea you were coming over today."

He was standing at her elbow. He stepped on the pedal of the diaper pail at the perfect moment, so that she could drop the soggy one in.

"I love them," he repeated slowly. "You're a very talented woman, Mary Brady. And Littletown is a wonderful creation."

She just looked at him, mute with idiotic delight. She hated herself for feeling so thrilled. She especially hated the overeager questions that came thronging to her lips. *Do you really like it? What's good about it? What exactly do you like about Littletown? Did you recognize Prince Dudley Do-nothing? How could I make the stories better? Do you think I could ever, ever, get them published?*

"Mary, I want to show them to my agent. She represents all kinds of authors, not just travel writers. I think she'll be as excited as I am."

Mary had to work just to swallow. Her throat felt suddenly dry. He sounded sincere, but she mustn't believe in this. The disappointment would be terrible if he didn't mean it. If he didn't follow through.

And he was Playboy Cahill's best friend, after all.

Scooping Stewbert into her arms, she turned to Troy.

"That's a very generous offer. And I'm not saying I wouldn't be thrilled. But I'm not going to thank you by sleeping with you." Her fear made her sound tough. But that was okay. She'd rather sound bitchy than pathetic. "I just thought you'd better know that at the outset."

"It hadn't crossed my mind," he said, grinning. "Tricks like that wouldn't work with a woman like you. After all, did Princess Cerulean kiss Count Fribbleslag just because he threatened to lock her puppy in the tower? Of course not. She nearly drowned him in the moat for suggesting such a thing."

He really had read them. In spite of herself, Mary smiled back. "In that case, if you're sure it's what you want to do… I mean, if you really think that the stories are…"

She took a deep breath and started over. "I would be absolutely, positively thrilled and grateful."

Troy nodded, businesslike. "Good. If you'll give me six or eight of your best stories, I'll send them first thing in the morning."

It was all Mary could do not to kiss him. He didn't look a bit like Count Fribbleslag, who had been based on a lazy, middle-aged millionaire who summered here years and years ago, back when Mary had been a housekeeper at the hotel. One day, the jerk had suggested that her tips might improve if she were a little friendlier. She had found it necessary to dump her full bucket of slop water on his lap.

Luckily, her foolish impulse to plant a big, sloppy, grateful kiss on Troy's cute mouth was short-circuited by the sound of footsteps running up the stairs and Heather's voice calling, "Mary! Mary, where are you?"

The meeting must be over.

Mary held her breath for a long second, praying. Well, as she had already admitted, she was better at being bitchy than being pathetic, so her prayer sounded more like a *Listen Up* letter, but she assumed that God was used to that. *You'd better tell me Cahill did the right thing today, because I know how you feel about murder.*

"Mary!" Heather burst into the nursery, breathless. "Mary, you should have been there! We won!"

Mary began to breathe again. She didn't need the details—it was enough to see Heather's face. She had never looked so joyous, her smile electrically radiant, her green eyes as bright as the crystal ones on Stewbert's stuffed bunny.

Though Heather had been her usual stoic self about the whole mess, Mary knew how much this decision meant to her. Owning Spring House, living here and working here, had been Heather's dearest dream.

Mary also knew that buying the house had shoved Heather's finances right to the brink. If the rezoning hadn't gone through, Heather would eventually have had to sell it. She might as well have sold her heart, with her left arm thrown in for good measure.

But now, thank God, the house, and the dream, were safe. No wonder Heather was walking on air, her usual overbred, uptight restraint thrown to the winds.

Mary, who was definitely underbred, pumped her fist in the air jubilantly. "Yes!" She hugged Heather hard. "You did it, girlfriend!"

Heather shook her head. "No. Griffin did it. He won't tell me precisely *how*, but—"

Griffin, who obviously had followed Heather up the stairs at a more leisurely pace, appeared in the doorway, his grin cute and cocky, the kind of grin Mary usually wanted to knock off his face. But right now it didn't bother her one bit.

"I told you. I didn't really do anything. I guess Alton Millner finally grew a conscience, that was all."

Mary snorted. "Grew a conscience, my foot. You can't fool us. He could just as soon grow another head." She grinned evilly. "No, wait. The man already has two faces, doesn't he?"

Everyone laughed, including the Stewberts. Heather hugged Mary again, and Troy clapped Griffin on the back, smiling. "Congratulations, pal. You did good."

Silently Mary and Troy exchanged a smile. What with her own excitement about Troy's reaction to her stories, and now Heather's victory, there was so much happiness floating around this nursery Mary was surprised the room didn't lift right off the house and fly away.

Still softly laughing, Heather picked up one of the babies and twirled him in circles, her lab coat swirling around her like a ball gown.

"Oh, this is a wonderful, wonderful day," she told the little boy. "Uncle Griffin is a miracle worker, Stewbert." She brought the baby up to Griffin. "Tell your uncle what a very good thing he's done today."

"Flam!" the baby cried excitedly, waving his arms. "Greek!"

Griffin chuckled, but Heather kissed the baby's chubby cheek. "That's right, Stewbert. Now tell Uncle Griffin how very, very grateful I am."

Griffin held Heather's gaze. "Why don't you tell me yourself?"

Heather hesitated, her cheeks flushing.

"No, no," Troy remonstrated playfully. "Ixnay on at-thay, bro. You'll spoil everything if she thinks you had an agenda. You're not allowed to ask for anything in return for a favor. Ask Princess Cerulean. Ask Count Fribbleslag."

Griffin smiled, though he didn't take his gaze from Heather's. "But I'm not Count Fribbleslag, Troy. I'm Prince Dudley Do-nothing."

Shocked, Mary laughed nervously. "How the heck did you know that, Griffin?" She scowled. "Besides, so what? Prince Dudley Do-nothing isn't allowed to black-mail anybody, either. Especially not for doing some-thing he should have done the first time around anyhow."

"It's not blackmail, Mary," Heather said quietly. "He already did his good deed, and he never asked for anything in return. This is…" She smiled up at Griffin so sweetly Mary thought she might yak. "This is different."

Mary sighed. "Oh, well, if it's *different,*" she said, rolling her eyes. "Then by all means give the hero a hug and get it over with."

But Heather hadn't waited for Mary's permission. When Mary looked back, Heather was in Griffin's arms, her head resting on his chest, the baby snuggled between them.

Griffin lay his cheek against Heather's shining hair. His lips moved. Mary wasn't quite close enough to hear, but she thought he said, "You're welcome."

"GRIFFIN CAHILL! The very man I wanted to see!"

Emma Tremaine Dunbar grabbed Griffin as he

entered the door of the Paper Shop and whisked him to the custom-order counter in the back of the store.

Griffin groaned. "I was afraid of this," he said sadly, allowing himself to be dragged by the sleeve. "One kiss, and you were hooked. You know, you're just going to have to forget me somehow. Your husband has a very big gun, and—"

"Shut up, Griffin." Emma gave him a dirty look as she plopped him onto a chair behind the counter. "Your kisses aren't nearly as amazing as you think."

"They aren't?" Griffin gazed up at her, offering her his best wounded expression. "You mean all those other women were..." he swallowed hard "...lying?"

Emma glared at him. Then her blue eyes softened and she crinkled her nose. "Oh, probably not," she said. "Damn your conceited soul. Probably not."

She glanced around the store, as if checking for eavesdroppers. Only one customer remained, a teenager looking at birthday cards over by the door.

"But that's not why I'm so happy to see you," Emma said, lowering her voice. "I've been hearing the most astounding gossip about you, and I want to know if it's true."

"Probably," he said equably. "Although if it's that thing about me and Justine Millner's baby, it's a dirty lie."

Emma grimaced. "Nobody's fool enough to think you'd touch a hair on Justine Millner's little airhead. Why, you're old enough to be her—"

"Be *very* careful."

"Older brother." Emma shoved a stack of card samples out of the way and hiked herself up onto the edge of the counter. "But quit trying to change the subject. Here's what I'm hearing—you and Heather Delaney are living together at Spring House, parenting a couple of babies you *say* are your nephews. You and she were seen smooching in the orchard behind Sweet Apples Sunday morning. And best of all, you first buried her rezoning request and then, for no apparent reason, revived it in an emergency council meeting in the predawn hours yesterday."

Griffin whistled softly. "Damn, Emma. You just got back from your trip late last night, right? Where did you come up with all that?"

"I'm connected," she said smugly. "And this is Firefly Glen, remember? Home of the high-speed grapevine. Just tell me if it's true."

"Okay. Yes, no comment and sort of."

Emma folded her arms. "Details, damn it. I want details."

"Consult your grapevine, then. You're not getting them from me."

Emma pressed her lips together irritably, which made Griffin want to laugh. God, Harry really had his hands full with this stubborn wife of his, didn't he? Emma was trying to bore her intensely blue Tremaine eyes into his soul. She probably had a rack in the back office, where she tortured information out of people like him.

He took it for a minute. Then he yawned broadly, tilted his head and smiled at her. "Give it up, Em. It's not working. Besides, you haven't even asked me why I'm here."

Emma grinned. "You said it yourself. One kiss, and you're addicted. But you're going to have to get over me, Griff. My husband has a big gun."

"I know. That's why I've come, not as a lovelorn home wrecker, but as a paying customer." He smiled at her look of surprise. "So. You might want to be a little nicer to me, huh?"

She grinned again. "Probably not."

He took a piece of paper from his pocket. "Good thing you're the only stationery store in town. Here. I need a hundred copies of this printed out on something nice, and I need them by this afternoon. Can you handle that?"

Emma took the paper from him and scanned it. It was an invitation to a surprise party Friday night, to celebrate the opening of Dr. Heather Delaney's new offices at Spring House.

"Oh, my gosh," Emma breathed. "It's true! Heather got her zoning variance!"

"A hundred copies," Griffin reiterated patiently. "This afternoon."

Emma's eyes glinted. "So that means the rest of the rumors must be true, too. You and Heather—"

"Are you listening, Emma? A hundred copies by two-thirty. No later than three. I want them to go out in today's mail."

The bell over the shop's front door tinkled, announcing another arrival.

"Oh, for Pete's sake." Emma looked up, growling. "What now?"

"They're called customers," Griffin said. "I hear some stores actually encourage them."

But this wasn't just any customer. This was Mary Brady. Griffin watched her approach with resignation, the way he might watch an incoming storm.

Completely absorbed in some sheet of paper she

held, Mary was striding purposefully toward the custom-order counter, where Griffin and Emma were huddled. She didn't look up, and consequently she was almost on top of them before she realized that Emma wasn't alone.

"Emma, can you do these up for me ASAP? They're the announcements of Heather's new offices, and we need them—"

Her reaction to the sight of Griffin was so dramatic it was almost comical. "You?" She recoiled, almost dropping the paper. "You? Here?"

Griffin sighed, realizing how it must look, the two of them tucked away behind the counter. Especially to Mary, who was always ready to believe the worst of him.

"Yes, me. Here." He pushed aside a sample book of wedding announcements and took Mary's hand in his. "But, please, you must promise not to tell anyone. You see, Harry has this terribly big gun."

Mary snatched her hand away. "God, Cahill, every time I think you couldn't go any lower—"

Emma was looking confused. "What on earth is the matter with you, Mary?" She glanced from Griffin to Mary, then back to Griffin. "Oh." She frowned. "Oh, good grief, I'd almost forgotten. Has everyone heard about it?"

Griffin shrugged. "Firefly Glen. Home of the high-speed grapevine."

Mary was sharply folding up the paper she'd brought in. "I'll just come back another time, Emma," she said stiffly. She turned around to exit the store, her shoulders rigid and squared, the picture of silent disapproval.

Watching her, Emma chewed on her bottom lip,

tapped her fingernails on the wood counter rapidly and finally hopped down with a sigh.

"Darn it, Mary," she called out. "Wait."

Mary turned around slowly. "Really. I'd rather come back later."

"Yeah, well, I've got something to tell you, and I want to tell you now."

"You don't have to do this, Em," Griffin said quietly.

"Yes, I do," she said. She went over to Mary and put out her hands. "Mary, listen to me. You've probably heard that Griffin and I were sneaking around, having this hot, illicit thing, and Harry caught us together. Is that about right?"

Mary flicked a hard glance at Griffin. "That's the edited version," she said tightly.

"And now you think he's some kind of coldhearted, black-hearted bastard who sneaks around with married women, right?"

Mary lifted her eyebrows. "That's the edited version."

"Okay. But here's what really happened." Emma took a deep breath. "Harry and I were having some problems. I didn't know what to do, so I asked Griffin to help me make Harry jealous. He didn't want to, but I pretty much forced him into it. We staged a kiss, Harry saw it, and it worked. Now Harry and I are back together, and everything's fine. That's the whole stupid, humiliating story."

Turning to Griffin, she smiled weakly, running her fingers through her short, black hair. "I'm sorry, Griff," she said humbly. "I don't know why you didn't just tell me to go straight to hell."

Griffin smiled back. "Because you were already there, sweetheart. Personally, I don't get it, but apparently for you life without that goofy husband of yours *is* hell."

Emma's eyes were suspiciously bright, but bravely she turned and faced Mary again. "I asked Griffin to keep it a secret because I was embarrassed, but now I see how selfish that was. He shouldn't have to look like a cad just because I don't want to look like a fool."

While Emma was explaining, Griffin could see Mary's indignation fading. The puffed-up disapproval seeped out of her like air from a leaky balloon.

"Well," she said uncomfortably. "Well, I don't know. I honestly don't know what to say."

"Don't say anything," Griffin suggested, suddenly afraid that they were rapidly approaching a tearful de-nouement. Standing knee-deep in wedding announce-ments with a couple of weeping women was not his idea of the perfect afternoon. "Don't let the sentimen-tality of the moment carry you away. I'm still Prince Dudley Do-nothing, remember? This wasn't my only sin."

"It was your worst, though," Mary said grudgingly. "I mean, your worst lately."

Griffin cocked his head. "Mary," he remonstrated. "Tell the truth, now. What about Heather and the Stewberts?"

Mary glowered. She made an irritated sound with her tongue against her teeth. "Okay, fine, you're abso-lutely right. I admit it. When I saw Heather in your arms yesterday, I thought I was going to have to—"

"What?" Emma grabbed Mary's arm. "Oh, my gosh! Come behind the counter. You have to tell me everything!"

Dear God. Griffin extricated himself neatly from the counter area and headed for the door. "I'm afraid," he said politely, "that this is where I came in."

"Griff, wait—" Emma was grinning. "Don't you want to hear what Mary has to say about the rumors?"

"Emma, my love," Griffin said, opening the door. "I'd rather have your darling Harry's gigantic gun pointed straight at my cold, black heart."

CHAPTER ELEVEN

HUMMING TO HERSELF, Heather slathered water all over the back of the eight-foot strip of prepasted wallpaper and then climbed on the ladder to press it in place. It went on perfectly, as if it were eager to cooperate.

As she smoothed the air bubbles out, she could just barely hear the deep, bonging tone of the grandfather clock out in the hall. Just one note? Was it already one in the morning? Good thing she was almost finished.

She climbed down and was preparing to wet another wallpaper strip when Griffin stuck his head through the doorway.

"I thought I heard noises. It's late, you know, especially for a doctor who has to wake up at five in the morning. Don't pregnant women get nervous when their obstetricians fall asleep in the middle of a delivery?"

He was right, of course. She ought to leave this for the workmen to finish when they came in the morning. She needed to get some sleep.

But the truth was, she had too much pent-up energy, and she had to do *something* with it. Wallpapering the last examination room in her beautiful new office was as good as anything else.

Besides, she enjoyed the work. She loved creating beauty and order in this wonderful place. Now that she knew Spring House was truly hers, that she would never have to sell it in order to pay rent on some concrete block office she hated…

She smiled. "I just want to finish this wall. Then I'm going straight to bed, honestly."

He surveyed the half-papered room. She wondered if he liked her choice in wallpaper—a soft green abstract swirl that she had hoped was both attractive and calming. But she didn't want to ask. His taste was so sophisticated, so masculine. He probably thought it was too frilly.

"Tell you what," he said. "The Stewberts are sound asleep. How about if, until they wake up, I pitch in down here?"

"There's no need," she insisted. "Really. I'll be fine."

"But I've been wanting to show you the orchard pictures. I was hoping you'd tell me which ones you think Granville would like."

She hesitated. Griffin was in his official sleeping uniform—though as far as she could tell he never slept more than a couple of hours at a time. He wore a loose pair of navy sweatpants, a butter-yellow T-shirt and not much else. And still he looked disgustingly elegant. Must be that long, low waist, and those broad shoulders. Made everything look like a tuxedo.

Heather thought of her own glue-spattered cutoffs and sticky sweatshirt and grimaced.

He came in, his bare feet slapping softly on the hardwood floor. He set a stack of photographs, all color eight-by-tens, on the examination table.

"Here. You look at these, and I'll put the next strip up for you."

Reluctantly she put down the brush. Probably he didn't need her approval of his photographs any more than she needed his approval of her wallpaper. Still, it was nice of him to ask.

"Okay." Picking up the pictures, she hoisted herself onto the table and began to study them.

The first two were innocent enough. Griffin had found an interesting perspective that hinted at an endless angled row of apple trees, blooming ever smaller, into eternity. The next was a close-up, just the intricate patterns and textures of brown branch and white blossom.

But the third one stopped her. It was a picture of Heather herself, sitting on the picnic blanket, leaning back on her elbows. Her face was lifted, open to the sun, her breasts pressing against her flimsy dress.

Heather tightened, barely holding back a gasp of displeasure. Had her dress really been that revealing? Had she ever posed in such a flagrant display of sensuality?

This wasn't one of Griffin's "spring" pictures—unless spring was merely the symbol for fertility. The sun was ripe, the trees were ripe, the woman was ripe. Even the babies that sprawled against her were as fleshy as sweet peaches that had become too heavy for the branch and rolled to the ground.

She supposed it was a good picture. Sensual, creative, well composed. And very flattering of her, in its way. But even so…

Looking at this woman, who was Heather and yet was not Heather, made her feel strangely edgy. And a little angry with Griffin, who seemed to be implying that he knew things about her, things she didn't even know about herself.

"I didn't realize you were taking pictures of me," she said. She tried to laugh casually. "At least I guess it's of me. This must be a kind of trick photography. I hardly recognize myself."

He paused, the brush in his hand. "It's no trick. It's what they call a candid shot. Candid, as in un-posed. Without pretense." He raised one eyebrow. "Or defense."

Looking back at the picture, she realized that he was absolutely right. What made her uncomfortable about this photograph was how utterly defenseless she looked.

Without question, this woman was prettier, softer, more accessible than Heather. But she was also more vulnerable. Unarmed and unaware, the woman in the photograph was weak.

The perfect prey.

She glanced at Griffin, who was standing on the ladder now, smoothing the strip of wallpaper into place. His back was to her, his long, powerful body outlined by the well-worn cotton. His hands, moving across the green swirls, were deft and sure. He was strong, supple and focused.

The perfect predator.

And the most alarming thing about it was that, somehow, looking at him, at the beautiful, coherent strength of him, made her feel, just for a moment, that perhaps things *should* be this way.

It made her believe that perhaps power *should* meet surrender. Thrust should meet yield. Take should meet give.

No! Her anxiety level rose like mercury in the sun. That was *not* what she believed. Oh, maybe she had made a terrible mistake, getting this close to him again. She had to get him out of this room—and, as soon as possible, out of this house—before she began thinking like a victim.

His victim. And just one of many.

She put the pictures down carefully and stood, though her legs felt strangely uncertain, as if she had caught some weakness, like a flu, from the woman in the orchard.

She moved toward the last precut strip of wallpaper. "I think I'll get started on this one," she said brightly, as he climbed down from the ladder. "That way we'll be finished sooner."

"Okay," he agreed, clearly unaware of the turmoil inside her. "I'll be working on the bottom, so if you start at the top, we shouldn't get tangled up."

But suddenly she was all thumbs, which was absurd. She was a doctor—her hands were unusually steady, trained to be skillful and quick. She'd already hung a dozen strips of this same paper without a single mistake.

This piece, however, was different. It had been cut wrong, for starters. Either that, or the ceiling was suddenly off plumb. Pleats, wrinkles, air bubbles and lumps rose up everywhere. She growled under her breath. What an unholy mess!

Determined to start fresh, she peeled it off, but the darn thing began to fold over her, over itself, like a crazy, limp accordion.

She reached over her head, and her hands met a wet mess of glue.

"Damn it," she mumbled, trying to back away without losing her toehold on the rung of the ladder.

The paper was sticking to her hair now, and, no matter how she twisted it, the glue side was always against her skin.

Finally she lost her cool. Indifferent to whether she preserved the wallpaper, she began to wad up every inch she could reach. "Get—off—me, you diabolical—"

Maybe she couldn't see a thing, but she could hear just fine. Griffin was clearly chuckling. She turned, ready to blister him, but she almost lost her balance. And then, thank heaven, she felt his solid steadiness just below her on the ladder.

"Hang on a minute," he said, repressed mirth altering his words. "Just hold still, and I'll get it off."

She stood there, fuming, while he slowly worked her free. He gradually unearthed her head, peeling her hair loose strand by sticky strand.

And, as she emerged, she met the amusement brimming in his blue eyes. "It's not funny," she said.

"Sure it is," he retorted, grinning. "Why, come to think of it, it's almost as funny as the sight of a grown man getting sprinkled by a naked baby."

She scowled, recognizing the echo. Okay, so she'd been insensitive that day. She should have known he'd pay her back with interest.

"Seriously, are you all right?" he asked.

"No." She really, really hated looking like such a fool. "The damn thing tried to eat me."

"It's okay." He smiled. "It's nothing that can't be fixed."

He led her to the sink, which, thank goodness, was already fully operational. He turned on the warm water and put her hands under it, scrubbing softly with his own to dissolve the glue. Then he urged her forward and splashed the water along her forearms.

"Thanks." She cast him a half-grudging look from beneath her lashes. "I could do this myself, you know," she said, but not very forcefully, so she wasn't surprised when he didn't let go.

"I've got it," he said cheerfully. "You just relax."

He must be kidding. She couldn't remember when she had felt this agitated and uptight. Maybe she was overreacting, but she suddenly realized that, for her, just standing this close to him was dangerous.

They had almost made it safely through their tricky three weeks together. She mustn't let herself start thinking stupid thoughts now.

He massaged between her fingers, working off the glue. It was efficient, and effective. But it felt oddly sensual.

She wondered if he had meant it to. She slanted another glance at him, but he looked perfectly business-like. She must be imagining things.

"Okay. Now the rest of you." Griffin led her to the examination table. Circling her waist with his hands, he lifted her up onto it. "You wait there," he said, turning back to the sink. "And don't touch anything."

As she sat there, on this table made for patients, she felt strange, as if her body were trying to contain two overwhelming and contradictory urges. One was the frantic impulse to run—just bolt, without warning, without explanation, without apology.

But the other was the absurd, self-destructive desire to have Griffin go on touching her.

He found several clean white washcloths beneath the sink. When he had them nice and damp, he lay them on the padded mattress beside her.

Her legs dangled over the side of the table, so he

parted them slightly, making room for him to come in very close. Her knees settled softly against his hips. Self-conscious, she tightened her muscles, holding her thighs a fraction of an inch farther apart.

He didn't seem to notice one way or the other. But she did. With his sexy body tucked between her legs like this, she could hardly think straight.

"Face first," he said, chuckling as he tilted her chin, letting the brilliant overhead light shine on the rapidly hardening streaks of glue. "Although, I don't know. You're kind of cute when you're covered in paste. Takes me back to our kindergarten days."

"I didn't even know you in kindergarten," she said, glad of anything to take her mind off the way his hard, lean hips shifted against her knees whenever he moved. "I only had eyes for James Loughlin. Now he was a *real* man. He actually ate the paste. *And* he had a Spiderman lunchbox."

Griffin grinned, taking one corner of the towel and addressing her eyebrow, which had glued itself to her hair. "The girls really go for that, do they?"

"You bet. It's the kindergarten equivalent of a Ferrari."

He chuckled, but he didn't say anything further, seemingly intent on his work, though surely she couldn't have absorbed that much of the paste. But she didn't complain. The cloth was warm, like the pampered, scented towels at an expensive spa, and he draped it over his hand like a glove.

He worked slowly, systematically, beginning at the brow. Then her nose and cheeks and chin. He took the most time with her mouth. He traced the outline of her lips first, then smoothed across the surface. Then, with a smile, he lightly pinched a fleck of paste from the soft, dipping curve of her upper lip.

Finally, with his forefinger, which was carefully shrouded in warm, wet cotton, he reached back and stroked the sensitive skin behind her ear.

"Now the rest of you." He traded for a fresh towel and, spreading it wide open, moved it up and down her throat, rubbing lightly. He found a spot of flaky paste on her collarbone. He worked it free, then slid the edge of the towel lower, just slightly below the neckline of her sweatshirt, to get the rest.

She felt a strange tingling in her midsection, as if this were a new and slightly kinky kind of foreplay. Idiotically, she began to obsess about the towel, about the wet warmth that left cool shimmers in its wake, about the slightly scratchy fibers that awakened each nerve ending separately.

And then she began to think about how all this would feel without the towel. He still hadn't touched her with his bare hand, and she realized that every inch of her body strained for the moment when he would.

Suddenly, out of nowhere, she was shivering. Goose bumps spread across her skin like dominoes falling. She crossed her arms, hugging herself.

He stopped immediately. "Are you cold?"

She shook her head. "Not really," she said. But she kept her arms wrapped protectively, clutching her elbows so tightly it almost hurt.

"What is it?" His voice was deep. "Heather? I didn't hurt you, did I?"

She shook her head, not trusting herself to speak. This was ridiculous. But that was the power he had over her. The power to make her weak. To make her ridiculous. She shut her eyes, and was horrified to feel a damp warmth seeping from the corners.

With a low, concerned murmur, he caught her tear in the towel. Touching her chin, he tilted her face toward his. "Sweetheart, what's the matter?"

She looked at him helplessly. "I don't know," she said. "It's just all so—" She blinked, forcing herself not to cry, which would be unbearably pathetic. She never cried. "I think I'm just tired. And a little bit confused."

He gently touched the towel to her other eye, absorbing the tiny drop of wetness. "About what?"

"About everything. About you. I don't understand why you are being so...so nice."

He smiled. "Well, thanks a lot."

"You know what I mean. You just keep doing things that are—"

He waited.

She didn't know exactly how to go on. She couldn't just say, *Without even trying to, you're turning me to jelly. You're seducing me, and you don't even know it. You don't even care.*

But she had to say something. "You've done too much. The vote yesterday was all your doing, no matter what you say, and—"

"I told you I'd try to help with that. After all, you're doing me a huge favor with the Stewberts, aren't you?"

"Yes." She tried to clear her mind, but it was difficult. He was still stroking her cheek softly with the warm towel, and it was painfully distracting. "And that should settle it, it should make us even. But you keep doing things, little things, but they add up. Like the night you helped with the class, or the times you've let me sleep through part of my shift. Or that picture, in the orchard. Or tonight, with the wallpaper…"

She swallowed hard. This was the important part, the only really honest part. "And now, the way you're touching me—"

She paused, expecting him to jump in, protesting, explaining, wielding his glib eloquence to dazzle or deflect.

But he didn't. He just watched her, his eyes dark and intent.

"What about the way I'm touching you?"

"I don't know." She took a deep breath. "I guess I'm not sure what you want, what you expect from me. I'm…I'm feeling things, things I never wanted to feel again. I don't even know whether you're doing this deliberately, or if I'm just trapped in some ten-year-old…"

She felt her voice rising, and she reined it back down. "I guess I just don't know what your agenda is."

"I don't have any agenda." He was half smiling, but his eyes, for once, looked somber. "Hasn't it occurred to you that maybe I'm trapped, too? That maybe we're both caught up in something we can't control?"

"No," she said flatly. "Not you. I've never seen you lose control, never in your whole life."

"Of course you have. You just never understood what you were seeing." He dropped the towel on the table beside her, and he put his hands, his hard, bare hands, on her shoulders.

"I lose control every time I see you, Heather. It's been that way since I was seventeen. It's that way now. I'm very much afraid it will be that way forever."

She looked at him, at that dark, determined look she knew so well, and for a moment her vision blurred again, splintering the bright light into a field of broken crystal.

Sex. He was talking about sex.

For him, the magic of their relationship had always been entirely physical, hadn't it? He had never understood how much more than that it had been to her. He'd never realized that, for her, his laughter fired up the yellow torch of the sun. His lips lit the silver candle of the moon. His smile tamed demons, summoned angels, made every day worth living.

He would have laughed at such maudlin sentimentality. For him, "love" was easy, fun and simple—and as multiorgasmic as possible. It was wet, possessive kisses, hard, hot passion, shivering sweat and sweet, satisfied exhaustion.

It was, in short, just good sex. And lots of it.

And yet, maybe her indignation here wasn't quite honest. She had to admit that she had always understood that part, too. She had often felt that pulsing, liquid heat rising up, like the subtle pump of an interior, invisible volcano, just because Griffin Cahill had entered a room.

She felt it now, in fact.

And he knew it.

"But you asked for answers, Heather, and you deserve them." His blue eyes scoured her face with a kind of hunger that was both a ghost from the past and a devil from her dreams. "It's really very simple. You asked what I expect from you. I expect nothing. You asked what I *want*. I want everything."

"Everything?" she echoed helplessly. Everything… But that was too much. That would leave her, when he left, with nothing.

"Everything." He hooked his hands beneath her knees and dragged her slowly toward him. "I want you to wrap your legs around me and never let go. I want to kiss you until neither one of us can breathe."

He brought their bodies so close together that she had to reach back, planting the heels of her hands on the soft table, to balance herself. The heat of him was a piercing ache between her legs.

"I want to look at you." He bunched the fabric of her sweatshirt in his hands and lifted it almost to her throat, baring her breasts to the light, which was terribly bright, bright enough for a doctor to work by.

She inhaled sharply. He had always loved her breasts. And she had loved the way he loved them.

"I want to touch you." He slid one hand between their bodies, setting off a sparkle of colored lights sizzling through her veins.

"And taste you." He lowered his head, and grazed his closed lips over the tingling tips of her breasts. She moaned lightly, wishing he would take her into his mouth. That hot, hungry mouth. She would remember his mouth, she thought, when she'd forgotten everything else in the world.

"And I want to make you call out my name, the way you used to do."

His breath was hot against her skin. "Do you remember that, sweetheart? Do you remember how my name was always the last thing you said? The last thing you whispered? Right before you began to scream…"

She tightened her legs around him, her body answering with a truth more compelling than words. She remembered everything.

"Do you want that, too?" He touched his tongue to

her, and she twisted helplessly. The world was fading, narrowing to two people, one hunger. "Tell me, Heather. Tell me that you want it, too."

"I want it," she said hoarsely, as if she'd already screamed his name till her throat was raw. "I want you. I—"

But the world had not really gone away. It roared back at that moment, like an enemy that had retreated briefly, only to regroup and attack again.

Right under his hand, on the waistband of her shorts, her pager suddenly went off. The buzzing noise, so close it felt as personal as a slap, was horrible. Loud, electronic, malevolent.

He yanked the pager free with a disbelieving curse. He stared at it for a long, numb, silent moment. And then he looked at her.

"I don't suppose there's any chance you won't answer it," he said.

She blinked, horrified to realize that, for one heedless moment, she had considered exactly that. Her feet had been wrapped around the small of his back, and she let them fall gracelessly away. She scooted back from him, farther onto the table.

She had to think. She had to breathe a little. Clear her head.

"It must be a patient," she said thickly, pulling her shirt down to cover her breasts. "Only my service knows the number."

Stepping back politely, he handed the pager to her. She looked at the digital display. Of course, it was her service. Only in a carefully scripted happily-ever-after fairy tale would it have been an error, a carelessly dialed wrong number, a glitch in the tiny little wiring.

She forced her weakened legs to carry her across the room. She picked up the telephone, called her service and listened, saying little.

It was Anna Mizell. She was in labor. Probably false labor, but she was at the hospital, in a panic, blood pressure skyrocketing, begging for Heather to come.

Heather hung up the telephone. As her mind cleared, she told herself this might be a blessing in disguise. She needed time to think.

She was under no illusions about what would have happened next. She would have become Griffin's lover. Again. And this time he wouldn't even have had to bother with the whole messy pretense of an engagement. He could have departed next week with a thoroughly satisfied libido, and a conveniently clear conscience, as well.

She couldn't deny she wanted him. Who wouldn't want him? He was six-feet-three-inches of raw sexual magnetism and breathtaking expertise. But did she want him that much? Enough to break her heart for him all over again?

"I have to go," she said with a fairly good approximation of professionalism and control. "I have to change. I have a patient in labor."

She had expected him to be furious. But though his face was etched with tension, to her surprise he merely nodded.

"I know," he said levelly. "It's all right."

She hesitated, but what else was there to say? She nodded, too. And then she took a deep breath, smoothed the wrinkles from her shirt and moved toward the door.

In spite of herself, when she reached him, she stopped.

"I'm sorry," she said. "But, you know, maybe this is

for the best. Things were getting a little out of control and this will give us time to—"

"Don't kid yourself, Heather," he interrupted gruffly. He was holding himself stiffly, as if his body hurt when he moved. "If ten years of waiting haven't put out this fire, the next ten hours aren't going to do it."

"Yes, but, if we think it over, we—"

With a low growl, he pulled her into his arms and shut her up with a very hard, very hot kiss.

"Accept it, sweetheart. This isn't over. It's just postponed."

CHAPTER TWELVE

ALL RIGHT, GRIFFIN CAHILL, listen up. If you think I'm suddenly going to start believing you're Mr. Nice Guy, just because you're making a big deal over Heather's new offices, think again. Just because you're going to a lot of trouble, and expense, and planning this swell party just to make her happy, well...

Mary stopped, abruptly aware that this *Listen Up* letter, which she'd been composing in her head, wasn't going at all the way she'd intended it to. Annoyed, she fiddled with the lacy edges of a beautiful tablecloth, just one of many available for rental at Temporarily Yours, Firefly Glen's most exclusive party shop.

She tried to talk herself back into her customary disdain. But it wasn't working. The truth was, Griffin *had* begun to redeem himself in her eyes.

A little.

He really was going all out with this surprise party. He had asked Mary and Troy to come here, to Temporarily Yours, to arrange for all the elegant necessities, like china and silverware, tables and chairs, linens and lighting.

And he wasn't just dodging the hard work, either. Griffin himself was over at the florist right now, Stewberts in tow, coordinating about a zillion dollars worth of flowers.

"Hey, what do you think about this?" Troy was standing next to a huge fountain, in which a curvaceous naked woman rode a dolphin that ejected a continuous spray of champagne out of its grinning mouth. "Griffin said get whatever we wanted, spare no expense."

She shook her head, shuddering. "I also heard him tell you nothing tacky."

Troy leaned his head against the statue's shoulder and gave Mary a piteous look. "Hey, that's not nice. I had one of these at my wedding."

"I guess that explains why you're divorced."

Mary moved toward the chafing dishes. If all one hundred people—and their dates—accepted Griffin's invitation, which they probably would, the caterer was going to need a lot of help.

Troy gave the statue's bottom a friendly goodbye pat and strolled over to the alcove where architectural features were displayed.

"So do you think we ought to get some arches, or maybe some columns? Now don't tell me they're tacky, too, because I've seen them at some pretty swanky parties. They fill 'em up with fake roses and little white lights and stuff. They look great."

Mary eyed the tall, plaster-of-Paris columns, the white latticework arches. "Still too kitsch," she decided. "You've seen Spring House. It's so ornate, with all that Victorian stuff going on everywhere. It really doesn't need a lot of extra froufrou, you know?"

Troy pouted. "Fine. I'll just go sit in the corner and let you decide."

Mary smiled. "Fine."

Troy wasn't the type to sulk for long, though. In

less than five minutes, he was up again, joining Mary at the champagne glasses. "So, Mary, have you ever been to Nepal?"

She laughed. "I haven't ever been anywhere." She held up two glasses, a classic and a continental. "Which one do you like?"

He frowned at them. "The fat one." When she looked surprised, he rolled his eyes. "I mean the skinny one. Who cares? After a couple of drinks, they all look exactly the same anyhow, right? Kind of like women."

She made a rude sound and kept walking. Maybe the frosted glasses would be nice…

"Well, as I was saying. Nepal is really exciting," Troy went on as if she'd never interrupted. "Even more exciting than a Friday night surprise party in Firefly Glen, if you can believe such a thing."

She ignored him. But he kept hovering at her elbow, fidgeting in a way that seemed almost nervous. She began to wonder whether this conversation might actually have a point.

"Yeah, and…?" she prompted him.

"And." He paused. "And, well, I'm probably going to have to miss this party, because my plane for Nepal leaves Friday afternoon." He sounded a little embarrassed. "I just wanted to tell you that ahead of time. You know, so you wouldn't rent an extra champagne glass on my account."

Mary was quite pleased with the way she kept her cool. She glanced at him casually. "Why? All the Saturday planes to Nepal were full?"

"No, nothing that easy to fix. There are time elements involved. People. Events. Deadlines. Stuff like that. I don't really have any choice."

"Oh."

She picked up one glass after another—etched ones, plastic ones, pink ones, black "Over the Hill" ones. She made absolutely certain that none of her irrational disappointment showed on her face.

Because what right did she have to be disappointed, anyhow? Troy Madison was just another rich guy blowing through their quaint little town. He had never even hinted that he might stay.

And besides, what difference did it make to her when he left? A couple of weeks ago, she hadn't known he existed. In a month or two, she wouldn't even remember his name.

Except that, darn it, she liked him. Not in that fluttery, romancy way. But as a friend. He was smart, and he was easy to be with, lighthearted and funny.

Most of all she respected him as a writer. She liked reading his work and letting him read hers. She liked talking to him about the craft, about the business. It had been very exciting for a little Firefly Glen wanna-be. He knew so much, and she knew almost nothing.

But it was over, and that was that.

She picked up a deceptively simple crystal continental champagne glass, one of the most elegant and expensive styles in the store.

"This one, I think," she said. "It's pretty, and—even better—it'll put a serious dent in Griffin's budget."

She had a sudden horrible thought. She turned to Troy. "Wait just a minute. Is Griffin going with you?"

She was sizzling mad at the very thought of it. If Griffin Cahill arranged this party, and then didn't show up for it... If he jetted to Pakistan—or India or Timbuktu or wherever the heck Nepal was—she'd have to hunt him down like a dog and beat him to death with his own expensive camera.

"I've been trying to talk him into it," Troy said with surprising candor. He must have missed the bloodred fire in her eyes. "But so far I'm not having much luck. He takes this uncle business pretty seriously."

"Damn good thing," she muttered.

Troy wrinkled his brow. "Why? I thought the more miles there were between you and Griffin the happier you were."

"It's complicated," she said. And it was. She wasn't even sure herself why she wanted Griffin to stay. A blind Martian could tell what was happening between Griffin and Heather these days. Whenever they were in the same room together, the sexual tension was so thick the rest of the people could hardly breathe.

All that edgy, uptight, panting, blushing, coy little touches. It made Mary want to yak. But she knew what it meant. It meant Heather was going to let Playboy Cahill break her heart all over again.

So did it really matter so much whether he broke it before Friday night, or after?

Yeah, actually, it did. She didn't know why, but it did.

She plopped the champagne flute on the counter so hard the crystal rang through the large showroom like a church bell. "Okay, that's glasses, china, linens and tables. All that's left is to decide on the chairs."

She had just about picked one out—the most expensive, of course—when Griffin came through the double doors of the store, rolling the tandem stroller in front of him.

The Stewberts seemed to be in high spirits. But the

one on the left had a couple of slobbery yellow daisy petals stuck to his lips, as if he'd just eaten a canary.

Mary opened her mouth.

"Don't even ask," Griffin said wearily. "Suffice it to say that my bill at the florist will be slightly higher than anticipated."

Mary chuckled. *Way to go, Stewbert,* she thought, giving him a mental high five. Between them, they were going to make Griffin pay big time for the chance to impress their dear, deluded Heather, weren't they?

"So what flowers did you decide on?" Mary knelt down and extricated the petals from the baby's mouth. "Daisies?"

"No, daisies were Stewbert's choice. But I vetoed that. I picked something the florist called the Splendor of Spring, which, though its name sounds a little hysterical, is actually quite pretty. It's mostly violets and lily of the valley."

"Lily of the valley?" Mary stood up slowly. She gave Griffin a suspicious look. Had the son of a gun just gotten lucky? Or did he really remember little details like that? "Heather loves lily of the valley. It's her favorite flower."

Griffin smiled. "Yes," he said. "I know."

"Well." Mary squinted at him. "That should make her very happy."

"Yes," he agreed. "It should."

"Which is what she deserves," she added pointedly.

Griffin nodded.

"Yes," he said, in a tone Mary decided to interpret as a promise. "It is."

IT WAS THE PERFECT DAY to interview a potential partner. Heather had never felt more certain that she needed one.

Actually, the *perfect* day would have been yesterday. Then she would have had someone already on staff, prepared to take over for her this morning.

And then maybe she could get some sleep.

Heather smothered her tenth yawn of the morning and tried to focus on the handsome, twenty-nine-year-old doctor who sat across the desk from her, explaining why he wanted to leave New York City and move to Firefly Glen.

Poor guy. He kept having to repeat himself. He must think she was very stupid—or very hung over.

Her eyes were red-rimmed and scratchy, her whole body slowed down by fatigue. She'd been up all night with Anna Mizell, making sure it was truly a false alarm. She had finally released her at 8:00 a.m.

But that meant Heather hadn't slept all night.

And she wasn't going to sleep today, either. Apparently sleep was a luxury single practitioners couldn't afford.

That's where…what was his name? She sneaked a peek at his flawless résumé. *Adam Reading*. That's where Adam Reading came in. Would he think it was odd if she hired him on the spot, told him his first patient was in Room One, and then curled up and took a nap?

Oh, well. It was a lovely fantasy.

"I've talked to your references," she said, looking down at her notes. "They were highly complimentary. Everything looks great on paper. But a partnership…"

She decided to be candid. She was too tired to bother sugarcoating things right now. "Sharing a practice is a very intimate relationship, a lot like a marriage. Frankly, I'm still not sure I'm ready to take anyone on, and if I did…"

He smiled. He had a very warm smile. And he looked like a very young Gregory Peck. The patients must love his bedside manner.

"If you did," he said, "you'd want to be sure it was the right partner. You'd want to be sure we saw eye to eye on all medical issues—and a lot of personal issues, too."

She nodded, glad that he didn't seem to be offended that his sterling credentials and Ivy League education didn't necessarily guarantee anything. Good doctoring wasn't done on paper. It was done on people.

"I'd also want to be sure that you were approaching this as a long-term commitment. Small towns aren't always as delightful as people think. And we're slow to integrate strangers. If you didn't stay, I'd have a difficult time persuading my patients to accept another new doctor anytime soon."

"I can imagine," he said, clearly unfazed. "But I love small towns. I was born and raised in one just a hundred miles from here. I wish they could use another ob-gyn, but they can't. My dad doesn't plan to retire for at least thirty more years."

So his father was a small-town doctor, too. Heather felt herself warming even more to this slightly old-fashioned young man. Though he was only a few years younger than she was, he seemed so serious and innocent. It was actually very appealing.

He leaned forward, his long, strong-boned face growing even more serious. "I am looking for a permanent position. I'm finished with big-city medicine. My wife and I have done a lot of soul-searching and a lot of research. Firefly Glen is the perfect place for us."

She raised her eyebrows. "Your wife?" She didn't

know if this was good news or not. It would depend on the woman. Firefly Glen wasn't crazy about glitzy women. And vice versa. "Does she like small towns, too?"

"She doesn't know very much about them," he admitted. "She was born in New York. Sally was a dancer. With the City Ballet."

Uh-oh. Heather didn't want to stereotype anyone, but a ballet dancer? She knew from tough personal experience that if people yearned for excitement, travel, adventure, crowds, culture…then Firefly Glen couldn't hold them for long.

"*Was* a dancer," he repeated, stressing the past tense. "She quit five years ago. She gives dance lessons now. And…well, we found out a few months ago that we're going to have a baby. In the fall." He finally smiled again. "That's what finally decided us. It's our dream to start our family here, in a place like Firefly Glen."

Heather hesitated. She had planned to cut the interview short, considering how exhausted she was. She had expected to thank Adam Reading, then send him on his way, with promises of a follow-up call sometime soon.

She wasn't an impulse kind of person. She liked to think things through, make careful decisions after weighing all the elements. But everything was a little weird today. And suddenly her instincts about this honest, gentle man were so strong she couldn't imagine dismissing him according to plan.

"Tell you what," she said impetuously. "Why don't you spend the day with me, here at the office?"

She stood, smiling invitingly. The waiting room was full. What better way to see if she liked him? What better way to see if he'd fit in—in her office, in her town, in her life? "Meet some of the patients, get a feel for what you'd be doing. Then come to my house tonight and have dinner. We've got a lot to talk about."

"I'd be honored." Adam was obviously surprised, and deeply pleased.

Heather was pleased, too. It all made perfect sense. He was by far the best candidate. She had liked him on sight. Getting to know him better right away would expedite the decision and *maybe* prevent a mass walkout by her staff.

And the fact that Adam's presence at dinner tonight would keep Heather and Griffin from picking up where they'd left off…

Well, that was just a lucky coincidence.

DINNER, WHICH THE THREE of them ate by candlelight on the side porch, where the wisteria smelled the sweetest, was a huge success.

By the time they reached the peach cobbler, Griffin and Adam Reading were the best of buddies. They liked the same plays, vacationed at the same resorts, read the same books. Griffin had even, it turned out, seen Adam's wife dance once, a few years back. He must have said all the right things, because Adam's smile was so profoundly grateful it moved Heather almost to tears.

Of course, that wasn't hard, given how exhausted and surreal she felt by then. She'd been up and working for thirty-seven hours straight.

Amazingly, the men didn't seem tired at all. The night was clear and starry, the spring breezes mild enough to encourage them to linger. So they poured another glass of wine and settled into a comfortable discussion of teething.

Heather had to smile. Griffin Cahill talking about teething. It was like seeing the sun set in the east.

Declining a refill—she'd already had two glasses—she stretched out on the porch swing just a couple of feet away, listening but too sleepy to participate much. She shouldn't have had the wine, not on top of two weeks of sleep deprivation. She felt as limp as overcooked spaghetti.

She used to be able to weather all-nighters better than this, she mused dreamily. But then, she hadn't ever had so many jobs before—doctor, civic militant, renovator of historic houses, mother to twin babies.

Not that she really was a mother, but…she felt like one. At least for the moment. A temporary, very tired, mommy. She rested her head against the arm of the swing, thinking, somewhat irrelevantly, how extraordinarily warm babies were. How their smiles lit up your heart.

Yes, they were exhausting. But having that sweetness in your life was probably worth it, she thought, closing her eyes just for a moment. It was probably worth whatever it cost.

She woke to the sound of rain, and the cool, earthy scent of wet grass. Confused, but too drowsy to care much, she burrowed a little further under her blanket.

But then a cold drop of water hit her cheek. At the same time, she felt a warm hand on her arm.

"Heather," Griffin's voice was saying. "Wake up. It's time to go to bed."

She sat up, vaguely anxious. Time to go to bed? What time was it? Even more disturbing, her bed shifted weirdly under her when she moved. But it wasn't her bed. It was the porch swing.

She pushed her hair back from her face and looked up at Griffin groggily. "Did I fall asleep out here?" She frowned. "What time is it?"

"It's about three," he said, taking the quilted blanket and placing it around her shoulders. "Come on in. It's storming."

"Three?" Vague anxiety gave way to real alarm. She felt in her pocket for her pager. Oh, God—all that wine! She almost never drank. She was always on call. So she had no head for it.

Oh, how foolish! What if one of her patients had needed her?

"I've got it," Griffin said, holding out the little black box. "I was afraid you wouldn't hear it, so I took it with me when I went up to feed the Stewberts. It didn't go off."

But she had to check anyhow. She scrolled hastily through the stored numbers. He was right. For once, nobody had called. Not even Anna Mizell.

Still, the fog in her head wouldn't quite go away. She tried to piece together the evening. She'd brought the new doctor home for dinner, and…

"Oh, no. What about Adam?"

Griffin smiled. "He finally left about midnight, but I practically had to throw him out. He was so fascinated by the Stewberts he could have stayed up there playing with them all night."

"He met the Stewberts?"

"They woke up—you didn't hear that either—and he was so excited. He begged me to let him help. He's trying to learn everything he can about babies." Griffin widened his eyes angelically. "I generously allowed him to learn all about the diaper-changing process."

Groaning, Heather leaned her head back against the swing. "Great. My best prospect for a partner, and I pass out in the middle of dinner, leaving him to the mercy of a total stranger and a couple of bawling infants." She sighed heavily. "He probably thinks I'm a drunk and a lunatic."

Griffin smiled. "He thinks you're a cross between Florence Nightingale and Mother Teresa. He couldn't stop raving on about how great you are with your patients." He tugged on the blanket. "*I'm* the one who thinks you're a lunatic. Any chance we could talk about this inside? I'm getting wet."

"Of course. I'm sorry." She stood, still heavy-headed and slightly groggy.

The blanket fell onto the swing. Griffin gathered it up and once again arranged it around her shoulders.

"Come on, Mother Teresa," he said. "Let's get you to bed before the Stewberts wake up again."

"The Stewberts...oh, no, Griffin—my shift!" She groaned one more time. Was there no end to the ways in which she'd been inept tonight? According to the schedule she had herself concocted, she was in charge of the Stewberts from eight to midnight. "I slept right through it!"

"No problem," he said lightly, holding the blanket under her chin and smiling down at her. "I had Adam to help, remember? The man has done his homework, I'll say that for him. Their baby's not due until October, and he already knows five complete verses of 'Little Bunny Foo-Foo.'"

Heather felt a little wobbly. Now that her anxiety was subsiding and the blanket was warming her up again, she realized she was still very, very sleepy.

"Five verses," she said, trying to keep her eyes open and her head upright. "Wow."

"I know. He'll make a great father. He has an almost godlike patience for 'This Little Piggy.'"

All of a sudden she gave up. She let her head fall forward, coming to rest against his chest. "I hate 'This Little Piggy,'" she confessed to his shirt.

Chuckling, he stroked her hair gently. "Me, too. I say give me peekaboo any day."

"Absolutely," she said seriously, as if they were discussing strategies for world peace. "Peekaboo is much better. It makes the Stewberts laugh."

He tugged on her earlobe gently. "You know, sweetheart, you're going to catch pneumonia if you don't come in out of the rain. Can you walk, or do you want me to carry you up to bed?"

Sweetheart. She loved the sound of his voice saying that word...

Sweetheart? Oh, no. She suddenly realized that the moment she'd been fearing had arrived. They were alone. Together. And she had pretty much fallen into his arms.

"Griffin," she said, tilting her head to look up at him. "I don't think we should— I know you said it wasn't over, but I'm just not ready to—"

He shook his head gently. "Don't worry, I'm not going to try to seduce you tonight. We've both had too little sleep to do it justice, don't you think?"

"Absolutely," she agreed, weak with relief. She let her head fall against his chest again. "And, I'm afraid, too much wine."

She could feel his lips curving against her hair. "Actually, my hopeless innocent, wine is one of the internationally recognized staples of seduction."

"Well, of course, I know that, but—"

He chuckled softly. "I said don't worry. I like my women wide-awake. And frankly, your adoring young doctor's rhapsodies are a little too fresh in my mind. *No one* makes a pass at Mother Teresa, sweetheart. Not even me."

CHAPTER THIRTEEN

"SO WHAT DO YOU THINK, Stewbert?" Griffin angled his cards so the baby, who was crawling around on the floor beside him, could see them. "Should I raise or call?"

Stewbert grabbed for the cards, eager, as always, to sample anything new and different. But Griffin held them out of reach. "No way, pal. This is the first decent hand I've had all night, and I'll be darned if I'm going to let you eat it."

Troy, who was also on the floor, growled as he tried to peel apart a mess of sticky notepaper. "Damn it. Did we decide the green Post-it notes were five or ten?"

Griffin sighed. "Try to concentrate, won't you? The greens are one. The pinks are five. The yellows are ten." He placed a yellow Post-it in the central pot. "It's really very simple."

"It is *not* simple," Troy said, ripping free a pink "chip." He tried to toss it into the pot, but it stuck to his fingers. "It's crazy, that's what it is. Sane people do not play poker on the floor. Sane people do not bet with Post-it notes. Sane people do not show their cards to slobbering infants and ask for their advice."

Griffin yawned. "Get over it, Troy. You don't care where we play. You'd play poker on top of a coffin if you had to. In fact, we did that, didn't we, that time in Louisiana?"

Troy was still trying to shake off the pink Post-it. "Yeah, so? There wasn't anybody in it."

"So, my point is you're not bugged because we're on the floor, or because we've had to hide the real poker chips from the Stewberts. You're bugged because you're losing."

Troy glared at him. "Actually, Einstein, I'm bugged because I can't make you come to Nepal. I'm bugged because I'm going to have to do the story with some other photographer, who won't be half as good. I'm bugged because you're playing nanny to these babies, when you know darn well you could hire somebody else to do it for you."

He leaned against the wall, ignoring the Stewbert who was attempting to unclasp his watch with his one tooth. "I know you, Griff. You could get bored covering the Apocalypse. You're a gather-no-moss, itchy feet, adrenaline-rush kind of guy. You've got to be going absolutely bonkers, stuck in this burg for a whole year. And now this babysitting gig…I'm actually starting to worry about you, bro."

Griffin shrugged. In theory, Troy was right. Griffin asked himself every day why he wasn't going crazy. Why had he been more or less content to spend almost three weeks puttering around Spring House, doing odd jobs to expedite the renovation, tending the Stewberts, waiting for Heather to get home from work?

And the pictures he'd been taking… A few nice shots of Spring House, which he intended to give Heather when their Stewbert job was over. Some cute pictures of the babies that would undoubtedly please Jared and

Katie. A few chamber of commerce photos for Granville Frome. Hardly Griffin's usual stuff.

"Maybe I needed a break from the road," Griffin said, drawing two new cards. "A hotel room can get pretty boring, too, you know."

And lonely.

"Not *your* hotel room." Troy wiggled his eyebrows like Groucho Marx. "So what's really going on here? You and I have been talking about this Nepal trip for years. Your brother is coming back Monday, right? You'd only have to leave your nephews three lousy days early."

"I promised I'd take care of them, and I'm going to. Just play cards, why don't you?"

Troy apparently hadn't even heard him. "It's Heather, isn't it? You've traded the international Parade of Pulchritude for the chance to play doctor with one ravishing redhead."

Griffin grimaced. "Do all writers talk in cheap alliterations, Troy, or is it just you?"

"All of us—but I'm the best." Troy smiled self-deprecatingly. "And don't try to change the subject. I think I might be onto something with this new theory. I think I've caught the scent."

"Your theory stinks, so that might be what you're smelling." Griffin grinned suddenly and pointed toward Troy's pile of Post-it notes. "Plus, I think you're being robbed."

Troy looked, and then he cursed. Stewbert had sat in Troy's stash of poker "money," and now was crawling away toward the playpen, colorful little pieces of paper stuck all over the bottom of his diaper.

"I give up," Troy said, slamming down his cards. "All I can say is thank God I'm out of here tomorrow.

I'm warning you, Griffin. You should come with me, or the next Stewbert running around here just may have your name on it. And that'll be the end of the road for you, my friend."

"Oh, relax," Griffin said irritably. "The Nepal assignment is good, but there will be others. I'll go next time."

"Griffin?" Heather's voice came floating toward them. Griffin looked up and saw that she had opened her bedroom door a crack and was peering out. "Can I talk to you for a minute?"

"Sure."

"Thanks." She shut the door.

Troy gazed knowingly at Griffin, nodding slowly in an extremely annoying I-told-you-so way. He leaned back against the wall and shut his eyes.

"End of the road," he intoned mournfully. "The absolute end of the road."

Griffin resisted the urge to knock Troy's head off as he passed. He scooped up one of the babies, instructed Troy to watch the other one and headed for the door to Heather's room.

He wondered why she wasn't asleep. Her shift had ended over an hour ago, and she had to get up early. Had they been too noisy? But these old houses had thick walls. He certainly couldn't hear anything that went on in the nursery when he was asleep in his room, which was on the other side.

Heather was sitting on the edge of the bed, waiting for him. She wore a long white cotton nightgown with green sprigged flowers. A matching robe lay across the foot of the bed, on top of a lacy white bedspread.

Griffin came in and pulled the door shut behind him carefully.

"Hi," he said softly. "We weren't keeping you awake, were we?"

She shook her head, smiling at the baby.

"Hi, sweetie," she said. She patted the bed beside her. Griffin understood that the invitation was purely for Stewbert, but after he brought the baby over and propped him up against the pillows, he sat down, too.

"Everything okay?"

"Yes, of course. I just forgot to tell you that Stewbert had been crying a lot earlier—teething, I think. I gave him some Tylenol about eleven, and I didn't want you to accidentally give him another dose."

"Okay," Griffin said, though he felt a little skeptical. Wasn't that the kind of thing she could have called across the room? Surely it didn't necessitate a private, middle-of-the-night chat.

Not that he was complaining. In spite of any warning Troy might have to offer, Heather could call Griffin into her bedroom anytime she wanted.

He watched her now, as she bent over Stewbert, kissing his tummy and murmuring an endearment. He'd like to have a picture of this moment, he thought. The slope of her back was so graceful. And in the honey light from her bedside lamp, her hair, which fell loose across her shoulders, looked almost golden.

He felt a strange twisting sensation in his chest. God, she was beautiful. Sometimes, when she was suited up in her intimidating lab coat, with her hair tightly bound and her manner strictly professional, he almost forgot how fine and fragile and feminine she really was.

Oh, hell. He was waxing as alliterative and ridiculous as Troy. It must be something about the intimacy of the hour, the shadowed light, the simple beauty of her slim, ivory-pale bare arms and the supple curve of her breast under the cotton gown.

Or maybe he was just horny as hell.

He breathed slowly to steady himself. Good thing he'd brought Stewbert with him, or who knows what he might have done now.

He'd been in Heather's bedroom before, of course. The exchange of baby shifts had required lots of moving back and forth through the three-room suite. And he had sometimes even let himself indulge in a fantasy or two…fantasies about what it would be like to sleep in that solid four-poster walnut bed, under that white, lacy spread.

Or rather, *not* to sleep.

But ever since that night in her downstairs office, when they had come so close to making love, the fantasies had been absolutely out of control. He couldn't look at her without desire flaring up like the blue fire of a gas jet. He walked around with a tension in his gut that wouldn't go away. The rope was so tight right now he felt half-bowed from the pressure of it.

At this moment, he would have given every Post-it note he owned for the right to make love to her one more time.

"Well," he said, struggling to be practical, "I guess Stewbert and I should get going. Let you get some sleep."

She turned toward him, her hand still resting protectively on Stewbert's tummy. "But there was one more thing," she said. "Something else I wanted to talk to you about."

He nodded. "I thought there might be. What is it?"

"I—" She looked uncomfortable suddenly. "I'm sorry. I didn't mean to eavesdrop, but I heard a little of what Troy was saying to you just now."

Griffin smiled. "Troy's a writer," he said. "He talks nonsense just for the joy of stringing words together. Don't pay any attention to him."

She smiled back, but she didn't look convinced. Oh, hell, Griffin thought. Troy and his big, unstoppable mouth. He wished he could remember exactly how far Troy had gone. He groaned inwardly, remembering that bit about playing doctor.

"I heard him talking about an assignment. Something special. Something you've been wanting to do for ages. And apparently you're going to miss it because you have to stay here with the Stewberts. Is that right?"

"More or less." Griffin shrugged. "But if there's anything I've learned through the years, it's that there's always another assignment."

Stewbert had begun to fuss, so Heather picked him up and held him comfortingly against her breast.

"Maybe," she said as she stroked the baby's head. "But I want you to know that it would be all right with me if you wanted to go with him. It's only a few days until Jared comes back, and I could manage the Stewberts until then."

"No, you couldn't," Griffin said. "What if one of your patients goes into labor?"

"It's only three days," she argued reasonably. "Mary could stay over to babysit. And actually Adam Reading is staying on for a week or so, too. We're seriously talking about a partnership. He's wonderful with the patients, Griffin. His skills are excellent. So he could always pitch in if the emergencies got out of control."

Griffin looked at her, too surprised to speak. She meant it, didn't she?

He knew he should be grateful. Objectively, he could

see what a generous offer it was. And yet he didn't feel grateful at all. He felt strangely raw, and irrationally resentful that she could so easily toss aside the last three days they had together.

Maybe the last three days they'd ever have.

Sometimes, when he was caught in one of those self-indulgent fantasies, Griffin told himself that maybe a love affair of some kind wasn't out of the question. Heather obviously felt the same sizzling chemistry that was burning away at him. Maybe, he dreamed, maybe when the twins were gone, if she really hired a partner, she would travel somewhere with him—somewhere exotic, somewhere romantic.

The Bahamas, maybe. He'd been wanting to photograph that one last waterfall for the book he was proposing. Yes, that might appeal to her. She liked waterfalls. Silver Kiss Falls had always been their favorite secret place.

So why not, the fool with the fantasy always insisted? Just because they were too different to create a permanent life together…surely that didn't mean they couldn't share something wonderful for a little while, something they'd both remember forever.

But then the fantasy would pop like cheap bubble gum. Heather wasn't the traveling type. And she damn sure wasn't the temporary fling type. Their differences had driven them apart ten years ago. And during those ten years their lives had twisted even further in opposite directions, like divergent vines growing out from a common root and ending up on different planets.

So realistically, what were the odds that this little oasis, this temporary truce, could last even five minutes beyond the departure of the twins?

No, these next three days were all they'd ever have. And he didn't intend to give up a minute. Not for Troy, or Nepal, or anything else on earth.

"I appreciate that, Heather," he said finally. "But I really don't have any interest in going to Nepal. And besides, I couldn't run off now. I can't leave you to break the news to Katie that I've mixed up her precious Stewberts."

"Oh, that's right." Heather smiled at him over the baby's now-sleeping head. "But actually that moment might go more smoothly if you're *not* here."

She put her hand on his arm. "Honestly, Griffin, it's all right if you go. I really can manage."

"I'm sure you can," he said softly, resisting the urge to touch her, too. Instead he reached out and traced the incredibly fragile labyrinth of Stewbert's tiny ear.

"But I don't think you understand me, Heather," Griffin said. "I'm staying because, for the next three days, there's nowhere on earth I'd rather be."

MARY WENT TO THE AIRPORT with Troy the next morning, even though she really couldn't spare the time. It was Friday, and the preparations for Heather's surprise party at Spring House were reaching a fever pitch. They couldn't begin until she left for the office, and they had to be finished before she came home at night. It was bedlam.

Even so, Mary simply decided to *make* the time. She didn't want to lose her last few hours with Troy.

Typically, the plane was late, so they sat companionably on the uncomfortable airport seats, watching people trundle luggage back and forth. It was peaceful, not having to chitchat just to fill the air. And it made

Mary feel particularly cozy because, though neither of them said a word, she knew they were both inventing histories for the interesting characters who walked by.

That was what Troy had given her, she thought warmly. A sense that she was not weird, living so much in her imaginary worlds. A sense that she was not alone.

She wished that she could give something back to him. But the only gift she had to offer was advice, and she felt pretty sure he wouldn't welcome it.

Oh, well. It wasn't her way to hold back.

"All right, Troy Madison," she began impulsively. *"Listen up."*

He grinned at her. "Yikes," he said. "That sounds ominous."

"Yeah, well, I've got something to say. And you know how I am when I've got something on my mind."

He nodded emphatically. "Yes, ma'am, I definitely do."

"Okay, so here it is. I know this trip to Nepal is important to you. It sounds absolutely fantastic. I wouldn't dream of suggesting you turn it down. But when it's over, I want you to do something for me."

He frowned quizzically. "Oh, yeah? What?"

"I want you to go home."

Clearly he hadn't been expecting that. He pushed his shaggy hair off his forehead and looked blankly at her. "Home? You mean to my wife? To Anita?"

"Yes. To your wife Anita and your daughter Vicky and your son Mark." When Troy turned his head away, symbolically rejecting the very notion, Mary took his chin and pulled his face back toward hers. "I mean it, Troy. Go home. It's not too late to sort things out."

He laughed unpleasantly. "Yes it is. You don't know Anita."

"No, but I know people. I know women. And if you ask me, that so-called affair of hers was nothing but one great big stick of dynamite set off for the express purpose of grabbing your attention."

"Bull." Troy's face was stony. "It was my best friend, Mary."

"Which made it almost inevitable that you'd find out, right? Is Anita stupid?" She saw his eyes flicker. "Okay, then I rest my case. Look, maybe you can't work it out. But you don't know that. You haven't even gone home since you heard about the affair. She probably thinks you don't give a damn."

Troy's jaw was tight. "She saw the divorce papers, didn't she? That ought to tell her I give a damn."

"Men!" Mary let her head fall back. "I swear, there isn't enough brainpower among the whole lot of you to run a flashlight. Listen to me, Troy, and listen good. Filing for divorce tells her you're mad. It tells her you're offended and furious and you by God refuse to share your own private female with anybody. What it does *not* tell her is that you give a damn about *her.*"

Troy squinted at her, obviously irritated. But he shifted uncomfortably. Her message was getting through. That was one of the many things Mary liked about Troy. He might hate the truth, but he didn't refuse to look it in the eye.

"So I'm just asking you to think about it. Think about going home and getting to know your family again. A lot of this is your fault, you know. Common sense ought to tell you it's hard to keep a family together if they're always apart."

"Wow," Troy said, almost smiling. "I'm actually getting my very own *Listen Up* letter."

She ignored him. She had heard the flight attendant announce the preliminary boarding for his flight, and they didn't have much time.

"Hush up," she said. "I knew there was a reason I always did this in writing. It's impossible to get a man to listen for more than five seconds at a time."

He folded his hands in his lap and waited meekly.

"Okay, well, anyhow, I firmly believe that you can find a way to mend the broken places. But you'll have to stay put long enough for the glue to set. You know what I mean?"

He nodded slowly.

The darn, insensitive flight attendant called for Troy's row. He glanced over, then looked back at Mary. Finally he stood up.

"I know," she said. "Just promise me one more thing. If I'm right, if you guys really do find a way to patch things up, you can thank me by inviting me to your next book signing."

He tilted his head, giving her that cute grin she had already grown so fond of.

"And you can invite me to yours," he said. He held out a little piece of paper. "Take this. It's my agent's name and telephone number. She wants you to call her."

Mary stared at his outstretched hand. "What?" She didn't dare touch it. This felt decidedly too good to be true, and she was afraid the paper would poof into fairy dust. "Why?"

"Women," Troy said, laughing. "They don't have enough brainpower among the whole lot of them…"

He picked up her hand and pressed the paper into it. "Because she thinks you have a future as a writer, dummy. In fact, she's pretty sure she can sell one of the syndicates on the idea of a hot new advice columnist with an in-your-face, no-nonsense, big-sister tone."

Mary felt lost. "An advice columnist?"

Troy nodded. "Yep. *The Listen Up Letters,* they'd call them."

Mary opened her mouth. Then she shut it.

"She has feelers out about *Littletown,* too, although she said that might take a lot longer. The children's fiction market's pretty hard to break into, but she wants to give it a try."

Mary shook her head, disbelieving. "I never thought you really meant it," she said numbly. "I thought you just wanted to sleep with me."

"I did, of course." Troy hoisted his carry-on over his shoulder, then leaned over and kissed her on the cheek. "But I knew you weren't falling for it. Besides, what would that have done to my chances with Anita?"

Mary squeezed his hand. She tried to smile. He kissed her cheek one more time, and then he was gone, leaving only the one magical piece of paper behind to prove he'd ever really been there.

She went to the picture window and realized she was so sad or happy or something that she was about to burst into tears.

Well, that would be ridiculous, wouldn't it?

All right, Mary Brady, she began firmly, touching the cool glass with her fingers as Troy's plane taxied toward the runway. *Listen up.*

CHAPTER FOURTEEN

ON FRIDAY AFTERNOON, Heather's last two patients of the day canceled. Though that was unusual, she was secretly relieved, because it meant she might actually be able to catch up on some of this paperwork.

But she had barely settled into her chair when Mary came bursting into the room, a dry-cleaner's dress bag slung over her shoulder and her most determined, militant gleam in her eye.

"Put those charts away," Mary commanded. "You've got a dinner engagement with your new partner and his wife in less than an hour. So lay down that pen and change into this."

Heather looked at her watch. "You know I can't go anywhere, Mary," she said. "I've got baby duty at six."

Mary had that dangerously stubborn look, as if she might actually start wrestling Heather out of her clothes single-handedly, so Heather tried to think fast. "Maybe I can scrounge something up to feed the Readings at Spring House. I might have some of that pasta left."

Mary tossed the dry-cleaning bag on the desk. "You are going out," she said. "Dr. Reading wants you to meet his wife. He wants to take you somewhere nice. You are not going to offend this guy, do you hear? He's perfect. We want him. Get dressed."

Heather still hesitated. She was tired, and besides…
"What about Griffin? Is he okay with this? He was
supposed to have the evening free."

Mary put her fists on her waist and narrowed her
eyes. "He's okay with it."

Heather smiled in spite of herself. "As if you gave
him any choice in the matter."

"Whatever. They're his stupid Stewberts, anyhow,
aren't they? He's okay with it. Now hurry up. Dr. Reading's wife has made a long trip. She's pregnant, she's
tired, and she is still eager to meet you. The least you
can do is hurry."

Heather recognized defeat when it stared her in the
face. She put down the pen. "Okay, Mother. What am
I wearing?"

Smiling happily now that she had emerged victori-
ous, Mary ripped the plastic covering off with a
flourish. "Behold! Your best dress."

Heather frowned. It was her green silk, very simple
but very dressy. It had a fitted bodice, almost no back
and clasps of silver rhinestone bows at the shoulders.
"God, Mary, where are we going? The castle ball?"

Mary beamed proudly, as if she'd made the dress
herself. "Remember, Sally Reading used to be a ballerina. We have to show her that Firefly Glen has style."

Heather sighed, fingering the cool silk. She hadn't
had much opportunity to wear this lately. She'd been
working so hard her social life had practically disappeared.

"Style, my foot. She'll probably just think I'm a
vulgar show-off who has no idea how to dress for an
ordinary Friday night dinner."

But Mary was starting to look cross again, so

Heather abandoned the argument. Sighing, she picked
up the dress, and the little case of accessories—underclothes, makeup, panty hose, black pumps and hand-
bag—that Mary had brought along as well. She'd even
brought a matching silver headband for her hair.

Wow. Mary sure did want to impress the Readings,
didn't she? Good thing Adam was married. Mary
probably would have instructed Heather to sleep with
him just to show him how great the sex was in Firefly
Glen.

"Okay," Heather said, "but I'm going to tell her the
truth. I'm only ridiculously overdressed like this
because my bossy assistant picked out my clothes."

Mary made sweeping motions with her hands, shooing
Heather toward the full bathroom adjoining her office.

"Oh, for God's sake, stop whining and just put the
dress on. I promise you, you'll thank me for it later."

But as she shut the bathroom door, Mary grinned
in a way that made Heather suddenly feel nervous, as
if she were being costumed up for some kind of sac-
rificial ceremony.

Heather stuck out the heel of her hand, jamming the
door so that it wouldn't quite shut. She gave Mary a
piercing stare through the narrow crack. "You're not
cooking up something dumb here, are you, Mary?"

Mary frowned, all innocence, as if the comment bewildered her.

"You know what I mean," Heather said firmly. "I'm
not going to get to this restaurant and find only Griffin,
a big vulgar bottle of wine, and some smarmy violin
player waiting there, am I?"

Mary snorted. "Get real. Do I look like I spend my
time hand-delivering chicks to Playboy Cahill?"

But Heather was no fool. She knew that Mary hadn't quite answered the question. She held the younger woman's gaze steadily.

Mary sighed, wounded. "God, have a little faith, would you? I swear to you, straight out, on my honor as a Brady. Griffin Cahill is at home with the Stewberts. He is *not* going to be waiting for you at the restaurant."

Heather breathed deeply, relieved. "Okay, then. Sorry. I'll hurry."

But as the bathroom door fell shut, she caught one last glimpse of Mary. And darned if the woman wasn't grinning all over again.

EVERYTHING WAS READY.

The purple and white color scheme looked great against the existing Victorian decor of Spring House. The florist, particularly, had created a work of art. The Splendor of Spring arrangements of lily of the valley and violets were gorgeous. Silver bowls of them graced every table, and deep green leafy garlands of the flowers swung from the staircase banister and along every mantel.

As for the food, Griffin had left the decisions to Theo Burke, asking only that she use a Victorian theme. When she arrived an hour ago, she had insisted on showing him every canapé, every hors d'oeuvre, every sauce and every pastry. The food looked wonderful— orange-rosemary chicken, mushroom bisque, chocolate-whiskey cake, quince-almond tarts, hazelnut truffles. And it smelled even better.

People began showing up around six. Of the one hundred he'd invited, only five had declined. An amazing percentage of the guests were delighted to come, particularly considering how short the notice had been.

Most of the Glenners who accepted honestly wanted to celebrate Heather's victory. She'd lived in Firefly Glen all her life, as had her father, the town's only obstetrician for decades, and she was much loved.

A few of the others came for more selfish reasons, lured by Theo's food or the chance to tour the beautiful historical Spring House. Griffin had tried to weed out the vultures who would be attracted only by the aroma of fresh gossip. He hadn't invited people like Bourke and Jocelyn Waitely, who would just love to see Griffin and Heather together so that they could test the temperature of every touch, dissect the meaning of every glance, and perhaps make nasty little predictions about how long the aloof Heather Delaney could hold out against Playboy Cahill.

But he wasn't naive. He knew that everyone, even the nicest people, would be curious. They'd all be watching. For Heather's sake, he'd have to be careful.

Maybe he could start by hiding his impatience a little better. By six-thirty, he'd already glanced at his watch six times. But where was she?

Suzie Strickland, one of the few teenagers who had been invited, appeared at his shoulder. She actually looked pretty good tonight. She'd toned down her eye makeup and removed her eyebrow ring, probably because she'd heard Mike Frome was coming, too.

She couldn't bring herself to be completely conventional, of course. Her dress was the color of radioactive owl puke, but Griffin decided not to comment.

"So you honestly believe that not one soul in this town spilled the beans to Dr. Delaney?" Suzie surveyed the decorated room phlegmatically, making sucking noises on some kind of candy drop. "Sorry. Echinacea and zinc. I'm getting a cold. Want some?"

Griffin declined with regret and addressed her earlier question. "I hope no one told her. Why? Do you think they did?"

Suzie considered, sucking loudly. "Naw. Probably not. They were getting a kick out of the cloak-and-dagger stuff. Makes their petty little lives seem important, I guess."

Griffin smiled. "I know it has done wonders for mine."

"Oh, your life isn't little," Suzie said. "You're an artist. You got loose. You went places. I've gotta give you props for that. As soon as I can, I'm going to bust out, too." She frowned. "But I'm *never* coming back."

Griffin looked at her. Never? Well, maybe. Maybe she was absolutely right. Maybe she'd hit Vanity Gap running, and she'd never look back.

But maybe not. *Never* was a long time, and the world was a very strange place.

"She's here!" Hissing whispers went up all over the house. Griffin hadn't been sure what ruse Mary would employ to get Heather to stop by Spring House on the way to her imaginary dinner with the Readings. But obviously Mary had prevailed, because Heather's car had just pulled up in the front driveway.

Only the dim hall sconces and the lights in the upstairs nursery had been left burning, so that the house would look completely normal. Everyone fell utterly silent as Heather's footsteps crunched across the oyster-shell driveway.

Finally her key scratched in the lock. He could hear

the collective intake of breath. Then Heather opened the front door, and assigned guests all over the first floor flipped switches. The whole house was suddenly ablaze with sparkling white light.

"Surprise!"

Two hundred voices all shouting at the same time packed a rather intense punch. Heather, who had been laying her keys on the hall table, froze so completely she looked as if she were made of wax.

From his spot near the staircase, Griffin saw Mary coming up the porch behind her friend. She paused, quickly surveying the entire scene, from the cascade of lily of the valley to the huge banner that read Congratulations, Dr. Delaney.

Mary's eyes met Griffin's. And slowly, almost grudgingly, she began to nod. *Imagine that,* Griffin thought with an internal smile. He had finally done something that Mary Brady approved of.

Now if only Heather felt the same.

But he was going to have to wait to find out. The guests had swarmed the hallway, crowding around Heather, laughing and hugging and offering their happy congratulations.

As the crush pushed past, Sarah Tremaine ended up at Griffin's side. "Why don't you shove your way through?" She was holding a champagne flute filled with water, which she was resting on her rounded tummy as if it were a table. "The party was your idea, after all."

Griffin watched Heather for a minute. She was flushed and smiling, gorgeous in green silk.

"I can wait," he said.

But even as he said it, he knew he couldn't wait forever.

"Hey. Stop flirting with other men," Parker Tremaine said playfully, coming up to wrap his arms around his wife. "You know it makes me jealous."

Sarah leaned her head back against her husband's shoulder as if it were her favorite pillow. "Nonsense. I was just telling Griffin that this party was his idea. He should get the first kiss."

But he had already done that, Griffin thought silently. Heather Delaney had given him her very first kiss, years and years ago. He could remember it still. It had tasted of strawberry-flavored lipstick, the kind all the fifteen-year-old girls were wearing that year, the tinny hint of braces, and terror. It had turned him on so hard and fast he almost fell down. He'd never, in his whole life, been so helplessly aroused by any other single kiss.

Parker chuckled, watching his friend watch Heather.

"I think," Parker said to his wife, "that Griffin may be a little like me. He doesn't care who gets the first kiss. Just as long as he gets the last."

TWO HOURS LATER, when Heather was dancing with old Ward Winters, Griffin finally cut in.

She'd been wondering if he'd come to her. She'd gone to him, right at the beginning, and tried to thank him for the wonderful surprise. But there had been so many people around, and someone had whisked her away almost immediately. All night long, she'd been fed and feted. She'd been kissed and congratulated, twirled and teased and toasted.

Surrounded by a chorus of oohing and aahing, she had opened a hundred wonderful presents—all the little office extras she hadn't been able to afford after renovating the house.

Mary and the staff self-servingly but sensibly gave her a coffeemaker for the office. Parker Tremaine gave a gift certificate for free legal service to draw up a partnership contract. Emma Dunbar donated a year's supply of free printing from the Paper House. Hickory Baxter sent a thousand pink tulips, and the man-hours to plant them in the side yard.

Others had been equally thoughtful, giving according to their means. She'd opened magazine subscriptions for the waiting room, toys and video tapes for the children's corner, gift certificates for medical supply stores, and, from one of the teenagers, batteries for her pager.

It was the most impressive outpouring of goodwill she'd ever witnessed. She would easily have the most splendid medical offices in the country.

But though she had enjoyed seeing all her old friends, she had often found herself looking around for Griffin. When she spotted him, he always seemed very busy, playing host, taking care of the party, tending bar and tending the socially insecure. He had kept Granville and Ward from getting into a fistfight, and he had even managed to get artsy Suzie Strickland and super-jock Mike Frome to share a couple of dances.

Nice of him, but it meant that somehow, through it all, Griffin and Heather hadn't had a single minute to really talk. Not a single minute alone.

Until now.

Ward Winters grumbled, but Griffin wasn't budging, so he finally relinquished her. Heather grinned at the crusty old man, who was one of her favorite people in the world, kissed him goodbye, and then turned to Griffin.

"Hi, there," she said with a smile, feeling his arms

come around her waist. "I've been looking for you. I wanted to thank you properly. Everyone tells me the party was entirely your idea."

"Yes," he said politely, his hands warm against the small of her back. "It was."

"Well, it was a wonderful idea, simply heavenly. But you really didn't have to do anything like this, you know." She sighed. "Didn't I tell you not to be so nice? Didn't I say you'd already done too much?"

"Yes," he agreed, his lips against her ear. "I believe you did."

She pulled away a little and smiled into his handsome, sardonic face. "You're not, by any chance, trying to impress me, are you, Griffin Cahill?"

"Yes," he said, smiling back. "I believe I am."

She sighed again. "It's working," she said helplessly. She rested her cheek against his shoulder. "I'm afraid it's working far too well. I'm within an inch of believing that you may actually have a heart."

He did, of course. She could feel it thudding hard beneath her cheek.

"Is that so? An inch?" He rubbed his chin slowly against her hair, which sent little goose bumps shivering down her spine. "Tell me, Dr. Delaney. What would it take to get you to go the rest of the way?"

He wasn't really kidding. She knew that. But she tried to sound jocular. It wouldn't do to show now, in front of all these people, how completely he had destroyed her resistance.

"Hmm," she stalled. "Let me think."

She closed her eyes and breathed deeply, taking in the familiar, exciting scent of him. Her body seemed to be molding itself into his.

"You don't need to think about it, Heather," he said, his voice low and insistent. "Tell me. What would it take?"

"I don't know," she whispered as his hands subtly caressed the curves of her hips. The silk seemed to melt to nothingness beneath his fingers. She turned her face into his crisp white shirt. "No, that's not true. I do know. Not very much, I'm afraid. All you'd have to do is ask."

IT WAS TWO IN THE MORNING.

The guests had all gone home. Griffin's housekeeper, Mrs. Waller, who had been babysitting during the party, had gone home, too. The Stewberts were bathed, fed and put back to sleep. Heather had taken a shower, washed her hair and carefully hung up her pretty green dress.

She ought to be exhausted. But she wasn't. She felt, in fact, as if she might never sleep again.

She stood by the window, watching the dark rain that had been falling heavily for the past hour. In the shining orbs cast by the landscaping lights, she could see flowers bending, leaves quaking, grass drowning in the silvery flood. The Stewberts should sleep well tonight. They loved the soothing grumble of a storm.

Finally, at almost two-thirty, she heard the sound she'd been waiting for. Griffin's low knock on her door. He must have been trying not to come, she thought. He must have been trying to resist.

But she could have told him it was futile. This night had been ten years in the making, and neither of them was strong enough to stop it from coming.

She opened the door and let him in.

"Hi," she said softly. She didn't pretend to be sur-

prised to see him. She had been waiting, ticking off the
seconds one by one. Surely he knew that.

He was still dressed, although he had taken off his
tie and unbuttoned his white shirt at the throat. His
sleeves were unbuttoned, too, and shoved up almost to
his elbows. She felt awkward, suddenly, in her sleeve-
less cotton nightgown, her hair damp and streaming
carelessly over her shoulders.

"Hi," he said. He held out a flat box wrapped in
green paper and tied with silver ribbon. He had taken
a sprig of violets, probably plucked from one of the
staircase garlands as he came up, and he had slipped it
under the ribbon. "I brought you a present."

She took the box, which was surprisingly light.
"What is it?"

"Well, everyone else gave you a gift at the party," he
said with a small smile. "But I thought you might prefer
to be alone when you opened mine."

Her nerves had begun to hum. She moved to the bed
and sat carefully on the edge. She freed the violets and
set them on the white sheets. Then she tugged at the
silver ribbon, which fell open easily.

It was a small stack of letters, maybe only eight or
ten of them, neatly tied with another silver ribbon.
Holding her breath, she took the packet out of the box,
but she knew what they were without even looking.
They were her teenage love letters to Griffin.

"I can't believe you've kept them all these years,"
she said slowly, turning them over and over in her
hands.

"I couldn't destroy them," he said simply. He was still
standing at the far side of the room. "They're all there,
just as I promised. The one about the falls is on top."

Oh, yes, the one about the falls. She had almost forgotten that he had offered to return these to her, back when he was trying to persuade her to help him with the twins. That seemed so long ago now. She couldn't imagine him needing to bribe her to participate. These had been the most gratifying three weeks of her life—and in some ways the most exciting. She would not have traded them for anything on earth.

She looked at him, wondering if it were possible to say any of those things. But she couldn't find words that made sense. She just opened the packet, unfolded the top letter and began to read.

Her first impression was astonishment—the handwriting was so girlish. She had imagined herself so grown-up at seventeen, had firmly believed that falling in love had made her a woman overnight. But this gawky, looping script could almost have belonged to a child.

And the infamous "vow" now seemed absurdly tame. Silly, even. "All right, I promise," she had written at his insistence. "I will stand under the falls—naked—while you take my picture. But you must never show anyone, Griffin. That's what you have to promise me. I couldn't bear for anyone to know the things that you can make me do."

And the rest of the letter—which had seemed so daring and X-rated at the time—it was just a collection of dreadful, unimaginative clichés.

"Your hands are made of fire." "When you touch me, I feel as if I am the waterfall." "I am a flower, Griffin, and you are my sun and rain."

But, back then, they hadn't been clichés, not to her. She remembered writing this letter, and she knew how it had felt—as if she and Griffin had *invented* love.

Like young pagan gods, they had created passion with nothing but the power of their bare bodies. Every metaphor of fire and flood and flowering desire seemed to have been born fresh the day he touched her.

"Oh, Griffin," she said sadly, folding up the letter. "I can hardly believe I was ever so young. So foolish."

"You weren't foolish," he said huskily. "You were the most beautiful thing I had ever known. I couldn't believe I was allowed to touch you. To make love to you."

The shadow of a smile crossed his lips. "I think that's why I wanted that picture. Because I wanted something to keep, something to prove it had all really been true."

"It *was* true," she said, laying the letters on the bed beside her, next to the sprig of already drooping violets. "I can still remember how it looked, standing there under the falls. I can remember every rainbow, every note the water sang as it hit the rocks, every gauzy plume that tore off in the wind and blew away."

She looked at him. "And I can remember how it felt. Can't you?"

For a moment he didn't even move. Then, slowly, he walked toward her and sat beside her on the bed. Reaching out, he took her hand and placed it against his heart.

"Heather, listen to me." He tightened his hand around hers. "Tonight, when we were dancing, you told me—" Shaking his head slightly, he started over. "You said that all I had to do was ask. Did you mean that?"

"Yes," she said. And then again, on an unsteady exhale. "Yes."

His eyes were very dark. He put two fingers under her chin and tilted her toward him.

"I'm asking, Heather." He lowered his head to hers. "I don't have the right, but, God help me, I'm asking."

She swallowed, hypnotized by his lips, so near she could feel their warmth.

"You know what the answer is, Griffin," she said. "The answer is yes."

"Yes," he echoed, like a prayer. And finally he kissed her.

His lips at first were gentle, but the fire caught quickly, as if the years had left both of them parched, dangerously easy to spark. They fell together on the bed, as eager and hungry as they had ever been—trying to make their questing hands find every thrilling place at once, murmuring sounds that were more than words, kissing hair and skin and cotton alike, struggling with buttons and zippers and sheets.

But finally, when they had shed their clothes and bared each other to the moonlight, he seemed to force himself to a slower pace. He took time to put on a condom. Then he knelt before her on the bed, gazing down at her with glittering eyes, and she knew, she knew with a sizzling thrill, that this time would be very, very different.

They weren't children anymore. His body was stronger, the muscles trained into sharp definition. And he held himself with a new, mature control. She knew that the desperate, impetuous boy was gone forever. This powerful, virile man knew exactly what she wanted—and how to give it to her. And he could make it last longer than the moon could hang in the sky.

But the real difference was deeper than that. It was in his eyes, in the new shadows there. The shadows spoke to her, told her that these past ten years had taught him some of the same hard lessons. He, too, had met loneliness. He, too, had forged a fragile truce with regret.

And they both had learned something about the ephemeral nature of joy. A night like this wasn't to be devoured thoughtlessly, as they once had done. It must be cherished, second by agonizing second. Such a night might never, ever come again.

All those truths, and more, were in his hands and lips and eyes as he stared down at her naked body.

"Yes, Heather, I do remember how it felt," he said, lowering his mouth to her breasts. It seemed a lifetime ago that she had asked the question. She shivered as his breath drifted warm across her flesh.

"I dreamed of it for years. I dreamed of parting your thighs under the water and sliding into you." As he spoke, he nudged her trembling legs apart. He touched between them with gentle fingers. "Every night, it was the same dream. Me, moving through the cold water into the incredible heat of you."

Desire knifed into her, following his fingers. Her heart was pumping so fast she could hear it in her ears.

"Do you still dream of it?" She looked at him, wondering if he could see the ache that pulsed through her like a second heartbeat. "Do you still dream of making love to me?"

"I had finally taught myself not to," he said, stroking her softly and watching her, as if he could read what her body wanted in her eyes. "But then I came home, and it began all over again. I dream of you all the time, Heather. I dream of this. Even when I'm awake."

He shifted then, removing his wonderful fingers, and she shut her eyes, trying to hold on to the feeling.

He rose above her, his hard, ready body touching her, and though he tried to hold back, she knew that he had waited almost as long as he could.

"It's all right," she whispered. "Come to me, Griffin. The answer is still yes. The answer will always be yes."

With a low moan of relief, he entered her. It was a hard, passionate claiming, fierce and swollen and oh, so familiar. "Griffin," she said helplessly, and in answer he began to move.

Instantly she felt deep, slow ripples of building passion. She clutched his shoulders. This was not memory. This was not a dream. This was Griffin.

He put his hands behind her hips, arching her back, controlling every stroke, every rhythmic ebb and flow of pressure. Within minutes, she was lost. It was too much. He was too sure. He knew everything, and she could hide nothing.

He shifted, a conscious friction. The tiny movement blinded her.

And suddenly it was washing over her. She caught her breath as the misty past surrendered to the flooding now. Her throat made a small, raw sound, a sound so full of fear and joy it might as well have been a word.

She knew that word, just as she knew his body moving ever faster, harder, into her. It was the word that meant yes. Still, yes. Always and forever, yes.

And, oh, Griffin, Griffin, help me. It was the word that meant love.

CHAPTER FIFTEEN

FOR ONE CONFUSED and wonderful split second when he woke up that radiant Saturday morning, Griffin Cahill felt—

Young.

He felt young. Buoyant, eager, brimming with the mindless physical joy a nineteen-year-old takes for granted. As if life and the world were full of pleasure, and all of it belonged to him.

Stretching on soft cotton sheets, he smelled lily of the valley and smiled. Only half awake, without even opening his eyes, he knew exactly where he was. He was in Heather's prim Victorian bedroom, in Heather's prim Victorian bed.

Heather. His body tightened, remembering the long, amazing, anything-but-prim Victorian night, and instantly wanting more, needing more, knowing with a hazy, sensual delight that he could never get enough.

But he was ready to try.

He turned and reached for her, murmuring her name. But the place beside him was cool and empty.

Heather was gone.

He sat up, brushing his hair out of his eyes, and looked around the room. Her nightgown, which had tumbled to the floor last night in an abandoned heap, was nowhere to be seen. His own clothes were folded neatly on the dresser.

He could smell the damp sweetness of a recent shower floating in from the adjoining bathroom. And then he knew. She wasn't just briefly gone, in the next room checking on the babies, or on the sleeping porch watching the clean spring morning come to life.

She was *gone.*

He looked on the nightstand by his side of the bed, and saw with relief that she had left him a note, and, thoughtfully, his cell phone. If she needed to call him, she wouldn't want to call the house line—it was noisy and often woke the Stewberts.

He picked up the note.

Mrs. Mizell again, it read. *I'm sorry. Back soon.*

The cell phone buzzed, and he picked it up before it could finish the first ring. "Tell me you're on your way home, damn it," he said gruffly. "I'm already going crazy without you."

There was a hesitation on the other end, and finally a young woman's voice said tentatively, "Mr. Cahill? Is that you?"

Griffin almost laughed out loud, recognizing the voice of his agent's young secretary. Damn, he really was nineteen again, wasn't he? That was such a classic idiotic teenager's faux pas.

"Yes, Jeannie, it's me." He cleared his throat, trying to sound awake. "What's up?"

Jeannie took a couple of minutes to recover from the shock of his greeting, but finally she relayed her message. It was good news. The best. His agent had a terrific offer on a book he'd proposed last year—a photographic essay of the world's most beautiful waterfalls. He'd been hoping someone would bite.

And now, he thought, punching the off button and disconnecting the poor, bewildered Jeannie, now maybe he could take Heather with him. He closed his eyes, briefly lost in the fantasy. Okay, maybe he was jumping the gun, assuming that she'd be willing to leave Firefly Glen. But she had already decided to get a new partner—that must mean something, some shift in her life outlook.

And last night.

Well, that had meant a lot. Maybe, he thought… maybe it had meant enough.

The cell phone buzzed again. This time he was more careful, preferring not to embarrass himself again. He looked at the digital display, though that really wasn't much help. It wasn't one of his preprogrammed numbers. The readout simply said, "Unassigned."

Maybe she was calling from the hospital…or Anna's house…or anywhere. He kept hoping it was Heather, right up until he heard his sister-in-law's voice.

"Griffin? Is that you? You're still alive? The twins haven't killed you yet?" Katie sounded happy and playful…and, though he knew you couldn't always tell for sure, she sounded *close.*

"Not quite," he said. "But they haven't given up yet. They've still got a couple of days to work on me."

"No, they don't!" Katie laughed merrily. "That's why I'm calling. I'm in Firefly Glen, and I'm coming to save you, Griff. And Heather, too. Like the marines, right? I'm marching right in to the rescue."

He sat up straighter. This wasn't supposed to happen today. She was due to pick the boys up on Monday. He and Heather were supposed to have two more days.

Heather, he thought again, instinctively knowing how difficult this was going to be for her. He had to call her. He had to warn her. If Katie took the boys away while Heather was at work…

He tried to think it through. "You're here? You're coming? When?"

"I'll be there in less than an hour. So you'd better hurry, Griff. Go wake those bad little boys up and tell them their Mommy is home."

What could he say but yes? He hung up the phone and stared at the nursery door. And right on cue, as if they'd heard everything, the Stewberts began to cry.

FINALLY, FINALLY, Anna Mizell was consoled, comforted and convinced.

Heather had never before found it so difficult to maintain her professional serenity. But somehow she managed. Yes, she assured Anna. Her backache was normal. Her baby was fine. The baby's head had engaged, so she might go into labor soon, within the week perhaps. But it would not be today. Definitely not today.

As soon as Anna left the room, Heather turned to Mary, who had come in ten minutes earlier to relay Griffin's terse message about the Stewberts.

"My next few appointments," Heather said urgently, pulling off her stethoscope and laying it on the counter. "Are any of them emergencies?"

But Mary was way ahead of her. "They're rescheduling them as we speak. We can free up at least an hour, maybe more. Don't worry about any of it. Just go." She grabbed the otoscope from Heather's pocket. "Hurry."

It took Heather only ten minutes to drive from Main Street to Spring House, but today it seemed to take forever. She didn't speed, but she drove with focus, not even glancing at the lush spring flowers that grew in window boxes and pots and yards. Usually, spring in Firefly Glen delighted her, but today it was no more than a fuzzy kaleidoscope of pointless colors.

Still, though she didn't waste a second, when she got to the house a large red minivan was already parked in the driveway.

So she would have no time to say goodbye in private. But at least the Stewberts were still here. That was something to be grateful for.

The front door was unlocked. Dropping her purse on the hall table, she flew up the stairs. Her heart was pounding by the time she reached the nursery, so she forced herself to take a deep breath before entering.

"Hi," she said as she opened the door, smiling with her best approximation of casual good cheer.

The woman standing beside the crib looked up. So this was Katie, Heather thought, coming into the room. The twins' mother was tiny, blond and beautiful. She had one of the Stewberts in her arms and was showering kisses on his bare back.

Griffin stood beside her, holding the other baby, who also wore only a diaper. He seemed to be in the process of packing a large blue duffel. That half-filled bag stopped Heather in her tracks. For the first time, she understood that the Stewberts were really leaving.

Katie beamed at Heather. "Hi, there," she said enthusiastically. "You must be Saint Heather. I've been dying to meet you. Thank you, thank you, thank you, for helping Griffin take care of my little monsters. Heaven knows what would have become of them if Griffin had been left to his own devices."

She grinned at Griffin. "They'd probably be smoking and cussing and whistling at big-chested women by now."

He smiled back. "How do you know they aren't?" He patted the baby's padded bottom. "Come on, Stewbert. Say something dirty for Mommy."

Oh, no. He had called the baby Stewbert. Heather held her breath. But Katie laughed, which apparently was Katie's reaction of choice.

"Stewbert? Is that what you call them? Like Stewart and Robert mixed together? That's too funny!" She leaned over and kissed the baby Griffin was holding. "Don't listen to him, Bobby. Give Mommy a kiss."

Bobby. Heather smiled, realizing that Katie hadn't had a moment's trouble separating the boys—and hadn't considered for an instant the possibility that anyone else had, either.

She should be glad. Griffin had dodged that bullet, at least. But, instead, Heather felt strangely wistful. It was sad, somehow, that now, when they were leaving, she was learning who they really were.

The one with the cowlick, the one who hated peas and always woke up when the telephone rang. That one was Robert.

And the other one, the one who could play peekaboo for hours, the one who tried to eat everything he could reach—that one was Stewart.

"Anyway, Heather, thank you so much. You were an angel to pitch in. I bet you could have killed me for being gone so long."

Heather shook her head. "No," she said honestly. "I loved every minute of it. The boys are absolutely adorable."

Stewart, who had been gnawing on his mother's top

button, turned at the sound of Heather's voice. "Geep!" he cried in profound delight, holding out his hands and straining toward her. "Barn fink!"

Though it made her arms ache to repress the urge to take the baby and kiss his silly, wet mouth, Heather didn't know what to do. Surely, after three weeks away from her sons, Katie would not want to share their affection. But Katie merely grinned wryly.

"Well, I guess that's what I get for being gone so long," she said, handing the fretting, wriggling Stewart over to Heather with yet another smile. "He's obviously forgotten all about me. He's clearly fallen in love with you."

Griffin was watching Heather with soft eyes. "Yes," he said. "They both did. I think Heather is what they call a natural."

When Heather took him, Stewart stopped fussing immediately. He folded himself contentedly against her breast and began sucking his fingers as if he might go back to sleep.

Katie watched the two of them for a minute without a hint of envy. Heather marveled that the other woman could be so relaxed, so assured of her ultimate place in her sons' hearts. Heather held Stewart closer, trying to soak up this last warm, sleepy hug, trying to internalize it, so that she'd never forget how it felt.

Perhaps Katie's easy confidence was the special magic of being the real mother—instead of the temporary one. She'd never have a *last* hug. For Katie, there would always be another.

"Yeah, I'd say you've definitely got a flair." Katie tilted her pert blond head speculatively, then looked over at Griffin. "Hey, make yourself useful, why don't you? I've left a suitcase out in the minivan, and I need it."

Griffin smiled at his sister-in-law's autocratic tone. "Yes, your highness," he said with a bow. "Don't let her boss you around too much while I'm gone, Heather," he said, chucking Stewart's chin as he passed. "She has definite slave driver tendencies. She makes Mary Brady look like an amateur."

Katie glowered at him. "Are you still here, Griffin?"

When his footsteps had receded, Katie turned back to Heather, obviously eager to take advantage of their privacy. "So. Are you married, Heather? Do you have any children of your own?"

Well, that was subtle. Heather shook her head.

"No," she said, aware that a ridiculous stinging had started behind her eyes. How foolish it would be to cry. She had always known the Stewberts were not hers. Not really. "No, not yet."

"Well, you definitely should hurry up and have some. You'll love it. It's the best thing in the world." Katie smooched loudly against Robert's head, and the baby looked up at her, laughing. "Although I have to say...I hope you're not counting on Griffin to be the daddy—"

"Katie, really, I—"

"Oh, I know, I know. He's gorgeous. And sexy as hell. But he's one hundred percent useless in the relationship department. Okay, so I know I'm butting in here, but you seem really nice. Just a friendly heads up. Do *not* bank on Griffin. I've never seen anyone so allergic to commitment."

Heather couldn't help feeling Katie was being a bit too harsh. "You know, he was wonderful with the boys. And even when he had the chance to leave, he didn't. He took this commitment very seriously."

"Oh, dear. He's got you deluded, doesn't he?" Katie

looked sad. "If he stayed, it was because he was enjoying himself." She eyed Heather anxiously. "I didn't mean with you. I meant— Oh, I don't know what I meant. He makes me nuts. He's so frivolous, you know?"

Heather shook her head. "I don't think you under—"

Katie was on a roll, though, and couldn't be stopped. "And he'll *never* have children, I'll tell you that. He'd have to grow up first himself, and he has positively no intention of ever doing that."

Her comments had a well-rehearsed quality, as if this was a frequent lament in the Jared Cahill family. *When will your irresponsible brother ever grow up?*

"Katie, really, it's all right," Heather broke in with polite firmness. "I really was just doing him a favor. Griffin and I are just good friends. We've known each other since we were kids."

Katie smiled in obvious relief. "Oh, then that's okay. If you really know him, you know better than to count on him for anything important. I almost killed Jared when he told me he'd left the babies with Griff. Talk about a short attention span."

She tickled her baby's ear playfully. "Little Bobby can focus on one person longer than Uncle Griffin, can't you, pumpkin?"

Heather didn't answer, but Katie didn't notice. Her conscience cleared, she had begun rummaging in the dresser. Pulling out a red romper, she plopped Robert on the changer.

"But I hope you do have *someone* in mind," she babbled on as she deftly wiggled Robert's foot into the romper's leg. She seemed utterly oblivious to

Heather's uncomfortable silence. "You really should get started pretty soon."

AFTER THE MINIVAN had pulled away—packed to the bursting point with toys and diapers, strollers and high chairs and cribs—Griffin and Heather walked back into Spring House slowly. Silently. Side by side, but not touching. Like people left behind after a funeral.

Instinctively they went upstairs. But the nursery, once a colorful hodgepodge of clutter and activity, was bare and silent. Heather could hardly stand to look at it, with its unbroken expanse of hardwood floors, one scruffy chest of drawers and a poignantly empty rocking chair.

She didn't like to go in her own room, either. Its memories were too recent, as well.

So she stepped out onto the sleeping porch. It had begun to rain again. She looked at the gray drizzle and hoped that Katie's minivan had antilock brakes.

It would have been kind of ironic, really, if it hadn't been so tragic. She wrapped her arms around herself, wondering how life could have managed to spring such a perfect and inescapable trap.

In the past three weeks, she had unearthed two long-buried truths about herself.

The first truth: With all her heart, she longed for a family. Children. Babies of her own.

And the second: With all her heart, she was still in love with Griffin Cahill.

The trap was that they were mutually exclusive. By choosing one, she would almost certainly give up the other. She could never have them both. She could almost hear fate laughing at her as she stood here, struggling in its cruel, shining jaws.

"Heather." Griffin had come onto the porch behind her. "It's all right. I know how much you're going to miss them."

"Yes," she said quietly. "I am."

He put his arms around her and rested his cheek against her hair. "I can't believe how quiet it is around here."

She nodded.

"But I have something exciting to tell you." He nuzzled her ear. "And something to ask you, too."

She didn't answer. She just watched the rain, which grew every minute more steady and dense, forming a silver curtain that she simply couldn't penetrate.

"I'm going to be leaving soon," he said. "I just got the call this morning. It's a photo assignment I've been negotiating for a long time, and it finally came through. I'll be going to the Bahamas, to shoot pictures of a waterfall there."

He tightened his arms. "I was hoping you'd come with me. You could leave your practice for a few weeks, couldn't you? Now that Adam Reading is here?" His voice sounded so eager, so full of anticipation. "I think you'd love it there. It's absolutely spectacular."

She felt a long, slow sinking, as if someone had dropped an anchor in her heart. Not an hour had passed since the babies were in his arms—not twelve had passed since Heather herself had been there. And all the while he had been making these plans to leave.

A waterfall in the Bahamas…

How could she have been such a fool as to believe he had changed? He'd just been taking a breather from *real* life. Just proving to his skeptical, critical sister-in-law that he could do it.

Just playing house.

But Heather had forgotten it was just a game. She had watched him with the babies, and she had imagined that he was learning to appreciate the joys of domestic life, with a loyal partner by his side and laughing children at his feet.

Instead, he had been impatiently ticking off the days. She remembered the smile he had turned on the other men, the daddies in her birthing class.

I've only got two weeks left in my sentence, he had crowed proudly. You're in it for life.

He had meant those words. Everyone had known it but her.

He touched her shoulder now, as if sensing that she wasn't paying attention.

"Did you hear me, Heather? I'm asking you to go with me."

"I'm sorry," she said in a low voice. "I can't."

The tension in his arms was subtle, almost imperceptible. But she felt it. "Why not?"

"I have commitments here," she said. "I have a home. I have a practice. I can't just dump my patients on a total stranger, no matter how pleasant Adam Reading may be. I don't approach life that way, Griffin. I couldn't just drop everything and go chasing after pretty waterfalls because you ask me to."

Griffin's arms slowly fell. He backed up a step. "Of course you could," he said concisely. "It's only for a couple of weeks. You could make it work if you really wanted to."

And he was right, of course. She could. It wouldn't be easy, but she could manage. She could leave Adam here, in charge of Anna Mizell and the others. She could pack a bag and follow Griffin blindly into a passionate, tumultuous affair. It would be hot and thrilling…and painfully brief.

And when it was over, she would be destroyed.

"Perhaps you're right," she said, trying to be honest. Surely she owed him that. She owed it to herself. "I guess the truth is that I don't really want to."

"Why not?"

"Because I think you'll break my heart." Heather turned and faced him, because, however painful, this was something that *had* to be faced. "Be honest with me, Griffin. Can you ever see yourself settling down? Having children? Staying with one woman for the rest of your life?"

He seemed to choose his words very carefully. "I can see us being together," he said slowly. "You felt what happened last night. It was magic. That's what we are together. I want more of it. I think you do, too."

She looked at his handsome, earnest face. "How much more? Another night? A month? A year?"

Griffin frowned. "How can I answer that? As long as it's good. I'm not sure I believe in forever, but I do believe that we could make each other very happy. We've got a fresh start, Heather. Let's not overthink it. Let's just see where it takes us."

She could see how it might look that way to him. No couple, when they first started out, could be sure where their relationship would end. They just played the cards and hoped for a winning hand.

She wasn't afraid to take an emotional gamble. But that was the important difference. With Griffin, it wasn't a gamble—it was Russian roulette with every chamber loaded.

Because he hadn't changed, not really. For him, the success of a relationship was still measured in months, not lifetimes. It was still measured in laughter and waterfalls and mind-shattering sex. The things she wanted terrified him. They had driven him away ten years ago, and they'd drive him away again.

"Come on, Heather," he said, frustration lacing his voice. "Don't let fear make you an emotional coward. You know last night wasn't enough for either of us. Let's go to the Bahamas. And then, when the trip is over, maybe then we can think about what comes next. About whether we want to consider…something else. Something more permanent."

"Marriage," she said tightly. "That word you can't say—it's called marriage. It's called commitment. You say I'm a coward. But I think you are. See how that word scares you? It scares you so much you can't even trust yourself to utter it."

"I uttered it once," he said, his voice suddenly very different, filled with a cold, impersonal amusement. "I got down on my knees, and I said it with tears in my eyes. I believe we both remember how that turned out."

That sardonic tone felt like a light whip, flicking carelessly against her heart. He hadn't taken that tone with her in a long time now. She'd forgotten how much it could hurt.

She turned away, fighting back the senseless tears it had stung into her eyes. There was another word he hadn't uttered.

Love.

And obviously he hadn't said it for one simple, fatal reason. He *didn't* love her. He wanted her, quite passionately. He clearly believed a few weeks in the

Bahamas would be a wonderful way to satisfy his hunger. But love, for Griffin, simply didn't enter into it.

"I can't talk about this anymore," she said, and her voice was full of unshed tears.

He cursed, hard, under his breath. Perhaps at her, perhaps at himself.

"The answer wasn't yes for very long, was it, Heather? One day, and you're already back to saying no. No to any kind of risk. No to me. No to life."

When she didn't respond, he took her shoulders roughly. "Damn it, Heather, talk to me. Why does it always have to be all or nothing with you?"

She turned, shrugging off his hands, which had too much power over her. She didn't trust herself to be strong as long as his hands were on her skin.

"Because," she said desperately, "if I give you one more day, that day will turn into a year. And that year will turn into another, just like it did before. And when you finally decide you're tired of me, that I'm not quite enough fun, that you'd rather visit your waterfalls with more exciting women, it will hurt too much."

His eyes were dark and full of anger. "Are you telling me it won't hurt if we end it now?"

"Yes," she answered honestly. "It will. But not as much." If he left her now, she could just barely survive it. Last night would become another one of those painful memories. But a year from now...or two.

"I'm not twenty-three anymore, Griffin. I'm making choices that will affect the rest of my life. If we end it now, I'll still have time to find the things I need. Roots. Commitment." Her voice faltered. "Children."

"And are those things so important to you?" He

narrowed his glittering eyes. "Even if it means you have to find them with another man?"

"Yes," she said, although the word was almost too painful to speak. "Even then. I won't end up one of your broken toys, Griffin. I deserve to find a better life than that."

In spite of the dismal gray light, his eyes were as suddenly brilliantly blue as sapphires, and as impossible to read. He looked shockingly like a complete stranger.

"I see," he said politely. "In that case, I had better get out of your way and let you start looking."

CHAPTER SIXTEEN

FOR THE FIRST COUPLE OF DAYS after Griffin left town, Heather did very well, carried along by the steamy momentum of anger and pride. She would not crumble. She knew how to handle Griffin's absence. It should be easier, in fact, than handling his presence. She certainly had more practice.

She threw herself into her work. She saw fifty patients and dealt with a dozen emergencies. Anna Mizell came in three times in three days. It was almost time. Heather asked Anna to stay close to home, just in case.

Then she drew up a partnership contract for Adam Reading, who signed it with his usual quiet pleasure. When the two of them returned from Parker's office, they were greeted by Mary and the staff doing a noisy victory dance in the waiting room. When Adam took Heather's arm, she let him twirl her around without resistance—right in front of all the patients.

At home at night, Heather tackled spring cleaning. She intended to throw away all the faded party garlands, but she found herself pressing one sprig of violets between the pages of her current novel. And when she ran across a yellow plastic key covered in tooth marks, she didn't throw it away, either. She slipped it into her top drawer.

So technically she wasn't brooding. She wasn't crumbling. But she wasn't quite herself, either.

To Mary's shock, Heather even went on a date, dinner at the Candlelight Café with a local C.P.A. If she was going to start looking for Mr. Right, she might as well get started.

But, while her date was nice, he was just barely Mr. Maybe. He ate with his elbows on the table, which caused Theo Burke to scowl at Heather, as if she'd brought a cockroach into the restaurant on a leash. And when Suzie Strickland walked in, it prompted the man into a twenty-minute rant about the horrors of multiple piercings practiced by this younger generation.

Bored senseless, Heather wished she had Stewbert with her. He'd know what to do. He'd give the man a very loud, very wet raspberry, slap his hands on the table and shout, "Flam!"

The image made her chuckle, which apparently wasn't the appropriate reaction. Mr. Maybe looked deeply affronted.

"Can you fail to appreciate," he intoned, "how such hideous self-mutilation demonstrates her abysmal lack of self-worth?"

"Geep fink" obviously wouldn't suffice, although it was the first response that came to mind. Heather looked at him, and thought what boring babies he would make. He went from Mr. Maybe to Mr. Never in the blink of an eye.

"Actually," Heather said calmly, taking a sip of wine, "I was thinking of piercing some body parts myself." She sounded, even to her own ears, a little like Griffin Cahill at his most sarcastic.

Mr. Not-in-this-lifetime looked horrified, as if she'd

sprouted green horns. He suddenly remembered an urgent tax return he needed to file.

Gathering her purse contentedly, Heather smothered a grin. *Double flam.*

It wasn't all superefficiency and irreverent amusement, though. There were other times, tough times. The night of her date, she woke up in the predawn hours, reaching out for Griffin. She hadn't done that in ten years, and, when she realized she was alone in the huge house, she turned her face into the pillow and cried like a child.

The worst times were at work. Often her patients brought their newborns along to their postnatal checkups. In the past, Heather had been delighted, offering the expected admiration, but always comfortably detached.

Now, with every tiny, sleepy face, she felt a wash of longing. Why had she never seen before what a breathtaking miracle birth truly was? The mothers weren't just happy. They were stunned with joy.

Sometimes the fathers came along, too. They held their infants with a special, awestruck caution. It was as if their large, clumsy hands had been entrusted with the world's only spun-glass basket of unicorn eggs and fairy wings.

That Thursday afternoon, Heather closed the door to her office quietly. It was three days after Griffin's departure, and she had just finished one of those family-style postnatal examinations.

This time, though, she had been so humiliatingly undone by her emotions that she needed a few minutes to compose herself.

She put the heels of her hands on her desk and leaned over it, breathing deeply. Dear God, she had to get a grip.

She heard the door click behind her. "Heather?" Mary said quietly. "Are you all right?"

Heather nodded, but she didn't turn around. "I'm fine. I'll be right out."

She could feel Mary's concerned gaze on her back. And she heard the deep sigh of worry.

"Oh, hell," Mary growled. "I think there's something I'd better tell you."

Heather shut her eyes hard. "Not now, Mary." She turned around and tried to smile. "Honestly, this is really not the right time for a *Listen Up* lecture."

"It's not a lecture." Mary backed up against the office door, as if she intended to use her body to block intruders. "It's just... Well, heck, probably I'm sticking my nose in where it doesn't belong."

"You?" Heather shook her head wryly. "Surely not."

"Oh, hush up, and let me say it. It will be quicker if you'll stop interrupting. I just wanted to say that...I don't know exactly what happened between you and Griffin. But I thought maybe...maybe you heard the rumors. About him and Emma Dunbar, I mean."

"Oh, good grief," Heather said on a sigh.

"I just wanted you to know that they weren't true. He wasn't fooling around with her, no matter what anyone says. So if that caused any trouble between the two of you—"

Heather had to smile in spite of everything. "For heaven's sake, Mary. You didn't actually believe those stories, did you?"

Mary lifted her chin. "Yeah, I did. Why not? There was a time when I wouldn't have put anything past that man." She frowned. "How did you know they *weren't* true?"

Heather laughed. "Emma is my best friend," she said. "I know how her wacky mind works. It was a colossally dumb scheme, but you've got to hand it to her. It worked."

Mary looked thoughtful. "If that's not the problem, what is? I thought you and Griffin might be getting back together. Not that I was so all-fired crazy about the idea, but, still, I thought so. Everyone did." She folded her arms across her chest. "But suddenly he goes screaming off on an airplane, and you start moping around here like a month of wet Sundays."

Heather drew herself up. "I am not moping," she said indignantly. "I've been very busy and productive. I work, I laugh, I hire partners." She gave Mary a steely look. "I go out on dates."

"*A* date," Mary corrected. "With a tall, thick slice of soggy bread who couldn't even take *my* mind off Playboy Cahill, much less *yours*."

"Mary," Heather said crossly. "I thought we were overbooked. Don't you have work to do?"

"Yes," Mary admitted. She put her hand on the doorknob. "But so, my friend, do you. And I don't mean those patients out there. I mean all that denial and confusion in here." She tapped the area near her heart with her fist.

"You'd better get yourself sorted out, Doc. Because the next time you burst into tears at the sight of a baby, we're going to start losing some business."

HEATHER HAD NEVER SEEN Silver Kiss Falls at dawn before. It was beautiful, like something in a dream.

The rising sun was dazzling, a silver-and-gold fire-cracker on the eastern horizon. Around it, the sky was white, as if it hadn't yet picked out what color it would wear today.

Heather worked her way down the ravine carefully, trying not to trample the lovely coltsfoot and columbine that grew in wide sweeping bands of spring flowers.

The falls were impressive right now, still swollen with spring meltwaters. Even from the top of the ravine, they had thundered so loudly she could hardly hear the morning song of the meadowlarks. Down here, at the foot of the falls, water roared in her ears, blotting out all other sounds.

The basin pool was alive, its bubbles spangled with gold dawn light. She took off her shoes and sat on the rocky banks, dangling her feet in the cold, swirling water.

She wasn't quite sure why she had come here. It wasn't terribly sensible. She had to be at work in two hours, and already her clothes were littered with tiny fleabane petals. Her feet were dirty, and her hair was frizzy from the damp.

But Mary's warning had struck home. It *was* time Heather sorted herself out. And she had instinctively felt that she could do it better here than anywhere else.

Maybe she'd been wrong to avoid this enchanted place, where the air was full of rainbows and her heart was full of memories. Avoiding Silver Kiss was like avoiding a piece of herself.

She had spent ten years trying to run away from the passionate, vulnerable girl she had once been. But then Griffin had come home, and she had discovered that she'd only been running in circles. She had ended up right where she had started. In his arms.

So she needed a new plan. If she wasn't going to run anymore, what was she going to do?

Spending those weeks with the Stewberts had awakened something maternal in her—that much was obvious. It was as if some hormonal trigger had been activated, and now she was filled with yearning for children of her own.

But was it merely children she longed for? Or was it *Griffin's* children?

What about her instinctive recoil at the thought of making babies with the sanctimonious C.P.A.? She didn't want his children, did she? She couldn't, in fact, think of a single human being whose children she *did* want.

Except Griffin.

And what about marriage? Wasn't that answer pretty much the same?

Her father had told her that an obstetrician needed a heart big enough to hold a lot of love, a lot of pain—and a couple of uncomfortable secrets. He'd been right, of course. As the Glen's baby doctor, Heather knew almost everything. She knew that Emma and Harry couldn't have children, which nearly killed Harry. She knew that Parker Tremaine wasn't the father of Sarah's baby, which didn't bother Parker in the least.

She knew which Glen wife had started taking birth control without telling her husband—and she also knew which wife had secretly stopped. She knew who greeted news of pregnancy with joy, and who shed tears behind the closed examination room door.

She knew, in short, that a big diamond wedding ring didn't guarantee happiness. And neither did a gleaming white cradle.

Nothing guaranteed happiness. Nothing.

But she knew one thing that came pretty close.

Love.

She smiled, remembering Griffin's beautiful young body knifing through this bubbling pool like a flashing golden fish. And his strong, knowing body finding hers in the moon-washed four-poster bed. And his sassy, up-side-down smile, as he rolled on the floor with his nephews.

How could she have been so blind? It was the moments filled with love that were the happiest. Love might not be a guarantee. It might not be permanent. It might not even be safe.

But it was the only real, spontaneous, soul-searing happiness she had known in her whole, entire life. And she had been a fool to send it away.

Suddenly she heard footsteps on the slope of the ravine. She looked up, her heart holding its breath.

Someone was coming down to see the falls.

A man. A tall man. Slim, blond…

The man looked up, glimpsed Heather sitting there, and smiled politely.

Her heart ached once, then began its normal rhythm once again. Not Griffin. Of course not Griffin. He was in another country.

But suddenly everything seemed perfectly clear. She stood, brushing flower petals and soil from her slacks briskly. She had two choices. She could either sit here forever, searching for Griffin in her memories, in her dreams, in every blond stranger who happened by.

Or she could go to the Bahamas and find him.

CHAPTER SEVENTEEN

THE SUN WOULD SET in about an hour. Griffin knew that if he didn't head out to the falls soon, he'd miss the sweet-light, those extraordinary minutes right before the sun goes down when the angle of the light is most dramatic, creating interesting texture and depth.

Maybe it would help. God knows he needed something. He'd shot the falls four times already, but it had been a criminal waste of film. What insipid pictures. It was as if he'd been in such a hurry to leave Firefly Glen that he'd forgotten to pack his talent.

The sweet-light just might make the difference. He should hurry.

But instead of picking up his equipment, he stayed where he was, on one of the resort's deck chairs overlooking the bright blue pool, which overlooked the glimmering green ocean. He'd been here almost an hour already, holding but not drinking a very expensive glass of spring water and listening to the wind clicking palm fronds like castanets.

And trying to figure out what the hell was wrong with him.

This was his chosen life. The footloose photographer, traveling to exotic locales at whim, searching for the perfect picture.

And until recently it had suited him just fine. No strings, no complications, no boredom. Five-star resorts and perfect-ten women, a new one every time he got restless. And, of course, photography to feed his creative side.

The perfect life, right?

Wrong. It didn't feel even remotely exciting anymore. It felt like a puffed-up collection of dust—no substance, no meaning, nothing that wouldn't blow away in the first wind.

Suddenly it seemed that he had nothing, nothing that mattered, anyhow. No Heather, no Stewberts, no Firefly Glen. And absolutely no interest in sex, perfect ten or otherwise. Just a series of impersonal, monotonous hotel rooms and small talk with strangers. Bad food, bad mattresses and, worst of all, very bad pictures.

He told himself it was only temporary. It would pass. He'd get over it.

He could start by getting out to the damn waterfall before the sweet-light turned into utter darkness.

But he didn't go. He crossed his legs and watched the water.

After a few minutes, a young man sat down on the deck chair next to him. He had a baby girl on his lap, all dressed up in a starched pink dress, lacy pink socks and tiny patent leather shoes. A rather foolish big pink bow had been propped on her little bald head.

"Hi," the man said in a friendly voice. He nodded toward the ocean. "It's nice, huh?"

"Gorgeous," Griffin agreed, welcoming the distraction from his own thoughts. He smiled at the baby, who looked red faced, fussy and a little confused, as if she had been crying so long she'd forgotten why. "How old is she?"

"Four months," the man said. He jiggled the baby nervously. "I don't know why she's so grumpy. I've tried everything, but she just keeps crying."

Griffin could have suggested taking off some of those hot, scratchy clothes, but it wasn't any of his business, so he kept quiet.

Apparently Griffin provided a momentary distraction, because the baby stared at him fixedly, her damp eyes intensely curious. Griffin met her gaze pleasantly but without any overeager interest of his own. Babies, he had learned, liked to make the first overture.

Her mouth was open, drooling, and she was frowning slightly, as if he were some strange new species she had yet to catalogue and wasn't sure she approved of. Griffin had to fight back a chuckle. It was a pretty uppity look, actually, as if she were the Queen Mother instead of a little bald blob who couldn't even sit up yet without her daddy's chest to balance against.

God, children's faces were wonderful, their emotions playing on their features as clearly as the wind racing across the water. His fingers itched to take out his camera and see if he could capture that hilarious, endearing expression.

He was shocked to realize that this was the first truly creative urge he'd felt since he left Firefly Glen.

For no apparent reason, the little girl began to wail. Her daddy patted her back and bounced her gently on his knee, obviously beside himself with anxiety.

"She's usually pretty happy," he said to Griffin apologetically. "I just don't get it. I've changed her, fed her, burped her." He looked down at his yowling daughter.

"Come on, Ginny, tell me what's wrong. We don't want to have to wake Mommy up. She really needs a nap."

But Ginny just arched herself furiously and cried harder. Poor kid, Griffin thought. It was hard to watch anyone in such inconsolable distress. She reached her little fist up and tugged at her ear—and the gesture triggered something in Griffin's subconscious.

"Could she be teething?" The Stewberts had tugged their ears like that when their teeth were hurting them. Now…if he could just remember what Heather had done. Oh, yes, those cold ring toys he had kept finding in the refrigerator. "I think ice helps to numb it."

The daddy looked at Griffin's glass hopefully. But Griffin, not having been driven mad by hours of this, still retained enough good sense to realize that an ice cube was one of the millions of things babies could choke on.

He transferred his glass to the other hand to remove temptation from the father, whose eyes were starting to look a little crazed. He remembered that feeling, when you would trade your soul for a few minutes of quiet—except that apparently no one was interested in taking the deal.

"Sometimes just rubbing your knuckle against their gums can give some relief," he suggested. "And there's some kind of lotion stuff you can buy at the drugstore."

The daddy was obviously so desperate he'd try anything. He rubbed the edge of his index finger across the baby's tiny mouth. The crying faded instantly.

"Wow," the young man said, looking at Griffin with awed gratitude. "You're good at this baby thing."

Griffin smiled. "Not really," he said, remembering Heather's gentle ivory fingers smoothing matted hair from Stewbert's damp brow. "But I'm lucky. I know someone who is."

"My wife's good at it, too. But she's so tired today." The young man sighed and stood, not removing his finger from his daughter's mouth. "Hey, listen, I'm Doug. Thanks a lot. If I can fix this by myself, it will really impress my wife. She thinks I'm hopeless."

"Nobody's hopeless," Griffin said slowly, wondering if that could be true. Wanting it to be true. "Believe me, Doug. If I can do it, anybody can."

The young man smiled. "I knew you must have kids. How many?"

"None." Griffin stood up. "But I am just about to go home and fix that. Assuming, God help me, that it's not too late."

"Too late?" Doug looked concerned. "Why would it be too late?"

"Because I'm a moron, that's why. I'm an unmitigated fool and—"

Griffin stopped, wondering what on earth had come over him. Not only was he spilling his guts to a complete stranger…he also thought he saw Heather Delaney walking toward him, dressed in a flowered bikini, with a soft, transparent green skirt wrapped around her hips and a yellow hibiscus in her hair.

Right. Heather Delaney with a hibiscus in her hair.

He'd finally gone completely crazy, that was the only explanation. Still, he couldn't take his eyes off the woman, who would probably notice it soon and call the police. He'd never spent the night in jail before. At least that would solve the monotony of cookie-cutter hotel rooms.

But she walked like Heather, with that special combination of sex and elegance that made his knees weak. She was ivory skinned, rare on this island of sun-worshippers. Her hair shone like cinnamon glitter.

Something deep in the pit of Griffin's stomach began to pulse out a beat of primitive recognition.

It was Heather. It was.

"Hey, are you okay?" Doug sounded worried.

"I'm fine," Griffin said softly. "In fact, I think I'm about to be the happiest man on this island."

Doug frowned, then followed Griffin's gaze. Heather was still gliding toward them. She had begun to smile.

Doug laughed, light finally dawning. "Oh, I see. So I guess the answer is no, it's not too late."

"I sincerely hope you're right," Griffin said without taking his eyes from Heather. He was afraid she might disappear if he so much as blinked. "I don't mean to be rude, Doug, but with any kind of luck the next few minutes are going to require a little privacy."

"Gotcha." Doug disappeared with a fascinated smile at Heather, who was now only a few feet away from Griffin.

She was, hands down, the most beautiful sight Griffin had ever seen. More beautiful than a golden October in Firefly Glen, a luna moth in Peru, or a roseate spoonbill over the Everglades—though those were three of the most stunning visions of his photographer's life. She made his heart pound harder than an earthquake, a charging lion, a war—though he had seen them all.

And with a flash of sudden awareness, Griffin understood that he was finished traveling forever. Without Heather, nothing would ever be exciting again. And, with her, nothing could ever be dull.

She came so close he could smell her. Then she tilted her lovely gaze at him and smiled.

"Well, as I live and breathe," she said, her voice

husky, as sultry as surf rolling in over pebbled beaches. "If it isn't Playboy Cahill."

He almost couldn't speak. He didn't have a single clever one-liner at his disposal. It was as if he had dropped his bag of tricks from weakened fingers, and everything glib was running out like sand.

"Heather," he said simply. His voice was hoarse. "I can't believe it's really you."

She came another inch closer.

"Maybe," she said gently, "if you touched me, you'd be sure."

Something ungovernable was rising within him. It felt like something he had believed dead. It felt a lot like hope.

He tried to smile. "If I touch you, sweetheart, I'll be lost."

"Wouldn't that be only fair?" She gazed at him thoughtfully. "After all, I am here, away from everything I thought defined me. I'm here on this island with only one thing to trust—the way I feel about you."

"And what is that?" His throat was dry. "What do you feel?"

"Love," she said.

Her pale cheeks were flushed, and her eyes were bright with a fever he recognized. "I love you, Griffin. I always have. I followed you here to ask you to forgive me. I was a fool. I don't care if you want me for ten minutes or ten years. Just want me. Please say you still want me."

The wind blew a strand of silky auburn hair across her porcelain cheek. He reached up and eased it away.

"I want you," he said quietly. "But what about what *you* want? What about the better life you said you deserved? The better man you said could give it to you?"

She closed her eyes, sighing. When she opened them again, they were as clear and green as the ocean.

"I wish I had fallen in love with him," she said. "With a quiet family man who wanted to spend his life in Firefly Glen, at Spring House with me, with our baby in his arms."

She shook her head. "But I didn't. God help me, I fell in love with you."

"Heather—"

"Please," she said, "let me explain. I have thought it through very carefully, Griffin. If I married that 'better' man, it would be the most horrible farce. I would hate him, and myself, before the wedding cake was stale. And even worse—if I had another man's child." She took a ragged breath. "I would spend my life searching his eyes, in vain, for some small sign of you."

He tightened his throat, the very thought a hot knife in his gut. Another man's child...

She made a weak attempt at a laugh. "So you have to agree, don't you? I'm not sacrificing myself by coming to you like this. I'm *saving* myself, and I'm saving that poor, unsuspecting fellow, too."

"God, Heather..."

He reached out then and gathered her into his arms. She came willingly, folding herself against him without any lingering trace of resistance. She meant it, he thought, humbled. He was the most unworthy, superficial, cheating bastard on the planet. He had broken her heart once, and he'd almost broken it again. But somehow, in spite of everything she loved him. She was willing to give up her dreams for him.

But, for once in his self-indulgent life, he was going to do the right thing. He was going to refuse the offer.

He bent his head, letting his cheek rub the sun-warmed silk of her hair. "That may be the most generous offer anyone has ever made," he said. "But I can't let you do it."

She twisted in his arms, but he held her tight.

"Shh," he whispered, the way he might have soothed Stewbert when he cried. "I don't know anything about marriage. Not about happy marriage, anyhow. My parents destroyed each other, inch by inch, over twenty horrible years. That's all I've ever experienced. So you see, you were right. The very thought of marriage terrifies me."

"I know," she said. "But I don't care. You don't have to—"

"I won't let you do this. You deserve everything you ever dreamed of, sweetheart. You deserve a wedding, a home, a baby."

She made a soft sound of frustrated distress. "You're not listening," she said.

"No. *You're* not." He put his hands on her cheeks and lifted her frantic face to his. "I believe with my whole heart that you deserve a better man, Heather. So I will just have to become one." He smiled. "Maybe you can teach me."

She stared at him, tears half-shed and trembling on her eyelids. She frowned, shaking her head, seemingly without even realizing it. "I don't understand," she said.

"I'm asking you to marry me. I'm asking you to take all that amazing, generous love you have inside and teach me to be a good husband." He kissed the edge of her mouth. "And then, when you're sure I'm worthy, you can teach me to be a good father."

Her breath was coming fast. "You don't have to do this," she said raggedly. "That's why I came, so that you'd know you don't have to—"

BABES IN ARMS

"But I *do* have to." He kissed the other side of her mouth. "I have to marry you because I can't live without you. When I stood up just now, I was coming home to ask you, to beg you, to be my wife."

"Oh, Griffin…" She swallowed, and the tears finally fell.

"If that's my answer," he said, smiling, "it's a little ambiguous. I could use a simple yes or no." He kissed her nose. "Of the two, a simple yes would actually be preferable."

"Yes," she said, smiling through her tears. "The answer is simply yes."

He kissed her, then, though he knew he should have waited. A dozen people were watching, probably some children among them, and if he lost control he was likely to get them thrown off this island for public indecency.

But he couldn't stop himself. She was his. His heart was spinning flaming cartwheels, and his whole damn body was on fire with wanting her.

He couldn't get her close enough. He drove his kiss hard, and she opened eagerly. He wrapped his hands around her waist, slid his fingers down the frothy nothingness of her skirt, into the tiny fabric of her bikini…

And encountered the dreaded pager.

He extracted it with a curse. "Bloody hell," he said. "You didn't. You didn't bring this damn thing *with* you?"

She smiled sheepishly, her lips slightly swollen and pink from the intensity of their kiss. "It's just for emergencies. Adam's in charge, but in case something comes up, I couldn't exactly—"

"Emergencies!" Griffin growled. "If that hypochondriac Anna Mizell calls you one single time, I'll throw it into the ocean."

"She won't." Heather settled herself back in Griffin's arms comfortably. "She went out of town for a family wedding, though I had told her not to, and she went into labor there. Some doctor in Rochester delivered her baby two days ago. Mother and child are both fine."

Griffin chuckled. "I guess now you have to admit that it might possibly be okay to take a tiny vacation now and then. Apparently you're not completely indispensable."

She wrapped her arms around his neck. "Apparently not," she agreed.

"Except, of course, to me." He slid the pager back into its makeshift pouch. His fingers touched the satiny skin of her buttocks, and Griffin felt himself tightening. They'd better get into the hotel room fast. Or maybe there was some gigantic sand dune nearby...

"Yes," she said, nuzzling his neck as if she knew he was in danger of disgracing himself and was devilishly enjoying the idea. "Except to you."

"Let's go inside," he said gruffly. "I'm on the top floor. Do you have a room?"

She smiled. "I'm on the first floor," she said proudly. "Wasn't that smart of me?"

"Brilliant," he agreed. "We'll use yours."

He took her hand and started leading her toward the lobby. But then he had a sudden annoying thought. He turned and, slipping his hand down her bikini panties one more time, he extracted the pager again.

"I'll keep this," he said. "I'll be damned if I'm going to have the wretched thing going off while I'm trying to make babies."

She stopped in her tracks. "Make babies? Why, Griffin Cahill. I thought you just said we were going to wait until I felt sure you were worthy."

"Ah. See how very bad I am?" Grinning, he pulled her close for another kiss. "I lied to you already."

Everything you love about romance...
and more!

Please turn the page for Signature Select™
Bonus Features.

FIREFLY GLEN

BONUS
FEATURES
INSIDE

Creating
Firefly Glen
by Kathleen O'Brien

FOUR SEASONS IN FIREFLY GLEN was my first series, so naturally I was scared to death. And here's a secret about me: whenever I'm nervous, anxious, lonely or depressed, I go to the bookstore. In the family, we call it my "happy place."

I'm sure the stock at Borders spiked that month. I started with inspirational "season" books, like *Seasons,* which has great nature pictures accompanying Robert Frost poems. I also got *Fall Colors Across North America, Stokes Guide to Nature in Winter, Fall Color and Woodland Harvests* and, my most essential resource, *Seasonal Guide to the Natural Year—New England and New York.*

Then came books for researching the houses: *Pictorial Encyclopedia of Historic Architectural Plans and Elements* for overall information. Then *Victorian Gothic House Style* (for the winter house); *Daughters of Painted Ladies* (for the

4

spring house); *Private Tuscany* (for the summer house) and *Cabin Fever* (for the autumn house)

Then books for researching the occupations and events: *Dictionary of Legal Terms*, *Dr. Miriam Stoppard's New Pregnancy and Birth Book*, *New American Pocket Medical Dictionary*, *Scarecrows*, *Ice Palaces*, *Capturing Drama in Nature Photography*, *The Criminal Mind*...and many more.

They weren't all bought in the first month, of course. Many of those decisions weren't made until much later. But gradually, as the world of Firefly Glen came to life, my bookshelves filled up.

I bought a couple of folders, too, for the smaller paper items I'd begun to amass. The first folder was entirely made up of sketches of Adirondack wildlife and plant life, including a great section on trees. Hand colored by me...after photocopying each page from an obscure little out-of-print book the library lent me. I have since destroyed the photocopies, feeling guilty about having made them in the first place!

The second folder was where I began building the town. Here are some of the odds and ends that eventually stuffed that folder to overflowing.

A *very* roughly sketched picture of the main downtown street, showing the sheriff's office and city hall at one end, and the retail establishments (including Theo's Candlelight Café) running down each side and the town square in the middle. I am a simply horrible artist. *The worst.* But still, this rendering, in my own elementary-school scratch, was very helpful in making the place come to life for me.

A page of statistics for Firefly Glen, including its population (2,937), how it's reached, what its characteristics are, etc.

Pictures of each of the four "Seasons" houses. Color-copied from books I bought and books I already owned so that I wouldn't have to destroy any books to get a picture into the scrapbook. Choosing the model for each house, each room, took forever. For me, the house is just as important as the hero or heroine, and I have to love it just as I would love the people.

Pictures of each character, major and minor. Usually I found inspiration in magazine ads or photo spreads. These are accompanied by half-typed, half-handwritten pages that list any pertinent facts mentioned about those characters. Eye color, ex-wives, addresses, height, favorite foods, anything I might need to remember! Very detailed—and yet, I still managed to get poor Theo's last name wrong once in the first of the books.

Several general pictures of Firefly Glen, found in *The Most Beautiful Villages of New England.* This is a spectacular book that seems to cover all four seasons, with that perfect Norman Rockwell look the northeastern U.S. so often has.

A downloaded article called "A Day in the Adirondacks," which included lots of vivid color and specificity about plant life.

A three-page chapter-by-chapter outline of each book as its turn came to be written. Earlier outlines were moved to the back of the folder, but never discarded.

Downloaded information about mosaics (for the pool in the summer house) and frescoes (for Suzie's work on the summer house for Natalie).

Notes on "acute stress reaction" and its symptoms and treatments, for Faith's traumatized nephew in the autumn house.

Several pages of handwritten notes from conversations with my friend Joan, who used to live in upstate New York. Joan had such fun, quirky, individual memories. She told me about the roadside fruit and vegetable stands, which invite payments made in an "honor system" cash box. This inspired one of my favorite scenes in the summer book.

Lots of notes about what happens to financial analysts who embezzle their clients' money. Handwritten from online and library research, including an e-mail request sent to an official CPA site online. The responses I received were great—so many and so forthcoming. Any mistakes are, obviously, mine.

"Baby Duty Schedule," a one-page printout detailing who—Griffin or Heather—has responsibility for the Stewberts at each moment of the day. Takes their schedule through one full week.

A scrap of paper with the ISBN of a book on winter carnivals. I never did find this one, but it sounded so great I can't quite let go of the info even today.

Five sheets of notes about Victorian houses and Gothic architecture, for the winter and spring houses.

A photocopied picture of the library in Horace Walpole's house, Strawberry Hill, in Twickenham, with lots of text info, as well. The inspiration for the library of the winter house.

A large envelope of chamber of commerce materials from Lake Placid/Essex County.

Recipes for apple pie, applesauce and date bars, apple butter, apple jam, apple cider, apple muffins. One for pumpkin pie, Parker's favorite at Theo's Candlelight Café.

Early brainstorming idea for the kinds of houses to be featured. Early suggestions, which were discarded for the simpler "season" concept, include a glass house near a waterfall, a crumbling abbey and a barn. These later became the spring, summer and autumn houses, retaining the mood—open and sunny, moldering, and close to nature—of the final choices.

A list of possible names for my little Adirondack town, which included Llewellyn's Glen (which later was used for the lake), Puddletown Glen, Halfpenny Glen, Goblin Glen, Oak Apple Glen, Vowchurch Glen. The first on the list was Firefly Glen, and there never really was any serious debate. It just felt right.

Magazines from the Adirondacks, rich with pictures, gardening information, specific names of flora and fauna and helpful ads. Also magazines about pool restoration, old house renovation, nature photography, etc.

Pictures, cut out of magazines, of clothing appropriate for each character. Faith, the autumn house heroine, came from New York, so her clothes came from *Vogue*. Suzie Strickland, the artsy high school smart-mouth, had to be pieced together, using bits from the edgiest pages I could find in *Seventeen* and *Cosmopolitan*... peppered with a few notes taken while people-watching at the mall.

A time line, expanded awkwardly over the course of the four books, tracking when babies were born, couples were married, etc. I always try this, but I always end up getting something wrong anyhow. Thank heaven for steel-trap-minded editors!

A couple of oddities here at the end. Probably during some rough moment, I felt the need to get to know Natalie Granville of the "summer" book better. I jotted down a list of the contents found when Natalie emptied her pockets after work one night.

- A piece of mosaic from the pool she and Matthew Quinn are restoring—she always half believes she'll someday find where it goes. Shaped vaguely like a crescent moon.
- Little bits of bow from her flower business, cut ribbons, little curlicues.
- Gold foil wrapper from a single chocolate truffle.
- Note to self—must find cheaper paint (crossed out), ribbon (crossed out) ...*everything*.
- Her favorite green pen.
- Little globules of granular plant food.
- A weed she'd pulled hours ago and stuffed into her pocket.
- Seven dimes, two quarters and thirty-six pennies. (The significance of these quantities escapes me....)

Also, a handwritten "dream" Natalie had one night. This was a pure brainstorming exercise. I had no idea where the dream would take me. As it turned out, I decided that she dreamed her house was burning down, and she didn't care. This helped lead me to the resolution of her story, in which she finds a way to "let go" of the house, which has become an albatross.

And last...for some strange reason, a copy of an article that was being e-mailed around the Internet at the time, titled "Before You Quit." I must have hit a *very* tough moment somewhere along the way!

Twin Legends
by Kathleen O'Brien

As you've just seen, the Stewberts are a force to be reckoned with. They take a very confident, capable cynic, and they turn him to mush. In a couple of weeks they manage to redraw his picture of the world, reawaken his heart and bring his dreams back to life.

But that's nothing new for twins. Across culture, across centuries, twins have always stood for amazing power. They represent the very energy that creates and drives the world. They stand for the basic duality of human nature: Good and Evil, Black and White, Creation and Destruction, Yin and Yang.

We need both forces, so that the earth will turn. Without both, everything slows down to a static nothingness.

Long before scientists ever uttered the word *monozygotic* or discovered the existence of DNA, everyday people created their own stories to explain the presence and power of twins. Here are some of my favorite "twin" legends, stories that are sometimes silly and illogical, sometimes weird and violent, but always lyrical and strangely touching.

1) Castor and Pollux, the twin stars of the Gemini constellation. Their mother, Leda, apparently was too beautiful for her own good. In one night, she was "visited" (a favorite euphemism of the old legends) by two men. One was her own husband, Tyndareus. The other was the god Jupiter, who appeared to her in the form of a swan. From that night, four children were born. (One was Helen of Troy, but that's another story.) Castor was human, the son of Tyndareus. Pollux was immortal, the son of Jupiter. But they were identical (in that totally confusing way myths have of leaping over logical hurdles), and they grew up together, inseparable. They had lots of adventures (some seafaring...they are credited with creating the St. Elmo's fire sailors still see today). But when Castor was killed, Pollux missed him so much he begged Zeus to let him join his brother in the Underworld. Zeus took pity on him, and allowed them to split the difference, spending half their time in the Underworld, half on earth. To honor their devotion, he supposedly created the constellation Gemini.

2) Romulus and Remus: Pretty Rhea Silvia's uncle took the throne from her father, and, in order to ensure that she didn't have any children who might become problematic later, challenging his right to be king, he forced her to become a Vestal Virgin. But he hadn't counted on the fact that the god Mars might "visit" her anyway. So when Rhea Silvia found herself pregnant with twins, her uncle ordered that they be set afloat on the river Tiber. He was hoping they'd die, of course, but Romulus and Remus got lucky. When they were abandoned, the Tiber was in overflow mode. When the river receded, their little basket ended up on dry land. They supposedly were suckled by a she-wolf (that part doesn't sound so lucky, actually), and then adopted by a shepherd family. When they grew up, they decided to found a great city (Rome). Unfortunately, they chose a rather illogical way to decide who would get the bigger share of the land. It all had to do with how many vultures flew overhead. Romulus won. Remus, predictably, got jealous, and Romulus had to kill him. Good practice for that Sabine women trick he pulled a little later in life.

3) Lisa and Mawu: In this legend from West Africa, Lisa, a male, is the god of day, heat, work and strength. Mawu is the goddess of the night, fertility, rest and motherhood. Their first son is

called Gu, and he apparently comes out in the shape of a sword. They use him to make the world, and then they have lots of other children, mostly twins, to run it. The most charming part of this legend is that whenever we see an eclipse, it means that Lisa and Mawu are making love.

4) The twin sons of King Ajaka: Way back when, having twins was considered a real problem. People thought it was bad luck, and sometimes they even thought it meant the mother had slept with two men. (See poor Leda, above.) In this legend from Nigeria, King Ajaka discovers that one of his favorite wives is going to have twins. Instead of killing them, he banishes them. When they grow up, they learn that their father is dead, and the kingdom needs a ruler. They toss a stone to decide which one will be king. (Hadn't anyone back then heard of a coin toss? Or, though this may be a stretch, sharing power equally?) The younger son wins, and he becomes king. The older son, the one who did not win the stone toss, gets jealous. He tosses his younger brother into the river to drown, then goes back to the kingdom and reports that his brother ran away. This seems to work for a while, but one day when he's passing the river, a fish jumps up and sings, "Your brother lies here." He kills the fish (he's apparently

getting used to the killing thing). But that's not enough, because the next time he's passing the water, the river itself rises up and sings, "Your brother lies here." This time he has witnesses. His subjects find his brother's body, and they reject the killer. He can't live with his guilty conscience (or perhaps the loss of all his riches and power), and so he poisons himself.

5) *The Parent Trap:* In this modern U.S. cinematic fairy tale, two little girls separated by divorce switch places and manipulate events in order to get their parents to fall in love again. It may not rise quite to the level of the ancient legends, but at least no one gets killed. And the myth of the innocence of childhood vanquishing the dark cynicism of adulthood is so sweet. It's definitely one of my favorite fantasies!

Extra Scene
with Ward Winters and Granville Frome
by Kathleen O'Brien

As you've seen, Firefly Glen is full of handsome heroes. Here's a snippit with Ward Winters and Granville Frome in their salad days.

WARD WINTERS HADN'T TAKEN his eyes off the two people at the table across the restaurant for the past forty-five minutes. Damn it, this wasn't going to work. He should have known any harebrained idea Granville Frome came up with would be a bust.

"Relax, for Pete's sake," Granville said, his mouth full of cherry pie. "It's got to happen sooner or later. Ginny could drive a saint insane, and we both know Bourke is no saint."

Ward growled. "Yeah, you know, and I know. But Roberta doesn't know. And if this doesn't work, she never will. They're already on coffee. If we can't get him to lose it now, she's going to walk out that door. She's going to get in his car, and—"

He had to take a sip of water, the idea made him so mad, and he almost choked on it. How could Granville eat?

"Hang on—there goes Ginny." Granville leaned forward, his fork dripping cherry juice onto the tablecloth. "She's going to dump his coffee into his lap. Believe me, that'll do it."

Ward drummed his fingers on the seat. "You said it would *do it* when Ginny brought the wrong steak. Or when she spilled his water. Or when she seated the screaming kids next to him. But it didn't. Look at him. I ought to go over and knock that grin off his smarmy face myself."

"You have absolutely no impulse control, do you?" Granville scraped his fork across his plate, trying to capture the last of the sweet red goo. "Isn't that what got you in this fix in the first place?"

"Shut up, Frome. You sound like my mother." Ward scowled. It just made it worse that Granville was right. Because of his temper, Ward had screwed up his one chance with Roberta, the smartest, prettiest girl in Firefly Glen High School.

For about six months he'd sat behind her in trigonometry, stuffing his hands under his thighs and praying he wouldn't grab her silky blond hair and start sniffing it like a dog.

Finally he'd found the courage to ask her out. She'd said yes, which had shocked the heck out of him—and everyone else in the senior class,

18

too. He was a Winters, which in Firefly Glen was a big deal. But he also looked like a six-foot-three stringbean, and he was always sticking his size-thirteen feet in his mouth.

Still, she'd given him a chance.

And then he'd blown it. Big-time.

Now she was dating Bourke Waitley, who, if the senior notables had a category for "Slimeball Most Likely To Sell His Own Grandmother for a Buck," would win it hands down. Roberta wasn't the first girl to fall for Bourke's toothy grin and his bright blue Cadillac convertible—just the best.

Word in the locker room was that tonight was The Night. Bourke planned to buy her an expensive dinner, then drive her out to Lost Logger Trail, where the starlight through the pines would mix with the bottle of sloe gin he had in his glove compartment, creating the perfect seduction scenario.

He'd even bragged about having six condoms in the glove compartment, too. Ward figured that was because it would take Bourke six tries to figure out how to use one.

He'd spent all week trying to figure out what to do. Then Granville had this idea. The one thing Roberta couldn't stand was a bad temper, right? Well, Bourke had one. Ask anybody on the football team. They'd seen Bourke Waitely toss things around the locker room after a loss. Red faced and bucktoothed, his voice high with rage, he'd looked like a rabid squirrel.

Now the mission was to be sure Roberta saw it, too.

So they'd recruited Granville's girlfriend Ginny to sabotage the dinner. Show Roberta that Ward wasn't the only one who sometimes lost his cool. Ginny worked at The Nine Candles, the one upscale restaurant within driving distance of Firefly Glen. They'd deduced that this was Bourke's destination tonight, and they'd been right.

What they hadn't been right about was Ginny's ability to ruffle the squirrel's fur.

Still...maybe Granville was right. Maybe this next ploy would work.

As they watched from the corner, Ginny grazed Bourke's cup with her hip, and bang! Bourke Waitely had a crotch full of hot coffee.

He jerked up, emitting a high-pitched sound, and Ward's hopes rose. But then Bourke took a deep breath, brushed at his slacks with his napkin and waved Ginny's apologies away brusquely. Not exactly princely grace and good humor, but not rabid, either.

"Damn it," Granville said under his breath. "We may have underestimated exactly how much he wants to get under Roberta's skirt."

Ward narrowed his eyes. Granville might be his best friend, but he could be a real jerk. "Don't talk about her like that, damn you, or—"

Ginny appeared at their table. "Look, guys, I'm going to get fired if I keep this up," she said, talking out of the side of her mouth while she poured water into their glasses. "Face it. He's not going to crack. Maybe he doesn't have a temper at all. Maybe that's why Roberta likes him better."

She gave Ward a pointed look as she said that. He scowled back at her. He didn't have a temper. He just...

Okay, he had a temper. Big deal. He wasn't dangerous. He was just impatient with fools, and he didn't like people who messed with Roberta.

And he said what he meant. Was that so rare these days that people thought it indicated he was nuts?

"Okay." He threw his napkin onto the table. "We're leaving."

Granville looked at him, his eyes wide. "We are? We haven't even tried the thing where she gives him the wrong bill."

"I'm not doing that." Ginny braced her hands on her hips. "Look, Granville—"

"Forget that," Ward said. "Ginny's right. It's not going to work."

"You're giving up?" Granville tilted his head suspiciously.

"Hell, no. We're just going to try something different. My idea this time."

Ginny groaned.

Ward stood, but Granville hesitated.

"Are you in or out?" Ward frowned. "I can do it alone if I have to."

Granville sighed. "What's your idea? Is it going to get us killed?"

"No."

"Arrested?"

"No."

"Humiliated?"

"God, you're such a mama's boy, Frome." Ward began walking toward the door. "Just forget it."

22

They had entered through the kitchen, so that Bourke and Roberta wouldn't see them, but he was through with all that. He walked out right past their table, and even when Roberta began to frown, and Bourke made a rude noise, he didn't stop.

He didn't know whether Granville was behind him until he got outside. As he stood there, breathing in the spring air, cool and clean from the afternoon's rain, he heard the restaurant door open and shut again.

"Okay." Granville stood beside him, his hands in his pockets. "What now?"

That was the good thing about a best friend. You didn't have to waste time with apologies. You fought, you got over it, you got on with it.

"Now we find the pretty boy's pretty car. It shouldn't be that hard, right? A brand-new Caddy is going to stand out around here."

Ward began scanning the parking lot. It was crowded on a Saturday night, but still...there it was. At the very end, parked so that it took up two spaces. God forbid anyone should open a car door and ding the shiny blue paint on Bourke's baby.

Bourke was so worried about that car, you'd think the spoiled brat had bought it with his own money, instead of getting it gift wrapped from his daddy.

The Waitelys, relative newcomers to Firefly Glen, didn't have half the money the Winters family had. But Ward's dad refused to pay a penny toward his son's car. Which was why Ward had a ten-year-old bottom-of-the-line Ford sedan. Luckily, the Fromes were just as tight with a dollar as the Winters family, so Granville rode around in his mom's cast-off Buick. It would build character, their dads said to each other, nodding smugly.

Maybe, but *damn it*. He felt himself drooling as he looked at the Cadillac, so shiny under the lights, as if it was a movie-star car. It had everything—style, speed, comfort. *Sex appeal.*

Bourke had left the top down, too proud of having a convertible to be sensible. Ward could see the leather seats. The back seat, in particular, looked much too big and comfortable.

Granville was staring, too, and Ward knew that between them they were generating enough envy to paint the whole parking lot green.

"You're not thinking about messing with his car, are you?" Granville sounded worried. "I mean, this is about Roberta, right? Not about the Caddy."

"I don't give a damn about his car." Ward couldn't quite meet his friend's eyes as he said that. He did want the car, of course. And someday he'd have one. But tonight was about Roberta.

24

He leaned over the passenger side door and popped open the glove compartment. That fool Bourke hadn't even locked it up. Ward pulled out the bottle of gin first. To tell the truth, he was almost relieved to find it. He would have felt pretty dumb campaigning against Bourke like this only to have him turn out to be a Boy Scout, with purely honorable intentions toward Roberta.

"Woo-hoo." Granville whistled softly. "Is that ours now?"

"You bet it is," Ward said. He kept rifling through the compartment. He found a wallet, but all it had in it was money. He tossed that back, irritated.

Where were the condoms? He didn't have all night. Bourke and Roberta could march right out that restaurant door any minute.

His fingers closed around a small box.

He wasn't sure whether he'd hit the jackpot or not. He knew what a box of condoms *looked* like. He'd seen them when the cool boys held them up like victory flags, and the other boys whooped their delight. He'd seen grown-ups buying them at the drugstore. They called them "safeties," mostly, and Mr. Fisher never batted an eye, just reached down, got a box and handed it over.

But Ward didn't know what the box *felt* like. He'd never held one in his own hands.

He pulled it out, and in the glow of the pole light he read it. Durex. A packet of three. He dug around and found another box. Two times three. *Six.*

"I'm going to kill him."

Granville peered over his shoulder. "Oh, man," he said. "I don't want to sound dumb, but do you think he could really... I mean, *six...*"

Annoyed, Ward ripped open the packet and pulled out one of the condoms. He unrolled it and shoved it over the gearshift, leaving the end drooping like a saggy balloon. It looked pale, pink and disgusting.

So there, stud. Once Roberta saw that, she'd know all about Bourke Waitely. And if she went with him out to Lost Logger Trail after that...

Granville began to laugh. At first Ward clenched his jaw, but then, looking at the pathetic, limp thing, he saw how funny it was. He began to laugh, too.

They ran, then, ran all the way to the back of the restaurant, where Ward's car was parked out of sight. The asphalt was slick from the rain, and Ward slipped once, getting muddy, but he didn't care. He wasn't like Bourke Waitely. He wasn't a junior exec, all Brooks Brothers and double-breasted ambition.

When he and Granville reached the car, they spent a couple of minutes looking at the box of condoms—it was pretty clear Granville hadn't ever seen one up close, either.

What a couple of geeks they were. And yet it was kind of nice, knowing that, geeky or not, virgins or not, at least they were the same.

Granville shook the bottle of gin, which they realized was already open. It wasn't even new. "He probably stole it from his dad's liquor cabinet."

Ward held up the condoms. "Where do you suppose he got these?"

Granville wiggled his eyebrows. "Same place? Once they saw Bourke, they probably decided they didn't want any more kids."

More laughter. They made about a dozen "Bourke Waitely, Poster Boy for Contraception" jokes, each one dumber than the last. They couldn't have acted any more ridiculous if they'd drunk that whole bottle of gin.

Yep, Ward thought comfortably, looking at Granville's familiar, basset-hound face, they were definitely geeks. The whole night had been pointless and immature. Losing a half-empty bottle of cheap gin wasn't going to hurt Bourke, and Roberta would probably go out to the trail with him just to show Ward she was her own woman.

So they'd accomplished nothing, in the end. But it was nice, having a good friend to help you deal with the sting of losing the girl you loved.

They were halfway back to Winter House, still laughing and singing, and maybe speeding just a little, when they saw the blue lights flashing behind them.

"Oh, no," Granville moaned. He looked down at the open bottle of gin between his knees. "Oh, man."

Ward thought of the condoms in his pocket. He didn't care about the sheriff...all he could think of was trying to explain this to his father. And then his mom, who would quietly cry and beg him to tell her where she'd gone wrong.

"We're dead," he said, groaning as he drew the old Ford to a stop. "It's as simple as that."

Two hours later, as they sat side by side in the one holding cell of the Firefly Glen sheriff's department, waiting for their parents to arrive, Ward had to appreciate that Granville had never once said "I told you so."

He had every right. Ward had explicitly promised that his idea wouldn't get them arrested. And look. Here they were. He remembered suddenly that, as a kid, Granville used to say he wanted to be president someday. Guess that wouldn't ever happen now.

The deputy who'd brought them in was Josh Tremaine. The Tremaines were good friends with the Winters and Frome families. That just made it worse. Now Ward's mother would have another lament. *You've humiliated us in front of our friends....*

"Ward," Granville said. "Are you awake?"

Was he kidding? Did he think anybody could sleep at a time like this?

"No."

Granville either didn't hear the sarcasm or didn't care. "I was just thinking. Probably we shouldn't have told him we took the gin and the condoms out of Bourke's car, huh? I just— I didn't want my mother to think that I..." He paused. "But I guess stealing stuff from someone's car is even worse, huh?"

Ward shrugged. "I don't know. Probably it's better to tell the truth. We wouldn't be very good at lying, do you think? I mean, we can't even keep the fake play book straight in our heads at football practice."

He heard a heavy sigh. "I guess so. But my mom. It's gonna be awful."

Ward knew exactly what Granville meant. *Moms.* They really knew how to make you feel lower than dirt.

So when he heard the sound of high heels coming toward the cell, he closed his eyes and said a prayer. *Let her come in screaming,* he asked. *Not the crying. Anything but the crying.*

"Well, if you two don't look the worst kind of pitiful."

His eyes flew open.

It wasn't his mother.

It was Roberta.

She was smiling that tilted smile that always made his knees weak. He rose nervously, but one of his feet had fallen asleep, and he almost lost his balance. *Hell.* He couldn't get anything right around this woman.

"Roberta," he said, his voice breaking. It hadn't done that since he was twelve. "I— What are you doing here?"

"I hope you came to help break us out of this cell before our parents get here," Granville said, sounding grouchy. "You should, you know. It's all your fault we're locked up in the first place."

Roberta laughed. "It's my fault you two are hopeless morons?"

"Well, it's your fault Ward's so crazy about you he can't see straight." Granville scratched at the crown of his head irritably. "And yeah, it's your fault we were morons tonight. Sir Galahad wanted to save you from the evil dragon."

She looked from one to the other. "Ginny told me about your plan at the restaurant. I swear, I don't think I've ever heard anything so stupid."

"Oh, yeah? Then I guess you didn't hear about what Ward put on the gearshift."

Ward felt himself blushing. "Shut up, Frome. Don't talk about stuff like that in front of her."

"*Talk* about it?" Granville was working himself up to a temper, which was rare for him. Usually the cussing and fuming was Ward's specialty. "*Talk* about it? Bourke wasn't going to *talk* to her about it, he was going to—"

"Frome!" Ward moved toward his friend, one fist up.

"Ward," Roberta said quietly. He stopped and looked over at her. In the dim light he could just barely see her blue dress, but he'd seen it at the restaurant, and he knew she looked fantastic.

"What?"

"Come here."

Feeling inexplicably chastened, he made his way toward her. "What?"

"Didn't I tell you that you don't have to fight my battles for me? I can take care of myself."

He frowned. That's what had gone wrong on their one date. He'd heard some kids making rude comments about her, and he'd gone up in a fury and shoved the biggest, loudest one. The guy was much stronger than Ward, so of course he'd cleaned Ward's clock.

And all for nothing. Turned out they had been her friends, and that's how they always talked to each other. Roberta was annoyed. They had argued. She'd made him take her home, and when they stood on her front porch, Ward with his black eyes and cut lip, she'd told him she didn't like violence, or pushy men, or chauvinists. She didn't want to go out with him again.

That's when he'd done the dumbest thing of all.

He should've apologized. He should've given her time to cool down.

Instead he'd shaken his head mulishly. She had to go out with him again, he'd said. She had to, because he was going to marry her.

She'd slammed the door in his face.

"I can't help myself," he said, leaning his forehead against the cold iron bars. "I don't know why, but I *want* to fight your battles."

"Then it's a shame you're always losing them," Granville put in from his perch on the bench.

Roberta gave Granville a quelling look. She was good at that. She was the strongest girl Ward had ever met. He wanted to tell her that. He wanted to explain that he didn't fight for her because he thought she couldn't handle her own problems. He fought for her because he loved her. Because she made him want to be a man strong enough to deserve her strength.

But he couldn't, not with Granville listening. A friend was good for some moments, but a real liability at a moment like this.

Roberta was looking at him, and the expression in her brown eyes was speculative. Musing.

"You've got a terrible temper," she observed.

He swallowed. "I guess so," he said. "But so does Bourke Waitely. Just because he didn't show it tonight doesn't mean—"

"I know what it means. It's kind of creepy, actually, to see a guy pretending that nothing makes him mad. Makes you wonder what he's so determined to hide."

"He's hiding that he's really a rabid squirrel," Ward said. "You should see him in the locker room."

She shuddered delicately. "I think I'll pass. Now...about you..."

He stood very straight, as if he had to pass an impromptu inspection.

"Your temper. I don't suppose there's any hope you'll ever change."

He frowned. "I could try." Then he sighed, too. "But probably not."

"Oh, well." She adjusted the purse on her arm. "At least you're honest. I guess that's all right, then."

"It is?"

"I guess it'll have to be, if we're going to get married." She looked at her watch. "Your parents should be here any minute, so I'd better go."

"Roberta—"

"You'll probably be grounded for a long, long time," she said. "Years, maybe. But when you get free, call me."

She was walking away. Ward put his hands through the bars. "Roberta, did you mean it? About getting married?"

She came back. She leaned in, found his face between the bars and kissed him softly.

"Tell you what. Get out of jail first, and then we'll see."

A Who's Who
of Interesting
Fictional Offspring
by Kathleen O'Brien

DREAM OFFSPRING

As Griffin and Heather head off to make babies, it might be fun to play with other pairings of fictional characters. Let's see if we can create a "who's who" of interesting fictional offspring.

Most Likely To Be Picked Last in Dodgeball

The child of Melanie Wilkes (*Gone with the Wind*) and Hamlet: ultrapassive gene pool. Poor Melanie can't do anything that involves an ounce of aggression. Hamlet can't make up his mind whether to throw the ball or not.

Most Likely To Be Shot by an Irate Husband

The child of Santa Claus and Cinderella: very sneaky gene pool. This child is likely to be adept at staging suspicious entrances and exits.

Most Likely To Get Yard-of-the-Month Prize

The child of Mary Lennox (*The Secret Garden*) and Indiana Jones: lots of decorating talent in this gene pool. Mary knows her flowers, and Indiana Jones would bring home lots of interesting statuary.

Most Likely to Have To Get Married in High School

The child of Tinker Bell and Icarus: lack of impulse control in this gene pool. Icarus has terrible judgment, can't do anything his father tells him, even if it's obviously good advice. And Tinker Bell does love trashy outfits and flirting with bad-boy pirates.

Most Likely To Become a Shoe Salesman

The child of Drusilla (Cinderella's stepsister) and Frodo (*The Lord of the Rings*). Surely this poor child would have an obsession with feet.

Most Likely To Get a Job at Kobe Steak House

The child of Zorro and Lady Macbeth: all those swords and daggers around the house. In this family, both nature and nurture are pushing the children in the same direction. This might be the best way to channel their talents for good.

Most Likely To Still Be Holding Enron Stock

The child of Pollyanna and King Arthur. Optimism is charming, within limits. But this gene pool would create a child who lived permanently in rose-colored la-la land.

Here's a sneak peek...

Quiet as the Grave
by
Kathleen O'Brien

*A much anticipated new Firefly Glen story...
Mike Frome's ex-wife is found suspiciously dead—
making him the prime murder suspect. Believing in his
innocence, Mike's ex-flame, Suzie Strickland, offers her
support. But sudden murder evidence against Mike is
discovered, testing their newfound trust and love...*

CHAPTER 1

EVEN AS THE DREAM PLAYED OUT, the man knew he was dreaming. Except…how could *dream* be the right word for anything so real? It was more like time travel. While his body lay there, helpless on the bed, twitching and whimpering and trying to wake up, his mind flew back to the cave and lived it all again.

Lived the stink. The air in the cave was wet. It had rained all day, and moisture clung to the slimy, pitted walls. Now and then a pocket of liquefied algae grew too heavy and popped from its secret pore, like a boil exploding. It slid across the gray rock slowly, an insect leaving behind a shining trail of ooze.

Everyone had come tonight, which was rare— but they must have heard that this would be special. Too many men crowded into the space, so the wet, stinking air was hot. He felt light-headed, as if the oxygen levels were too low. He wondered if they'd all die here, breathing foul air until they collapsed where they stood. How long would their bodies lie in their black robes before anyone discovered them?

Maybe they'd never be found, and they'd rot here. Poetic justice, surely. They were already rotted on the inside.

His mask was too tight. He couldn't breathe. He adjusted the cloth so that the eye and mouth holes lined up better.

When the girl was brought in, it was obvious she'd been drugged. They had to hold her up just to get her clothes off. Her head kept dropping. She made small sounds that weren't quite human, more like a puppy whining in a cage.

From there the dream went black. No sight. All sounds. The sound of metal against metal. Metal against rock. Metal against skin.

And always the puppy sound, begging. Struggling to find its way out of the cage. Sometimes the noises escalated a little, but they never got very loud. The cage held. The puppy had almost given up hope.

The cave seemed to come alive then, as if it was being sucked into a whirlwind. Weeping and low moans. Wet noises, as if someone gargled fear. Heavy breathing that rode the naked back of animal grunts. Babbling, somehow religious, from the blind trance of terror.

And then, finally, at the very end, one heart-breaking human word. The word to which everyone, even the dreamer, could be reduced, if things got bad enough.

"Mommy," the girl cried, though God only knew where her mother was. Not here, not in this cold stone room full of infected air and sweating men. The girl hadn't been more than a child when she came in, but she was a baby now. They had peeled fifteen years from her in fifteen minutes.

"Mommy, help me!"

And it was at that moment—every time, no matter how hard he prayed it wouldn't happen—that the dreamer felt his body jerk and release, spreading shame all over his pajamas, his sheets, his soul.

THE TUXEDO LAKE COUNTRY Day School Open House was the highlight of the elementary school season, and the Tuxedo Lake mothers knew it. They spent the entire morning getting ready. Manicures, pedicures, facials, eyebrow waxing and a hundred other little rituals Mike Frome had never known existed until he married Justine Millner.

The six years of their marriage had been an eye-opener, that was for sure. Her sunshine-colored hair, which used to mesmerize him the way a shiny bell on a string mesmerizes a cat, apparently was really an ordinary brown. Without its makeup, her face seemed to have different contours entirely. At home, he rarely saw that ivory skin. It was almost always buried beneath green cream and hot towels. Sometimes, when he turned to her at night—in the early days, when he still bothered to—he found her hands encased in gel-filled gloves that slid and squished when he touched them.

He would have been able to live with all that. It was called growing up, he supposed. Like discovering there's no such thing as Santa Claus. He could have coped, if only she hadn't been such a bitch. If he lived to be a million years old, he'd never understand why he hadn't seen sooner what a *bitch* she was.

Still, he'd put up with it for six years, for Gavin's sake. Gavin, who had been conceived when Mike and Justine were only teenagers, loved his mother, so Mike had tried to love her, too.

He'd tried for six whole years that felt more like six hundred. Then he just couldn't pretend anymore. He had to get out, or he'd die. He figured Gavin was better off with a part-time dad than a dead one.

Since then, he'd worked hard to make this split-parenting thing a partnership. For the past two years he and Justine had attended every single one of Gavin's Little League games together, and all the kiddy birthday parties, and of course all the deadly dull PTA functions.

To attend this one, he'd stopped right in the most critical stage of a job. The Proctors' boathouse was almost finished, and he should be there. But he'd told the carpenters to take the afternoon off—which had surprised the hell out of them, since ordinarily at the end of a job he was hyper-focused.

The open house was more important. The fifth graders were staging a musical play to welcome the parents to a new school year. "Learning Is Fun" featured historical characters who had demonstrated a love for education. Apparently Gavin's role was as the teacher in a one-room country school—a fact Justine had only this minute discovered.

"This *must* be a mistake," she was saying to Cicely Tillman, the mother of one of Gavin's friends. Cicely wore a small name tag shaped like a bow tie that read "Cicely—Volunteer Mommy."

"No," Cicely, the Volunteer Mommy, said. "It's not a mistake."

BONUS FEATURE

"It *must* be," Justine said again, and Mike recognized that tone. Volunteer Mommy would be smart to back off. "Gavin was supposed to be the narrator. He was supposed to be *Abraham Lincoln*."

"I know, I know, it's a shame, but he said he didn't want the part," Cicely explained, her voice brimming with the fakest sympathy Mike had ever heard, even from Cicely. "He wanted something smaller."

Justine scanned her program. "But this…this *farmer* isn't even a named part. What about Socrates? Or even Joseph Campbell?"

"We're five minutes from opening curtain, Justine." Cicely reached out and patted Justine's arm. "Some children just aren't comfortable in the spotlight," she said. "I'm sure Gavin shines in other areas."

Oh, brother. Well, even if Cicely didn't have the sense to get away, Mike did. He found a folding chair fifth row center and claimed it. While the ladies' drama continued, he watched the stage. Someone new must be running the spotlight. The glowing circle lurched all over the blue curtain, leaped to the side and hit the American flag, then slid down the stairs, only to pop up again on the curtain.

When the overhead lights flickered, warning that the show was about to begin, Justine finally arranged herself next to him with a waft of Chanel. She hummed with fury.

"Did you hear that? Not comfortable in the limelight! Did you hear that? Can you believe how rude?"

Mike rolled his paper program up into a cylinder and kept his eyes on the stage, where the curtains were now undulating with restless lumps. The kids, no doubt, trying to find their places.

"No, I didn't hear it." He didn't want to get into this. "I was too busy wondering what exactly it means to be a 'volunteer mommy.' Do you think they're implying that…"

But he should have known Justine wouldn't respond to any satirical attempt to change the subject Justine didn't have much of a sense of humor at the best of times. And this was definitely not the best of times. She could really be like a dog with a bone, if she thought she'd been slighted.

"That self-important little pencil pusher," she whispered sharply, leaning her head toward his. "She's an accountant. Her husband sells thumb-tacks, for God's sake. And she has the nerve to say Gavin isn't comfortable in the limelight. Right to my face."

Mike sighed and looked at his ex-wife. She was gorgeous, of course. She never ventured out of the house without looking perfect. But someone really should tell her that if she didn't stop disapproving of everything, her lousy temper was going to gouge furrows between those carefully waxed-and-dyed eyebrows before her thirtieth birthday.

"Gavin *isn't* comfortable in the limelight," he said, deciding to ignore the non sequitur about the thumbtacks. "Why would it be rude to say so?"

Justine glared at him a minute, then, flaring her elegant nostrils, turned her head toward the stage and tapped her program on the palm of her hand.

44

"For God's sake, Mike," she said under her breath. "Don't play stupid. Don't pretend you don't know what I'm talking about."

"I *don't* know what you're talking about. Frankly, that's the case about ninety percent of the time. No, make that ninety-nine."

She whipped her head around, but he got lucky. Taped music filled the air, the curtains began to open, two jerky feet at a time, and a pint-size Abraham Lincoln, complete with beard and top hat, stepped forward. It took the spotlight a few seconds to find him, and when it did Justine growled quietly.

"See? See what I mean? That's Hugh. She

took it away from Gavin so she could give it to her own *son*."

He didn't answer. He had spotted Gavin in the background, on the small risers that had been set up on either side of the stage. Mike had been to enough of these performances to know that, one at a time, the students would climb down and take center stage for their two or three lines. Mrs. Hadley, the music teacher, was careful never to leave anyone out entirely. She knew all about Volunteer Mommy Syndrome.

Gavin looked nervous as hell. Mike stared at him, sending "it'll be okay" vibes. He hadn't liked this kind of thing much either, when he'd been in school. He'd been tons happier on the football field, and he had a feeling his son was going to take after him. Which would, of course, piss Justine off in a big way.

About halfway through the play, her cell phone began to vibrate. These folding chairs were close enough together that, for a minute, he thought the rumbling against his thigh was his own phone. But he'd turned his off completely. He gave Justine a frown. Why hadn't she done the same?

To his surprise, she stood up, and got ready to edge her way down the aisle. She glanced back at him, holding her phone up as explanation.

God, she was absolutely unbelievable. Gavin

was due up any minute—he was one of only about two or three kids who hadn't performed yet. He grabbed her arm. He must have squeezed too hard, because she let out a cry loud enough to be heard up on stage.

"Sit down," he whispered. He jerked his head toward the stage. "Gavin."

He ought to let go of her forearm. He knew that. She was obviously strung out. She was humiliated because her son had a piddly part in the school play. She was mad at Mike for not caring. Plus, she'd had to repress all that resentment against Cicely Tillman, and self-control wasn't her strong suit.

She was probably as hot and high-pressure as a volcano ready to blow.

But he didn't let go. He was pretty damn angry, too. He knew who was on the other end of that cell phone. Her new boyfriend. The one she was going to be spending a month in Europe with, starting tonight. The guy was welcome to her, but, goddamn it, couldn't she at least pretend to put her son first, for once in her life?

"Let go of me, Michael," she said. Her whisper was so shrill it turned heads three rows away. "You're hurting me."

He hesitated one more second, and then he dropped his hand, aware that, in their section of the audience, they were now more fascinating than what was happening onstage. She rubbed her arm dramatically and then, with a hiccuping sob, made her way down the row.

Mike stared hard at the stage, ignoring the curious faces that were still turned in his direction. Gavin, who had just put on an old-fashioned hat, came forward.

"Our schoolroom is small, but it has to hold us all," he sang in a horribly off-key soprano. "My students walk for miles, and I greet them with a smile."

That was probably where Gavin was supposed to smile, but he didn't. He finished his tiny part, then he scurried, head bowed, back to his spot on the risers. Mike felt his stomach spasm. Was this just stage fright, or had Gavin actually heard his parents out here squabbling?

Justine didn't return even when the show was over, and Mike was fuming, though he managed to hide it fairly well, he thought. He ate cookies and drank fruit punch with the other parents until the kids joined them, enduring the awkward silences while everyone tried to figure out what to say about Justine's absence.

Finally Gavin came racing out, beaming. He barreled into Mike, trying to knock chests like the professional sports figures, but instead hitting

Mike's ribs with his nose. Mike's heart forgot Justine, and he pounded Gavin's back with a couple of heavy thumps of typical proud-daddy love. The kid was growing like crazy. In a year or two, that chest-bumping thing just might work.

Best of all, Gavin looked ecstatic now that his ordeal was over. He grinned up at Mike with those knockout blue eyes that were so like Justine's. "It's over!" He laughed. "I sucked, huh?"

Mike smiled back, relieved that the episode with Justine apparently hadn't quite reached the kids' ears. "Yep, you're pretty bad, pal. You're definitely no Pavarotti."

48 This was the kind of candor that would drive Justine nuts. She had the theory that admitting any inadequacies was bad for the boy's ego. But Mike knew that Gavin's ego was perfectly healthy. Maybe too healthy. Gavin was as gorgeous as his mother, he lived in a 6,000-square-foot mansion with his own boat and plasma big-screen TV, he pulled down straight As and he boasted the best batting average in his Little League conference.

It would do him good to face the facts—Hugh Tillman was a better singer.

"I know," Gavin agreed happily. "I can't ever get the tune. Mrs. Hadley hates me. Where's Mom?"

Mike felt the eyes of the other parents once again.

"She's outside," he said as casually as he could. "She got a phone call."

"Oh, well, tell her I love her, okay? I gotta go." Gavin and his buddies had plans to celebrate the success of the play with a pizza party at the Tillmans' house. "Hugh's mom is already waiting in the minivan for us."

"Go tell her yourself," Mike said. He knew Justine didn't particularly care about seeing her son, but if he let Gavin leave without saying goodbye, she'd carp about it all the way home.

The boy flew off, with Hugh and about four other boys trailing behind him. Mike grabbed a napkin, wiped cinnamon sugar off his hands and tossed his empty punch cup into the big trash bin.

"Three points," Phil Stott, his next-door neighbor, said with a smile. Mike appreciated that. He knew Phil, a nice guy who didn't have kids but was here to watch his nephew sing, was trying to bridge the embarrassment gap.

Gavin was back in a flash. "Found her! She says to tell you she's waiting for you in the car." He held up his hand for Mike's goodbye slap. At home it would be a hug and a kiss, but with Hugh and the other "dudes" standing by, a high five would have to do.

Mike obliged, and then did the same for all the other boys, who were accustomed to parading by him this way after every Little League game. He'd coached these boys since they were in T-ball. They were good kids. But he couldn't help thinking his own smart, silly son was the best.

He wished Gavin were coming home with him right now, but he realized that was pretty cowardly. Yeah, the ride home would be a bummer, with Justine pouting or ranting, but he could handle it. He didn't need to use his ten-year-old son as a buffer.

By the time he got out to the car, Justine wasn't speaking to him. Good. Pouting was ridiculous, but it was easier to ignore than the ranting.

She'd rolled back her silk sleeve and was rubbing conspicuously at the discoloration just above her wrist. He checked it out of the corner of his eye, just cynical enough to wonder which way the finger marks were facing. He was pretty damn sure he hadn't been rough enough to bruise anything. She'd probably done it herself, while she waited for him to come out.

He considered trying to make conversation, but it seemed like too much trouble. Woodcliff Road was kind of tricky, with a twenty-foot drop through wooded slopes on the passenger side. He needed to concentrate.

Let her sulk. She loved that anyhow.

Eventually, though, her resentment simply had to bubble out in words. She swiveled in her seat and glared at him. "So? Don't you have a single thing to say for yourself? After what you did to my arm?"

Damn. He'd almost made it. They were only a couple of miles from Tuxedo Lake. He negotiated a curve through some overhanging elms which were just beginning to go yellow. He glanced at her face, which looked slightly jaundiced in the glowing light. The shadows of the trees passing over her made it seem as if her mouth were moving silently, though he knew it wasn't. It was a disagreeable sight.

He turned away and shrugged. "Sorry," he said. "I just couldn't believe you were actually going to leave right when Gavin's part was coming up."

She waved her hand. "You call that a part? I can't believe he dragged us all the way out there for that. He made a fool of me, that's for sure."

Clenching the steering wheel, Mike tried not to react. This was pointless, and he knew it. He'd tried for six years to make Justine think about any situation, anywhere on this earth, without viewing it through the prism of her own self-interests, but she simply couldn't do it. He'd looked up "sociopath" once, and it fit perfectly. It was kind of scary, actually.

But like an idiot, sometimes he just couldn't stop himself from responding. He accelerated, whipping the passing trees into a batter of lemony green.

"He made a fool of *you*? Sorry, but you're going to have to explain to me how Gavin's school play can possibly end up being all about *you*."

She didn't answer right away, and he knew that was a bad sign. She was lining up her ammunition, and that meant this wasn't going to be just a skirmish. It was going to be war.

"That's just so like you," she said finally. "The perfect Mike Frome can't make mistakes. If anyone dares to point out that you've done something wrong, like rough up your own wife, you just launch a counterattack, trying to change the subject. Well, I won't be put on the defensive. You manhandled me, and I ought to go to the police."

"You're not my wife," he said. That was stupid, too. That wasn't the point. But she did that to him—made him so mad his brain shut off.

"I'm your son's mother. I think that is just as important, don't you?"

"No. I think it's tragic."

"God, you're so melodramatic." She narrowed her eyes. "Tragic? Because I took a call on my cell phone? I'm sorry to tell you, but that doesn't make me a bad mother."

He'd had enough. "No," he said. "What makes you a bad mother is that you're a raging bitch. You're the most self-centered, foul-tempered bitch in the state of New York. That's what makes you a bad mother."

He half expected her to slap him. He definitely expected her to start yelling epithets at him. But she didn't do either of those things. Instead, she did something that shocked the hell out of him.

She opened her car door.

"Justine!"

"Stop the car."

"Damn it, shut the door."

"No. Stop the car. I'm getting out."

He was already applying the brakes, but he had to be careful. She had one leg out. He didn't want to fishtail on these narrow, curving roads. He was mad as hell at her. He might wish he'd never met her, but he didn't want her to get hurt.

He maneuvered the car to a safe spot and turned to her. "Are you insane? Do you want to kill yourself? Shut the damn door."

She didn't answer. She just picked up her purse

and got out of the car, slamming the door shut behind her.

He rolled down the window. "Justine, for God's sake."

"Go to hell," she said without looking at him. "Go straight to hell where you belong."

He looked at her, so messed up with contradictory, heart-racing emotions and adrenaline that he couldn't even decide what he felt. It was about five o'clock, and the trees behind her were already full of shadows. She had on high heels, the better to impress the other Volunteer Mommies with, but no damn good at all for walking along an up-hill cliff road.

"Justine. Okay, look. I'm sorry. Get back in the car."

She didn't even answer. She simply began to walk.

He trolled along behind her for a few yards, leaning over to beg her through the window and steering the car with one hand. He felt like a fool, which was bad enough, but when another car came up behind him and honked impatiently, the embarrassment of it finally was just too much.

"Justine, get in the car right now, or I'm going to drive away, and you're going to have to walk the rest of the way home. It's nearly a mile."

No response, except another short toot from the car behind.

"Justine, I mean it. It's getting cold. I'm not coming back to get you."

She didn't even turn her head. She shifted her purse to her other shoulder and kept walking. The people behind him probably thought he was a stalker, or a serial killer.

Honk…

Well, screw her, then. If she wanted to walk all the way home in a snit, fine. She logged about five miles on the treadmill in the home gym every single day of her life. He figured she could handle three-quarters of a mile out here.

He rolled up the window and hit the gas. He watched her in the rearview mirror, getting smaller but never once looking his way or acknowledging her predicament by the slightest twitch of a muscle.

Finally he came to a curve, and when he looked in the mirror again she was gone.

That was the last time anyone—except perhaps her killer—ever saw Justine Millner Frome alive.

Look for *Quiet as the Grave* in bookstores in March 2006 from Signature Select.

A forty-something blushing bride?

Neely Mason never expected to walk down the aisle, but it's happening, and now her whole Southern family is in on the event. Can they all get through this wedding without killing each other? Because one thing's for sure, when it comes to sisters, *crazy* is a relative term.

The
GOOD KIND
OF CRAZY

TANYA MICHAELS

Signature Select ™

**All's fair in love and war…
So why not do both?**

BOOTCAMP

Three brand-new stories in one Collection

National bestselling authors

Leslie Kelly

Heather MacAllister

Cindi Myers

Strong-willed females Cassandra, Rebecca and
Barbara enroll in the two-week Warfield crash
course to figure out how to get what they
want in life and romance!

Experience *Bootcamp* in March 2006.

If you enjoyed what you just read,
then we've got an offer you can't resist!

Take 2 bestselling
love stories FREE!

Plus get a FREE surprise gift!

Clip this page and mail it to Harlequin Reader Service®

IN U.S.A.	IN CANADA
3010 Walden Ave.	P.O. Box 609
P.O. Box 1867	Fort Erie, Ontario
Buffalo, N.Y. 14240-1867	L2A 5X3

YES! Please send me 2 free Harlequin Intrigue® novels and my free surprise gift. After receiving them, if I don't wish to receive anymore, I can return the shipping statement marked cancel. If I don't cancel, I will receive 4 brand-new novels each month, before they're available in stores! In the U.S.A., bill me at the bargain price of $4.24 plus 25¢ shipping and handling per book and applicable sales tax, if any*. In Canada, bill me at the bargain price of $4.99 plus 25¢ shipping and handling per book and applicable taxes**. That's the complete price and a savings of at least 10% off the cover prices—what a great deal! I understand that accepting the 2 free books and gift places me under no obligation ever to buy any books. I can always return a shipment and cancel at any time. Even if I never buy another book from Harlequin, the 2 free books and gift are mine to keep forever.

181 HDN DZ7N
381 HDN DZ7P

Name	(PLEASE PRINT)	
Address	Apt.#	
City	State/Prov.	Zip/Postal Code

Not valid to current Harlequin Intrigue® subscribers.

Want to try two free books from another series?
Call 1-800-873-8635 or visit www.morefreebooks.com.

* Terms and prices subject to change without notice. Sales tax applicable in N.Y.
** Canadian residents will be charged applicable provincial taxes and GST.
   All orders subject to approval. Offer limited to one per household.
   ® are registered trademarks owned and used by the trademark owner or its licensee.

INT04R   ©2004 Harlequin Enterprises Limited

THE FORTUNES OF TEXAS: Reunion

**Coming in March…
a brand-new Fortunes story
by *USA TODAY* bestselling author**

Marie Ferrarella…

MILITARY MAN

A dangerous predator escapes from prison
near Red Rock, Texas—and Collin Jamison,
CIA Special Operations, is the only person who
can get inside the murderer's mind. Med student
Lucy Gatling thinks she has a lead. The police
aren't biting, but Collin is—even if it is only
to get closer to Lucy!

**The Fortunes of Texas: Reunion
The price of privilege. The power of family.**

Where love comes alive™

Signature Select™

COMING NEXT MONTH

Signature Select Collection
BOOTCAMP by Leslie Kelly, Heather MacAllister, Cindi Myers
Strong-willed females Cassandra, Rebecca and Barbara enroll in the
two-week Warfield crash course to figure out how to get what they
want in life and romance!

Signature Select Saga
QUIET AS THE GRAVE by Kathleen O'Brien
Mike Frome's ex-wife is found suspiciously dead—making him the
prime murder suspect. Believing in his innocence, Mike's ex-flame
Suzie Strickland offers her support. But sudden murder evidence
against Mike is discovered, testing their newfound trust and love....

Signature Select Miniseries
COFFEE IN THE MORNING by Roz Denny Fox
A heartwarming volume of two classic stories with the miniseries
characters you love! A wagon-train journey along the Santa Fe Trail
is a catalyst for romance as Emily Benton and Sherry Campbell
each find love.

Signature Select Spotlight
VOWS OF SILENCE by Debra Webb
A secret pact made long ago between best friends—Lacy, Melinda,
Cassidy and Kira—resurfaces when a ten-year-old murder is
uncovered. Chief Rick Summers knows they're hiding something,
but isn't sure he can be objective...especially if his old flame Lacy is
guilty of murder.

Signature Select Showcase
LADY'S CHOICE by Jayne Ann Krentz
Juliana Grant knows she's found "the one" in high-octane real-
estate developer Travis Sawyer—even if *he* doesn't realize it yet.
But Travis has arrived back in Jewel Harbour for retribution, not
for romance. And it doesn't help that the target of his revenge is
her family!